FINDING LOVE AT HOME

THE BEILER SISTERS

FINDING LOVE AT HOME

JERRY S. EICHER

THORNDIKE PRESS
A part of Gale, Cengage Learning

GALE
CENGAGE Learning®

Copyright © 2014 by Jerry S. Eicher.
The Beiler Sisters #3.
All Scripture quotations are taken from the King James Version of the Bible.
Thorndike Press, a part of Gale, Cengage Learning.

ALL RIGHTS RESERVED

This is a work of fiction. Names, characters, places, and incidents are products of the author's imagination or are used fictitiously. Any resemblance to actual persons, living or dead, is entirely coincidental.
Thorndike Press® Large Print Christian Romance.
The text of this Large Print edition is unabridged.
Other aspects of the book may vary from the original edition.
Set in 16 pt. Plantin.

LIBRARY OF CONGRESS CATALOGING-IN-PUBLICATION DATA

Eicher, Jerry S.
 Finding love at home / by Jerry S. Eicher. — Large print edition.
  pages ; cm. — (The Beiler sister ; #3) (Thorndike Press large print Christian romance)
 ISBN 978-1-4104-7407-0 (hardcover) — ISBN 1-4104-7407-0 (hardcover)
 1. Amish—Pennsylvania—Fiction. 2. Large type books. I. Title.
PS3605.I34F56 2014b
813'.6—dc23   2014030673

Published in 2014 by arrangement with Harvest House Publishers

Printed in the United States of America
1 2 3 4 5 6 7 18 17 16 15 14

FINDING LOVE AT HOME

ONE

It was a beautiful fall morning as Debbie Watson sat on the front porch swing of the Beiler home. She smiled as she listened to the creak of the swing chains on each side of her. She hadn't been born Amish or raised in the faith, and yet God had done a good work in her heart, just as He'd done in the hearts of the Beiler family. They had welcomed her into their home well over a year ago, and so much had happened since then. Good things as well as tragic things.

That she was well accepted in the community was one of the good things. Widower Melvin Kanagy's passing last spring, only weeks before his planned wedding with Ida Beiler, had been one of the great tragedies. That Ida had managed to rebound so quickly after her heart had been fully given to Melvin still surprised Debbie. Of course, she had her own heartache regarding Alvin Knepp. He still hadn't asked her home after a Sunday hymn singing. When Alvin returned from his brief time of living in the *Englisha* world, he'd practically promised he would ask to take her home.

Debbie pushed thoughts of Alvin aside and took in the sweep of fall colors beginning to roll over the hills around her. It was the second week of September, and Snyder County's Amish country always put on its best face this time of year. The Beilers' corn crop had been cut and stacked in the fields, awaiting the annual silage filling. Debbie planned to stay home from work when that day arrived. She'd wanted to take in the full flavor of an Amish silo filling for some time now — and this was the year!

The men of the community would gather for the day, and Saloma and Ida would have tables in the yard spread with an awesome noon meal. The community was a peaceful place filled with people who possessed deep faith and worked close to the soil. Debbie had chosen to become part of them, and each day she was drawn further in. And now, incredibly, tomorrow would be the day of her baptism! It had been so long in coming, and now that it was here, Debbie was finding it hard to hold her joy in. How she made it through all the baptismal instruction classes, with the long lectures by

Minister Kanagy on the *Ordnung* rules, was still a miracle. Minister Kanagy wasn't the bishop, but he acted like he was sometimes.

Minister Kanagy had been skeptical of her true intentions and had regarded her with steely eyes as she sat with the other applicants on Sunday mornings. Surely the others were also at risk of not keeping the *Ordnung.* Minister Kanagy didn't have to single her out — but he did.

Still, she would never wish calamity on Minister Kanagy, but disaster had struck anyway. Horrible tragedy. His wife, Barbara, had been diagnosed with cancer at nearly the same time his brother Melvin had passed, back in the spring. The doctors had recommended the most aggressive treatment for Barbara, but this had done little to halt the cancer's rapid advance. They had buried her last month, only yards from where Melvin's body lay.

Debbie sighed. How closely sorrow and joy walked together. And here among the community, the cutting edge of each emotion was felt to the maximum. These people drew support from God and from each other. That was how they survived and flourished in a modern world that often rushed past them. And tomorrow she would become part of them. Bishop Beiler would ask her the questions, she would answer, and water would be poured over her head. Debbie's hands tingled at the thought.

She'd truly become Amish. Her baptism would just confirm what she already knew in her heart. Despite his eagle eye, Minister Kanagy had failed to catch her in any *Ordnung* transgressions. She'd been careful about that, often questioning Ida Beiler for hours on how things were done. Ida would mention things like comportment, how to fold her hands on her lap in the instruction classes, and to look up only when the others spoke or a question was asked of her. Ida had personally supervised the sewing of her dresses, and she'd seen to it that her head covering was large enough. If Minister Kanagy had found fault with any of that hard work, Debbie would have corrected the error at once. That was another character trait the people of the community admired — the willingness to change one's ways to conform. And she *had* changed her ways. She'd come a long way from her *Englisha* roots.

Debbie's thoughts drifted to the sweeping lawns of the college of Franklin and Marshall in Lancaster. There the trees would also blaze with their fall splendor. The students were rushing about this week on their way to classes. She'd once been one of them, only she hadn't been eager or excited. Their world had never been hers, even when she completed four years and graduated with honors to please her mother. Callie had thought she'd won the struggle with her only child once Debbie had her degree in hand. Hoping her daughter's fascination with the Amish had been forever purged or at least neutralized by her college education, Callie had been sorely disappointed. With the world open before Debbie, and now able to choose for herself, she'd followed her heart first by becoming a boarder with the Beiler family and then by embracing their Plain faith. Her mother had openly disapproved of Debbie's decision. But at least her mother wasn't in shock like Adam and Saloma Beiler were when their youngest daughter, Lois, deserted the Amish faith and moved into the *Englisha* world. The Beilers were still reeling from the blow.

Debbie had grown up next door to the Beilers and was friends with the three Beiler girls: Verna, Ida, and Lois. But between Lois and her there had always been a vast difference. Debbie admired the Amish community, while Lois longed for *Englisha* life. Now Lois lived at Debbie's parents' place, where she'd moved earlier this year. Debbie

11

thought it was as if she and Lois had swapped places and corrected some error of birth. But there hadn't been an error. She was Herbert and Callie Watson's birth daughter, just as Lois belonged to Adam and Saloma Beiler.

Debbie brought the squeak of the swing to a halt for a moment. Next week Lois would marry Doug Williams, of all people. Mother must have introduced the two soon after Lois moved in. Debbie was sure her mother had eagerly pushed Lois down the path of social success that her own daughter refused. What irony, Debbie thought. She'd dated Doug on and off but was never really impressed by him.

Debbie pushed with her foot to start the swing again. The subject of Lois's wedding was a sore one around the Beiler household. Lois's wedding invitation was in the bottom of one of Saloma's dresser drawers, and it would remain there. None of the Beiler family planned to attend the wedding. And Debbie couldn't go either, although she would have before she began the baptism instruction classes. Tomorrow she would be baptized, and she certainly wouldn't jeopardize her new standing in the community by doing such a thing.

The front door squeaked open. Ida's face

appeared. "Hiding out, are we?"

"In plain sight." Debbie smiled. "Come join me."

Ida did so, gazing off into the distance as she sat down.

Debbie reached over to squeeze her friend's hand. "Are we troubled on this fine morning?"

Ida gave her a strained smile. "Your baptism is tomorrow. I'm so happy for you, Debbie. You'll have found your home amongst us at last."

"Thank you." Debbie didn't let go of Ida's hand. She wasn't fooled by Ida's cheerfulness. Her friend's heart was always toward others and seldom on her own troubles, but something was off.

"Do you want to talk about it?" Debbie tightened her fingers.

Ida shrugged. "I'm okay. Just thinking, that's all."

Debbie didn't back down. "You'll feel better if you talk about it."

Ida's response was a sharp intake of breath as she looked away.

"Did Barbara's funeral bring back memories?" Debbie tried again. "I know it did for me, so I can only imagine what you must still go through."

Ida's voice choked. "Melvin's body was

13

lying over there, Debbie. So close. The man I almost married. I could still see the outline of the grave. And Melvin's boy Willard, the eldest, couldn't stop looking at it. I got to thinking of him finding his *daett* under the cultivator tines. No nine-year-old boy should have to see such a thing, and with no *mamm* to comfort him . . ." Ida wiped the tears from her cheek. "I almost went over last week to put my arms around him, Debbie. But Willard isn't my son, and he never will be. Oh, why did *Da Hah* do this to us? Why, Debbie?" Ida struggled to control her sobs.

Debbie slipped her arm around Ida's shoulders and pulled her close. "God knows what's best," Debbie whispered, surprised that the words were more than just words. Conviction rose in her heart.

"*Yah, Da Hah* does." Ida collected herself. "And here I am blubbering all over the place."

"That doesn't mean that you don't trust Him, Ida. It just means that it still hurts."

Ida's shoulders shook. "First Melvin's six children are left motherless and fatherless, and now Minister Kanagy's two have no *mamm*. It seems so wrong."

Debbie let go of Ida and gave her friend a sharp look. Should she say something?

14

Hadn't she seen Minister Kanagy's gaze on Ida at the Sunday service — and Ida's weak smile in response? Or had her imagination been running wild?

Did Ida have ideas in her head? Like marriage to Minister Kanagy so she could take care of Melvin's orphaned children and Minister Kanagy's semi-orphaned children? Surely Ida wouldn't marry the man — even if Minister Kanagy asked. Would she? Shivers ran through Debbie at the thought of Ida as Minister Kanagy's *frau*. What a loveless match that would be. Debbie decided she shouldn't say anything about it. What if she said something, and Ida hadn't thought of it? Would she have planted seeds that could take root in Ida's kind and selfless nature? Then Ida's open heart might draw Minister Kanagy's attention even further. "That's terrible!" Debbie gasped out loud.

"I know." Ida nodded. "It's awful what has happened this year. And now Lois's wedding to that awful *Englisha* man is next week. Our family ought to go about the community in sackcloth and ashes."

Debbie let the subject of Minister Kanagy go. "People don't blame your family like you think they might." Thankfully Ida hadn't caught the true meaning of her gasp.

"I guess things look dark right now.

Maybe you're right." Ida lapsed into silence.

Perhaps Lois's upcoming marriage was the more urgent concern anyway. Debbie knew Doug well. She had, after all, dated the man. He wasn't quite the awful *Englisha* man the Beilers thought he was, but she understood their point of view. To them Doug had lured Lois deeper into the outside world. On the other hand, Debbie remembered what the Beilers were overlooking at the moment. Lois had found her way into the *Englisha* world on her own, well before knowing Doug.

Ida shifted on the swing. "I'm sorry. I shouldn't be speaking such harsh words about Doug. My heart is broken and sorrowful, I suppose. But that's never a *gut* excuse for wrongdoing."

"I'm sure *Da Hah* understands." Debbie reached over to squeeze Ida's hand.

"I hope so." Ida attempted a smile. "I'll be needing His blessing soon. If I don't miss my guess, Minister Kanagy will be calling before long. He needs a new *frau* — and quickly, I would say."

Shock sent Debbie to her feet. "You shouldn't say that, Ida. It's not decent. The man's wife is barely in the ground."

Ida appeared puzzled. "There's nothing indecent about it. *Da Hah* made that choice,

16

and Minister Kanagy is free to marry again since Barbara's gone. And we could bring all of Melvin's children into the family."

Debbie trembled. "He's a horrible man, Ida. Have you ever had to deal with his harsh eyes looking for any flaw in you? Well, I did. I lived through many an instruction class with the man. And what about what he did to Joe and Verna? He would've liked to put Joe in jail on his suspicions alone if Henry Yoder hadn't found another witness to testify for Joe."

Ida eyed Debbie. "He's a hard man, Debbie. I know that. But I also know I'm sitting here wasting away my life as an old maid when I could be mothering Melvin's six children." Ida paused to wipe her eyes. "Would you keep me from that, Debbie?"

Debbie's mind spun. Maybe there was hope yet. Ida hadn't said that Minister Kanagy had spoken to her. Perhaps there was no basis to this conclusion Ida had drawn. Perhaps Debbie had imagined it moments ago.

Ida seemed to read Debbie's thoughts. "He was watching me last Sunday at the services, Debbie. I know that look in a man's eye. So don't say I don't know what I'm speaking about."

Debbie wanted to protest in the loudest

voice possible. This wasn't right! Minister Kanagy was way out of line. He shouldn't look at another woman so soon after his wife had been buried. But her protests would be in vain, Debbie told herself as she took her seat on the swing again, her body now limp.

"It might be *Da Hah*'s will." Ida reached over to touch Debbie's arm. "*Da Hah* will give me love in my heart for the man — if not before, then after we've said wedding vows."

Debbie groaned but said nothing. What was the use?

Two

Debbie hurried about to clean her room. There would be no visitors to the Beiler place tomorrow after the Sunday services that she knew of, but it seemed like one's room should be freshly cleaned in preparation for a baptism. Sort of cleansing the space before cleansing the soul.

Saloma had smiled when Debbie stated her intentions downstairs after lunch. She seemed to understand. "We're doing a thorough fall cleaning soon, so don't work too hard."

Well, it wasn't a matter of hard work, Debbie thought. It was the principle of the thing. And Ida probably had her bedroom spotless — baptism or no baptism. Emery, the Beilers' youngest boy, still lived at home. He never cleaned his room, so maybe Debbie would do him a favor after she finished with her bedroom.

Emery was in his early twenties and

needed a wife, in Debbie's opinion. As the heir apparent to the Beiler farm, he should have no problem with his choice of any marriageable Amish girls in the community. Emery only had to say the word, and the girls would line up. Yet the young man seemed perfectly content to allow each day to roll by. He showed not the slightest concern about his single status. Still, who was she to criticize people about their married status? She was approaching twenty-four and was still single. But it certainly wasn't because she hadn't shown interest in someone.

Emery was such a decent man. Maybe she should make a try herself for his hand. Debbie laughed at the thought. Emery had never shown any romantic interest in her, and neither should he. She lived at the house after all, so it was almost like they were brother and sister. And what a scandal that would be if they did date. She'd be seen as a gold digger for sure. Few in the community would think otherwise.

Maybe her baptism tomorrow would push Alvin off his perch. The man was the limit! He'd made such promises before and after he came home from his stint in the *Englisha* world — a stint that had resulted in his excommunication. But thoughts of Alvin still made Debbie smile. There was much she could be thankful for with him. He'd seen his mistake and come back from Philadelphia with a humble and manly confession of his sins in front of the baptism instruction class and then the membership. Alvin had even admitted to a few dates with an *Englisha* girl named Crystal Meyers. Debbie figured Alvin had been surprised when she'd had a front row seat for his confession. But she had, and this was no doubt due to Minister Kanagy wanting to embarrass Alvin. Though in the end the maneuver had worked to Alvin's favor. Much of the respect she'd lost for Alvin had been restored by his broken and honest words. Alvin had said he was done with the *Englisha* world, and that he'd left Crystal Meyers behind for good.

Alvin had spoken to Debbie after the services that Sunday — an accomplishment for him, indeed. He was usually shy and timid. Maybe his time in the *Englisha* world had done him some good after all. She'd allowed her hopes to soar as Alvin expressed an interest in pursuing their relationship — after he made his life right with the church, of course. And he had done that a few weeks later with a knee confession in front of everyone. He was granted full restoration back into the fellowship of the community.

But then nothing had happened all summer. Nothing more than a few smiles exchanged at the Sunday services and the youth gatherings. What had gone wrong? Debbie asked herself that question a thousand times. She'd made her interest in him known even before she moved into Bishop Beiler's household. Debbie blushed as she thought of the times she'd driven all starry-eyed past Alvin's farm and watched him work with his team of horses in the fields. Thankfully Alvin must have never told anyone about it, even though he'd seen her and waved many times.

Debbie sighed. Surely Paul Wagler's continued interest in her didn't still deter Alvin. It had before he left for the *Englisha* world, but she figured Alvin would have gotten over that by now. There were reasons aplenty for Alvin to see that she cared for him more than she did for Paul — dashing and handsome though Paul was. She had settled in her mind that she would marry a down-to-earth, humble farmer. Not someone like Paul, who reminded her of the men she'd dated in her old life in her former world.

A rattle of buggy wheels jerked Debbie out of her thoughts. Surely Deacon Mast hadn't come to speak with her! This *was*

Saturday, the day the deacon usually made his rounds to deal with church troubles. Had Minister Kanagy thrown one last wrench her way? She felt a little paranoid as she raced to the window and pulled the curtain back. *Whew!* Verna Beiler had climbed out of her buggy and was tying her horse to the hitching rack.

Debbie left her broom and dustpan by the dresser and hurried downstairs. Saloma looked up from her knitting on the couch with a smile as Debbie rushed by.

"It's Verna, isn't it?" Saloma's face glowed.

"Yes! I'm going out to walk her in." Debbie continued her dash out the front door.

Verna waved from the buggy and hollered, "*Gut* morning."

Debbie ran across the lawn and down the sidewalk to grab Verna in a tight hug. "It's so good to see you!"

Verna gave a little gasp. "And you, but oh, watch out for my stomach. It just keeps growing."

Debbie grinned as she stood back to regard Verna's swollen middle. They ended up in each other's arms again in giggles.

"I probably shouldn't have come out." Verna gave her midsection another glance. "But I couldn't resist with how glorious the day is. And soon I'll be laid up with labor pains, and then the whole winter lies ahead with a young *boppli* in the house. Better enjoy the outside while I can, I told myself."

"I agree! And your *mamm*'s glowing with happiness that you're here," Debbie said. "Yours won't be her first grandchild, but you're the first of her girls."

"I know." Verna sighed. "I love it. And Joe — he's such a darling husband. No child will ever have a more doting *daett.*"

"Come!" Debbie offered Verna a hand.

Verna pushed it away. "I can still walk, though I waddle like a duck."

The two giggled again as they made their way slowly toward the house. The front door soon burst open, and Ida ran out to envelop Verna in a sisterly hug.

"I'll be having the *boppli* right here and now!" Verna groaned. "That is, if the two of you aren't more careful."

"She's not serious," Debbie said when concern flashed on Ida's face.

Ida recovered. "It's so *gut* that you've come. We needed your comforting presence in the house. Debbie and I were talking this morning about Barbara's funeral."

"Oh, you poor thing! Did that stir up so many sad memories?" Verna took Ida's hand, and the two continued toward the

24

house with Debbie beside them.

Obviously it had, Debbie thought as she noticed Ida's tears. She should tell Verna about Minister's Kanagy's advances at the Sunday service, but she bit her lip instead. Verna would be sympathetic, but that wouldn't stop Ida. With Melvin's children in the balance, Minister Kanagy wasn't likely to fail in his pursuit of Ida as his new *frau.*

Saloma met them at the front door, a big smile on her face. She gave Verna a much gentler hug. Her arms lingered around her eldest daughter's shoulders. "You look well, Verna. And the child?"

"The midwife had a *gut* report last week." Verna's glow matched her mother's. "It won't be long now."

"*Da Hah* be praised!" Saloma said. "Come in. I'm sure we can stir up some hot chocolate for you, if nothing else. And we have all afternoon to talk. The girls were puttering around, but they don't really have pressing work."

A warm rush ran through Debbie when Saloma called her one of the girls. She would never cease to give thanks for how the Beilers had taken her in. Adam and Saloma had treated her like their own child from the start. That was what she'd wanted for so long but hadn't dared hope would ever happen.

Ida disappeared into the kitchen. Debbie was ready to follow when Saloma motioned for her to be seated. "Ida can handle the hot chocolate."

Debbie thought of protesting but gave in. This was so like Ida. She sacrificed for everyone. It became almost expected. Still, Debbie couldn't do more than be in the way while Ida heated the milk for the hot chocolate.

Verna leaned forward from her seat on the couch. "So Ida's still mourning?"

Saloma's face was sober. "*Yah.* It's been hard. *Daett* says Minister Kanagy has also taken it very hard."

Apparently not hard enough if the man is making eyes at Ida, Debbie thought. She almost choked out a protest but held her tongue.

Verna looked pensive. "Don't you think it's a little early for Minister Kanagy to be, you know, thinking about another *frau*?"

Debbie drew in a sharp breath.

Saloma regarded Verna steadily. "So you saw it too on Sunday?"

Verna shrugged. "It was plain enough to see since Minister Kanagy never looks at women that way. And I'm sure Ida has put

26

two and two together by now. And there's Melvin's children — at least the two oldest who live at his place. Ida won't turn him down, *Mamm,* will she?"

Saloma didn't hesitate. "I've thought some about the matter, and I know this might not be the usual, but neither is the situation the usual. I think Ida should accept — if things come to that. Minister Kanagy would make anyone a *gut* husband."

Verna gave a little grunt. "Maybe so, but I don't like him all that much."

"It's in *Da Hah*'s hands." Saloma nodded as if that settled the matter.

Debbie stifled her words. She had best stay out of this conversation.

Verna grabbed her stomach moments later, and Saloma's face flashed alarm. "Is something the matter? The child?"

Verna shifted on the couch. "No. I'm just thinking about Ida and Minister Kanagy. I don't like it one bit. Ida's always been too self-sacrificing. I don't want to see her hurt."

Saloma shook her finger. "I don't want you to say one word to your sister, mind you. Not everyone can have a storybook ending like you and Joe. Now mind me — not one word!"

Verna groaned but settled back on the couch.

In the silence that followed, Ida appeared in the kitchen doorway. "Chocolate coming right up!"

"She's such a dear," Verna said as Ida disappeared again.

Tires crunched in the driveway, and Debbie caught a glimpse of the car through the window. She knew who it was.

Saloma got up to look out the living-room window.

"Who is it, *Mamm*?" Verna asked when her mother didn't move or provide information.

"It's your sister!" Saloma stepped back and grasped the back of a rocker.

Verna struggled to get up. "Dear *Hah,* help us. That girl is nothing but trouble."

Saloma headed for the front door as she muttered, "How can one apple in the bushel turn out so bad?"

Verna ignored the comment and hollered toward the kitchen. "Ida, our sister's here."

"I already know," the answer came back. "I'll heat another batch of milk if necessary."

As usual, Ida's first thought was of service instead of her sister's transgressions. Debbie got to her feet. She would help Ida now, protest from Saloma or not.

Ida glanced up with concern when Debbie walked into the kitchen. "Did you see how she's dressed?"

"No." Debbie didn't add that she didn't have to. Lois likely wore one of Debbie's old dresses she'd had the sense not to wear around the Beilers. Lois would have no such inhibitions. Lois was more of an *Englisha* girl at heart than Debbie had ever been — even though Lois was born Amish!

Ida pasted a smile on her face. "I've got everything ready, but you can help carry in the cups. At least we can give Lois a nice afternoon — show her what she's missing."

That won't happen, Debbie thought. Lois doesn't appreciate the quiet ways of Amish life. But Ida always saw the best in everyone — even Minister Kanagy apparently.

Debbie followed Ida into the living room holding steaming mugs of hot chocolate in both hands just as Lois bustled through the front door with Saloma at her side. Lois's dress was well above her knees.

Lois grinned and gushed, "Well! If it isn't the whole family back together again. And hot chocolate. Am I glad I stopped by!"

Debbie smiled and handed over a mug as Lois took a seat. "I'm glad you stopped in."

Ida spoke up. "*Gut* to see you, Lois."

Lois took a quick sip of the hot chocolate. She wasted no time to get to the point of her visit. "So, will I see everyone at my wedding next Saturday?"

Lois knew good and well no one from her family would come, but she had to make one last attempt, Debbie supposed.

Saloma's voice was weary. "You know we can't come, Lois. It's an *Englisha* wedding. We cannot approve of this. You know that."

Lois's face fell. "I told Doug that would be your answer, but he just doesn't understand. I had to try one more time to convince you." Lois's voice caught, and she wiped one eye with a quick sweep of her hand. The hot chocolate remained clutched in the other.

"I'd come," Ida said with sympathy, "but it can't be, Lois. We can't show any approval of this choice of yours. Surely you know that."

Lois gulped. "I guess so. It's just sad and painful, that's all."

"You should have thought of that before you left." Saloma's voice had a bite to it.

Lois braced herself before she took another quick sip of hot chocolate. "But I love my new life. And Doug is such a catch. And I'm in my first year of college in Shamokin. We're setting up housekeeping after the wedding in a small rental in Selinsgrove. What more could I ask for?"

There was silence in the living room. Not

because they didn't know the answer to Lois's question, but because Lois wouldn't listen even if they spoke the truth. Lois had chosen her life, which was a jump over the fence to the Amish. And there was nothing anyone could do about it.

Saloma moved first. She reached over to touch Lois's arm. "But at least you've come home today. I'm glad for that. Maybe you can visit again after the wedding — and bring this husband of yours with you."

Lois pasted on a bright smile and settled in. The conversation soon flowed easily enough — now that the hard part was out of the way. The talk was all about Verna's baby and the Amish wedding season ahead of them. Lois's face fell momentarily when that subject came up, but she recovered quickly.

Finally, just before she left, Lois spent some time alone with Ida. The two whispered together near the front door when Saloma went into the kitchen. Debbie watched the sisters with no little sadness that things would never be as they had been. Lois's happiness in the *Englisha* world made that only too apparent.

THREE

The next morning as Bishop Beiler preached the main sermon, Debbie shifted to a more comfortable spot on the bench. The group of baptismal candidates had their seats set up near the ministers. She wasn't used to sitting right out in the open where everyone could see her. Usually she was seated behind a row or two of younger girls. Debbie tried not to move, but that had been difficult for the entire three-hour church service. She clasped her hands on her lap and forced herself to focus on the bishop. The clock on the living room wall crept toward twelve. The sermon would close soon, and she wasn't about to embarrass herself on the day of her baptism by squirming like a three-year-old.

Debbie sat up even straighter when Minister Kanagy's gaze came her way. He hadn't paid much attention to her all morning, even during their last instruction class upstairs. Perhaps Minister Kanagy thought he should make one last check before it was too late.

I look perfect! Debbie wanted to yell. But that wasn't even remotely the attitude a baptismal candidate should have. She smiled to think how her lack of being raised Amish sure showed at times. Minister Kanagy, of course, wouldn't take that as an excuse.

At least Minister Kanagy hadn't paid any attention to Ida, who was seated over in the unmarried girls' section. If he had, Debbie might have glared at him, baptism or no baptism. But a glare at Minister Kanagy could have no good end — even after one was baptized.

She hadn't caught sight of Alvin all day. He was seated somewhere among the row of unmarried men, she was sure. Alvin would be here for her baptismal day, even if some emergency had come up on the farm. Alvin's *daett* would cover for him, although Edwin was officially retired and lived in a *dawdy haus* with his wife, Helen, who had suffered a serious stroke this year.

Debbie focused again on Bishop Beiler's preaching. The bishop had his hands clasped now. He paused for a long moment before he turned toward the row of baptismal candidates. "We have come to this important step in the lives of these young people. All summer we as a ministry have tried to instruct them on how a godly and humble life is to be lived before *Da Hah*. We have found them submissive and willing to obey. For this we are grateful, and our hearts are glad. So without further words, if these are still willing to confess their faith before *Da Hah* and this congregation, they may kneel."

Debbie waited until the others moved first. Since she was the only girl in the class, all she had to do was follow the boys. Debbie slipped to her knees and brushed the long folds of her dress behind her. She bowed her head as Bishop Beiler began to ask the questions at the other end of the line.

The bishop's voice trembled when he reached her. "Do you, our sister Debbie, confess before *Da Hah* and these many witnesses that you will forsake the devil, the world, and your own flesh, and that you will obey the voice of *Da Hah* alone?"

"Yah," Debbie said softly.

A light touch of a hand came down on her *kapp*.

Deacon Mast, who stood beside the bishop, tipped his water pitcher three times as the bishop intoned, "I baptize you in the name of the Father, of the Son, and of the Holy Spirit. Amen. You may stand to your feet."

Saloma had made her way out of the married women's section by the time Bishop Beiler had helped Debbie to her feet. Saloma took her hand and kissed her on the cheek. The two embraced. Saloma didn't release Debbie right away as a soft sob escaped her. When Deacon Mast cleared his throat, Saloma held Debbie at arm's length and gave her a teary-eyed smile.

Debbie wiped her eyes. On the way back to their seats, she almost stumbled over a satchel set up against a bench leg. Saloma noticed and reached back with a hand to steady her. Saloma's eyes shone with happiness. Thankful for the help, Debbie's thoughts turned inward. It was almost as if she were born anew today. She'd become someone she hadn't been by natural birth. But wasn't that the way it should be? Her heart pounded as she kept her eyes on the songbook for the last song. On this her baptismal day, would Alvin finally make up his mind and ask her home? Surely this would help. If Alvin did ask her, she could move on to the next important goal all Amish girls had — saying marriage vows with the man they loved. And beyond that to raise families for the next generation of people of faith and community.

The singing finished, Debbie remained seated for a moment, catching her breath from all the excitement. Deacon Mast's *frau,* Susie, was the first to come up and greet her with a hug and a kiss on the cheek.

"You made it, Debbie!" Susie was all smiles. "We all knew you would."

"Thanks to the Beilers' help," Debbie replied at once. Even in triumph, she knew one gave thanks to others for the parts they played.

"You did plenty yourself," Susie told her. "And now you're really one of us. Well, I'm glad for you." Susie's face fell for a moment. "*Da Hah* gives and *Da Hah* takes, that's what I told David this morning. Not that long ago we lost a member, but today we gain new ones."

Debbie's voice caught. "That was so sad about Barbara's passing."

Susie nodded. "One should never question *Da Hah* though. He always knows what's best."

"It's still so hard." The words slipped out.

Susie didn't appear offended. "That's the part we must work through, trusting Him. Well, let's not spoil the joy of your day, Debbie. Welcome again."

"Thank you," Debbie whispered as Susie moved on. Others came and shook her hand, wishing her God's best and telling her what a blessing and inspiration she was to many of them. She was surprised to hear that. The community had been a blessing to her more than anything.

Ida soon pulled on her hand. "Shall we go help with the tables?"

"Of course," Debbie agreed. She didn't expect royal treatment, even though it was her special day. Back to work it was. There had been no sign of Verna seated among the women today, but she hadn't expected her friend to venture out again until the birth of her child. Ida seemed to read her glance as they made their way to the kitchen. "I don't see Verna either, but I'm sure she's thinking of you."

"Thanks." Debbie smiled. The kitchen was crowded, with women and girls every-where. Ida found Deacon Mast's wife, Susie, and tapped on her shoulder. "May we help somewhere?"

Susie thought for a moment. "The unmarried men's table in the back of the house needs help."

Debbie's feelings sank as Ida moved toward the bowls of peanut butter and red beets lined up on the counter. She had no choice but to follow Ida's lead, although at the moment she'd rather do almost anything else. Debbie loaded her hands with bowls. Maybe she could drop out of line and serve the married men's table instead. But that would provoke strange glances from the other girls since that table apparently had plenty of servers assigned to it.

She still hadn't seen any sign of Alvin, but Paul Wagler was here, plain as day. He looked up and smiled at her as they approached the unmarried men's table.

"What an honor!" Paul cracked. "Our food ought to be so blessed today, being freshly baptized and all."

"You can shut up!" Debbie snapped before she could seal her lips. This would only encourage Paul further. Why couldn't she keep her mouth shut when Paul teased? The room teetered with laugher, and Paul's look was triumphant. Ida placed her bowls on the table with a quick sideways glance at Paul. Ida used to have her heart set on the eventual capture of the man's attention, but that had never happened. Why didn't Ida try again? Debbie wondered. Instead she planned to settle for Minister Kanagy. Such an effort would so be like the self-sacrificing Ida. She probably didn't even know how to pursue her own interest in Paul. And Paul wasn't interested anyway. He wanted a flashier girl — like Debbie, Paul claimed.

"Oh, she's still in dreamland . . ." Paul leaned over to coo in Debbie's direction. "Well, I say I'm glad to see it myself."

There was weak laughter from the other men. Paul sounded half-genuine in his appreciation. Debbie's heart softened toward him for a moment. Surely on one's baptismal day she ought to think nice thoughts — even of Paul Wagler.

Paul had a big grin on his face. "I see Deacon Mast's water didn't wash away any of her beauty."

"That's enough out of you!" Ida gave Paul a glare.

Paul appeared chastened for a second before he joined in the laughter all around him.

As she followed Ida back to the kitchen, Debbie stared at her friend in astonishment. What had come into Ida to speak up like that? Normally she didn't dare stand up to any wisecrack Paul made.

"Thank you!" Debbie whispered. Emery had sat at the end of the table, but he acted like he approved of Paul's actions. Thankfully his sister disagreed. It would have been nice if Emery had also stuck up for her.

Ida glanced back, appearing pale and

surprised at her words to Paul. "That wasn't a nice thing for him to say."

Debbie smiled. "At least you noticed. But I know that's just Paul."

Ida continued as if she hadn't heard. "You're good looking and very decent, Debbie. On that he was saying the truth."

"Hush!" Debbie felt a rush of heat run up her neck. "Don't say that." Now if Alvin said such things she would have accepted them — but not from Paul.

Ida gave her a weak smile. "I guess it isn't decent to say such things."

Debbie leaned closer in the press of the crowd of women to whisper, "You ought to pursue him yourself, you know."

Ida choked for a moment. "Now you're thinking crazy. You ought to accept who *Da Hah* has laid out for you, Debbie. The two of you are made for each other like peas in a pod."

Ida's words stung deep. She meant them as a compliment, but Debbie knew she and Paul were not in any way a match. Paul was an arrogant man. Despite Ida's own feelings for Paul, she'd tried to push Paul and her together all of last year. Ida acting in her usual self-sacrificing way, of course.

Debbie stepped closer as Ida leaned toward her. "Debbie, did you notice Alvin

40

wasn't here on your baptismal day?"

Debbie winced. She'd been too distracted by Paul's teases to see for sure if Alvin was at the unmarried men's table.

Ida continued. "I really should tell you this, Debbie. It's not right that you don't know."

Debbie gave Ida a quick glance. Ida wasn't one to spread rumors, so she had to think this was serious news.

Ida came even closer. "Alvin's *mamm,* Helen, hasn't been well for some time — since her stroke this summer."

Debbie nodded and waited. She already knew that.

Ida struggled for the words. "The Knepp family hired on Mildred Schrock the week before last. Alvin's *daett* won't move in with any of the sisters-in-law. Not unless he absolutely has to. Anyway, Mildred's living right there on the farm, Debbie. You know what that could mean. And Alvin could have forbidden it — if he had objected. You do know Alvin pursued Mildred when they were in school?"

Debbie caught her breath. Would this explain Alvin's hesitancy all summer after he'd almost promised her a date? Had Alvin fallen for his old sweetheart? It made way too much sense. Debbie grabbed the edge

41

of the counter in front of her. "Yes, I knew."

Ida clutched her arm. "I'm not trying to startle you, Debbie, but it's time you knew. Alvin not showing up today may mean something."

A fire shone in Ida's eyes that Debbie didn't see very often. What had gotten into her? Probably the injustice she perceived in Alvin's continued play with her affections while a man like Paul stood on the sidelines ready to sweep her up the first chance he had.

"It's probably a coincidence," Debbie managed. "We mustn't read too much into this."

They filled their arms with bowls of food again. Ida was obviously not convinced, and neither was Debbie, if truth be told. This did look like a real threat to her future with Alvin. She knew from the stories Verna had told her before she married Joe that Mildred had shown Alvin attention before they joined the youth group. Why Mildred stopped, Verna never ventured to guess. Likely because of the Knepp reputation for being poor farmers. But now with the revelation that Alvin wasn't to blame for that, things might be different. Alvin had taken over his father's farm and it was prospering, so perhaps Mildred regretted her original decision and was interested in Alvin again.

No wonder Alvin hadn't asked her home all summer. Debbie shook her head to clear the spinning world in front of her eyes. She pasted on a bright smile. This was her baptismal day, and she wouldn't allow Alvin Knepp to spoil it . . . even though her heart throbbed with deep pain.

FOUR

That Sunday evening the hymn singing drew to a close, and Debbie sat on the front bench trying to concentrate on the songbook Ida held with her. Ida didn't know what had transpired just before the evening meal. She should have told her friend at once, but Debbie couldn't bring herself to speak the words. The problem was she couldn't believe the conversation with Alvin had occurred or that she'd agreed to allow him to drive her home tonight. Not after what Ida had told her this afternoon.

Even now Mildred sat further down the row of girls beaming a big smile straight across the aisle at Alvin. She'd done so all evening. Alvin at least had the decency not to return the attention. But how did Mildred dare give Alvin such open attention if there were no feelings between the two of them? Debbie scolded herself for returning to those dark thoughts of doubting Alvin.

44

Wasn't his asking her home answer enough? It was, after all, the moment she'd so longed for.

Alvin had been all smiles when he spoke to her. He hadn't looked at all like he had anything he should be ashamed of. "Sorry to miss your baptism this morning, Debbie," he'd said. "The cows were sick with mastitis again, and I was waiting for the vet."

"And your *daett*? Where was he?" she'd managed to choke out.

"Oh . . ." Alvin shrugged. "He doesn't get involved in running the farm any longer."

As if that answered all the questions. Why was Mildred at his *daett*'s house to care for his *mamm* when other girls were likely available?

Alvin hadn't seemed to pick up on her rumpled spirits. "I . . . I'm finally ready to take you home, Debbie. Like we spoke of last spring. I'm sorry it's taken so long. Is tonight okay? I mean, if there's a problem, I can wait until next Sunday."

The man at least had the decency to act a little hesitant. But that was usually Alvin's problem, not his virtue. Debbie knew she ought to be thankful Alvin had gained as much confidence as he had. His time spent in her world hadn't been entirely wasted. Perhaps that was why she'd decided not to

snap at him. There might be nothing between him and Mildred, although if Ida
thought so, how could it be just imagination?

Alvin had regarded her with a question on
his face. "Is everything okay, Debbie?"

"Oh! Yes, of course," she'd chirped. "Tonight's just fine."

Now here they were, almost time to go
home, and Ida still hadn't been told. Down
the bench Mildred was still smiling like a
sunflower that followed the sun. Debbie
couldn't remember that Mildred had acted
like this last Sunday, but then Mildred
hadn't moved in with Alvin's parents until
recently.

Debbie focused back on the service as the
last song was given out. Mildred would find
out soon enough that she had allowed Alvin
to take her home. That would cool Mildred's
obviously revived ardor. And Debbie and
Alvin had way too much history together to
throw it all away on an innocent thing like
who had moved in next door to help Alvin's
parents in their time of need. The community girls did that kind of thing all the
time, and no one thought twice about it.

The song ended and the soft murmur of
young people's chatter began. Debbie didn't
move as a few of the men who dated steady

jumped to their feet and went outside to get their horses. Their girlfriends gave them brief glances and went on with their conversations with the other girls. There was no sense in rushing outside to wait in the cold before the men had their horses and buggies ready.

Now was the time when she had to tell Ida. Alvin might leave at any moment. And sure enough — as if Alvin had heard her thoughts — he got to his feet and left, followed by the admiring look of Mildred Schrock. As Alvin slipped out the door, Debbie forced herself to nudge Ida.

"I'm not going home with you and Emery tonight."

Ida turned around, a look of surprise on her face.

Debbie whispered, "Alvin's taking me."

Ida gasped and a few girls glanced their way.

"Please! Don't make a fuss," Debbie said. "I'll explain later."

Ida collected herself. "Of course!" she squeaked.

This didn't go well, Debbie thought. She had to get out of here whether Alvin was ready or not. Several of the girls were still staring at her as Debbie fled toward the washroom. They could all figure out tomorrow what the fuss had been about. By then the whole community would know Alvin had taken her home.

Debbie found her shawl in the bedroom and stepped outside. The evening air had cooled considerably. She wrapped her shawl tightly around her shoulders. Now to find Alvin's buggy. A line of girls stood at the end of the sidewalk and gave her quick glances. Well, they would just have to be curious. She wouldn't announce the news, but she also wouldn't stand here in uncomfortable silence. Why couldn't she find Alvin's buggy and help him hitch up? It wasn't exactly the custom of dating girls, but neither was she the normal Amish girl.

Debbie moved on past the line of girls, navigating around the buggies lined up to go to the driveway. She soon found Alvin's buggy without any problems. He hadn't arrived from the barn with his horse, so she waited in the shadows until he appeared leading a snorting horse by the bridle. He appeared pleased to see her. He must have interpreted her early arrival as eagerness to have him drive her home. Hopefully this misconception warmed his heart more than Mildred's smiles had all evening. But she mustn't think about Mildred anymore. Debbie had wanted this for so long. Why spoil the evening?

Debbie fastened the tug on her side in sync with Alvin's movements. She climbed in, and he threw her the lines before he got in himself. She handed him the reins as soon as he was settled.

Alvin gently slapped them against his horse's back. "Get up, Star."

Well, now she knew the name of his horse! Debbie hid her smile. She didn't want Alvin to know she valued any information about him she could gather. He didn't need to know that.

Alvin steered his buggy around the others, and it bounced in a ditch once before they reached the blacktop. Debbie settled back in the seat. She actually was on a ride home with Alvin Knepp! It was hard to believe.

"Chilled off a bit," Alvin commented, offering her more of the buggy blanket.

Debbie tucked the edge under her. "Does this cold weather affect your cows?" She didn't know much about cows, but it sounded like an intelligent question.

Alvin grimaced. "Cold is never good for sickness, but the vet thinks we'll be okay. I milked the sick ones out and dumped the milk. All I can say is we can't afford much more of this."

"How is the farm doing?" Debbie already

knew the answer, but she wanted Alvin to talk about it.

"Dad took the change hard." Alvin glanced at her. "I suppose you wondered why I took so long getting back to you . . . about taking you home. It's not because I was having doubts, Debbie. But I was busy and having to deal with *Daett*'s disapproval of . . . well . . . lots of things." Alvin slapped the reins again to get Star to speed up. "I guess I should explain. Things weren't the best around the farm growing up. I had to make a lot of changes this year to get the place working right. None of this was easy, but things are going smoothly now. And with your baptism out of the way, I thought it was time."

Debbie swallowed hard. "My baptism, Alvin? You didn't trust me before this? And your *daett*? Does he not approve of me?"

Alvin swallowed hard. "Of course I trusted you, Debbie. But . . . I mean . . . how do I explain? It's like this. I saw so much out there in your world. What with being with Crystal Meyers on a few dates and seeing how her life had turned out. And I wondered . . . Well, it doesn't matter now. I know you're not Crystal."

Debbie couldn't keep the disappointment out of her voice. "But you thought I might

50

be? And your *daett* thinks so too?"

Alvin turned to face her. "Okay, *yah,* I did. The thought crossed my mind, and I had to be sure. Plus, *Daett* was highly disapproving — actually still is highly disapproving of us. And I had already challenged him on enough things. It was best that I waited. Please try to understand."

Debbie felt her body turn cold. She tried to keep her words warm. "I do understand that your parents are among the best *Ordnung* keepers in the community. And now that their son is back from jumping the fence, I can see they don't want him polluted at any cost. But you made your mistakes too, Alvin. What were you doing out in my world to begin with? Then you wouldn't have learned what *Englisha* women are capable of. Like leaving their husbands after they say the wedding vows. I'm not like that, Alvin."

Alvin let go of the lines with one hand. He grasped her hand and held it firm. "Debbie, listen to me. I love you. I do. I'm not perfect. I have my problems. And one of them is watching that Paul Wagler making eyes at you every Sunday, knowing all the time he'd make a much better husband than I ever could. How do you think that makes me feel? It took a lot of courage just to ask you home, Debbie. So please, let's not quarrel."

Debbie willed herself to calm down. She wasn't perfect, and obviously Alvin wasn't either. She couldn't hold that against him. And she knew he had fears. Alvin had always had them. At least he worked to overcome them. And he was honest about things tonight. That went a long way, didn't it? This still didn't answer her questions about Mildred Schrock, but right now that had best be left alone. They'd quarreled enough for one evening.

Debbie gave Alvin a warm smile.

He relaxed.

"Sorry if I was too harsh," she said.

He smiled back. "I like your spunk, so don't change that."

Both of Alvin's hands were back on the lines as he concentrated on driving.

"I don't have anything ready to eat at home," Debbie said. "This was kind of sudden."

He gave her a kind look. "I'll be with you, that's all I need. I get enough to eat at home."

The thought of Mildred over in the *dawdy haus* flashed through Debbie's mind. Had Mildred brought food over to Alvin this week? Without a doubt she had, and Mildred had also used that time to moon over Alvin, if Debbie didn't miss her guess. She snuggled up against Alvin's shoulder, and he didn't pull back. She spoke with an uplifted face. "It's still a wonderful evening. Remember how I used to drive past your place in my car to admire you working in the fields? That seems like a long time ago."

Alvin smiled down at her. "It hasn't been that long, but I know what you mean. I used to be so fascinated with the *Englisha* girl in her fancy car. I never dared dream she'd be in my buggy one day."

"My Dodge Shadow wasn't fancy," Debbie protested as she sat up. She thought of the many students at Franklin and Marshall who drove BMWs, Audis, and Porsches.

"It was fancy to me." Alvin's voice was soft. "But now you're with me in *my* buggy."

"I like it better this way." Debbie nestled back against his shoulder.

"So do I." He gave her a sideways glance.

She wondered if she should be leaning against his shoulder on a first date. Was that a little too much for the Knepps who kept a strict *Ordnung*? No doubt it was, but Alvin had been out in her world and would likely be practical about it. Because that's what they were, she thought with a smile. A practical couple. She'd been drawn to Alvin

53

for his simple ways, and he to her because of her perceived fancy ones. It all made perfect sense.

"I think we do have some pie in the pantry," Debbie said as Alvin slowed down for the Beliers' driveway.

"I told you it doesn't matter." He brought Star to a halt by the hitching post.

Debbie climbed out and waited while Alvin secured the tie rope. This would be a good first evening together, she decided. There was no reason why it shouldn't be.

FIVE

The predawn air had a nip to it the next Monday morning as Alvin stepped out of the washroom of the old farmhouse for a moment. He glanced up at the sweep of bright stars overhead and smiled. Last night had been a success! *Yah,* Debbie had been a little feisty at the start, but he could understand why with the long wait after he had practically promised to take her home. After they had arrived at the Beiler place, Debbie calmed down. For the rest of the evening she'd treated him with the utmost respect and affection. But she always had, and much more than he deserved. He must not doubt her any longer or question her devotion to the community.

It was his time spent in the *Englisha* world that made him nervous. Why he had ever done such a thing was beyond him. To risk and receive excommunication had been so stupid. How had he dared? And now that he had taken Debbie home from the hymn singing, a new fear niggled at him. Hadn't Crystal said something about a visit to the community? That she had relatives in the county? *Yah,* she had, but surely she wasn't serious.

Alvin sighed as he remembered how things had been before he'd left and met Crystal in Philadelphia. His *daett* had run the farm and allowed Alvin no say in the day-to-day operations. As a result, *Daett* had managed to run the farm into the ground and accumulate debt. Alvin had fled rather than face the scorn of the community. He'd also been convinced he could never win Debbie's heart when Paul Wagler was showering affection on her all the time.

How wrong he had been! And how wrong he had been about some other things as well. The *Englisha* world had been worse than he'd imagined. Crystal Meyers had taught him that. How could a nice woman like Crystal leave her husband? Maybe the man had been a horrible person. Crystal hadn't really said so, but still remarriage after a divorce was out of the question for anyone in the community. As was divorce itself. Yet Crystal had wanted to strike up a relationship with him. She would have married him, he was sure. But hers was a world he couldn't understand — nor did he want to understand it. But Debbie wasn't *Englisha* anymore, Alvin reminded himself. Debbie was not like Crystal.

Alvin blew on his hands and retreated inside the washroom. He used the kerosene lamp to find his way into the basement, where he stoked the old furnace back to life after a night set on low. He still slept upstairs even though his *mamm* and *daett* had moved into the *dawdy haus.* Though most single men didn't live by themselves, Alvin's *daett* had insisted they build the *dawdy haus* this year. They had, and Edwin and Helen had moved in at once. Likely because of their past tense relationship, Alvin figured. Or maybe it was because he now ran the farm, and it was a little easier for *Daett* to face that reality if he lived at the *dawdy haus.*

I need a *frau,* Alvin thought. And the old farmhouse needed a woman's touch. He was old enough to have a *frau.* But he had dawdled around all summer being nervous about Debbie, and now there was no way they could get a wedding in this fall. Not with the Beilers acting as Debbie's family. They would want things done decently and in order. And Debbie wouldn't consent to such a rushed schedule anyway. Neither would he like it, he supposed. Although it would be nice to have a *frau* in the house to clean and fix his meals. He didn't look forward to another whole year living here alone.

His *mamm*'s health had begun to deteriorate in the spring, and then she had suffered the stroke. And if he didn't miss his guess, his *mamm* had the onset of Alzheimer's on top of everything else. His *daett* didn't think so, but at least he had summoned Mildred Schrock's help, which would have been awkward if they still lived in the same house. Not that the community would say much, since both *Mamm* and *Daett* would have been in the house. But it was best that the three stayed in the *dawdy haus*. And that Alvin didn't date Mildred. He wouldn't have liked to anyway. There were too many memories he didn't wish revived between them. Some of them were quite painful.

Not that the good ones could be revived. There was too much bitterness in his heart for him to think of Mildred Schrock as anyone other than *Mamm*'s caretaker. And he didn't even like to think of her as that. But *Mamm* and *Daett* needed help and Mildred was available, so he hadn't objected. And it was a credit to Debbie's character that she hadn't brought up the subject last night. No doubt Debbie saw the foolishness of any idea of romance between Mildred and himself. Anyone could see that if they looked.

And if Debbie had protested, he would have told her that Mildred in the *dawdy haus* was nothing like what he had to put up with watching every Sunday as Paul vied for Debbie's attention. And if he didn't miss his guess, Paul would keep at it. His attempts might be a little better hidden, but Wagler wouldn't give up on winning Debbie's affections until wedding vows were said. Another reason a fall wedding would be perfect — only now it was too late. And he had no one to blame but himself.

Maybe he was more of his father's son than he wished to admit, Alvin thought. He might know how to run a farm, but he wasn't good with a woman's heart. He climbed the basement stairs and, in the glowing hiss of lantern light, pulled on his coat and headed outside. He paused and took another glance at the blaze of stars overhead. They fell clear to the horizon, accenting the shadowy tops of the trees. When dawn broke, the deep red and gold fall colors would be visible. Hopefully he'd be in the fields hard at work by then. Alvin pushed open the barn door and called to his cows as he entered. They answered with soft moos.

He loved this part of the morning. The stillness of *Da Hah*'s creation was all around him. The animals were moving quietly and the gentle smells of the barn rose around him.

Alvin jumped when a woman's voice spoke behind him. "*Gut* morning, Alvin. I see you know how to get up early."

Alvin whirled around. "Mildred! What are you doing out here?"

She held a lantern in her hand and smiled up at him. "Helping with the chores. Your *daett* said it was part of my job."

"But . . . but . . ." Alvin sputtered. "He never told me. And you've been here almost a week."

Mildred shrugged. "You can't expect me to organize everything so quickly. I had your mother to settle into her new routine first."

"You're not helping out here." Alvin stood his ground with his lantern swinging in his hand. "I won't have it."

Mildred laughed. "Your *daett* said you'd throw a fit. Seems you and he don't always get along, but on this one he told me he's right. You're struggling in the barn with so many chores, and I am to help you."

His *daett* was right, Alvin had to admit. He hadn't been able to make it into the fields until after daylight, and that was valuable time lost. But Mildred helping with the chores wasn't wanted. Not morning and night each and every day.

"I won't be able to help in the evenings," Mildred said, as if she could read his mind. "So take what you can get, Alvin, and be thankful for the help."

She was brisk enough about the matter, Alvin thought. Maybe he should give in. He stood rooted in one spot. Mildred regarded him with a tilt of her head. "Well, we don't have all day. What do you want me to do first?"

Alvin let out a breath. Debbie would understand. He hung his lantern on a hook on a ceiling beam. Without a backward glance, he went to open the gate for the cows.

Mildred had spread the feed and was snapping the stanchions shut as the animals put their heads through to eat when he came back.

She's efficient, Alvin thought. Unlike Debbie, Mildred had grown up on a farm, so of course she was.

"Water in the millhouse?" Mildred asked, giving him a smile even as she disappeared through the swinging barn doors.

She knew good and well where the water was. Mildred was trying to keep him at a disadvantage. And she would know how to do that. Mildred knew all about him — his anxieties, his timidity, his inability to stand up to his *daett*. The only reason he ran the farm now was because the church committee had taken over while he was in the *Englisha* world. They'd given him charge when he returned. Otherwise his *daett* would have destroyed the farm before he would have asked Alvin to help.

Mildred appeared again carrying a wash bucket and a cloth. "I guess you wash down the udders, don't you?"

"Always do," Alvin muttered. Feelings like he hadn't felt in a long time swept over him. How did Mildred do it? She made him feel like a small boy sitting at his school desk.

Mildred stepped out from behind a cow with a mournful look. "Do we really have to start out this way, Alvin? I guess it's mainly my fault. I want to make that plain. I did things I shouldn't have in those years after we left school. I really am sorry. I hope you're not still holding them against me."

"You didn't really do anything," Alvin said. He didn't look at her. His heart throbbed with pain.

Ida shru
Emery
slowed fo
Once Em
Debbie h
and Ida
undone a
reached h
appreciat
while the
With Em
they set t
"Want h
Emery
back.
Debbie
house, ar
Both Sal
rockers w
better th
thought.
home thi
bad cold.
over Lois
Bishop
tion, "I s
rived!"
Debbie
Ida can
"There v

Mildred regarded him for a moment. "Well, maybe I didn't. That's what I've told myself at least, but you know what I mean. I could at least have come and spoken with you . . . told you that my affections had moved elsewhere instead of just cutting you off like I did."

Alvin still didn't look at her. He just couldn't. He remembered how badly he'd felt too well. The cold, slicing pain when Mildred had turned up her nose at him those first youth gatherings he had been to. *Yah,* she was right. She hadn't really done anything — but at the same time, she had.

Mildred continued. "We were young in those days, Alvin. I was a schoolgirl and silly on top of it all. The thought never dawned on me how much stock you placed in our little chats and glances. I liked you, Alvin. I wasn't making that up. But we grew up. And I made mistakes. Can you forgive me? I really am sorry. I could have been much more tactful in how I handled things."

"It was nothing." Alvin lifted a piece of milking equipment from the rack on the wall.

Mildred obviously didn't plan to let this go. She didn't move. "We should at least come to some kind of terms, Alvin. I'm working for your *daett* and *mamm.* I'm

63

doubt if she's staying past this afternoon. She's *Englisha*, after all. Maybe it's just curiosity."

"I agree." Debbie went to join Ida in the kitchen. She would see Alvin next Sunday evening, and they would have a conversation about this and go from there. Alvin shouldn't run away from his problems.

Ida had the popcorn popper on the stove when Debbie walked in. She glanced up. "This is all the more reason you really should consider Paul. Alvin has *Englisha* girls following him home now!"

Debbie groaned. "Ida, please! Alvin and I have been through a lot. For one thing, I came from the outside, so how can I fault Alvin for problems with that world too? But I can assure you that Alvin isn't in danger of falling for Crystal. I admit I had a few fears fluttering around in my stomach when I first saw her, but I know how Alvin feels about Crystal now."

Ida grimaced. "Paul Wagler truly loves you, Debbie. I've known that for a long time. I don't understand why you don't see it."

Ida had her mind made up. Debbie groaned. But maybe she was the one who had lost hers. All they needed now to top this awful day off was for Minister Kanagy

74

Ida shrugged but left the subject alone.

Emery didn't seem too concerned as he slowed for the turn into their driveway. Once Emery came to a stop by the barn, Debbie hopped out on one side of the buggy and Ida on the other. They had the tugs undone and the snaps off by the time Emery reached his horse's bridle. He grunted his appreciation and led the horse forward while the two girls held the buggy shafts. With Emery leading the horse to the barn, they set them gently on the ground.

"Want help?" Ida hollered after him.

Emery shook his head but didn't look back.

Debbie turned to lead the way toward the house, and Ida followed close behind her. Both Saloma and Adam were seated in their rockers when they walked in. Saloma looks better than she did last night, Debbie thought. She and the bishop had stayed home this morning. The bishop to nurse a bad cold, and Saloma because of her grief over Lois's wedding to an *Englisha* man.

Bishop Beiler boomed through his congestion, "I see the popcorn makers have arrived!"

Debbie smiled as she took off her shawl.

Ida came to a stop in front of her mother. "There was a strange *Englisha* woman in doubt if she's staying past this afternoon. She's *Englisha*, after all. Maybe it's just curiosity."

"I agree." Debbie went to join Ida in the kitchen. She would see Alvin next Sunday evening, and they would have a conversation about this and go from there. Alvin shouldn't run away from his problems.

Ida had the popcorn popper on the stove when Debbie walked in. She glanced up. "This is all the more reason you really should consider Paul. Alvin has *Englisha* girls following him home now!"

Debbie groaned. "Ida, please! Alvin and I have been through a lot. For one thing, I came from the outside, so how can I fault Alvin for problems with that world too? But I can assure you that Alvin isn't in danger of falling for Crystal. I admit I had a few fears fluttering around in my stomach when I first saw her, but I know how Alvin feels about Crystal now."

Ida grimaced. "Paul Wagler truly loves you, Debbie. I've known that for a long time. I don't understand why you don't see it."

Ida had her mind made up. Debbie groaned. But maybe she was the one who had lost hers. All they needed now to top this awful day off was for Minister Kanagy

74

to show up this afternoon and begin his heavy-handed courtship of Ida.

"Sorry if I hurt your feelings," Ida said. "I wasn't trying to be hard on you and Alvin."

Debbie smiled understandingly. "These are big problems that Alvin and I have. I'm not saying they aren't. But I want to work through them, not run away."

"I just don't like the way Alvin's been using you." Ida turned to pour in the popcorn kernels. She asked over her shoulder, "Will you get me the bowl?"

"Sure." Debbie rushed to the counter even though there was no need to hurry. The popcorn wouldn't pop for two minutes or so. Ida gave her a concerned look but said nothing as she twirled the popcorn popper handle. Debbie smiled back, waiting until Ida dumped the first batch of white kernels into the bowl. While Debbie added the salt and butter, she caught sight of a buggy in the driveway. Joe Weaver was climbing out to tie his horse.

Debbie caught her breath. Verna's time must have arrived! Ida had a suitcase packed upstairs all week in preparation for this moment.

"Joe's here!" Debbie tried to quell her excitement. This was exactly what they needed to distract themselves from all their troubles.

Ida set the empty popcorn popper on the stove with a bang. Her hands flew to her apron strings, and she jerked them open. Without a word, she dashed up the stairs.

Debbie grabbed the popcorn bowl and went to the living room doorway.

"What's gotten into the girl?" Saloma asked. Apparently she hadn't noticed the buggy drive in.

"Joe's here!" Debbie told them. "Verna's baby must be on the way!"

Saloma's face lit up and the section of the *Budget* she'd been reading flew across the floor.

"Don't do that," Bishop Beiler chided. "You'll be tearing the pages so I can't read them."

"Verna's baby!" Saloma gushed.

"It's happened before," the bishop said with twinkles in his eyes.

Saloma ignored him and made her way to the living room window just as Joe came up the front steps. Saloma jerked open the door. "Is it time, Joe?"

He took his hat off, a worried look on his face. "*Yah.* Verna had me pick up the midwife an hour ago, and then she sent me here for Ida."

"Cheer up!" Bishop Beiler boomed from

his rocker. "Babies are born all the time."

Saloma waved her hand at her husband. "Don't pay any attention to him, Joe. Of course you're worried. It's a big undertaking. I'll see if Ida's ready."

Before Saloma could take a step toward the stairs, Ida bustled down with her night satchel. She'd changed into her chore clothing. She didn't say a word as Joe led the way outside.

Saloma stared after them. "*Da Hah* gives, and *Da Hah* takes away. Blessed be His name!" she called.

"Amen!" Bishop Beiler said loudly from his rocker.

Debbie fled back into the kitchen. She was blessed to be a part of this family in their sorrows and in their joys. Someday, if the Lord willed it, she and Alvin would experience this very thing. She would do everything in her power to make that happen — even with Crystal Meyers and Mildred Schrock around.

Seven

Joe urged his driving horse, Isaiah, onward as Ida clung to the buggy front and tried to remain calm. After all, there really was no rush. She would help with the birth where she could, but the full responsibility for that lay in the capable hands of the old midwife Sadie Graber. By the means of her considerable skills, half the Amish babies around Lewistown had been brought into the world. Ida's job was to help take care of the *boppli* once he or she was born.

"Sadie knows what she's doing," Ida said reassuringly as she clutched tightly to the side of the buggy when Joe took a corner at good speed.

Joe's face twitched. "I know, but I'm awfully worried."

"*Da Hah* will do what He wishes," Ida said.

"That's what's got me afraid." Joe made no pretense of hiding his doubts about the matter.

Ida tried to hide her smile. One's first child must be the worst for causing fears, but in the end Joe would submit as they all did to the inevitable revelation of *Da Hah*'s will. But that didn't mean one didn't pray sorrows wouldn't come or that the birth would be as easy and as safe as possible.

Joe's lips moved in whispered prayer. "Dear *Hah,* You know I love Verna and the *boppli* that's coming. If it's not against Your will, please keep them both safe. How could I live without Verna? And how could either of us go on if the child is lost?"

Ida reached over and squeezed Joe's arm.

He smiled in gratitude, but his face was still tense. Joe regarded her for a moment. "You've had your share of sorrows, Ida." Joe turned his attention to the road as he navigated another sharp corner.

"*Da Hah* has seen me through all of them," Ida said. "And He will be with you and Verna."

Joe nodded but kept Isaiah moving at high speed. *Yah,* he trusted *Da Hah,* but he still wanted to get back home. He slowed the horse as they neared home. "I must admit that I'm feeling tense and have a headache. But it's nothing compared to Verna's pains."

Ida leaned forward to pick up her satchel

she'd set on the buggy floor. She rummaged through it and pulled out a bottle of aspirin. Ida shook two into her hand and held them out to Joe. "Take these. It's going to be some long hours, I'm thinking."

Joe snorted. "I'm not a baby." But he took them, tossed the pills into his mouth dry, and swallowed.

"Now relax!" Ida commanded.

Joe smiled. He pulled into the driveway and stopped alongside the midwife's horse and buggy at the hitching post.

Ida helped Joe unhitch Isaiah and headed for the house. Halfway across the lawn, she paused. Did Joe know enough about how long birthing might take to think of unhitching Sadie's horse? *Nee,* likely not. She ran back to the barn door and hollered, "Joe, you do know that Sadie might be here all night?"

"I'll see to her horse then," Joe hollered back. "Thank you."

Ida chuckled. Joe hadn't admitted his not realizing these things, but that's how men were. They didn't like confessing their lack of knowledge. Just as Minister Kanagy hadn't wanted to admit this afternoon to his total ignorance on how to proceed with courting her. The poor man. She couldn't blame him though. This was an awkward situation for both of them, made all the worse by the man's sorrow over his *frau*'s recent death. She hadn't told anyone about the exchange. She deliberately blocked it out of her mind on the drive home with Debbie and Emery. But now she let the memories rush back.

For once Minister Kanagy's nervous twitches and fumbles had seemed completely appropriate. He'd motioned her out on the back porch when she walked by after the services. She'd obeyed, praying that no one would interrupt them in the midst of their talk. Not that they were doing anything wrong, but still . . .

Was this going to be a new start for her as Minister Kanagy's *frau*? It certainly seemed so. But Minister Kanagy was just standing there, totally at a loss for words once he had her attention. He'd appeared confident enough earlier when he'd watched her during the services, but that was gone now.

"I . . . uh . . . sometimes . . . Ida . . . um . . . I don't really know . . . You'll have to forgive my clumsiness, Ida. T–t–this is very h–h–hard," he stuttered.

What came over her, Ida had no idea. Maybe it was *Da Hah* giving her boldness and a willing heart because, truth to tell, she wasn't attracted to the man. Not like she'd been to his brother, Melvin, and, before that, to Paul Wagler. Paul didn't really count though. And as for Melvin, love had come slowly into her heart. There was no reason it wouldn't do that for his brother. With time, she told herself.

Ida reached out and took Minister Kanagy's hand. She used his first name. "Ben, I understand. And I'm so sorry about Barbara's passing. I really am."

He gulped hard even though his fingers lingered in hers. "You understand then? About the children? And my inability to take care of them well enough? And that the wedding season will soon be over?"

She'd smiled. "I understand all that."

He'd stood there dazed.

Before long someone would walk past, so she'd prompted him. "Are you asking me to be your *frau,* Ben?"

Relief had flooded his face. *"Yah,* Ida. *Yah!"* I know I'm not that *gut* a husband for you, but I'm pressed greatly in my soul. And you are a godly woman."

Ida had smiled. The man had a poetic side to him. She hadn't expected that. "*Da Hah* will help us, I'm thinking. And *yah,* I'm willing."

His eyes had widened. "You move my heart to great depths, Ida."

Ida had pulled her hand from his. She could appreciate that he was grateful for the easy conquest, but even now footsteps sounded near the porch door.

Minister Kanagy rushed out, "I will come by your home then? This week sometime? For making the plans?" He hadn't even waited for her nod before he fled.

Debbie had glanced strangely at Ida when she arrived back at the kitchen. Thankfully Debbie had apparently attributed Ida's distracted condition to the trauma associated with Lois's wedding the day before.

Ida had struggled for more than thirty minutes to compose herself. She was thrilled to gather her shawl around her shoulders in the washroom when it was time to leave. She'd allowed Debbie to lead the way outside to Emery's buggy. Thankfully she'd been able to turn her thoughts and the conversation elsewhere for the ride home. The conversation about the strange girl in church, who turned out to be Crystal Meyers, had served as a convenient distraction.

She would soon be Minister Kanagy's *frau*! Ida pushed open Verna and Joe's front door. No thrills ran up and down her spine, but neither was that a requirement. She was happy with what *Da Hah* had apparently planned. And she would get to care for

Melvin's children. That would be one of the first things she'd speak with Minister Kanagy about. He would have to agree to bring them all into his house if he wanted to wed her.

Pausing to listen, Ida heard soft sounds coming from the downstairs bedroom. She headed that way.

Sadie met her at the door with a smile. "I thought I heard someone drive in. Is Joe still beside himself?"

Ida grinned. "I gave him two aspirins. He'll be in after he's put your horse up."

Sadie laughed. "I'm not surprised he's in such a state."

Ida joined in the laughter. "Can I do anything to help?"

"See your sister for a moment." Sadie waved toward the bedroom door. "Then keep the water warm in the kitchen. I'm going that way now. We're going to need lots of it for coffee . . . hot chocolate . . . towels." Sadie laughed again. "*Bopplis* don't ask us when to arrive."

That they don't, Ida agreed as Sadie disappeared toward the kitchen. The front door slammed, and Joe said something to Sadie. The midwife murmured something back. Ida eased herself into the bedroom. Verna was propped up in bed with pillows, her

84

face red and sweaty. Ida rushed forward. "You poor thing! Is it that bad?"

"Keep Joe out of here!" Verna gasped. "I have enough to take care of right now."

Ida hid a smile. How she was going to accomplish that, she had no idea.

Verna caught her breath and whispered, "Why did Eve ever eat that apple in the garden?"

"We're not such saints ourselves, you know." Ida reached for Verna's hand. "They always say the first *boppli*'s birth is the worst."

"And they're right," Verna said, taking another deep breath. "Did *Mamm* say anything about coming?"

"Nee." Ida squeezed Verna's hand. "We didn't know you wanted her here."

"Neither did I." Verna grimaced. "*Mamm*'s comforting presence would be nice right now."

"Shall I send Joe for her?" Ida let go of Verna's hand to turn toward the door.

Vern grabbed for it again. "*Nee,* let's stick with the plan. You're here! What more could I want?"

"I'm not sure I can do much," Ida said as Sadie came back into the room with wet washcloths.

Sadie waved her hand toward the bedroom

doorway. "Ida, you can keep Joe out of here. That's your job right now. I told him he's to come no closer than the living room. He's an emotional wreck, that man is. You'd think the husbands were having the *boppli* sometimes." Sadie placed a cool washcloth on Verna's forehead.

A grateful look crossed Verna's face. She relaxed into the pillows. "How long will it be now, Sadie?"

"Only *Da Hah* knows that, dear heart," Sadie said. "The *boppli* is turned right, which you can be thankful for. So we wait until it's time, and we pray."

"*Yah,*" Verna whispered. "We must pray."

Sadie closed her eyes. "Dear *Hah,* we ask for Your peace tonight as we gather for the miracle of birth. Bless Verna and Joe. Calm their troubled hearts. Help Verna through the pain by making it bearable. I will do what I can in the hours ahead, but You know that's precious little without Your wisdom and guidance and strength. Amen."

"Amen," Ida echoed.

Verna managed a smile.

Ida stayed with Verna a few minutes longer before she stepped outside the bedroom. Joe jumped up from the couch when he saw her, but she motioned him to sit again. "You might as well get used to the fact that it's

86

going to be a long time. Just relax, Joe. There's no sense in wearing yourself out."

Joe snorted. "It's going to take more than aspirin for me to relax."

"Have you had supper?"

Joe appeared startled. "I guess not."

"Well, that might help," Ida said. "I'll make you some."

He didn't object — and even looked grateful.

Ida went into the kitchen and opened the refrigerator. She found leftover casserole. There was enough for the three of them. Ida started the fire in the oven and found half a cherry pie in the pantry while the stove heated. A head of lettuce and a few carrots became a tossed salad of sorts. It would have to do. Bread, butter, and jam were also in the pantry. With milk for the pie, that would be supper.

Once she had everything ready, she let Joe, Sadie, and Verna know there was hot food in the kitchen.

Joe came in immediately and sat down. He prayed and then helped himself.

Ida took her place at Verna's side while Sadie went to fix a plate for herself.

"How's Joe doing?" Verna asked.

"He's eating," Ida chuckled.

"He'll be a great *daett.*" Verna tried to

87

smile through a contraction. "We just have to get through this part."

"You will!" Ida squeezed Verna's hand. "Both of you will."

"You're such a comfort," Verna whispered. "Thank you for being here."

Should she tell Verna about Minister Kanagy? The news rose up inside of her and pushed at her lips. This seemed such an inappropriate moment. *Nee*, she would focus on Verna's needs. Her own happenings weren't that important right now. It was best if *Mamm* were told first anyway.

"Are you sure there's not something I can get for you?" Ida asked as she took Verna's hand.

"Just be with me for a moment," Verna said. "Sadie thinks things might be going faster than she expected, even if it is my first one."

"You're doing okay!" Ida encouraged.

Moments later Sadie came back. Ida left to fix herself a plate in the kitchen. Joe was gone, so she sat at the table and ate alone. Sadie had put the coffeepot on the stove to heat, so the aroma filled the room. Joe must have taken her advice and gone upstairs to lie down while he could. The house stood silent. Ida's thoughts wandered to Minister Kanagy again. If she married him, her life was about to change in radical ways. Overnight she would become the mother of eight children and the wife of a minister. Becoming a mother was a hope she'd not dared to dream since Melvin's death. She'd let go of his children, figuring they were gone forever from her life. But apparently *Da Hah* had other plans.

"Help me do my duty," Ida whispered into the air of the silent kitchen. "And help me love them all — including Minister Kanagy."

She finished her meal and cleared the table. On the stove the coffeepot hissed as steam rose into the air. This was so like life, Ida thought. You lived and then you were gone, just like vapor that rose upward and vanished from the world. At least her life would have meaning and purpose.

"Thank you, dear *Hah* for this change." Ida glanced at the ceiling. "And let Verna birth a healthy child. If it is not against Your will. Otherwise help us bear the sorrow with Your grace."

EIGHT

That same Sunday evening, Alvin sat bent over at the table, his head resting in his hands at his parents' kitchen table in the *dawdy haus.* He was here to visit his *mamm,* yet he knew that wasn't the real reason. He should be at the hymn singing, but he wasn't. Mildred had gone there an hour ago. She'd driven her own horse and buggy. He'd watched her by peeking around his living room curtains. He'd almost gone out to help her hitch her horse to the buggy, but that wouldn't have been right. Mildred would get more ideas in her head about their relationship than she already had. And she would have asked him why he wasn't going.

She could see that his buggy was still here . . . it sat in plain sight. He would still have to answer her question eventually. But now he could do that tomorrow morning when she came to help with the chores.

Hopefully by then he'd have a satisfactory answer for his strange behavior. His real concern tonight was Debbie. What would she think when he didn't show up at the hymn singing? She had to know Crystal Meyers had been at the church service this morning. Debbie had probably even recognized her when she arrived because Crystal was sitting with Deacon Mast's *frau,* Susie. And that was why he'd kept his head down all day and rushed home before the noon meal.

Would Debbie think he had anything to do with Crystal's sudden appearance? He should have driven over to see Debbie this afternoon, but he couldn't bring himself to face her right now. And it wasn't because he still had feelings for Crystal. He was sure he didn't. But Crystal must still have an interest in him, otherwise why would she have come? Debbie would think he'd done something to encourage that. He hadn't. But how was Crystal's presence explainable? Who would believe him? Especially not after he'd admitted to Debbie just last Sunday that he'd feared she might in some ways be like Crystal. After all, Debbie *had* come from the *Englisha* world. *Yah,* he had been wrong to think that, but now with Crystal showing up, what would Debbie think? It was a horrible mess, and he was to blame for it.

Alvin stood. His *daett,* Edwin, had stirred in the living room. Alvin hadn't wanted to sit alone with him, and his *mamm* hadn't been up from her Sunday afternoon nap, so he'd settled in the kitchen. Now she must be out of the bedroom.

Alvin stepped through the kitchen doorway and winced. The sight of his *mamm* in her crippled condition tore at his heart. His parents weren't that old — at least to him. Yet almost overnight his *mamm* had lost so much. Her left hand was immobile, and her speech was slurred. She couldn't walk without the help of a walker. His *daett* was by her side now. Edwin was trying to help, but he seemed helpless as he fumbled beside her. Alvin rushed forward to take his *mamm*'s hand. "Have you had supper?" he asked. It was a stupid question, he figured, but better than nothing.

His *mamm* stared at him for a moment. "Are you visiting?"

"It's Alvin!" *Daett* hollered near her ear. "He stayed home from the hymn singing to pay us a visit."

"That's *gut,*" *Mamm* mumbled. "I'm glad to see him." A faint smile crossed *Mamm*'s face.

Alvin leaned forward to give her a hug. She didn't respond other than to look up at him. "I love you, *Mamm,*" he said, giving her a peck on the cheek.

"We should get her something to eat," *Daett* said, looking concerned. "There are leftovers in the refrigerator that Mildred left. I'm supposed to heat it in the oven when she gets up."

Daett is likely to burn the house down, Alvin thought. *Mamm* had always tended to the kitchen duties. But perhaps Mildred had drawn hidden talents out of *Daett.*

As if he could read his son's thoughts, *Daett* said, "I had to make do for a while before Mildred came. I know how to make a fire in the oven."

"Come then." Alvin took *Mamm*'s hand and gently pushed the walker toward the kitchen table.

His *daett* stopped him. "*Nee,* she'll rest more comfortably in the rocker until I get her food ready."

Alvin shrugged. "Okay." He helped ease *Mamm* into her rocker. She settled in with a smile on her face. "It's *gut* you're visiting, Alvin."

"*Yah, Mamm.*" He stroked her arm.

Daett was at the kitchen doorway. "If you want, there is enough for you to eat from what Mildred has in the refrigerator, Alvin. Unless you've had supper."

He hadn't, and he was hungry. Alvin nodded his thanks. He stood and followed his *daett* into the kitchen. This is strange, he thought. He'd grown up and worked with his *daett* in the fields but never in the kitchen. This was women's work — duties men didn't perform. Yet here they both were and at the same time.

For the first time in a long time, Alvin's heart stirred toward his *daett*. Alvin had always been so sure he was different from his *daett*, but now he was no longer so certain. And there was still the fact his *daett* had never done what his youngest son had done. He'd never fled to the *Englisha* world like a scared rabbit rather than face his problems. And his *daett* had never stayed home from a hymn singing because he'd seen his old girlfriend at a church service.

As his *daett* built up the fire in the stove, Alvin got the leftovers from the refrigerator. From what Mildred had left in the refrigerator, the girl knew how to cook. But then he expected that. Mildred had been raised Amish. Did Debbie know how to cook? But of course she did, he told himself at once. He must not question or doubt her.

"How was the service this morning?" *Daett*

asked as Alvin handed him the food to put in the oven.

"Okay," Alvin replied. What would *Daett* say if Alvin mentioned that an *Englisha* girl from his past had been in attendance? Alvin shivered. There would likely be words of rebuke spoken like he hadn't heard since he was a child.

"I hope *Mamm* can go again someday." *Daett*'s voice was wistful.

It probably wouldn't happen, but Alvin wasn't about to say so. "Perhaps I can stay with *Mamm* some Sunday while you go," he offered.

Daett seemed grateful. "*Yah,* perhaps. I haven't been wanting to ask such a sacrifice from Mildred. She does enough for us already."

He couldn't stay next Sunday, Alvin thought. That was the day of his next date with Debbie — if she wasn't upset with him. But why would she be? Debbie had been nothing but reasonable last Sunday. He must pay her a visit some evening this week and, at least, explain his erratic behavior. He couldn't explain Crystal's presence, but Debbie would understand.

Daett spoke. "Mildred tells me you're getting along well with her at the barn in the mornings. She likes helping with the chores."

Alvin cleared his throat. "You really didn't have to send Mildred out. I'm fine alone."

"A man is never fine alone," *Daett*'s voice rumbled, "You need a *frau*, Alvin. That house is mighty empty all by itself, especially with no *kinner* in it. But I suppose your *mamm* should be telling you this. She would if she could."

Alvin stared at the floor. "I took Debbie home last Sunday night."

Daett glared at him. "So Mildred told me. I had hoped you'd forgotten that girl after waiting all summer."

"Debbie was baptized the other Sunday," Alvin said. "She's Amish now."

"Water only goes in so deep, Alvin. That girl was *Englisha* once, and you know how them *Englisha* live. Will you take a *frau* who leaves you at the first sign of trouble coming down the road?"

The words stung. Alvin was like his *daett* and hated to admit he had the same fears. But he wasn't about to say so now.

"You done thought the same thing, didn't you, Alvin? So why don't you follow your better sense and take Mildred as your *frau* instead? She seems like a real decent woman. She's interested in you, if I don't miss my guess."

"Daett." Alvin tried to smile. *"Daett,* I love Debbie. And, well, Mildred and I have a bad history, and I'd like to just leave it alone."

"History is *gut,* Alvin." His *daett* opened the oven door and touched the food with his finger. "Ouch! Ready to go, I think. Go bring *Mamm.*"

Alvin had no plans to renew a romantic relationship with Mildred. That was certain, and his *daett* knew that. There was no sense in arguing about it.

Alvin helped *Mamm* to the table. She had just sat down when headlights came down the driveway of the old farmhouse. Alvin was ready to go outside to see who it was when the car moved right up to the sidewalk of the *dawdy haus.* That made sense, Alvin thought, sitting down again. Some *Englisha* neighbor who knew his *daett* was calling. The person had seen that the farmhouse was dark but there were lights on further back. *Daett* could meet them and see what they wanted.

Daett glanced at Alvin. "You can pray with your *mamm.* I'll go see who it is."

Alvin nodded. He reached over to hold his *mamm*'s hand. They bowed their heads and gave silent thanks.

Mamm reached for her spoon when she

97

was finished praying.

Alvin was thankful *Mamm* could still feed herself. He dreaded the day when the indignity of not doing so would be heaped on her. But perhaps *Da Hah* would have mercy and spare *Mamm* that humiliation. He sincerely hoped so.

Daett's voice from the front door filled the house. "*Gut* evening. May I help you?"

And then the voice that sent shivers up his spine seemed to reverberate throughout the house. "Is this where Alvin Knepp lives?"

Alvin was already on his feet when his *daett* asked, "What business do you have with Alvin?"

"Well . . ."

Alvin rushed to the door and wondered how to handle this situation. He should have known she'd make contact. She hadn't come just for the church service that morning. He'd hoped his rapid departure after the meeting would have sent the message that he had no interest in seeing her. Apparently the message wasn't received. And now his *daett* was involved.

"Excuse me," Alvin said as he pushed past his *daett*. "I'll speak with Crystal outside."

"What is this?" His *daett* sounded suspicious.

Alvin ignored him and plunged on toward Crystal's car. He figured Crystal would follow him, and they'd be out of earshot for whatever this conversation might entail.

"Alvin, please stop! Have I done the wrong thing in coming here?"

Alvin stopped and faced Crystal. He held his anger and tried to even his breathing. "We're not in Philadelphia, Crystal. I'm home, and you know what home is to me. Why have you come?"

"Alvin . . ." She reached out and touched his arm. "Please, Alvin. Let me explain."

He drew back. "Explain what? There's nothing to explain. It's over between us. I have no more feelings for you."

Her voice was soft. "I know that, Alvin. And that's why I've come tonight. I respect you. I wanted you to know that I'm not here for that."

"Then why are you here?" His voice sounded unnecessarily harsh, but he couldn't help it.

"I wanted to see where you came from, I guess. What kind of world produced a good man like you." Crystal's expression was intense.

"Crystal, please. Your being here isn't going to work. There are too many questions that will come up. You can't just come here

99

without expecting to cause problems. People will talk."

She held out her hands. "But I haven't done anything, Alvin. I went to church with your deacon and his wife this morning. I did that after asking around in Beaver Springs and being directed to the deacon's residence. I told them I had family in the area and wished to visit an Amish church. And the Amish people couldn't have been nicer! I was shocked that after the service you raced outside and left without speaking to me. That's when I decided I'd better look you up to make sure you understood I wasn't here just to see you."

"Deacon Mast told you where I live?" Alvin choked out.

Crystal paused for a moment. "Yes. Was that bad? I was visiting family and was curious about your community. That's all."

There were a dozen things wrong with this situation, Alvin thought. Among those was what Debbie would think. And what the ministry would do when they discussed Crystal. On top of that, he had to deal with his *daett* on the subject now. "Your presence complicates everything, Crystal."

"I see." She seemed deeply hurt. "I meant no harm, Alvin. But you know how life is out there. Do you blame me for coming here? I'm looking for something better. Is that wrong?"

Alvin took Crystal's hand. "I don't blame you, and I'm sorry for my outburst. But it's better if you leave and go back to where you came from."

Pain showed on her face. "Did you have to change this much, Alvin?"

"You can't stay, Crystal. It's that simple." He forced out the words.

"I'm making it uncomfortable for you. I didn't mean for that to happen." She began to tear up.

Alvin was at a loss.

Crystal continued. "So you won't help me? No one here will help me?"

Alvin glanced up at the sky for a moment. He reached out and took her hand. "Come, Crystal. I want you to meet my parents. I will leave this situation in *Da Hah*'s hands."

NINE

Alvin awoke in the morning darkness to the jangle of the alarm clock. He gave the clock on the dresser a whack. That didn't stop its racket, so he groped until his thumb found the shut-off button. He felt on the floor for his clothing and noted his head was throbbing. He had a splitting headache, which explained why he'd slept until the alarm went off. Normally he was up a few minutes before . . . if not sooner.

Alvin stood and shook his head as the memory of last night flashed into his mind. Crystal Meyers had paid him a visit, and he had introduced her to his parents. Those brief moments had been awkward but necessary. The gesture had seemed the least he could do. They'd walked in and Alvin noticed the astonished look on his *daett*'s face. Alvin had taken Crystal up to the rocker where his *mamm* sat.

"*Mamm,* this is Crystal. Crystal, this is my

102

mamm, Helen. She had a stroke earlier in the year and is still struggling with the effects."

"It's nice to meet you, Mrs. Knepp," Crystal said, reaching down to shake Helen's hand.

"*Gut* evening."

Mamm appeared to not comprehend what was going on, but this whole situation was incomprehensible, Alvin thought.

When they turned to *Daett,* his face looked like a thundercloud. Apparently he'd put two and two together. Alvin tried to keep the tremble out of his voice. "*Daett,* this is Crystal. Crystal, this is my *daett,* Edwin."

"It's good to meet you," Crystal said, offering her hand.

Daett shook it after a brief hesitation.

Then Alvin said, "We really have to be going." He took Crystal's hand and headed for the door. He urged her on when she turned to smile and say goodnight over her shoulder.

Once he escorted Crystal to her car and opened her door, he said, "Crystal, you can't come back here. Please understand."

"I'm not sure I do," she replied. "I mean no harm. I'm interested in the kind of lifestyle that produces quality men like you."

She hesitated. "I might even want to become . . . Amish."

Alvin almost laughed, but he thought better of it. He kept his voice firm. "Crystal, you would not be happy here. Believe me. And as for you and me, our former relationship out there in your world can't be continued in my world. I'm dating someone else now, Crystal, and . . ." Alvin paused.

Crystal hesitated. "I guess she did wait for you then. I understand." Crystal gave his arm a quick squeeze and then started the car, shut the door, and drove out of the driveway.

Alvin fled to the farmhouse without a glance at the *dawdy haus.*

And now he was barely up and out of bed. There was pounding on the front door. He didn't normally lock the doors, but he had last night. An instinct from his childhood, no doubt, after all the times he'd been dragged out of bed and his bottom strapped for transgressions his *daett* had found out about. There would be no punishment this morning, but there would be words said he'd rather not hear.

Alvin lit the kerosene lamp. The noise at the front door was louder now, but it stopped when he stepped into the living room. Alvin set the lamp on the desk and

104

unlocked the door. It flew open as he stepped back and awaited the inevitable.

"Alvin Knepp," the first words out of his *daett*'s mouth were clipped, "I will have an explanation for this. Who was that *Englisha* girl you brought into my house last night?"

Alvin sank down on the couch. "I used to date Crystal when I was living in Philadelphia." Alvin waved his hand in the general direction of the living room window. "I've told the ministry about her. I held nothing back in my confession. I even told them about going to a bar and grill with Crystal. That's when I 'woke up,' you could say, and came home. Most people thought it was because of Melvin's passing, but I'd already made up my mind to return home."

"You've *been* with this woman then?" Horror dripped from his *daett*'s voice.

Alvin sighed. "*Nee, Daett.* Crystal is more honorable than that. I don't know about myself in that regard, but we did nothing like that."

"But you. . . . you . . ." *Daett* searched for the right words. "Your hands were freely on her, and hers on you."

Alvin groaned. "That's the *Englisha* way, *Daett.* Perhaps I learned it out there. They touch the arm . . . the hand . . . to show casual affection . . . to show concern."

"Someone who is not your family?" *Daett* took a step back.

"*Yah,* it is so." Alvin rubbed his head again. "Is this lecture over now? I have a headache and choring to do."

Daett regarded him for a moment. "All I can say, Alvin, is that I'm deeply disappointed in you. If you say you've told the ministry everything, and they are okay with your confession, then what can I say on the matter? But as your *daett,* I say you're a failure. Oh *yah,* you may know how to run a farm and make it profitable. That's something I didn't do, and the committee let you take over . . . all because I don't change my ways. Well, my ways worked for my *daett,* and they should have worked for me. They would have if I'd been given enough time to try them."

Alvin sat up. "*Daett,* this is not about farming."

His *daett* snorted. "Maybe not farming exactly." He waved his arms about. "I'm talking about raising a family in *Da Hah*'s ways. That's something you don't know anything about, Alvin. You got your heart fixed on an *Englisha* girl. You can't handle women, Alvin. Not even Debbie, whom I guess the ministry has now baptized. But my heart is not settled on the matter.

Debbie was the reason you ran out into the world. Why, I don't know, but you did. And now you bring another *Englisha* girl into the community? What is wrong with you, Alvin? You are nothing but a flop when it comes to the things that really matter. And all the time, you've had a good Amish girl waiting for you. Mildred would take you back with open arms, Alvin. If only you had the sense to see it."

You were the real reason I left the community and got myself excommunicated, Alvin almost said. Instead he bit back the words. It wouldn't help. His *daett*'s words weren't totally correct, but some were close enough that they cut deep. He, Alvin Knepp, *was* unskilled in the things of the heart. He knew how to run a plow and a disk. He knew how to cut hay. But that was child's play compared to what really mattered. In that, *Daett* was right.

"I hope you come to your senses on Debbie before it's too late!" *Daett* turned and left after delivering this last volley. He didn't wait for a response.

Alvin groped for the side of the couch and stood. His head swam as he grabbed the lantern and staggered into the washroom for his coat. He shielded his eyes from the light and made his way into the yard. A soft glow through the barn windows caught his attention. Another groan escaped his lips. Mildred was already at chores. Shame upon shame was being heaped on him this morning.

"*Da Hah* help me," Alvin prayed as he pushed open the barn door.

Mildred stood by the stanchions regarding him with skepticism. "You look rough. Should you be up this morning?"

"You can't do the chores by yourself," he said without thinking about how it might sound. Actually, Mildred probably could, for all he knew.

"You look like you were up all night." Mildred raised her eyebrows. "Were you with that *Englisha* girl who was in church?"

"Mildred, please don't you start on me. I did nothing wrong — unless introducing Crystal to my parents was wrong. And it probably was."

Mildred didn't appear convinced. "An *Englisha* girl follows you back to the community — at least that's what the buzz was last night at the hymn singing — and you're not sure if something is amiss? Why would an *Englisha* girl come in like that and then go to your place last night?"

Alvin shook his head. "It's not what it appears, Mildred. What do you care? I'm the one who has the explaining ahead of me. I have Debbie to explain to. Imagine how that's going to go."

Hope flashed across Mildred's face for a moment.

Alvin noticed and frowned. Apparently he'd said the wrong thing. But he really didn't care what she thought. He cared only what Debbie would think.

"I think you did some awful things out there, Alvin. I don't know about last night, but you're obviously being tempted. I mean, who wouldn't be attracted to a beautiful woman like Crystal, or even Debbie for that matter. But they aren't doing you any *gut.* Can't you see that?"

"Stay out of this, Mildred!" Alvin left her to open the back barn door for the cows.

Mildred had the feed spread out by the time the cows filed in. She gave Alvin a sharp look. "I'm not trying to destroy your life, Alvin, or take you away from anything. I'm just speaking my heart to you. And with what has been happening over the weekend, I think I have at least that right. You and I — we go back a long time. To those days in school when we smiled at each other from our desks. I thought you were so handsome and shy all at the same time. That was the combination that attracted me. I used to

109

love those whispered conversations we had, Alvin. I really did. Yes, I left you back then. But I was wrong, Alvin. I was puffed up in my mind. I thought of other boys who appeared better than you did right then."

Mildred glanced at him. She continued when Alvin ducked behind a cow. "I don't know if I can ever make that right, Alvin. Maybe I have no right to even try . . . but like I said, yesterday shook everyone up. I hope you understand that. Crystal won't be explained easily. I'm sure Deacon Mast will be making a visit to see you. But you already know that. What I want to say is for myself, Alvin. I'm sorry. I couldn't see the man you were becoming. It takes a lot of nerve to live out there in the world . . . facing being put in the *bann.* And then you came back and repented. Or at least you're trying to repent. And now you have your *daett*'s farm. I see now that it wasn't you who was running it into the ground. If there is ever a chance again of a fresh start for us, Alvin, please consider it. If not, well, I'm still sorry. I wish you nothing but the best. But always remember that I, for one, understand. And I'm willing to understand even more, whatever is revealed or said in the days ahead."

Alvin finally looked at her. "Mildred, it can never be — you and me. But thank you for understanding."

"You're a *gut* man, Alvin." Her smile was weak. "Keep up your courage."

She wouldn't give up, Alvin thought. He ducked his head down again to check the equipment on the cow. He'd thanked Mildred for her concern, and he owed her nothing further. Although, he had to admit, it would be so easy to just let go and fall back into the way things used to be when he was growing up. Mildred would be a safe *frau*. She was raised in the ways of the community and stirred no suspicions in anyone's heart. But one couldn't go back to the past. He had changed, and so had Mildred. More than even she might be aware of.

Right now he wanted the pounding in his head to cease and for the misunderstandings from yesterday to simply vanish like the dawn outside was overtaking the darkness. But that wouldn't happen. Again he'd have to face his troubles. He couldn't continue to run away from them.

TEN

The baby's cry rent the still, morning silence as Ida held Verna's trembling hand. Old Sadie held the baby facedown against one arm while she operated a hand suction with the other. Verna threw her head back against the pillow with a soft gasp and closed her eyes as she panted.

"*Yah,* it's a girl!" Sadie announced. Her wrinkled face glowed. "Another birth and so precious — once again. *Da Hah*'s ways never cease to amaze."

"Can I do anything?" Ida let go of Verna's hand.

"Give me a minute, and you can call Joe. The man must have the living room floor worn bare by now."

Ida thought about Joe. He'd been shooed away from the bedroom door by Sadie sometime before dawn. He'd gone out to the barn, but the front door had slammed a half hour ago. Joe was either finished with his chores, or he couldn't stand another minute away from his *frau.*

"Did I hear right?" Verna's voice trembled. "It's a girl?"

"*Yah,* you heard right." Sadie eased the now blanket-wrapped infant into Verna's arms.

The glow in Verna's face was instant as the color rushed into her face. "Our very first *boppli,* Ida! Oh, she is so beautiful!"

Ida ran her hand between the tiny fingers of her niece. A rush of love rose up inside of her. "That she is, Verna!"

"She's a little jaundiced, but some babies are," Sadie said as she washed her hands in a warm bowl of water on the dresser. "You'd better get Joe, Ida. The poor man." Sadie chuckled.

Ida took one last look at the tiny crinkled face before she opened the bedroom doorway. Joe nearly tumbled in on her. Ida gasped.

"I'm . . . I'm . . . I'm so sorry," Joe stammered, grabbing the doorframe. "I thought I heard a baby's cry."

"That you did." Sadie gave him a warm smile. "Your daughter's over there, Joe." Sadie motioned toward Verna with her chin.

Joe took cautious steps forward and reached for Verna's hand.

"It's a girl, Joe!" Verna whispered. She opened the blanket wider to show both wiggling arms. "Isn't she beautiful?"

"Sarah Mae," Joe said, his voice awed. "You said it would be a girl, Verna."

Verna beamed. "I wanted you to be the first to say the name."

"That's a nice touch." Sadie was still smiling. "Sarah Mae. I like that. It's been a while since I've heard the name used."

"Are you okay?" Joe touched Verna's forehead.

"I am now," Verna said. "Did they keep you outside all this time? You poor thing. But it was for the best, Joe. It really was."

"We'd better leave them alone for a few moments." Sadie pulled on Ida's arm.

Neither Verna nor Joe noticed them leave. They gazed together at the child in Verna's arms.

"A most beautiful thing, a child's birth," Sadie whispered. "Have you ever thought of doing midwifery, Ida? You were quite *gut* helping me." Sadie gave her an appraising glance. "And you're still on your feet after being up all night."

"Anyone can do that," Ida said at once.

Sadie smiled. "Not everyone, believe me. I do declare, you're not even wobbly on your feet. Think about it. That's all I can say. I'm not a young woman anymore, and I'll be glad to start taking you along on births if you're interested."

Ida swallowed hard. "But if I should marry?"

Sadie laughed. "I have twelve children myself. Are you forgetting that? A woman like you . . . there's always room in your heart for the little ones."

Ida's mind whirled. She loved helping bring lovely Sarah Mae into the world. Could she not also enjoy this in the future? What worthwhile work it would be! Would Minister Kanagy consent?

Sadie studied her and offered a short laugh. "Have you a man picked out then? Is there someone we don't know about?"

Ida felt heat rise up her neck. Obviously not everyone had noticed Minister Kanagy's glances her way.

"Come on now," Sadie teased. "Your secret will be safe with me. *Da Hah* knows I have plenty of those already, working amongst the people like I do."

But she hadn't even told *Mamm* yet, Ida thought. There hadn't been time yesterday before Joe arrived with the news that Verna was in labor. Still, her heart had bonded deeply with Sadie over the nighttime hours. To tell Sadie about Minister Kanagy felt

like the most natural thing in the world —
and she greatly longed to tell someone.

"Well, we'd better get busy then." Sadie
gave her a warm smile.

Obviously the midwife didn't intend to
push the matter further. Ida blurted the
words out. "Minister Kanagy inquired after
me yesterday. I told him I'd be willing to
wed him."

Sadie's eyebrows went up. "And his *frau*
barely in the ground."

Ida winced. "There are his children and
Melvin's children to consider. They are the
real reason for the rush."

"Oh . . ." Sadie paused for a moment. "Of
course! How could I forget? That's so sweet,
Ida. And you wish this? Are you sure?"

"I want it with all my heart," Ida whispered. "Melvin's children, that is. And the
Kanagy children. Minister Kanagy — he's
okay, I guess."

Sadie shrugged. "You're thinking it's *Da
Hah*'s will then? And Minister Kanagy? You
could do worse, I suppose. You do know
though that much hard work lies ahead of
you. Minister Kanagy has two children of
his own, and Melvin had six, didn't he?"

Ida nodded. "I wish to have them all
together."

Sadie continued. "And with any *Da Hah*

gives the two of you. That could be quite a houseful. You're still young, Ida. Of course, it's not twelve like my brood."

Ida turned all kinds of red. Of course Sadie would speak plainly. Hadn't the work they'd been doing all night made it obvious what married couples could expect?

"I still want it," Ida managed.

"Then you'd better be plain-speaking with Minister Kanagy." Sadie gave Ida a steady look. "Take it from me. Speak your mind from the start — *before* the wedding vows are said."

"I was going to tell him." Ida nodded.

Sadie shook her finger at Ida. "You tell Minister Kanagy you want *all* of Melvin's children brought under his roof. Don't assume he knows this. Men must be told, you know."

"Oh, I'm sure he'll agree." Ida's voice trembled.

Sadie's voice was firm. "You tell him there will be no marriage vows unless he brings all these children home. I've seen the kind of person you are, Ida. You'll be giving that man more than he deserves in a *frau.* So make sure you're getting your end of the deal."

Ida glanced away as her face burned. "*Yah,* I'll do what you say."

"You do that!" Sadie squeezed her arm and disappeared toward the kitchen.

Ida followed, trying to collect her thoughts. With how Sadie said the words, Ida decided she would apparently need to stand up to Minister Kanagy. The thought sent chills up and down her spine. She could almost see his piercing eyes staring at her. Her insides would turn to jelly, but Sadie was right. She must insist on his agreement *before* they said the vows. If Minister Kanagy told her after the wedding that all of Melvin's children wouldn't live with them, she would wish to curl up and die.

Sadie glanced at Ida over her shoulder. "And tell him you want to help me with delivering babies. That he has to agree to also!"

Ida drew her breath in.

Sadie laughed. "I'm only teasing. Looking out for myself, that's all. But the offer still stands. If you wish, of course. And if you can work things out with Minister Kanagy."

Ida breathed evenly again. "I will pray about this. But now I'd better fix breakfast or Verna will think I'm up to no *gut*."

Sadie smiled. "You do that, and I'll wrap things up in the bedroom. I might have to hitch the horse to pull Joe out of there."

Ida joined in the laughter as Sadie left the kitchen. Moments later, with an egg carton on the counter and a slab of bacon brought up from the basement, Ida paused to listen. She was certain that car tires had crunched in the driveway. But who would have stopped by at this time? Likely someone who had business with Joe. Sure enough, she heard Joe's quick footsteps go past the kitchen doorway. Voices murmured on the porch, and then moved inside.

It's Debbie's voice, Ida thought. She must have stopped by on her way to work to see how things were going with Verna. Her friend Rhonda still gave her a ride each workday into Lewistown. This was a pleasant surprise! Debbie would get to see baby Sarah this morning. Ida rushed into the living room just in time to see Joe ready to lead both young women back to the bedroom.

"Good morning, Ida!" Debbie greeted her. "I just had to stop by and see for myself."

Rhonda gave Ida a warm smile.

"I'm so glad you could both stop in," Ida told them. "Little Sarah was born just an hour ago . . . after an all-night effort, of course."

Debbie smiled. "I can imagine! I can't

119

keep Rhonda for long, so let's see what has come from God's hand."

"A wonderful, beautiful *boppli*," Joe told them. He waited near the bedroom door and motioned for them to hurry.

"The happy *daett* can't wait," Ida commented. She felt the glow again of when Sarah Mae had been born. Sadie might be right that she loved this. But Ida doubted whether she could take on the extra work after her marriage to Minister Kanagy. Not with eight *kinner* in the house — and all of them acquired in one day.

"Visitors already!" Sadie announced with a smile as they all squeezed into the room. "Now take it easy. This woman's had a lot of excitement today already."

"Don't pay her any mind!" Verna spoke up from the bed. "This is such a treat. Joe's been busy enjoying our little wonder, and now you can share in it with us. She is such a darling, our little Sarah Mae."

Ida hung back as Debbie and Rhonda cooed over the baby. She would have plenty of time to give little Sarah Mae attention in the next few days while she stayed here to help Verna and keep house. These days would be such wonderful times, full of quiet joy. Then she'd have to face Minister Kanagy again . . . and the busy life that lay ahead of her.

"Thank you, dear *Hah,* for this opportunity," Ida whispered.

Debbie and Rhonda had already moved away from Verna's bed. Ida stepped back to let them past. Debbie pulled on Ida's sleeve and gave her a quick look with a toss of her head toward the kitchen. Ida followed the two women out of the bedroom.

"I'll be right with you," Debbie told Rhonda in the living room. "I promise. I just have to say a few words to Ida."

Rhonda glanced at her watch and shrugged. "We have some time, but hurry."

Debbie's smile was gone when they arrived in the kitchen.

Ida faced Debbie. "What's wrong?"

Debbie wrinkled her brow. "Minister Kanagy came by the house after you left last night. Is this really going to happen, Ida?"

Ida looked away. "It's a little soon, I suppose, but I wasn't surprised."

"You have taken total leave of your senses! Do you know that?" Debbie's voice was tense and loud.

"We've spoken of this before, and I have to do what I think is right, Debbie. Can you understand that? We can't have this conversation every time Minister Kanagy stops by

121

the house."

Debbie let out a long sigh. "I hoped you'd changed your mind."

Ida shook her head. "And what about you and Alvin?"

Debbie's face fell. "Alvin wasn't at the hymn singing last night. I'm not really worried about . . . well, Crystal. But Alvin's disturbed about something, and I don't know what I should do. I overheard Emery asking where Crystal is staying. I feel a little bit like the world's falling sideways."

Ida reached over to touch Debbie's arm. "Don't worry about Emery. He never does anything wrong. Maybe you should be the one changing your mind about Alvin."

"Maybe we should both pray," Debbie said. "We need it."

Ida didn't hesitate. "I agree. That's the first thing we should do instead of the last thing." With her hand still on Debbie's arm, the two bowed their heads together in silence.

Almost at once Rhonda's voice from near the front door interrupted them. "Debbie, time to go!"

Debbie looked up and forced a smile. "Have a good day now. Enjoy that baby. I'll keep praying for both of us."

"So will I!" Ida assured her.

Debbie dashed out of the kitchen.

"Dear *Hah*, help us all!" Ida prayed out loud. "We so need Your grace."

ELEVEN

Early Friday evening Debbie rushed about the barn helping Emery and Bishop Beiler with the chores. Ida was still at Verna's place, and Saloma was busy preparing supper.

When Debbie arrived home from her job at Destiny, there had still been a glow on Saloma's face that had begun Monday night when she and Adam had visited little Sarah Mae. Even Emery had harnessed up his horse and gone to visit his sister and new niece. Debbie smiled at the memory of how Saloma had exclaimed when she returned home, "The first of my girls to bear me a grandchild. I'm so blessed in my old age! And I'm still in *gut* enough health to enjoy the *boppli.* There was many a year I thought my eyes would never see this day. But not only has the day arrived, but little Sarah Mae is the sweetest thing."

Ida had been gone all week, but Debbie

had handled Ida's jobs and chores without much trouble. Thankfully, Ida would be back after the weekend so things could return to normal.

What hadn't been normal were the things going on in Debbie's life. All week the problems had simmered, and now it was like they were bubbling to the surface with force. She was sure Alvin was in no danger from Crystal Meyers. The danger lay in some other direction, but from where? Alvin had been behaving so strangely. Could he be rekindling his interest in Mildred? Debbie sighed. No matter what, she planned to stick with Alvin and make their relationship work. She had come too far to bolt now. And where would she go? Alvin was the man she'd hoped to date for so long and perhaps someday marry. She would have to pray more; that was the solution. But even as she prayed, her mind churned and whirled. A new wrinkle was that Emery had continued to ask her about Crystal, even though Debbie assured him she didn't know the woman beyond recognizing who she was.

What had possessed Crystal to pay the community a visit? Was she as innocent as she appeared? Alvin might not be in danger, but that didn't mean Crystal had the purest of motives. Why had Alvin rushed out after church on Sunday morning without a backward glance? To make matters worse, Alvin hadn't shown up for the hymn singing that evening. She would have liked to visit Alvin this week. That's what she would have done not that long ago. But that was the old Debbie, the *Englisha* Debbie, the Debbie she wanted to change. Amish women didn't throw themselves at men. No, she would just have to pray, and trust God, and hope Alvin had a decent explanation for his actions this Sunday evening.

Debbie climbed down the haymow ladder. What did Emery think about all this? Surely he hadn't fallen for Crystal. That would be way out of character for Emery. He needed a decent, steady Amish girl as his wife. One who would do him good all his days and not evil. Crystal would bring plenty of trouble with her, of that Debbie was sure. Maybe she should ask Emery what he'd seen about Crystal that interested him. Emery's questions about Crystal had been brief but genuine.

Surely Emery wasn't . . . Debbie stopped short. Her mind had gone wild now. She'd thought too much about Alvin and what he might be up to. Emery wasn't known for his rash decisions, so he couldn't be serious about pursuing an *Englisha* woman. And the Beiler family couldn't stand another shock like that. Not after Lois. And Debbie cared a lot herself — an awful lot about how Emery turned out. The thought that Emery might leave the faith for an *Englisha* woman turned her blood cold. He was Bishop Beiler's youngest son, the heir to the home place, and Crystal was divorced. Alvin had told her that much. This could lead nowhere but to disaster — if there was any truth to her wild thoughts.

Debbie took the last rung of the haymow ladder with a quick jump. This was enough thinking! Hadn't she resolved only moments earlier to cease and desist? Debbie reached up to squeeze her forehead, but the thoughts still churned. She might as well have this out with Emery — if Bishop Beiler wasn't around. Bishop Beiler didn't need to hear her distress. Emery would tell her the truth, and that would clear up the whole matter. And she would even admit to him that her wild imagination was getting the best of her. Emery would laugh and understand. He was that kind of man.

Debbie glanced around and caught sight of Emery as he turned the last row of cows loose from their stanchions. Bishop Beiler was nowhere in sight. She dodged the moo-

127

ing cows and worked her way closer to Emery.

Emery looked up with a grin. "Got all my hay bales down, I see."

"So you're watching," she said. "I might not be as efficient as Ida, but I try."

"You do *gut.*" Emery gave her a sweet smile. "Just like you make food."

Debbie glared at him. "That wasn't necessary, Emery! I do try, you know."

"I'm just teasing," he said with a laugh. "I like your cooking."

Debbie took a deep breath. "Tread softly when you talk about a woman's cooking."

Emery slapped the last cow on the rump. "I'll try to remember that."

Debbie stepped closer. "I need to ask you something, Emery. If you have a moment."

He gave her a questioning look. "What did I do now?"

This was nonsense, Debbie told herself. She should back out of this before she said anything. Emery was Bishop Beiler's youngest son, and he would never do what she had been imagining. But she didn't want him to have an interest in Crystal. Not at all!

"Hel–lo! Deb–bie!"

Emery's voice broke through her thoughts. Debbie rushed in. "I was wondering . . .

128

since you've made a couple of comments about Crystal Meyers . . . although romance isn't something you normally show an interest in . . . Emery, please tell me you don't have an interest in that divorced *Englisha* girl."

"Hey, I like *Englisha* girls!" Emery's tone was lighthearted. "I like you."

"Don't tease me." Debbie's tone was tense. "And I'm Amish now, not *Englisha*."

Emery's face softened. "You really care, don't you?"

Debbie tried to gather her wits. "I'm sorry, Emery. I know this is none of my business, but my nerves are kind of raw, what with Alvin and Crystal and Mildred . . ."

Emery regarded her with interest. "I kind of like this concern of yours. I didn't figure you'd care one way or the other."

The world spun at Emery's compliment. It was the nicest thing he'd ever said to her.

He went on. "I guess I should be honest, Debbie. I did speak with Deacon Mast and told him I hoped he'd be encouraging if Crystal wanted to stay in the community. I'd heard that Crystal went over to speak with Alvin on Sunday night and received quite a rebuff, so I felt I should give my encouragement to Deacon Mast."

Debbie drew in her breath. "So that's why

129

Alvin wasn't at the singing."

Emery shrugged. "Alvin told her not to come around again, if that's what you're worried about. But the community supported you with your decision to join the community, and I think they should do the same for Crystal. If she wants to make the same decision. It's only right. Surely you of all people can see that."

Debbie tried to breathe evenly. What Emery said made sense, and yet it didn't. That Crystal would seek out Alvin was no surprise. That validated her opinion of the woman. Alvin's reaction was also expected. It was Emery's interest in Crystal that bothered her.

Debbie focused on Emery's face. "I think you should forget about Crystal. She's divorced."

Emery's words came quickly. "That's no reason to reject the woman out of hand. I hope she stays around and finds the peace she's obviously looking for."

This was worse than Debbie had thought. Clearly Emery had spent considerable time thinking about Crystal. His conclusions could in no way be trusted. Not when it came to *Englisha* women.

Debbie tried again. "There are dangers out there you might know little of, Emery. I care about the wife you end up with. You deserve better than Crystal. She'd be a disaster. You know that. Your faith would be at stake. You'd lose everything you love."

Emery laughed. "Now you're thinking wild. Don't be so suspicious. I'm not falling for a divorced woman, if that's what you think."

Debbie ignored his comment. "Do you know what the woman's up to this week? Has she left the community?"

Emery hesitated. "How would I know? I just wanted to give my encouragement to Deacon Mast."

"But you do know." Debbie couldn't keep the edge out of her voice.

Emery tried to smile. "*Yah,* I guess I do know. Deacon Mast told me. Crystal's staying around for a while at her relative's place, which is not far from here. And I did tell Deacon Mast I'd introduce her at our young-folk gatherings — if she came. And what's wrong with that? Everyone deserves a chance, Debbie."

Debbie's fingers dug into her palm. "You know none of that's going to work, Emery. Crystal will no longer be welcome at the services once people find out she's divorced. She'd have to work a long time to overcome that obstacle. Look at me! I barely made it,

131

and I . . ."

Emery moved away a step as the bishop appeared around the corner of a horse stall. "I know, Debbie. That's why I'm going to help where I can. Help people understand that Crystal's intentions are *gut*. Get them to trust her and give her a chance."

Have you told your father this? Debbie wanted to shout after him.

Emery gave her a tense smile over his shoulder as he walked away.

Clearly the man knew he was on dangerous ground in spite of his denials. Would Crystal be able to weave her spell completely around Emery's heart? What hold did this woman have on Amish men? First Alvin and now Emery. Her worst fears were indeed true.

The bishop interrupted her thoughts. "Thanks so much for helping us chore this week, Debbie. I've been wanting to say something but haven't gotten around to it until now. You're almost like a daughter to us. But then you already know that."

"Thank you." Debbie smiled. "I'm glad to help."

"How are you and Alvin getting along?" Bishop Beiler's voice seemed to boom inside the barn.

Debbie swallowed hard. "Okay, I guess.

132

We have a few rough spots, but we've always had those."

Bishop Beiler appeared pleased. "I must say, I've heard nothing but *gut* things about Alvin lately — other than that deal with Crystal, which I hope is over with. He's really taking care of his *daett*'s farm. The committee has disbanded now, having given Alvin full charge of everything. I'd say you've got a *gut* man there. And he's getting a *gut frau* . . . if that's how things work out between you."

Debbie felt heat rise up her neck. "It's only been one date so far."

Bishop Beiler laughed. "I'm thinking you and Alvin have been working on this for a long time. But then who can question the ways of *Da Hah*?"

That was true, Debbie thought, even if the bishop didn't know the half of it. But his blessing was something she could be thankful for.

"We're trying," Debbie managed.

The bishop smiled and moved on.

Debbie gathered her wits together and walked out of the barn and across the lawn toward the house.

Saloma looked up in surprise when Debbie hurried into the kitchen. "Chores done already?"

"Yep!" Debbie chimed. "May I help you?"

"Certainly!" Saloma motioned toward the stove. "I'm almost done, but you can finish the bacon. I guess I drifted off thinking about Verna's baby. What a blessing we've been given in our old age."

"I know." Debbie bit back further words. She wasn't about to spill the beans about Emery. And perhaps this was just an innocent gesture done out of the compassion in Emery's heart. But she doubted it. Doubted it with all her heart. All she knew for sure was the Beilers couldn't lose Emery to the world. They just couldn't.

TWELVE

Later that evening after supper, Ida knelt as she poured warm water into the bowl set on the living room floor at Joe and Verna's place. She tested the temperature with her fingers before she lifted the squirming Sarah Mae and set her inside. Ida kept a firm grip and washed her new niece with one hand. Gently she rubbed the soapy washcloth into the baby's creases. Verna sat on the couch wrapped in a thick quilt and watched with a concerned face.

Joe was on the rocker and seemed to have no worries about how a baby should be washed. He cooed, "She's such a darling."

"Be careful. Don't break her." Verna pushed the quilt aside and tried to get up.

Joe laughed. "She's too cute to break."

"Those are the ones that break," Verna asserted as she sat down again.

"I'm being careful." Ida lifted Sarah Mae out of the water and dried her with the softest cotton towel she'd found in Verna's linen closet. It was deep blue with stitched edges. Still, the cloth deepened the reddish hue of the baby's wet skin. Sarah Mae kicked her legs and protested with a cry.

"She wants her *daett.*" Joe made a move to get up, but Ida gestured him down and made him wait until she'd dressed Sarah Mae. She handed the baby girl to him. He cuddled the infant in his arm, the picture of happiness. Verna leaned toward the two with a glow on her face.

Ida too smiled at the sight. This week had been among the most enjoyable of her life. Oh how she loved babies and the attention they received. *Daett* and *Mamm,* along with Emery, had visited on Monday night. Joe's parents had come the following night. Ida had made hot chocolate and popcorn both times, and she kept her eye on Verna lest her sister tire herself too much. But Verna seemed to know when she'd had enough activity. Both parents were also sensitive and had left at a decent hour — after one last round of exclamations over the little bundle.

Things had gone so well Ida could almost forget what faced her next. Verna and Joe's joy had drawn her in like a cocoon and wrapped her in a glorious glow of love and expectation. Verna already talked of Sarah

Mae's first Sunday visit to the services and how the *boppli* would again be the center of attention. This was, after all, the first of Bishop Beiler's girls to bring a child into the community. And through it all *Mamm* would glow like a lamp with the wick turned on high.

This was also Lois's honeymoon week with her *Englisha* husband, Doug. The comparison of joy on the one hand and grief on the other was hard to fathom. How could Lois jet off to that Mexican city Lois had called Cancun? The place must be full of fancy things. Surely Lois knew this, and that's why when she was home on her last visit she'd only whispered the information to Ida when *Mamm* couldn't hear. None of the family had gone to the wedding. What a sight that must have been, with Lois in an *Englisha* white dress and a long, flowing veil. Lois hadn't said exactly how she'd be dressed, but that's how brides appeared in doctor offices' magazines in Mifflinburg. Ida knew that Lois loved all things *Englisha,* and she would certainly have copied the best.

There would be pictures of Lois's wedding and of Cancun. Lois would have them in her car when she visited after the honeymoon. She'd come over to the house without Doug that first visit. That was a given. Would Lois dare bring pictures into the house? That would take a lot of nerve even for Lois. But if Lois did, *Mamm* would need to throw them right out on the porch. There was no question about that.

Maybe she could sneak a look sometime when she visited Lois in Selinsgrove. But that might never happen now that Lois was firmly *Englisha.* And as Minister Kanagy's *frau,* visiting Lois might be even more difficult to explain. Bishop Beiler's daughter might get away with such a thing, but not a minister's *frau.* That was just the way things were. Lois was responsible for the choices she made, and she would have her new position as *frau* and *mamm* to consider.

Ida emptied the bath bowl into the sink as memories of Melvin's children flooded her mind. How she'd loved all six of them. But she didn't want hope to rise in her heart just yet. That was why she hadn't allowed thoughts of Melvin's children to enter her mind this week. It hadn't been that difficult, surrounded as she was by the joy of Verna's new *boppli.* But now the weekend lay ahead, and Minister Kanagy would surely pay her a visit before Sunday. He might even come tonight. He'd know she was at Verna's place, and he'd also know a visit was necessary to plan the wedding.

She would keep the wedding small, Ida told herself. But she'd said the same thing about her planned wedding to Melvin, and *Mamm* had overridden her. They had been in the midst of plans for a wedding the size of Verna's when news arrived of Melvin's passing. The baked pies and purchased food items had already filled the basement. But this time there really would be a small wedding. No matter what *Mamm* said. But first she would have to tell *Mamm* that she was going to wed. A whole week had gone by, and *Mamm* still didn't know anything about Ida's sort of engagement to Minister Kanagy.

Ida pinched herself. She was promised to Minister Kanagy! This was hard to believe, and yet it was true . . . just as true as when she'd consented to be Melvin's *frau*. There had been no thrills or chills when they'd spoken last Sunday on the back porch. No butterflies raced around Ida's stomach. But that didn't matter. She hadn't felt that way about Melvin at first. Now with Minister Kanagy they were both older and practical. Minister Kanagy needed a *frau,* and Ida wanted Melvin's children as her own. The exchange was fair enough. She would make this plain to the minister when he visited.

He would agree, and that would be the end of the matter.

Ida returned to the living room where Joe was still cooing over baby Sarah Mae. She left them again to prepare Verna's bed for the night. In the bedroom, she stripped off the sheet and slipped on a fresh one. Wash day had been every other day this week with the amount of dirty diapers Sarah Mae created. The wash line filled with white cloth diapers had been a beautiful sight. They'd flapped in the wind as the day warmed. All the hard work involved with *kinner* contained many rewards. *Yah,* the gift to bring *kinner* into the world to serve *Da Hah* in their generation must be one of the greatest privileges allowed *Da Hah*'s people.

Ida looked out the window and caught sight of buggy lights turning into the driveway. That would be Minister Kanagy! She smiled. Already she had the man figured out, and she hadn't even said the vows with him. Wasn't that a *gut* sign?

Oh! Verna and Joe didn't know about Minister Kanagy's interest in her. They would be surprised, and they must be told right away. Ida raced back into the living room. She tripped over the edge of the couch, and barely stopped her fall in time with a quick grab of the sofa's back.

Verna and Joe looked up in alarm. "Is something wrong, Ida?" Verna asked.

Her words rushed out. "Minister Kanagy's coming for a visit. I don't know for sure, but it's possible he's coming to see me. You see, he and I . . . we've been . . . oh!" Ida paused to catch her breath. "He may be here because we need to speak of our wedding."

"Ida!" Verna reached over to grab her sister's arm. "You're speaking with Minister Kanagy this soon after his *frau*'s passing?"

At least Verna wasn't objecting to Minister Kanagy, just to the timing. Ida hadn't expected Verna to object though. Joe looked a little skeptical, but he didn't say anything.

Ida gulped. "It may be a little soon, but there are *kinner* involved. Minister Kanagy's and Melvin's. So it seemed right to me when Minister Kanagy asked."

Verna waved her hand toward Joe. "Go to the door then, Joe. Welcome the man in. Oh, where can they go to talk? I guess we can hide out in our bedroom."

"*Nee*, you won't!" Ida said at once. "We'll go upstairs to my room."

Just then the women heard Joe speak. "*Gut* evening, Ben."

"*Gut* evening, Joe."

Minister Ben Kanagy's voice squeaked a

141

little, Ida thought. The man was obviously nervous again. But what man wouldn't be under the circumstances? He probably figured Verna and Joe didn't know why he was here.

Ida stood straight and walked to the front door, even as the minister stepped inside. She gave him a smile and a little nod. That should let him know everything was fine.

He seemed to relax as he turned to Joe first and then to Verna. "Congratulations on the birth of your first child. I was so glad to hear everything went well. *Da Hah* has blessed you with a great gift."

"That He has," Joe agreed. His voice changed to a teasing tone. "Has little Sarah Mae gotten herself into church trouble already?"

Joe laughed and Minister Kanagy joined in. His laughter was a bit nervous.

Ida gave him another smile, and she could see him relax.

Minister Kanagy cleared his throat. "I guess you know why I'm here — to speak with Ida."

Joe nodded. "She just told us moments ago of your *gut* news."

"It's . . ." Minister Kanagy obviously was searching for what to say.

"You don't have to explain," Verna said.

"Ida thinks you'd be most comfortable visiting upstairs in her room. But if you prefer, Joe and I can take little Sarah Mae and hightail it for our bedroom. That way you two can have the living room to yourselves . . . if you think that best."

Minister Kanagy's hand twitched. "I wouldn't wish to disturb you. Not in the least. *Nee*, upstairs is fine. We'll behave ourselves."

Verna tried to smile at the nervous laughter that followed between Joe and the minister.

Ida figured the joke wasn't any more funny to Verna than it was to her. Minister Kanagy should stick to the business at hand. He shouldn't try to lighten the mood. But he must still hurt over the loss of his *frau,* Barbara. Ida would need to cut the man a lot of slack, even if he made cheesy jokes.

Without a glance at Minister Kanagy, Ida retrieved the lit kerosene lamp from the kitchen table and led the way upstairs. The steps soon squeaked behind her as Minister Kanagy followed. He'd caught up by the time she arrived at the bedroom she'd been using. Ida stepped inside and motioned toward the only chair. "I'll sit on the bed, if you don't mind."

Minister Kanagy nodded and sat down.

143

Ida put the lamp on the dresser. She turned the flame up until it threatened to smoke. The flickering light played on the minister's dark beard.

Minister Kanagy smiled and glanced up at her. He didn't seem a bit nervous now, which was *gut*. She didn't want a man who was always nervous around her. Apparently once Minister Kanagy was through the first part of an awkward situation, he calmed down. And she seemed to help him along that way, rather than hinder him. That was also *gut*. Ida gave him a smile as she seated herself on the edge of the bed.

The minister cleared his throat. "I'm glad to see you tonight, Ida. I hope this is a good time and that I'm not inconveniencing you."

Ida's smile came easily. "I was half expecting you, so I'm happy you've come."

"I'm happy to hear that." Minister Kanagy thought for a moment. "If you don't mind, Ida, I'd like to tell you about Barbara first. I want to make it clear that I'm not expecting you to replace her. I will always have a special place in my heart for Barbara. I want no secrets on that matter between us. I thought it would be better if I told you about her right up front. Then, if you wish, you can tell me about Melvin. He was my brother, and I know you loved him."

"I did." Tears sprang unbidden to her eyes. "And, *yah,* I wish to hear about Barbara."

THIRTEEN

Minister Kanagy had spoken for thirty minutes now, and Ida felt a little guilty that she hadn't been totally wrapped up in his story. Her mind had wandered even with her initial interest in what he had to say. The tale of his former *frau*'s life was important to Minister Kanagy, so it was important to her. And Minister Kanagy had said she was to speak about his brother Melvin after he finished. But truth be told, she really didn't want to speak of Melvin. Their love had never been lived out day-to-day like the story Minister Kanagy was telling. Ida had only dreamed of having a life together with Melvin. They had never had even a fraction of what Minister Kanagy had with Barbara.

She forced herself to focus.

". . . the year Wilma was born. We'd waited so many years for the first one. Barbara thought *Da Hah* had decided we were to remain childless, but I kept up my hope.

And it did happen. I can remember my joy. I must have looked like Joe did downstairs tonight. Perhaps even more so because we had waited so long. John came a year later. I thought we were well on our way to a large family. A little late, but still time, I told myself." A hint of a smile spread over his face.

Ida decided she couldn't think of him anymore as Minister Kanagy. He must become Ben to her. *Ben.* Ida ran the name through her mind a few times. It felt okay. Not as fearsome and frightening as "Minister Kanagy." This man in front of her would soon be her husband — if *Da Hah* so willed it. Minister . . . *nee,* Ben should no longer strike uneasiness in her.

"Perhaps I should say something, Ben," Ida interrupted. She gave him a warm smile when he appeared surprised. "I want you to take as long as you wish to speak of Barbara, but I'd like best to be able to say things myself when they come to me." She gave him another smile. "It works for me that way."

"Yah," Ben said, regarding her with surprise.

He seemed to adjust rather quickly, for which Ida was grateful. She took a deep breath. "It's this thing about Melvin's children. I know you have two of them at your house — Willard and Rosa — in addition to your own two."

"Oh!" A smile spread across his face. "Of course you will wish to see all six of Melvin's children at times. That won't be a problem. It's most understandable that you would. We can start right soon, if you wish. I'll come pick you up on Sunday afternoon, and we can visit them."

He wasn't quite understanding what she was trying to say. Ida steadied herself. "*Nee,* Ben, that's not what I mean at all. In fact, I don't wish to spend time with them before our wedding." Ida glanced away as heat rushed into her face. She took a moment to gather herself together. "I want *all* of them in our home after the wedding, Ben. Your two children plus Willard, Rosa, Amos, Ephraim, Lonnie, and Lisa. *All* of them."

He was startled, even shocked. "All of them, Ida? But they have settled in with others of the family. We can't disrupt that."

"This is what I want, Ben." Ida tried to keep her voice firm. "This is partly why I am willing to say vows with you. For the children. Melvin's and yours. I was sure you already knew this."

The struggle on his face was severe. "But, Ida, this cannot be. I have four children at

148

my home now. Mine and two of Melvin's. Four more would be eight! And then with the ones *Da Hah* perhaps will give us . . ."

Ida forced a smile. "You just said moments ago that you wished for a large family. Maybe *Da Hah* heard you."

Ben's face turned a little pale.

Obviously he wasn't used to such plain talk from a woman, especially plain talk that was correcting him. Ida let out a breath and silently thanked *Da Hah* for having Sadie speak to her on this matter. It was a good thing Sadie had insisted she bring this up before saying vows.

"You seem to have made up your mind, Ida."

Ida met his gaze. "I will not marry without agreement on this condition. Either all of your brother Melvin's children come to live in our home after the wedding, Ben, or . . . or it's best we not say the vows."

He was silent for a long moment. "You are sure of this, Ida? You really mean it? This is what you desire?"

Ida nodded and affirmed, "I do, Ben."

His face softened. "Well, Melvin was my brother, and we did love each other. Perhaps this is *Da Hah*'s will."

"It is." Ida didn't hesitate. "And it is mine. *Da Hah* listens to a *mamm*'s heart, does He not? And if you promise me this and then take this from me, Ben, I will never be the *frau* you wish for. A part of my heart will die — a part you will wish hadn't."

Ben was an honorable man and wouldn't go back on his word once it was given, but why let it even be a temptation? She wanted to make it plain where she stood, that part of it would require having eight children in the house, plus the ones she would bear for him if *Da Hah* willed. Ida looked away as her face flamed again.

He thought long before he spoke. "You're a *gut* woman, Ida. Your heart is in the right place. You have not asked for ease, or pleasure, or for a gentle rule from my hand. Rather, you have asked for hardship, and trouble, and for helping the hearts of troubled children who have lost their parents. I cannot but give you what *Da Hah* has already given, Ida. It would be a sin for me to deny such love. I only hope you will one day see *me* in such a way. Such a love as yours is truly holy and righteous, and I am unworthy. *Yah,* Ida. I will make arrangements to bring all of Melvin's children to our home a week or so before the wedding."

Ida choked for a moment as hot tears rushed down her cheeks. This she had not expected. Such *wunderbah* words! They burned in her heart. Ben understood! Ida stood and stepped toward him.

He hesitated, but stood also and opened his arms. They embraced. Stiffly at first, and then with ease. His hand reached for her face. He touched her cheeks, his eyes intense. "Ida, I love you already. More than I can ever say."

She stilled his words with her fingers on his lips. She angled her head up even more to receive his kiss. Her first thought was that he kissed as Melvin had. The passion was the same. He kept his arms around her for a long time, but he finally relaxed his hug and gently separated from her. "This is not yet right, Ida. We have not said the vows, and I was once a married man. I want to be careful and honorable."

She nodded and sat on the bed again. He walked to the window and pushed aside the drapes for a better view. As he gazed out the window, Ida studied the back of his head. She was glad she had kissed him. It comforted her heart even though she'd been certain this course was *Da Hah*'s will. Confirmation was *gut*. But how would she compare with Barbara? Ben seemed to like her and even said so. Their relationship might not be a flame of fire like she'd eventually felt for Melvin or the raging river

Paul Wagler used to stir in her. But this feeling was something *gut* nonetheless. Wholesome even as it was tempered by the deep sorrow they had both experienced. In many ways they were one already in spirit. Ben would probably laugh at her if he knew how much she read into their one kiss, but she was glad he had spoken his heart. She would never have dared approach him with her heart open without his words. And now she knew. She would not dread his kisses or his love.

Ida shifted her weight on the bed. "We had best speak of the wedding date, should we not?"

"Of course." He took the chair again.

She gave him a tender smile. "Tell me what your thoughts are."

He ran his hands through his hair, obviously still distracted. "It makes no difference to me, Ida. Other than having it occur quickly during next month's wedding season. People will understand."

Ida nodded. "So *Mamm* and I can pick the best date for us?"

He appeared relieved. "*Yah,* that's okay. Whatever works. And I will begin telling the others about Melvin's children living with us."

"*Yah,* thank you. What about the witnesses

for the wedding? Do you have a preference for your side of the family?"

He waved his hand about. "I don't care, Ida. Phillip, my youngest brother, would be the natural choice for me, but he's still sore at me, I'm afraid." Ben gave a nervous smile. "I was a little harsh with him once, but I'll ask him anyway. Feel free to ask whomever you wish for your side of the family." He got to his feet and took her hands in his. "I just want to wed you, Ida."

"Ben . . ." she whispered, feeling the heat rise in her face again. "Thanks for saying such *wunderbah* things about me tonight."

He smiled. "Now I'd better go. I've kept Joe and Verna up long enough."

Ida remained seated. "You haven't finished the story about Barbara and you."

A smile played on his face. "I have said enough, Ida. Barbara was a *wunderbah frau* for me — while *Da Hah* allowed it. But she has gone on to a better place where I fear she has long forgotten me in the wonder of that splendid land. *Da Hah* has given me you, Ida. To comfort my heart, to bring joy to my old age, and to bring happiness into my home. You mean much to me."

He sat down again and pulled his chair closer. "I'm sorry I haven't taken the time to properly court you, Ida, such as taking

153

you home after the hymn singing in a buggy with a fast horse." He laughed. "My old plodder, Misty, can hardly pick one foot up after the other anymore. I really must get a better horse for you. I can't expect you to drive around the community looking like your horse is ready to die on you. I will see what I can find in Lewistown soon — before the wedding."

Ida laughed. "You don't have to. From the looks of things, I won't be leaving the house much anyway!"

He still looked concerned. "So you don't mind the lack of a proper courting?"

Ida felt the sting of tears and made no attempt to hide them. "I've had my proper courting from your brother. We loved each other, Ben, with all our hearts. We were looking forward to a long life together. I never could understand why it couldn't be." Ida paused to wipe her eyes. "So a proper courting? *Nee*, I think it's best this way. We'll make our own memories in life. They'll just be different from what we've had before. But isn't that how it should be?" It had been many months since Melvin passed, and Ida was surprised at her tears. Ben had drawn surprising emotions out of her.

He squeezed her hand. "You're a very wise

woman, Ida. But I really must be going. Perhaps I can see you again soon? Maybe some Saturday afternoon?"

Ida nodded as she searched for her handkerchief.

Ben stood and smiled down at her. "Are you coming with me to the front door?"

Ida stood. She gave her eyes one last dab before she followed him down the stairs. Verna and Joe were waiting, sitting quietly with Sarah Mae. Ida did her best to hide her tear-stained face. No doubt both Joe and Verna were curious about what had gone on upstairs, and she couldn't blame them. This was all so unexpected to them.

Ida gave Ben one last smile at the front door and then closed it.

"Well!" Verna said before Ida had even turned around. "Tell us what happened!"

"Is it going to . . . work out okay?" Joe asked, cradling his daughter in his arms.

"*Yah,* it's going to work out just fine. The wedding will be sometime in November. *Mamm* and I will get down to the planning as soon as I'm back home."

"Well!" Verna exclaimed again. "If that doesn't beat all!" She rose to give her sister a hug. "I'm so happy for you," Verna whispered.

Ida pressed back the sudden sting of tears again.

FOURTEEN

Saturday afternoon Ida sat beside Joe as he pulled into the Beiler driveway and came to a stop by the hitching post. Her long week at Verna's house was at an end, but the glow of happiness remained. Now with the meeting with Ben having gone so well, she must begin her wedding plans at once. There was so much to report and discuss with *Mamm* she could almost explode.

Joe glanced at Ida. "Do you want me to help you down?"

Ida laughed. "I'm quite capable, thank you. And I only have a satchel."

"I feel like I should do something special for you." Joe held the reins tightly as Ida climbed down. "You have been so *gut* with the baby."

"Just take care of Verna." Ida smiled up at him. "And don't drop little Sarah."

Joe grinned as he slapped the reins and guided the horse, turning the buggy around in the driveway to head home.

Ida took a deep breath as she looked around. The home place still looked the same. But then why shouldn't it? She hadn't been gone that long, even though it seemed a year. A life had come into the world in that time, and, in a way, a new life had begun for her. She'd felt a stir of love for Minister Kanagy . . . for Ben.

Verna had teased her this morning in the kitchen. "I think you're really in love with that stern old man, Ida."

Ida had smiled and allowed Verna to think what she wished. She had, in fact, thought of the oldest of Melvin's boys, Willard. He'd be ten now. He had begun to show his *daett*'s build, but there remained a sorrow that hung about him. Ida had so longed these past months for the opportunity to pull him close in a tight hug and whisper words of comfort in his ear. That wouldn't have been appropriate, but all that was about to change — and very soon. Hopefully Willard's heart was still reachable. But surely it would be or *Da Hah* wouldn't allow her this opportunity.

Ida moved toward the front porch.

The door burst open and Debbie raced toward her across the lawn.

Ida dropped her satchel and opened her arms.

Debbie paused a few feet away before she wrapped Ida in a hug. "You look so happy. Must be taking care of babies suits you well."

"You only know the half," Ida gushed. "So much has happened the past week, my head is spinning."

Debbie smiled. "Then you'd better start talking. You know I want to hear everything. Especially about Minister Kanagy. Are you expecting him to call on you soon? I'm surprised he hasn't been here already, knocking down the door looking for you."

"Maybe we'd better begin there." Ida hid a smile. "Ben came over to Verna's last night, and we had a *gut* talk."

Debbie was shocked. "The man hunted you down at your sister's place?"

Ida laughed. "You make it sound horrible. But things went very well. And I have permission to set the wedding date with *Mamm*. And all of Melvin's children are coming home to live with us."

"Whoa! Whoa!" Debbie held up her hand. "Isn't this moving a little fast? Are you telling me you were engaged last night?"

Ida felt heat rise up her neck, and she figured she couldn't hide this from Debbie.

And she wasn't ashamed of how things had happened. "Actually, Ben sort of asked me last Sunday on the back porch after the service at Deacon Mast's place . . . and I sort of accepted. And then last night we worked out the details. We don't have much time until the wedding season."

Debbie's shock didn't go away. "You knew on Sunday . . . and you hid it?"

Ida winced. "I wasn't trying to trick anyone. It was a little sudden for me, you know. I needed some time to process it."

"Oh, you dear!" Debbie groaned before she wrapped Ida in another hug. "If you're fine with the stern man, why should I care? But doesn't he just freeze the blood in your veins?"

Ida looked away, but Debbie would still see the rush of red. This part she wouldn't share. Debbie had no need to know that she and Ben had kissed last night. What a scandalous thing to even think about, let alone do. But she had done it!

Debbie eyed her skeptically. "Well, to each her own, I guess. You don't have to tell me more right this minute. Come! Your *mamm* is waiting impatiently for news."

Ida pulled on Debbie's sleeve. "How's Emery doing? Has he tormented you with any more teasing about that *Englisha* girl?"

Debbie glanced away before she answered. "We'd better not talk about Emery. I spoke with him last night. I'm worried that he's not just teasing. He knows all about Crystal and wants to support her efforts should she decide to join the community."

Ida shrugged. "Emery puzzles me. I don't understand why he doesn't show more interest in the community's girls. What about you and Alvin? Anything going on there?"

Debbie lagged a step behind. "I have to face Alvin on Sunday night. He'll have some explanation I'm sure."

Ida frowned. "You know how I feel about Alvin. Getting rid of him wouldn't be a bad idea."

Debbie managed a smile. "Then it looks like I'm telling my troubles to the wrong person."

Ida appeared pensive. "You do have other options, you know. Alvin can take care of himself."

Before Debbie could respond, the front door opened again and *Mamm* hollered out, "Are you girls going to chatter on the lawn all day? This old woman is waiting for news."

Ida laughed and rushed forward to give *Mamm* a hug.

Mamm protested. "You're going to

161

smother me, Ida. Has Verna's *boppli* so affected you?"

"She's such a sweet bundle," Ida gushed. "And growing even more beautiful since you saw her on Monday night."

"I should have visited today, I suppose." *Mamm* led the way inside. "But there will be plenty of time. Is Verna coming to church on Sunday?"

"I don't think so." Ida took a seat on the couch, and *Mamm* settled into her rocker.

"Thank *Da Hah* she has that much sense," *Mamm* said. "Some of our young women are being influenced by the *Englisha* ways the past few years, thinking they have to bounce right up after only a few days of rest."

"I made sure Verna got plenty of rest," Ida assured her. "And Joe wouldn't let Verna out of the house even if she wanted to. That man is the most doting *daett* I've seen in a long time."

A slight smile crossed *Mamm*'s face. "You never got to see your *daett* and the way he acted. The way he cooed over the crib for weeks after your births."

Ida could imagine that. *Daett* had kept that attention up over the years, even to the present day. She could only hope Ben would be as attentive.

She had been so eager to talk to *Mamm* about her wedding plans . . . but now that she was home, she decided that could wait a few hours more. This evening she would take in the full flavor of life here, the place where she'd grown up. She'd help with the chores and later with the supper dishes. But *Mamm* should be told about the engagement.

Ida took a deep breath. "I'd best confess something, *Mamm*. Minister Kanagy spoke with me last Sunday, and I'm promised to him. He came over to Verna's last night, and we spoke of it again."

Mamm didn't say anything for a moment. "So that's why he stopped by the other evening. I thought something might be up."

"You don't object, do you? Will *Daett*?" Ida waited.

Mamm shook her head and sighed. "It's for the best, I suppose. A little soon, perhaps, but people will understand."

Silence fell between them as the seconds ticked past. *Mamm* felt the same as she did. Neither of them wanted to speak further on the matter. It was as if they both tried to hold off the inevitable but knew that was impossible. In the meantime, these last few savored moments of how life once was would give them strength for the journey ahead.

FIFTEEN

That evening Alvin rushed through his chores alone. Mildred wasn't scheduled to help, so he was by himself. The stillness of the barn was broken only by the moos of the cows and their bangs against the metal stanchions. Star neighed once and stuck his head in the back barn window to plead for a bucket of oats. But the horse would get none tonight. He'd give Star extra feed tomorrow after they made the trip to the service in the morning, and back to the hymn singing, and then to the Beilers' place in the evening.

Alvin dreaded the whole coming day. He dreaded the moment when he'd have to face people again — especially Debbie. But there was something he dreaded even more — the expected arrival of Deacon Mast, perhaps even yet this evening. Surely the deacon would visit. And yet dusk had almost fallen, and the deacon still hadn't made his appearance. Maybe the man was running late. Or maybe he wouldn't come tonight. Alvin stopped in the middle of the barn floor at the thought. If Deacon Mast considered Alvin's actions so serious that he wanted to discuss the matter first with the ministry on Sunday morning, Alvin was surely in more trouble than even he'd imagined.

How had this happened? Alvin groaned out loud. He had come home from his time in the *Englisha* world and thought he'd left it all behind. Why had the past returned to haunt him? How would he bear the shame of Deacon Mast's questions? Now it would almost be a relief if the deacon arrived so they could get this over with.

He wished Mildred had been scheduled to help in the barn tonight. Her presence would soothe him, he was sure. Her looks were plain enough. She certainly didn't match Debbie in beauty. Why Mildred ever got her nose up in the air about him was a mystery. Maybe she thought she could find greener pastures. Alvin let out a bitter laugh. Mildred had experienced about as much success with that venture as he had with his ill-fated rush into the *Englisha* world.

But it was also true that Mildred's personality was steady, she was scandal-free, and her reputation was above reproach. All of which he couldn't say for himself right now. Thankfully, Debbie wasn't involved with Crystal in any way. Debbie shared that advantage with Mildred. Now if he could settle this matter with Deacon Mast and assure him that Crystal would cause no further trouble for him or the community, this problem might go away. Hadn't he sent her away last Sunday night? The deacon would stroke his beard in worry over all those details. *Daett* had probably seen to it that the news reached the deacon's ears. Alvin had watched his *daett* drive off in his buggy several times this past week. He could have stopped in at Deacon Mast's on any of those trips.

Alvin glanced down the road. It was still empty of buggies. Maybe he should visit the deacon after the chores and tell him personally. Such a move might even work to his favor if he showed up voluntarily and confessed willingly. Alvin moved even faster. He shoved the feed in front of the stanchions for the next round of cows. He had them in and secured just as he heard buggy wheels turn in the driveway. Alvin rushed to the window. Sure enough, Deacon Mast was climbing out of his buggy. Well, the cows could wait. There were more important things right now.

Alvin met Deacon Mast at the barn door. "*Gut* evening, Deacon. I was expecting you." Alvin's smile was crooked.

"*Gut* evening, Alvin." The deacon took in the row of cows with a quick glance. "I see I caught you in the middle of chores. I was afraid that would happen, but I've been running late all afternoon."

"That doesn't matter. They can wait."

Deacon Mast gave Alvin a weary smile. "I'll help you, and then we can talk."

"With the cows?" Alvin knew alarm filled his face. This was a favor he couldn't easily repay.

"*Yah,* of course." Deacon Mast nodded. "I'm a farmer too, you know. And a man shouldn't be kept from his work. Not when he's milking cows."

Alvin swallowed hard. "Well, this is the last round."

"Then where can I help?" Deacon Mast looked around and didn't wait for an answer. He helped himself to a set of milking equipment.

Alvin joined in as Deacon Mast bent down beside a cow. He wasn't exactly comfortable with this arrangement, but this was the deacon after all, and the deacon was in charge. What could he do but follow along? Mildred would laugh if she were here and saw him in this predicament. And he deserved laughter. This was his own fault because of his habit of running away from problems. If he'd never gone to Philadelphia, none of this would be happening.

Deacon Mast looked over the cow's back. "Alvin, maybe you can answer some of my questions while we work."

Alvin nodded but said nothing. What was there to say? The deacon was polite to even ask. Amish people held conversations all the time while they did the chores. The deacon would of course wait for any major lecture until they were face-to-face. And a lecture would surely come. There was little doubt about that.

Deacon Mast cleared his throat. "Your *daett* stopped by this week. He's quite concerned about what happened last Sunday night. He says the *Englisha* girl, Crystal, who came to my place, came by to speak with you. You also did not attend the hymn singing. Did you know she was coming to the community, Alvin?"

"Nee," Alvin said, his response muffled by the cow he was working with.

"That's *gut* to hear, Alvin."

The deacon doesn't sound convinced, Alvin thought.

"Why did Crystal come then, and why did you stay home from the hymn singing?"

Alvin took a deep breath as he considered what to say. He had to tell the truth, hard as that was. "*Yah,* I admit Crystal came," Alvin said. "Seeing Crystal did disturb me considerably at the service . . . it was unexpected, though she had hinted she might visit. I was worried what Debbie would think. But why Crystal came, I know only what she told me. She said she was drawn to the community. She wanted to see what our way of life is like because she is searching for peace."

The deacon probed. "Was this not the girl you confessed to dating while you lived in Philadelphia?"

These were the exact questions Alvin didn't want to face. He couldn't speak at the moment.

The deacon took his silence as a *yah.* "You must still have feelings for the girl then. Is this not correct, Alvin?"

"I do not!" Alvin exclaimed. "Crystal had no reason to come in like this, disturbing me and the life of the community. I told her so!" Alvin tried to calm himself. Vigorous denials would accomplish little.

"You spoke these things to Crystal on Sunday night . . . when she came to see you?" Deacon Mast stood up to look at him.

"*Yah!*" Alvin coughed and ducked behind a cow. He didn't have anything to hide, yet his face burned with shame.

"And you told Crystal . . . about not having feelings for her?"

"*Yah.* And that is the truth!"

"Yet there was some need to say it?"

Alvin stood up straight. "Crystal told me she came because she wants to find out more about the community. That I had stirred a desire in her to learn of our life in her search for peace."

Deacon Mast's voice was pensive. "That's what she told us — when she first came. She also said she had family in the area. Do you know if this is true — about her family?"

Alvin shrugged. "She never mentioned anything of her family to me."

"And yet you spoke of love?" The deacon's voice dug deeper.

"*Yah,* but not love as you are thinking. We spoke of the *possibility* of love. We did go on a few dates, *yah.*" Alvin beat the barn wall with his hand. "How many times must I confess to this thing? We did go out, but I left it all behind when I returned. I did not make any kind of commitment with Crystal. Isn't that plain enough? I'm here, am I not?"

The deacon's face was sorrowful. "Your anger does not speak well of you, Alvin. There are many questions raised by all of this. You should still have known better than to associate with a divorced woman."

"I did not know she was divorced until our last date just before I returned to the community. I am sorry for what I did," Alvin whispered, all the fight having seeped out of him. "I will bear my shame before *Da Hah* and His church. I tell you plainly that I have no further interest in Crystal."

Deacon Mast stepped back from the cow he worked on. "I accept your apology, Alvin. That is always *gut.* But with the history that Crystal has with you . . ." Deacon Mast paused.

"Crystal would never do anything indecent." The words slipped out. He wished he hadn't said them. Why did he defend her? He didn't know the woman nearly as well as he'd thought he did. Otherwise he would have thought earlier of the possibility that she might show up.

Deacon Mast shrugged. "Only *Da Hah* knows the hearts of men, Alvin. Maybe Crystal has only *gut* motives. Emery Beiler spoke with me about Crystal. He wants me to encourage her to learn more about our faith and to join the community if she so desires. Emery only wants to see her settle into a decent life that befits holiness and godliness. Crystal says she might move in with her relatives in Penns Creek. Her nearness increases our concerns about you and the issues that have come to the surface. Are you telling us all of the truth? Is your heart perhaps still out there in the world, Alvin?"

All his blood seemed to drain to his feet, and his body turned icy cold. Alvin couldn't get a word out of his mouth. Not that his denials would do much *gut*.

Deacon Mast continued. "Did you perhaps come home, Alvin, so you could take over your *daett*'s farm?"

Alvin had nothing to say. What was the use?

Deacon Mast's tone grew more serious. "Your *daett* says he found letters you and your *mamm* wrote each other while you were in Philadelphia. He says there's a lot in there about coming home so the committee would let you run the farm. Why have you not told us this, Alvin? And now we find out that Crystal is divorced, which you knew. You knew even then that this would never be acceptable to the community. Is that why you left Crystal — maybe with her feelings hurt and her not understanding why you cut off the love between the two of you?"

Alvin groped for the clips on the stanchions. He released the cows one by one and shooed them out the back door of the barn. Then he settled down on a three-legged stool set against the wall.

Deacon Mast waited for him with a sober face. "Perhaps it's time you begin confessing your sins for real, Alvin?"

"None of what you say is true," Alvin's voice croaked.

"You should not deny the truth, Alvin. Your *daett* did find the letters." Deacon Mast's voice was insistent.

"It's not what it seems," Alvin managed. "*Yah*, the farm did have a pull on my heart. *Yah, Mamm* did encourage me to come home. But I came home for the right reasons, Deacon Mast. I wanted what we have here . . . not what is out there."

Deacon Mast's voice stayed calm. "So now you tell us. After you must. But what if there are other things you are not saying?"

"Things such as what?" Alvin forced himself to take another deep breath.

Deacon Mast shrugged. "About Debbie maybe. Were you honest about all things in your relationship with her?"

Alvin couldn't yet find the strength to

speak about how Debbie used to drive past the farm to catch glimpses of him in the fields before she joined the community.

Deacon Mast regarded him with a tilt of his head. "There is something more, is there not?"

His words came out in a rush. "Debbie and I noticed each other . . . before she moved in with Bishop Beiler and joined the community. She drove past here at times, and *yah,* my heart did beat faster. But what is wrong with that? We never met or spoke until much later."

"This might explain much, Alvin." Deacon Mast's words were clipped. "Your heart seems much drawn to the *Englisha* world. And then you leave for that world, even accepting excommunication. Just think about that, Alvin. Why would one do that? Why would a person throw his soul into the risk of darkness? And yet you did. Maybe it was because you had doubts about your ability to win Debbie's hand once she joined the community. Was that the problem? So you left to find another *Englisha* girl, one more fitting to your lusting heart? But once your *mamm* told you what was going on with the farm, you couldn't resist coming back and being put in charge. And when Debbie was still available, everything kind of fell into your lap. And you thought all was going well until *Da Hah* revealed your sins by having Crystal come. Is that it, Alvin? Does that sound pretty close to right?"

Alvin frowned. "None of it is right even if some of it is true."

"Now what kind of sense does that make?" The deacon regarded Alvin with a steadfast gaze.

Alvin met his look. "It doesn't, but I still speak the truth."

Deacon Mast sighed. "These are serious matters, Alvin. They are also complicated. You deny them, so what can I say? I will speak to the ministry. I know we will not rush into any conclusions, and I'm not sure what can or should be done. I exhort you to search your heart and repent of any evil you find there. It would be *gut* if you confessed to Debbie about why you came back. Bishop Beiler seems to think her heart is in the right place. And Emery speaks well for Crystal, so she may have honest motives as well. In the meantime, I'd pray, Alvin, that *Da Hah* will open the truth to you so you can see clearly."

Alvin put his head down and leaned his forehead on both his hands. He listened as the barn door swung open and shut. Moments later he heard the deacon's buggy wheels roll down the driveway. The sound of horse hooves hitting pavement soon died away.

He would never live this down, Alvin thought. Not in a dozen years.

SIXTEEN

Early the next morning Alvin walked toward the barn, his gas lantern swinging by his side in the brisk morning air. He was still tired after a restless night, but the chores wouldn't wait. Each hour of the night had been a torment. Wild dreams he hadn't had since his childhood kept him first on one side of the bed then the other. Deacon Mast had chased him with his buggy over open ground while thunderclouds moved across snowy fields. Winter lay heavy on the land, and from behind the deacon's buggy had come strokes of lightning that broke through the ice on the pond. The heat had sizzled the ice as the bolts struck. The more Alvin ran, the more the rain fell from the skies, turning into steam before it reached the ground. He'd awakened gasping several times. Each time he had to assure himself this was a nightmare, only to have it begin all over again when he dozed off. There was no need for the alarm this morning. He'd waited for this hour long before it arrived.

He must calm down, Alvin told himself. He must do that before he made something out of Deacon Mast's visit that wasn't there. The deacon had nothing against him other than questions about the motives of his heart. How could he be disciplined for that? And even if Deacon Mast stood firm in his wrong conclusions, unless Alvin committed some further transgression there would only be the shame he had to bear. Hopefully the community would eventually forget about the entire situation. This comfort was slim. Alvin's heart told him something else entirely. There were screams of "Run, run, run!" But to where? There was no place to hide. Not unless he wished to bolt for the *Englisha* world again, which he did not.

Alvin pushed open the barn door, and hung his lantern on the ceiling hook. Before he turned around, light from Mildred's lantern bounced off the barn walls. She's out early, he thought. It was a *gut* thing Mildred hadn't been here last night. If she learned what the deacon had to say, her nose would go right back up in the air like it had after their school days ended. And this time her rejection would burn even deeper. He paused. He hadn't known he cared so much about what she thought, but he did.

Alvin stiffened and turned to face her. "*Gut* morning," he said curtly.

She looked him over for a moment before she spoke. "My, you look rough. The deacon did you over *gut,* I see."

He searched her face for signs of scorn and found none. There was only compassion and concern. "He came . . . but it's not like it might seem, Mildred."

Mildred gave him a sad smile. "I'm sorry you have to go through this, Alvin. Your *daett* gave me the full load last night after we saw the deacon's buggy over here. I can't say I blame Deacon Mast for thinking such things about you, but I told your *daett* I think he's wrong in questioning your character."

"You did? But it doesn't look *gut* for me. You have to admit that." Even as he said the negative, Alvin felt jabs of pure joy run up his back. Mildred believed in him. Mildred! The girl who had rejected him all those years ago.

She stepped closer and touched his arm. "Not everything is like it appears, Alvin. It makes perfect sense to me that your *mamm* would want you home to take over the farm. You know how things used to be run around

180

here." She gave him a meaningful glance. "I used to think you were made of the same stuff as your *daett* — incompetent when it comes to running a farm. But your *mamm* knew you weren't. So what's wrong with her wanting you home again? And of course you jumped at the chance. What man wouldn't? I'd disrespect you if you hadn't come back."

"But," Alvin sputtered, "but I really came back because I didn't like the world out there."

Her smile was sweeter this time. "I know that. And in their hearts the people of the community know that. I even think Deacon Mast knows it. He just has to consider the worst. And your *daett* is speaking out of his bitterness right now, Alvin. You must forgive them all. And with time your *daett* will see that he's wrong, that you weren't trying to take something away from him that didn't belong to you."

"Crystal is still here," he admitted. "As long as she's around, people like Deacon Mast will get the wrong idea."

Mildred's look was direct. "I understood that you didn't invite her or give her any encouragement to come. That you don't have feelings for her."

"Of course I don't!"

Mildred's smile was back. "Then there you go, Alvin. Keep your chin up. It'll be okay. Things might be rough for a while, but if you don't do anything foolish, you'll make it. Now, shouldn't we be doing the chores? It's Sunday morning, and you don't want to be late for the service." She stepped closer to pat him on the shoulder. "And do put on a more sunny face, Alvin. You look guilty, and there's no reason for it. You don't want Debbie thinking there's something to all of this, do you?" She gave him another pat. "Debbie will be right by your side tonight, and everything will be just fine."

"Thank you!" Mildred seemed like a sister to him . . . even more than that perhaps. Her words made that plain enough, although she was likely trying to make up for her actions all those years ago. Alvin gave her a warm smile before he turned to open the barn door for the cows. What a *gut* heart the girl had. *Da Hah* had supplied exactly what he needed during this difficult time. If he'd had this kind of support before, he never would have bolted for the *Englisha* world. He slapped the back ends of the cows as they pushed past him toward the feed bins.

Mildred had the feed spread out when he returned and snapped the clips shut on the

182

stanchions. She gave him another smile before she began to work in silence.

Alvin allowed her presence to soothe him. She worked so efficiently without words. She didn't need instructions. It was as if she belonged here . . . and had always belonged here. She was one of their people, just as he was one of them. And like Debbie was, Alvin reminded himself. Except Debbie had joined from the outside. The thought troubled him. He wished it didn't. He shouldn't blame Debbie. She hadn't done anything wrong, and Bishop Beiler had the utmost confidence in his boarder. So should he.

Alvin finished his share of the cows and turned them loose. Mildred shoveled the next batch of feed while he shooed the cows out and brought the next round in. She still hadn't said anything more by the time they finished and he let the cows out again.

Now she spoke with a warm smile. "You're coming over for breakfast, Alvin. After you've finished the rest of the chores, of course. I'll have bacon and eggs with biscuits and gravy ready. I can even make sausage, if you like."

His mouth fell open.

Her smile never dimmed. "You're not eating by yourself this morning. I will not have it. Not after the night you've had. You still look awful. And I can't stand it anyway. Being over there at the *dawdy haus* and thinking about you in that cold kitchen all alone and trying to stir something up to eat. All I have to do is add a little extra, and there we go."

He wanted to protest, but what came out was, "You're way too nice, Mildred. But how can I?"

She raised her eyebrows. "How hard is walking over on your two feet? You don't expect me to carry you, do you? The deacon wasn't that hard on you."

When he still hesitated, she gave another push. "You and your *daett* really need to talk, Alvin. You can't go on living next door to each other with these bad feelings between the two of you. I don't know if one breakfast will fix things, but why not try? Be nice to the old man, Alvin. He's your *daett*. And you have taken over his farm."

Alvin's resistance vanished like the dreams of the night in the light of day. "Thank you, Mildred. This is very nice of you."

"Think nothing of it," she replied. "Now don't dawdle." And she was gone.

Alvin's head spun as the light of her lantern disappeared through the doorway. What had he just agreed to? Breakfast at his *daett*'s place? But what was wrong with that? And he did need to speak with his *daett.* Mildred was right on that point. Alvin could feel the need in his bones, even though she was also right that the conversation might lead nowhere. He still needed to try. And a hot breakfast? His mouth watered at the thought of hot biscuits and gravy, to say nothing of eggs and bacon. Cold cereal from a box was a horrible comparison to that.

Debbie need never know, he told himself. Not that she should care. There was nothing between Mildred and him in a romantic way. She worked for his *daett* and, of course, wished to comfort her friend Alvin in his troubles. Breakfast was just one way Mildred could do that. *Nee,* Debbie would have no problem if he ate breakfast once in a while at the *dawdy haus.*

Alvin rushed to finish his chores. He turned off his lantern and stepped out to the dawning sky. The last faint twinkle of stars overhead drew his attention, and he paused for a moment to look upward. It amazed him how much *gut* the thought of a hot breakfast did for him — that and Mildred's encouraging words this morning. Who would have thought she would stand by him in such an hour of trouble?

Alvin approached the *dawdy haus* and entered without a knock. His *daett* was seated on the rocker, his *mamm* on the other. He didn't appear surprised so Mildred must have told him.

"*Gut* morning," Alvin greeted.

"*Gut* morning," his *daett* returned.

Alvin approached his *mamm*'s side to give her a quick hug. A sorrow swept over him at the sight of her. Not that long ago *Mamm* had been so alive and full of love for him. No doubt that love still beat inside her heart that was gradually freezing within her crippled body and mind.

"I love you, *Mamm*," he whispered. She gave him a weak smile. He turned in the direction of the waves of delicious smells rolling out of the kitchen. The aroma of baking biscuits and frying bacon almost took his breath away.

Mildred's cheerful face appeared in the kitchen doorway. "Sit down and wait for a minute. Breakfast will soon be ready."

He did as he was told. The living room was wrapped in silence. He almost stood to join Mildred in the kitchen but decided he probably shouldn't. That wouldn't look decent. Allowing her to help with barn chores was one thing, but him helping in the kitchen was going too far. Instead he

186

picked up the copy of *The Budget* that arrived faithfully at the *dawdy haus* each week. He scanned the pages until Mildred announced, "I'm ready! Will you help your *mamm* to the table, Alvin?"

He turned to catch Mildred's smile. His *daett* stood and walked over to *Mamm*. Together they helped her to her seat at the table.

Now was the time when he should speak, Alvin told himself, or it would only get harder. He'd already wasted precious moments in the living room reading.

"*Daett*," he began, once his *mamm* was comfortable and his *daett* had taken his seat at the table, "Deacon Mast told me what you said about me last week. I want to tell you that some of it was true. I did read and respond to *Mamm*'s letters. And, *yah*, the promise of working the farm did partly draw me home. But there was more to it than that. I want the life that you have created here. I want what the community has. I want what our people believe. I don't want what's out there in the *Englisha* world. I'm sorry if I've led you to think ill of me."

Mildred flashed him an encouraging smile when he finished. She glanced between his *daett* and him.

His *daett* grunted and responded, "That

may be as it is, Alvin. I don't pretend to know a man's heart. But with that *Englisha* girl running around last weekend and coming right into my house like she owned it, I thought the deacon should know everything that has gone on. So that's why I told him. You shouldn't hold that against me."

Alvin swallowed hard. "It's okay, *Daett*. I understand."

Mildred looked pleased as Alvin took his seat.

Alvin relaxed a bit. He'd done the right thing.

Without a word *Daett* bowed his head for silent prayer. When they'd finished, Alvin pushed his troubled thoughts away and concentrated on the delicious breakfast Mildred had prepared. The woman knew how to cook, no doubt about that.

Alvin dug into the biscuits and gravy. It almost melted in his mouth. And the bacon was fixed to a golden brown, still juicy enough to chew. That was how bacon should be prepared. It had been a long time since he'd had such food to eat, so perhaps his opinion was tainted. Still, he gave Mildred a grateful smile when she glanced his way. She smiled back and beamed with joy.

SEVENTEEN

After the Sunday evening hymn singing, Debbie pulled herself up into Alvin's buggy and settled into the seat. Silence filled the air. She'd longed to speak with him all week, but now that the moment had arrived the words lay frozen in her mouth.

"*Gut* evening." Alvin glanced over from his side of the buggy. He tried to sound cheerful.

Debbie did her best to echo his mood. "*Gut* to see you again."

"And you too." Alvin glanced each way at the end of the driveway before he guided Star through the turn and let him dash down the road. His hooves beat a steady rhythm on the blacktop.

Debbie knew she should say something, but she could think of nothing to start an easygoing conversation. Alvin had appeared troubled all day, but at least he'd stayed around for the meal after the service. He

189

had gone home but showed up for the hymn singing. Now he was taking her home. If Alvin did his part to face their troubles, Debbie would also do hers. At least one *gut* thing had happened today. Paul Wagler had been more restrained with his teases when she'd served food at the unmarried men's table. Maybe he was finally accepting the inevitable.

Alvin laughed a bit too hard and then said, "At least Crystal didn't bother me today. Still, I was surprised to see her at the service."

Debbie drew in her breath and replied with care. Crystal wasn't really the problem, and she didn't want to make her one. "I was surprised too." What could she say next to keep the conversation going? She decided just to speak up. "Alvin, I'm glad I finally have a chance to speak with you. It's been two weeks, you know."

He grunted. "There's nothing to speak about when it comes to Crystal. I told her it was over between us, and she understood. I've told you that too."

Debbie smiled a bit. "I'm not worried about you and Crystal."

"Really?" Alvin sounded surprised. "So what are you worried about?"

Debbie kept her voice steady. "Maybe you

should begin with last Sunday and tell me what happened. Why did you leave in such a hurry after the service?"

Alvin took his time before answering. "It wasn't what it may have seemed. I was startled and upset by Crystal's sudden appearance. I guess I ran."

Debbie sighed. "I know you don't have feelings for Crystal. Were you afraid to face me about her? Don't you trust me? Or care how it looked to the others? You don't have to run, Alvin. Not anymore. And not away from me."

"I guess you've seen my faults again, and to that list you can add the ones Deacon Mast sees."

Debbie reached over and touched his arm. "I'm not trying to scold you, Alvin. I want us to learn to work *together* through any trouble."

Alvin's eyes were wide as he looked at her. "Do you know what Deacon Mast thinks?"

"No." Debbie didn't hesitate. "And I don't need to. I just want you to work on your problems. You're going to have to face things, Alvin, not run."

Alvin frowned. "I know. I don't know why I run away. I'm trying to do better. Seeing Crystal in church for the first time last week . . . that . . . that was too much for me to handle, Debbie. I thought I'd left that life out there, and then she shows up to bring it all back. It was awful!"

"I'm here to help you." Debbie squeezed his arm.

His voice low, he said, "I know you said you don't care what Deacon Mast thinks, but I'm in a lot of trouble right now, Debbie. Not with you, but with the community. They're thinking what you aren't thinking. And they won't be easily persuaded otherwise. Plus there are some things my *daett* has been saying . . . about coming back just so I could take over the farm."

Debbie leaned against his shoulder. "Either way, I believe the best in you, Alvin. We can make it through this together."

Alvin's voice was mournful. "I can't disprove the things Deacon Mast thinks. And what he thinks is what matters when it comes to my standing in the community. Maybe you ought to bail while you have the chance. This is only our second date, so I can't have done much harm to your reputation."

Debbie stared at him. "Alvin, really! Stop this! We're in this together. I'm standing with you!"

Hope flickered on his face. "So you

wouldn't bail on me then? Even if everyone says I still hanker after the *Englisha* life — and *Englisha* women? Deacon Mast believes this is why *Da Hah* had Crystal follow me home."

Debbie gathered herself together. "I don't believe that! No, I won't bail on you." She almost added, *I don't run away from things like you do.* Instead she bit her lower lip.

His hand sought hers. "Thank you. I appreciate that. I guess we'll make it. I really should tell you everything Deacon Mast thinks about me. Can you handle that? Will you listen?"

"Of course." Debbie drew closer to him and searched his face.

His words came slowly. "Deacon Mast said some things last night about my motives for dating you. I'm sorry, but I told him how you used to drive past my place before you joined the community. I told him I had noticed you. So Deacon Mast knows I was drawn to you even back then. He doesn't think my heart was in the right place, and he's not sure it is yet. Not when it comes to *Englisha* girls. I'm afraid the deacon's not going to easily forget his doubts about me."

"You told him, Alvin?" Debbie stared out the buggy door into the dark shadows. "You told him about that? Why? That was just between us!"

"The deacon dug deep, Debbie. He wanted to know everything. And I'm tired of hiding things — even the little things."

Debbie tried to keep the desperation out of her voice. "I wish you wouldn't have told him."

Alvin winced. "I guess I don't know myself anymore, Debbie. The deacon thinks I should tell you why I really came back from Philadelphia."

She hadn't expected the conversation to take this turn. Her voice quivered. "Perhaps you should tell me, Alvin." She glanced at him.

Alvin's face turned pale in the dim buggy lights as he pulled into the Beiler driveway.

Was it true then? Was Alvin in love with Mildred? Debbie wondered.

Alvin brought Star to a stop by the hitching post. He said nothing as Emery's buggy pulled up next to them. Then Alvin cleared his throat. "I came home because *Mamm* told me the committee might let me run the farm. I came home because I had hopes I might be able to make a go of it."

"That's okay," Debbie responded. "I thought you were so brave facing your sins in front of all those ministers, to say noth-

194

ing of the community and me. That couldn't have been easy, Alvin. Was I wrong in my judgment of you? Tell me I wasn't."

"I hope you weren't," Alvin whispered. "The truth is, there is yet a greater motivation behind all of this — my love for my people, for our farmland, for our traditions, for our community. I came home, Debbie, because I love it all too much to leave it forever. If I learned anything during that time in your world, it was that truth. Unfortunately, Deacon Mast doesn't believe me. He thinks there's more."

Debbie let her breath out slowly. "I believe you, Alvin. But you said, 'If I learned anything during that time in *your* world.' In your mind am I still from that world? Do you still consider me an 'outsider,' an *Englisha*?"

Alvin said nothing.

Emery pulled in the lane to park near them. Ida glanced their way as she climbed out of the buggy but headed for the house without a word.

Debbie shifted on the seat. "We'd better go inside, don't you think?"

Alvin climbed out of the buggy and grabbed the tie rope. He tied Star to the hitching rail. As they walked toward the house, he moved beside Debbie and took

195

her hand in the darkness.

Debbie didn't resist. She liked his boldness, if the truth be told. This attitude was something Alvin didn't have before he left for Philadelphia. If he could only see that some good came from his time in the world perhaps some of his fears and doubts of her would subside. Because that was the problem. Alvin was afraid of what she represented. Hadn't he said as much even before Crystal's arrival? He'd waited until she was baptized before he set a time for their first date. That still stung.

Ida had left the front door ajar for them, but there was no sign of her when they stepped inside. That was Ida's way, Debbie thought. She turned to Alvin.

"Why not sit on the couch while I get some brownies and milk from the kitchen?"

Alvin smiled as he sat down.

Debbie hurried into the kitchen as Emery entered through the washroom door.

"*Gut* evening. Are you and Alvin behaving yourselves?" Emery teased.

"We're perfectly behaved," she responded.

He laughed and then disappeared through the kitchen doorway. There was a murmur of voices as Emery spoke with Alvin. Silence followed.

At least Emery hadn't given in to Crystal's

charms, Debbie thought. Crystal had been at the hymn singing this evening, and she had not so discreetly sent smiles Emery's way. But Crystal wouldn't know how to "behave properly" at an Amish youth gathering, Debbie reminded herself. She was irritated that Emery had shown concern for the woman, and Debbie admitted that wasn't a very Christian attitude for her to have. If Emery cared for the *Englisha* girl, why shouldn't she give Crystal a chance?

Debbie pushed the thought away at once. She was on a date with Alvin, so why ask such a question? Didn't she have enough to deal with in her own life? But Emery was so good and decent . . . Debbie felt her cheeks get warm. She focused on her search for the brownies. She found them and slid two pieces on separate plates. She took a moment to compose herself before she took glasses from the cupboard and filled them with cold milk.

Alvin smiled when she walked in with his plate and glass. He was still smiling when she came back in with hers. "These are *gut*. Did you make them?"

Debbie shook her head. "Saloma made this batch. But I've tried the recipe and no one died." Alvin laughed but Debbie thought he sounded nervous. She looked over to ask "How's Mildred doing?"

Alvin didn't hesitate. "Debbie, there's nothing to say about Mildred. She works at my *daett*'s place. It's you I love. You pull and draw on my heart — like you've been doing since I first saw you driving past my place. And I'm sorry about spilling the beans to Deacon Mast. Please don't worry about Mildred. She's working for *daett* because *daett* won't go live with one of his daughters-in-law." Alvin smiled. "*Daett*'s a cranky old man, I guess. But the farm is doing well enough now so we can afford paying Mildred. Beyond that, Debbie, my heart is safe with you."

Debbie's head spun. After a moment she said what any Amish girl would say. "Okay. I can live with that."

Alvin attempted a smile. "I have my times of fear. I can't deny that. But my heart is with you. Thanks for believing in me."

"Let's forget about Mildred then." Debbie nodded. "Tell me how your mother is getting along."

Alvin's face darkened. "Not well, I'm afraid."

Debbie listened as he spoke about his mother's condition. She squeezed his hand once, and his troubled look vanished for a moment. We will be good for each other, she told herself. Just like she'd always imagined they would be.

"Communion will be soon," Debbie said when there was a break in the conversation. "Now that Bishop Beiler announced pre-communion church in two weeks, I can hardly wait. It'll be my first communion as a member of the community."

"*Yah*," Alvin said with a smile, "you really are one of us now. I'm very happy about that."

EIGHTEEN

Ida hung the third load of wash on the line. It was still early Monday morning. Her gaze turned again toward the road. She'd been watching for Lois's car ever since she got up. Ida was sure her sister would stop by soon to report on her honeymoon. Lois wouldn't be able to contain her excitement for long.

Ida sighed at the thought of Lois and Doug. Then she chided herself. There were so many other things she should spend her thoughts on this morning instead of her wayward sister. For one, *Daett* had announced at the breakfast table that the threshing crew would arrive Thursday morning.

Debbie had squealed with delight as the troubled look on her face vanished for a moment. Something wasn't right between Debbie and Alvin. The two had seemed tense last night when she and Emery had driven in after the hymn singing. But then maybe they should be tense. Alvin was in deep trouble with the community. For what, Ida wasn't totally sure. But Debbie was a grown woman and a member of the community now. Debbie had objected to her upcoming marriage to Ben, but she had the decency to temper her words. Ida decided she would also behave herself and say no more against Alvin.

What she ought to think about was her own wedding plans. She still hadn't spoken at length with *Mamm* on the matter. Ida wanted a day or so to pass before the finality of what was coming descended upon her. Her departure would leave *Mamm* and *Daett* in a fix and needing help on the farm. And now they had the noon meal on Thursday to plan for the threshing crew. Still, they would have to talk — today. The sooner the better.

Ida pinned the last piece of wash on the line and took another glance toward the road. Surely Lois would be here soon with her pictures from Cancun. The photos would not be allowed in the house, but Lois would certainly try. And there would be tears, but *Mamm* wouldn't give in. Ida was sure of that.

Maybe after the next load of wash she'd

speak with *Mamm* about the wedding plans. Lois might be here by then, and the matter would be pushed back maybe until evening. Maybe the rest of the wash should wait. At least if someone drove by he or she would see a wash line half full and know that the Beiler women hadn't grown lazy.

Ida took the hamper with her as she entered the house by the washroom door.

Mamm was working on a list at the dining room table. She was talking softly when Ida walked in. "Why *Daett* didn't let us know sooner, I don't know."

Ida knew *Mamm* was thinking about the threshing crew coming. She ignored the comment and sat on a kitchen chair.

Mamm looked up in surprise. "Are you finished with the wash already?"

Ida shook her head. "I thought we should talk about the wedding. I'm sorry to add to the list of stuff we have to do this week, but I don't know if we can wait any longer. Ben wants to wed this season."

Mamm laid her pencil down and studied her daughter. "Ida, are you sure about this?"

Now Ida was the one who was surprised. "*Mamm,* when I told you on Sunday night, you seemed fine with it. Now you're having doubts? There's nothing wrong with our plans or any reason we should be hesitant.

Our marrying is well within the customs of the community, even if the wedding may seem rushed."

Mamm hesitated for only a moment. "I still want to know how this all happened so quickly."

"Ben first spoke to me the other Sunday, and I accepted his proposal . . ."

Mamm interrupted. "He asked to marry you right from the first?"

Ida admitted, "Well, not really. I thought I'd save him the embarrassment, so I said I was open to the idea if that's what he was hinting at."

Mamm sighed.

Ida went on. "Ben visited me Friday night at Verna's and said he wants to say the vows this wedding season. He said we could pick any week that works for us. And *Mamm* . . ." Ida tried to look stern. "*Mamm,* the wedding will be small. I mean it this time."

Mamm settled into her chair. "He's a stern man, Ida. I guess you know that. But Minister Kanagy will be *gut* for you. I was thinking of Lois this morning, and right now I'd take a stern man instead of the husband Lois has chosen. Ben Kanagy is a *gut* man. *Daett* told me last night how thankful he is to have him by his side when difficult church problems come up."

203

Ida let out a long breath. "I guess being *Daett*'s son-in-law will make them even closer."

A hint of a smile played on *Mamm*'s face. "I suppose so. But tell me, Ida, does it bother you that you have so little feelings for the man?"

Ida let out a little gasp before asking, "Why do you say that?"

Mamm shrugged. "You cared so much for Melvin, and I don't suppose the heart changes that quickly."

Ida hesitated for only a moment. "Ben said the most wonderful things about me, *Mamm*. Even when I insisted that all of Melvin's children must come live with us after the wedding."

"So . . ." *Mamm* studied Ida's face. "So is this all about Melvin's children then? That's why you want to marry him?"

Ida reached over for *Mamm*'s hand. "There's nothing wrong with that, is there? Wanting to mother Melvin's children . . . and Ben's too, of course?"

Mamm clucked her tongue. "*Nee,* Ida, there's nothing wrong with that. No one says our hearts must pound when we accept a man's hand in marriage. But surely you have *some* feelings for the man? I know you have respect for him. And it certainly

204

sounds like you made it plain what you wanted. That took courage. Does he love you for that, Ida?"

Remembering their kiss, heat rose up Ida's neck. She was sure her whole face was aflame with color. There was no way she would admit to kissing Ben and how he'd embraced her with such passion. "I already told you he said nice things," Ida said. "I believe he loves me, *Mamm*."

"As he should." *Mamm* snorted. "You're a decent girl, Ida. The beauty you have goes all the way to the heart. I'm glad you're getting a husband who understands that. And may *Da Hah* give you a love between each other that makes both of you happy. On my part, I believe *Da Hah* will."

"*Da Hah* already has," Ida whispered. "Much more than I expected."

Mamm regarded her daughter for a moment. "How are we going to do this wedding of yours what with all the other things going on this fall?"

Ida felt a moment of panic. "Maybe we don't have to have one? We could just say the vows on a Sunday at the service. I'm sure Ben would understand."

Mamm gave Ida a quick glare. "Wipe that plan out of your mind, Ida. No daughter of mine is saying vows without a proper wedding. That is . . ." *Mamm*'s face darkened as the sounds of a car pulling into the driveway reached them. "That is unless she goes *Englisha*. Help us, dear *Hah*. I think Lois just arrived."

"I'll go let her in." Ida rose and went to the front door.

Lois's face glowed when Ida opened the door. Thankfully Lois had on a dress that came down well past her knees. Any little thing will help this morning. She saw Lois was carrying a satchel. "Leave the photographs outside, Lois, and come on in."

Lois pouted. "How do you know I've brought pictures?"

"Because I know you." Ida gave her a stern glare.

"It's a laptop computer with pictures on it," Lois corrected. Her face changed to reflect total happiness. "And so many lovely ones, Ida! Of the ocean, and the beach, and of the absolutely *wunderbah* place we stayed . . . and of Doug all glowing and happy because I'm his *frau*. Aren't you even a little, teeny-weeny-bit curious, Ida?"

Ida stood firm. "I see you can still speak German. And it's not about being curious, Lois. It's about resisting temptation. Something you should have taken to heart a long time ago."

More pout showed on Lois's face. "And miss Cancun, and Doug, and my *wunderbah* life out there? How can you even think that, Ida? You should experience it for yourself. Then you'd know what you're missing."

It was useless to argue, Ida decided. She might as well change the subject. Ida pointed at the porch. "It stays out here. If you're interested in anything besides yourself, you might like to know that Verna had her baby — a girl! Her name is Sarah Mae. I helped take care of her for the first week. She's beautiful!"

Lois leaned her satchel against the outside wall of the house. She grabbed Ida and gave her a long hug. "That is *wunderbah* news! *Mamm*'s first grandchild from us girls. I hope to give her one myself before long. Did you know that Doug's very open to having a *boppli* once I'm out of college? Though not too many, he said. He doesn't want that part of my Amish heritage brought with me!"

Ida blushed and looked away. She didn't want to hear about her sister's family plans. Lois was *Englisha* now, and she'd obviously taken to their ways like a duck to water. That wasn't a surprise.

Lois walked into the house and made her

way to the kitchen. "It's so *gut* to see you, *Mamm*! I had such a *wunderbah* time down in Mexico on my honeymoon!"

Ida arrived to find Lois with her arms wrapped around *Mamm*'s neck. *Mamm* hugged her daughter and then held her at arm's length. "I don't see any picture packages, for which I'm thankful. At least you have some decency and respect for our ways left in you."

Lois frowned. "I brought some, but Ida made me leave them at the door."

Mamm groaned. "Won't you ever learn, Lois? But do sit down and tell us about your week — wherever you were."

Lois's face glowed as she took the offered chair. Ida and *Mamm* sat down also.

Excitedly, Lois shared, "*Mamm,* there were stunning sunrises on the ocean. It was like nothing I've ever seen. At night we walked out to the water to watch and hear the waves come in. They climbed around our bare feet, ever higher and higher. Doug loves me, *Mamm,* like no Amish man ever did. I can't tell you how happy I am."

Mamm clucked and said, "That's because you never had the sense to let a man from the community love you. You chased them away with all your talk about how you loved the *Englisha* world." *Mamm* sighed. "But

Doug is your husband now, and we will live with it. Your children will now be lost to the world, I suppose. Do you care about that?"

Lois placed a finger across her *mamm*'s lips. "Let's not be dark today, okay? Let's be happy and joyful and thankful. I have so much to be thankful for." Lois clapped her hands. "And Ida said Verna has a baby! I'll have to stop in on my way home and take a peek. I'm sure little Sarah Mae is just a darling. Verna couldn't have anything but *wunderbah* children."

Mamm glanced at Ida. "So you told her about the baby. Did you tell her about *your* wedding?"

Lois gasped and stared at her sister. "Ida, you're getting married? To whom?"

"To Minister Kanagy," *Mamm* said. "We were just ready to plan the wedding when you drove in. Do you want to help?"

Lois fanned herself. "Let me get my wits about me first. Ida is marrying that stern old man? It's so hard to believe. Ida, is it really true?"

"*Yah,* it's true. And he's not stern on the inside," Ida protested. She remembered Ben's kind gaze in Verna's upstairs bedroom. She blushed at the memory.

Lois stared at Ida. "And you think *I'm* weird."

"Don't say that, Lois," *Mamm* spoke up. "Ida's making her choice for very decent and honorable reasons. She and Ben will be taking in Melvin's children. Now that's the kind of choice a Christian woman makes. She doesn't set her heart on trips to Mexico with an *Englisha* husband."

Lois shivered. "Minister Kanagy kissing a woman? The very thought! *Da Hah* help us."

Ida glared at Lois. "There's nothing wrong with his kisses!" She immediately realized what she'd admitted and turned as red as a beet.

A sly smile crossed Lois's face. "Aha! So you've kissed him already!"

Before Ida could salvage the situation, *Mamm* took charge. "No more talk like this, the both of you. Are you going to help with the planning, Lois?"

"Of course!" Lois settled into the kitchen chair. "Fire away."

As they talked, Ida noticed that Lois kept giving her quick glances accompanied by smiles. It was as if her sister realized what she was doing for Melvin's children. I think she admires my courage, Ida thought. And that courage had led to the kiss with Ben. Ida smiled as she remembered the kiss . . .

NINETEEN

On Thursday morning Debbie was up and in the kitchen before either Saloma or Ida stirred. She lit the fire in the cookstove and set the water to boil. The threshing crew would need plenty of coffee all day long, especially at lunchtime. *Yah,* today was the big day when the men would make their annual stop at the Beiler farm to put up the corn. By dusk tonight the Beilers hoped to have their silo filled to the brim. And that meant an early start for everyone.

Debbie had awakened an hour ago. Unable to fall back to sleep from the excitement, she decided to get up. Alvin would be on the threshing crew, she was sure. She hadn't dared ask whether Paul would also come. That would likely have encouraged Ida to ask how things had gone with Alvin Sunday evening. Thankfully Ida was wrapped up in her own wedding plans.

The truth was that Debbie wasn't sure

211

how to think about what had gone on last Sunday. Crystal was still around, presumably visiting her relatives, but she was also attending the community's services and hymn singings. But Crystal wasn't the problem — at least when it came to Alvin. Something else wasn't quite right though, Debbie thought. Although they both had tried hard to make it a pleasant time, there was obvious tension. She'd thought everything had gone quite well . . . until after Alvin had left. Then the dark thoughts had crept back in — thoughts about Mildred Schrock being in such close proximity to Alvin. And Debbie had been shocked about her own feelings when it came to Emery. His fascination with Crystal bothered her a great deal.

Debbie forced her odd thoughts away. This was to be a cheerful day, full of excitement and joy. She would not spoil it. Already she'd done all she could to help make things run smoothly around the Beiler household. She'd offered to stay home from work an extra day yesterday to help with the large noon meal, but Saloma would hear nothing of it.

"One day off your job is enough." Saloma gave her a stern look followed by a smile. "We appreciate you taking one day off to help us."

Saloma probably knew her real reason for wanting the day off — so she could watch the activities. Since Debbie hadn't been raised Amish, seeing events such as this close-up hadn't occurred very often. Debbie smiled as she thought of Verna and baby Sarah Mae. They would both be here. Verna had stopped by yesterday with the *boppli* for a few moments after Debbie had arrived home from her job at Destiny Relocation Services. Verna insisted she'd be back today to help. Saloma had made a fuss, of course.

"You shouldn't even be out yet," Saloma had lectured. "Let alone coming to help with the silage filling."

"Now, *Mamm,*" Verna had chided, "you know it's time for me to get back to my regular routine. If it makes you happier, I'll sit in the rocker all day and watch. But I'm coming."

Saloma had given in after that. Although there wasn't much she could do if Verna showed up — just as Saloma couldn't do anything if Lois showed up. Ida had dropped a wistful sigh yesterday about Lois not liking the *gut* things of Amish life, so maybe she shouldn't be here anyway. "But at least she's coming to my wedding," Ida had added. "I can't give her any special part being my witness like I wish I could." Ida hadn't gone on to say who her witness would be, but the decision would have to be made soon.

Debbie paused as sounds stirred from upstairs. Either Emery or Ida must have gotten up to begin the chores. Debbie took kitchen duty on most mornings in her feeble attempt to fill Lois's space. That was impossible, of course. She didn't come close to Lois's cooking abilities, but the Beiler family didn't complain. Even Emery stayed quiet, and he was the one who would most likely speak up if things weren't just right.

She wondered what Emery thought of how she cooked. He would be too gentlemanly to complain, and he probably didn't want to hurt her feelings. It was the rare *Englisha* girl who could match the cooking Emery was used to. Debbie wasn't sure she fit those shoes. Did Crystal know how to cook? But maybe Emery would sacrifice food for love. That was, if Emery would consider an *ex-Englisha* girl as a future *frau. Nee,* he wouldn't. And these were outrageous thoughts to have anyway. Why was she acting jealous of Emery's interest in Crystal? She must stop such thoughts! But how could she when she was sure she saw an extra gleam in Emery's eye in his unguarded moments. She recognized the signs of awakening love. *Yah,* unless she missed her guess, love was stirring in Emery's heart — and Crystal was to blame.

Debbie jumped when Saloma spoke behind her. "*Gut* morning! You're already up."

"I couldn't sleep." Debbie smiled. "I'm too excited about the silo filling."

"Well, it's going to be a big day, there's no question about that." Saloma bustled about the kitchen.

Morning bustling was something Debbie still hadn't grasped. An Amish woman could wake up early and hurry about at once. More than likely, this came from a lifetime of habitual early rising, something Debbie hadn't acquired in her childhood. She would learn though, she told herself as she picked up her speed. And she would make a decent *frau* for Alvin once they said the wedding vows. And she *would* say the vows with Alvin. With what they'd both been through, they should be able to weather any storm Mildred Schrock or anybody else cooked up.

Moments later Ida appeared with Emery and her *daett* close behind. They mumbled their "*gut* mornings," pulled on their overcoats and boots in the washroom, and then plunged out into the darkness with their gas lanterns. Debbie paused for a moment to watch the bobbing lights vanish through the barn doorway. A thought ran through her mind that left a chilly trail in its wake. Did Mildred's duties at the Knepp farm include helping with the morning chores?

They would almost have to, Debbie decided. Alvin had been doing the chores alone with close to as many animals to take care of as what the three Beiler family members handled together. In extreme cases, Emery or Bishop Beiler did the chores by themselves, but it took much longer. Likely Mildred was in the barn with Alvin right now. Mildred would be hard at work with Alvin under the hissing light of the gas lanterns. Alvin couldn't help but be affected by such close help from his former beloved. Was that, perhaps, the real reason Alvin had agreed to Mildred's care for his mother in the first place?

But Alvin had said nothing on Sunday evening about Mildred helping with chores, Debbie reminded herself. Surely he would have been honest if Mildred spent much time in the barn with him. He would know where that could lead . . . wouldn't he? Especially now that Mildred had so clearly shown a renewed interest in him? Granted things had been a little less obvious with

Mildred at the services now that Alvin was dating Debbie, but the gleam was still there in Mildred's eyes.

"Debbie!" Saloma's call made her jump again. "Will you watch the bacon?"

"Of course!" Debbie rushed over to the stove. She had to stop this jealousy of Alvin and Mildred! She trusted Alvin like he would trust her. And it was a disgrace for an Amish woman to get distracted in her own kitchen. She obviously had a lot to learn.

Debbie turned the pieces of bacon frequently, soon bringing them to the golden perfection the Beiler family liked. Debbie lifted them out with her fork — all but two pieces that needed a few more seconds. As she waited, thoughts of Alvin returned. With Ida marrying so soon, could she and Alvin do the same? It might be good to say the vows soon so all her foolish imaginings would stop. And yet it wasn't up to her. Alvin hadn't really said anything firm about marriage.

Debbie glanced at the bacon pan and gasped. She pulled the last two pieces of bacon out, but they were burned a deep brown and would be uneatable — at least by Beiler standards. "I burned them!" she said aloud.

"That's what comes from not getting your sleep," Saloma offered with a smile. Saloma was teasing, but it didn't help Debbie's feelings. She had to get control of herself. This was an important day for the Beiler family, and she was supposed to help — not be a distraction. She quickly set aside the two pieces of bacon for herself and helped move the food to the table.

They'd just finished spreading the table when Ida came in from the chores. She put on an apron and helped fill the water glasses. When Emery and Bishop Beiler arrived, they seated themselves, followed by the women. Debbie took her place along the back bench across from Emery. He gave her a quick smile before they bowed their heads in prayer.

"Now unto You, O God, we give thanks again," Bishop Beiler led out. "To You, our most gracious and merciful Father. Bless our home this day and the food the women have prepared. Give grace to their hearts for all the hard work they do and will be doing today. Be with us men as we try to supply the needs of the farm. Give us all protection and safety. We give You thanks as always. Amen."

Debbie passed the bacon to Emery, followed by the eggs. He took what he wanted and passed the plate on to his father. What went on in Emery's head? Debbie wondered. Soon she would get up enough nerve to ask him again about Crystal. Perhaps sometime when she could catch him alone in the barn. Not today, of course, but soon. Maybe she could yet prove her usefulness to Bishop Beiler and warn Emery of what might lie ahead if he had thoughts of being interested in an *Englisha* woman.

Bishop Beiler interrupted her thoughts. "So *Mamm* tells me you're staying home to help today, Debbie."

"Yes! It's an exciting day for me," Debbie said, choosing to sound upbeat.

"We'll put you on the wagons," Emery said with a grin, obviously teasing.

"I can try that!" Debbie offered, though she wasn't sure what work on the wagons entailed.

Bishop Beiler smiled. "We'd best leave that work to the men. Throwing corn bundles on and off can be quite a chore."

"You can keep us supplied with plenty of lemonade and coffee." This came from Emery. "That might be more appropriate for a woman."

"You don't have to patronize us, Emery," Ida shot at him. "Debbie and I could load those itchy corn bundles just fine. But this

219

is a man's day, we know, and we women can't be around to interfere with all your horsing around."

Emery laughed. "Don't look at me! I behave myself perfectly."

A shadow crossed Bishop Beiler's face. "I will lecture everyone before we start this morning. I agree that things have been getting a little rough the past years . . . what with the teasing among the young men." Bishop Beiler's face softened. "But some of them are getting older, thank *Da Hah,* and the wedding season's just around the corner."

"That's still no excuse for rough play," Saloma spoke up. "I heard the women say last week that Joe Weaver's younger brother, Virgil, and his cousin Roy were racing each other on who could throw in the most bundles. They ended up nearly knocking Virgil into the blades."

"Yah," Bishop Beiler agreed. "I heard that too, so I will be saying something this morning when the crew arrives. I know *Da Hah* watches over us, but tempting Him is never the right thing. We are supposed to use our heads."

"Young men don't always have a lot of sense." Ida gave Emery a sharp glance.

"Hey!" Emery protested. "I don't act like

220

that. And speaking of the wedding season, you and Minister Kanagy are getting married soon . . . too soon, if you ask me."

Ida looked ready to fire something back, but she must have changed her mind because she looked at her food instead.

The bishop spoke for her instead. "Ida's plans are perfectly honorable, Emery. She's taking on a needed work, and she will make Minister Kanagy an outstanding *frau.* You should take lessons from her."

Emery didn't answer, but he too kept his gaze on his plate of food.

Were thoughts of Crystal spinning around in his head? Debbie wondered. Did Bishop Beiler know about the attention Emery was paying Crystal?

Wagon wheels rattled in the driveway at that moment, and Emery appeared relieved. The bishop gulped down the last few bites of food and led out in the closing prayer.

TWENTY

Debbie stood at the living room window stirring the first batch of lemonade for the day. Verna had arrived an hour ago with baby Sarah Mae. The two were now in the kitchen with Ida and Saloma. Debbie had offered her share of exclamations over the fast-growing baby before she left the Beiler women to their private conversation. She didn't know exactly what they wanted to talk about, but it was only right that she give them some time together alone. Though she was Amish now and fully accepted in the Beiler household, she was still very aware of her difference from the other Beiler girls. She was a Beiler daughter . . . and yet she wasn't. Emery, whom she admired, was a brother . . . and yet he wasn't. That thought made her think again that the sooner she and Alvin married the better. But at the rate Alvin was moving, he wouldn't propose for another two years or maybe more.

Debbie shook her head and took in the scene outside. The barnyard resembled chaos. That was no doubt because she still wasn't used to silo-filling day. She was sure there was an order and rhythm to the men's work that didn't yet make sense to her. All morning, long lines of wagons filled to the brim with corn bundles were driven in from the fields and past some contraptions set up near the silo.

The massive unit with the long chute that went up the side of the silo was the silage chopper, Ida had pointed out. The tractor with the long belt that sat many yards away ran the whole thing. The noise was what had taken Debbie the longest to get used to. It was deafening, assaulting the ear with unending racket.

Each wagon pulled up close to the chopper, with the man who drove the horses hollering to the animals as he maneuvered the lines. There was no way the horses could hear any of the instructions in the racket, so Debbie figured the yelling was more instinctual than anything. No wonder Bishop Beiler had prayed for everyone's safety this morning.

She'd caught sight of Alvin's form on one of the wagons earlier, and now Paul Wagler was riding high on the next load of corn bundles. He appeared his usual cocky self as he stood balanced on top of the load as it bounded along. Every few seconds Paul would throw out his arms to maintain his balance. The man was clearly showing off. He even went so far as to jump around on one foot for a moment. Debbie gasped as she watched him. She didn't care for the man, not in a romantic way, but she cared about his well-being. It would be an awful sight to see any man, even Paul Wagler, sail off into the blue from the top of that load. There could be no good end to such an incident.

Ida must have heard her gasp because she joined Debbie at the living room window. A pleased smile spread over her face. "Paul's always been *gut* at such things."

"You shouldn't be admiring the man!" Debbie didn't keep the alarm out of her voice. "You're probably encouraging him. He's showing off."

Ida laughed. "Paul doesn't need any encouragement, and he can't see us from here anyway."

That was true, but Debbie still stepped back from the window. She regarded Ida for a moment. She still had her gaze glued out the window. The words just kind of slipped out. "You still have feelings for Paul, don't you, Ida?"

Ida didn't even flinch. "It's not like that, Debbie. Paul's a decent man under all that showy stuff, but he's not for me. I stopped pining for him a long time ago." Ida sent a quick glance Debbie's way. "Now, Paul and *you* — that's another matter."

Debbie forced a smile. "Sorry. I deserved that. Maybe we'd better go back to staying out of each other's business."

Ida nodded and a slight smile played on her face. "Perhaps so."

Debbie looked away momentarily, but she jerked her head back when Ida screamed. The sound rent through the living room. Debbie leaned toward the window, searching the yard around the silo with a quick glance. She could see nothing but the wagons lined up, with the one Paul had been on now in place to unload. Everything was how it should be. What had disturbed Ida? Ida stood silent, frozen in place as Saloma and Verna ran into the room.

All at once, the thought of what wasn't on the wagon went all the way through Debbie. Paul was gone! His place was empty on top of the high stack of corn sheaves.

"We must go help!" Ida's voice finally screeched.

"What's going on?" Saloma asked.

Since no further words came from Ida, Debbie said, "Paul must have fallen off the wagon. We saw him clowning around, and now he's not up there anymore."

"Help us, dear *Hah*!" Alarm rang all the way through Saloma's voice. "That man!"

Ida's voice trembled in a low whisper. "He's hurt bad. I know he is."

"Then we'd better go help!" Verna said.

Debbie leaned forward to peer out of the window. She agreed with Verna, but before she raced out there and made a fool of herself, she wanted to know whether Paul was really hurt. He'd never let them forget it if several of the women rushed out of the house to his aid, only to find him in perfect health and bent over with laughter somewhere behind the wagon. And the other men wouldn't forget for a long time either. But then Debbie caught sight of several men running toward the wagon. And the men in the teams behind Paul's wagon had wrapped their lines around the wooden trestles in front and leaped to the ground to run toward the huge chopper.

Clearly something was wrong. Saloma had obviously drawn the same conclusion. Her words were clipped. "Ida and Debbie, come with me. Verna you're staying in here with the baby. If you want to do something, heat some more water on the stove. If nothing's wrong, we'll use it for something else later."

Saloma's words cut through Ida's stupor. Without a sound she raced for Saloma's bedroom and came out with a pile of sheets. Saloma took a quick glance toward Ida but made no protest. Debbie stayed close behind the two as they hurried out the front door and across the lawn. If she needed any verification that something serious had happened, it was by the silence that greeted them. Someone had shut off the tractor and, with it, the massive chopper. Bishop Beiler would never allow this in the middle of a day of silo filling, unless the need was grave or it was dinnertime.

Saloma and Ida were at a full run by the time they reached the first wagons. No men were in sight as they slipped between the wagons and into the open field near the silo. There the huddle of men became visible, with a few of them bent over on the ground, and several on their knees, apparently in prayer.

Paul must be really hurt, Debbie thought. That was the only explanation. But how was that possible? The fall from the top of the wagon was far, but didn't seem to warrant this level of concern . . . unless perhaps he'd broken his neck. Debbie's heart pounded as they drew closer. The men parted to allow Ida and Saloma through. No one said a word. The sight in front of them was answer enough. How it had happened, she couldn't imagine, but Paul lay on his side, his arm mangled beside him. He was bleeding profusely.

"Call 911! Get an ambulance!" she screamed.

The form of Bishop Beiler took shape beside Debbie. He pulled on her hand and whispered in her ear, "Alvin already went." Bishop Beiler pointed across the fields. "Do you know what should be done until they get here?"

The bishop was asking if she'd learned anything in the *Englisha* world that might be helpful. Debbie's head was swimming. Besides, she had no medical training.

The bishop's voice was insistent. "*Think,* Debbie. Is there anything you can do?"

"I'll try," she finally managed. She forced herself forward. Saloma had Paul's head cradled in her arms as she murmured softly to him. "Don't move now. Help's coming. Don't move."

Ida was kneeling on the other side. Her hands lightly touched Paul's bloodied left arm. The man's eyes were glazed. Ida's sheets lay heaped beside her.

Debbie grabbed one of them and ripped it into long streamers. This much she knew. She gave the first piece to Ida. "Wrap his arm up!"

Ida didn't move.

"Ida! Now!"

"But I'll hurt him." Ida's voice sounded strangled.

"You'll hurt him worse if he bleeds out," Debbie said, kneeling beside the two.

That seemed to spur Ida into action. She wrapped the cloth around the bloodied arm.

"Tighter!" Debbie commanded. She didn't want to sound harsh, but Ida's caring spirit got in the way of what needed to be done. This would at least stop the blood loss.

Ida pulled tighter on the sheet even when Paul groaned and rolled his eyes. When the third piece of sheet had been used, the bleeding seemed to slow.

Debbie picked up another sheet, but paused when the sound of sirens pierced the distance. The medics would likely take off what they'd put on Paul anyway. The problem now was shock. That she also remembered. Paul should be kept warm. Debbie threw two of the sheets over his body.

If she had to make a guess, Paul's mangled arm was not repairable, but then she wasn't a doctor. Perhaps Paul would be spared the humiliation and agony of the loss of an arm. A lost limb was no small matter among the Amish, where physical labor was a necessity.

The sirens wailed to a halt behind them. Soon two men appeared with a gurney. They brought it to Paul's side. Several of the men offered to help, but the two medics waved them away. A woman who was with them patted Ida on the arm while Paul was transferred to the gurney. "Looks like you did a good job controlling his bleeding."

"That was Debbie," Ida said, nodding in her direction.

The woman gave Debbie a brief glance. "Any family going with us?"

There was silence for a moment. None of Paul's family was here, but someone should go with him. But who? All the men were needed to continue the day's work. It must go on, Debbie was sure. And men weren't of much use at hospitals anyway. Should she offer? Surely she could overcome her dislike for Paul enough to aid him in his injured state. But before she could speak, Ida whispered, "I'll go. I'm not family, but . . ."

Both Bishop Beiler and Saloma nodded without hesitation.

The two paramedics slid the gurney with Paul into the ambulance. The woman medic got in front. Ida climbed in, and the ambulance sped down the driveway and out onto the road, siren blaring.

The silence was broken by Bishop Beiler. "What exactly happened here?"

"I was driving the wagon," Joe's younger brother Virgil offered. His voice trembled. "We hit a rut hard coming in, and the next thing I knew Paul was flying through the air over my head. I'm sorry. I should have been more careful."

"You're not to blame," Bishop Beiler said. "Wagons hit ruts all the time, and we have to expect that. So what happened then? Did Paul fly into the belt?"

"*Yah.*" Virgil looked at the ground. "He hit on his stomach and was pulled toward the wheel."

Bishop Beiler's voice was sober. "This could have been much worse. Thankfully *Da Hah* has spared Paul's life. I'm glad this accident didn't happen because of any foolishness. Let's pray for Paul now — that the doctors will have wisdom in repairing his arm and that *Da Hah* will give him grace to bear the pain."

The hats came off the men's heads as they all paused to bow in silent prayer. As Debbie joined in, she couldn't help but think that the accident had indeed happened because of foolishness. But she wasn't going to correct Bishop Beiler, especially in front of everyone. And apparently no one else who had witnessed Paul's antics planned to offer a contrary opinion either. She caught a glimpse of Alvin standing toward the back of the group. He must have come back from making the phone call, but he'd wisely chosen to stay out of the way.

"Amen." Bishop Beiler finished the prayer. "Let's get back to work. Please be extra careful everyone. We mustn't have another injury. Not this year — and not ever."

Debbie followed Saloma back to the house as the roar of the machinery resumed behind them. Verna, her face pale, met them holding little Sarah Mae in her arms. Saloma stayed to fill Verna in on the details, while Debbie went back to the kitchen. Should she take the lemonade out now? The men would be even thirstier after the scare they'd been through.

She took the glasses and a dipper with her out the washroom door and set up inside Emery's buggy. She dipped glasses of lemonade for the men on the wagons as they drove past. She would run over and hand the glasses up and receive hearty words of thanks from all of them. When she accumulated empty glasses, she hurried to the water pump by the barn, rinsed out the glasses, filled them again, and handed them out.

When Alvin came by, he gave her a weary smile but didn't chat while he gulped down the lemonade. They couldn't talk anyway. Not in this awful racket. Clearly Alvin had been affected by the tragedy, as they all had. He was right to maintain a sober attitude. But it would have been nice if he'd noticed how well she fit in today. She was an Amish woman now.

In contrast, Emery both noticed and complimented her. "That was *gut* work on your part, Debbie. Paul might have lost too much blood by the time the ambulance arrived if you hadn't taken action."

"Thanks." Debbie lowered her head as she'd learned to do from watching when Amish women were complimented. Oh, if only those words had come from Alvin . . .

TWENTY-ONE

Late Saturday afternoon Alvin drove his team of horses in from the field. As he neared the barn, Mildred walked out from the house and greeted him with a cheery, "*Gut* evening."

Alvin pulled the team up short and returned her greeting. There was something about Mildred tonight that told him she was after something. He'd have to wait until she was ready to share it with him.

"Paul's going to lose his arm," Mildred said. "His *mamm* hasn't left his side at the hospital since the night of the accident." Mildred regarded him for a moment. "Did you see it happen, Alvin?"

Maybe that was what Mildred wanted. Details . . . gossip. But that seemed a bit beneath her. He shook his head. "I was several wagons back. But he fell into the belt from the top of the wagon when Virgil hit a big rut right in front of the chopper."

"Ida went with Paul to the hospital." Mildred sounded interested.

Alvin gave her a perplexed glance. "What's wrong with that? Someone had to go with him until the family could arrive. It wouldn't have been decent not to."

Mildred returned a sly smile. "I'm just surprised Debbie didn't grab the chance."

Alvin gave her a glare. "That's not fair, Mildred. Debbie wouldn't have gone unless there had been no one else. And even then . . ."

Mildred's smile sweetened at once. "*Yah,* that was very naughty of me, Alvin. I'm sorry. It just slipped out. I didn't mean anything by it."

Alvin didn't look convinced.

Mildred continued. "Alvin, would you like to come down tonight for supper at the *dawdy haus*? I've fixed a little extra, and there's no reason for you to sit and eat alone in that big house."

Alvin hesitated. He wouldn't see Debbie this weekend, so there shouldn't be anything wrong with his acceptance. Not that there was anything wrong with supper at the *dawdy haus,* even on the Sundays when he took Debbie home. But it might get complicated if Debbie found out he'd eaten Mildred's food the evening before. But surely

Debbie would understand. Just like Debbie had understood his explanation about Mildred's presence on the farm. Debbie trusted him.

"*Yah,* I'll come."

"I'll look forward to it then." Mildred glowed and dashed off.

Alvin's gaze swept down the road to where a buggy was fast approaching. Who would come by this late in the day? As the buggy neared, Alvin caught a glimpse of the man inside and drew in his breath. Deacon Mast! What did he want? Hopefully not more conversation about his supposed attraction to the *Englisha* world. Whatever it was, it couldn't be *gut.* Alvin jumped down from his wagon and waited while Deacon Mast arrived and pulled up. He got out and tied his horse to the hitching post.

"*Gut* afternoon," Deacon Mast greeted him. "Getting in some last-minute field work before *Da Hah*'s day of rest?"

Alvin nodded. "*Yah,* there's always more to be done."

Deacon Mast nodded. "That was quite a shock about Paul's accident on Thursday. As a result, I trust everyone's being more careful than they were before."

"I try." Alvin nodded again.

"Young men can get a little rambunctious

sometimes." Deacon Mast gave him a smile.

What was that supposed to mean? Alvin wasn't sure. But if the deacon offered no more startling advice then this, Alvin decided he'd be more than happy. Doubtless though, more serious things lay ahead.

Alvin nodded and bowed his head.

Deacon Mast cleared his throat. "I have shared my concerns with the other ministers, Alvin. About Crystal Meyers and your relationship with her."

"Her appearance here is not my fault," Alvin protested. "I left the woman a long time ago."

Deacon Mast silenced him with a direct look. "That's not how the ministry sees it, Alvin. Crystal seems to be conducting herself like a Christian woman should even if she's been divorced. They think this calls a lot of things about you into question just as I said they might. Bishop Beiler is quite worried about the matter. Especially since you're apparently so fond of Debbie. He thinks upon her almost as a daughter."

Alvin choked but couldn't get any words out.

Deacon Mast continued as if he hadn't noticed. "You do know that Ida Beiler and Minister Kanagy are saying their vows soon?"

"*Yah,*" Alvin answered, not seeing a connection.

Deacon Mast continued. "Anyway, Minister Kanagy obviously has even a greater interest now in seeing that the Beiler family is kept in *gut* standing. And we feel that any question about your character must be cleared up."

"So I'm being made the scapegoat for Minister Kanagy's fears?" Alvin said. "I protest this in the strongest terms. I have confessed my sins, and that's all there is to it."

"Your temper will get you nowhere, Alvin." Deacon Mast gave Alvin a firm look. "I counsel a humble attitude and a forgiving spirit. Your family has always been among the most faithful in keeping the *Ordnung,* especially your *daett.* How were you able to leave all that, and so suddenly, and face excommunication so willingly?"

Alvin hung his head again. "I've already been over that, and no explanation is going to persuade you, I'm afraid." Alvin struggled to keep his voice steady. "So, what is to be done with me?"

Deacon Mast's face grew even more mournful. "You aren't helping yourself, Alvin. Surely you can see that with your record, of being out there in the *Englisha* world, and why you came back — to take over your *daett*'s farm. We have a right to have questions."

Alvin stared at the ground. Bitter thoughts raced through his mind. His *daett* was at the root of this. He had run over to Deacon Mast with the news that Crystal had stopped by. His *daett* was always at the root of his troubles. But Alvin wouldn't give up easily — which was a new thought for him. He usually ran from his troubles, but right now there was little he could do but ride out this storm.

Deacon Mast's voice cut through his thoughts. "Have you got anything more to say, Alvin?"

Alvin shrugged. "*Nee,* not really."

Deacon Mast appeared grim. "We think you should voluntarily stay back from communion this fall, Alvin, until this blows over. It would show humility on your part and help restore our trust in you. We'd know that you intend to respect our concerns and listen to our counsel."

Shocked, Alvin tried to breathe. "You want me to stay back from communion?"

Deacon Mast nodded. "*Yah.* This would give us all time to figure out what is going on, Alvin."

Nothing is going on, he wanted to say, but

he didn't. Protests were useless right now. "But what reason shall I give?" he asked slowly.

Deacon Mast shrugged. "Pre-communion church is in a little over a week. That's the place to deal with this, Alvin. I wanted to let you know, so you'd have plenty of time to think this through. But it would be simple really, and everyone would understand. You can say that you regret bringing in an influence from the outside world, and that you question your own heart on the matter and wish to clear yourself with a few weeks of mourning and withdrawal. You can say you desire all our prayers for the health of your soul. That would be the least you can do."

"And if I refuse?" Alvin couldn't believe he'd asked the question, but the words blurted out. A glimpse of Mildred's face from earlier in the evening flashed through his mind, but he wasn't sure why.

Deacon Mast appeared troubled. "I make no threats, Alvin. But you know the community works on trust. It would not be *gut* if we couldn't trust you any longer. And rejecting our counsel would raise even more questions about your motives and character."

Alvin nodded. "Then I will accept your counsel. I don't think it's fair, but I also don't wish to make trouble. And I did do what you say I did — rush out into the world and bring shame on my family and the community. What possessed me, I don't know now. So perhaps this could be a time of cleansing and sorrow for myself."

Deacon Mast appeared relieved. "It is *gut* to hear you say these things, Alvin. My heart is much lighter now. Maybe this whole thing can be taken care of with this one small action, and we can all move on." Deacon Mast held up his hand at the look on Alvin's face. "I know it doesn't seem small to you, but in the large scheme of things, it is but a bump in the road. What you have already faced in being excommunicated is much worse than this, Alvin. Remember that."

But he hadn't had to actually face people for long while he was excommunicated, Alvin thought. That had been all done at a distance with letters written between him and the deacon. This shame would have to be faced head-on in full view. He'd have to sit there in communion services and allow everyone to see his shame. Alvin paused as another thought burned through him. This would be Debbie's first communion, and she would partake while he couldn't. That seemed to add to his shame.

Deacon Mast didn't seem to notice his

discomfort. "Soon this will be all over, Alvin. This gesture on your part will go a long way toward settling the ministry's mind. I'm sure Bishop Beiler's heart will be encouraged and comforted that Debbie is getting a man who is worthy of her. The bishop thinks quite highly of the girl, almost like his own daughter. So I have nothing but the highest hopes for the two of you. So take courage, Alvin. This is really a small matter."

"I'll try to," Alvin managed, as the deacon untied his horse and climbed back into his buggy. Alvin didn't move until Deacon Mast was clear down the road and out of sight. He shouldn't take this so hard, he told himself. It was after all his own fault, but still . . .

Alvin began to unhitch his team. When he finished he took them into the barn for the night. He shoveled extra oats into their feed boxes and listened to the draft horses noisily chomp their food. This was the life he loved, Alvin reminded himself. And the deacon's words had been true enough. In the grand scheme of things, one missed communion was a small matter. Still, it didn't seem right. But what could he say? Rebellion was out of the question. He was through with that option.

Twenty-Two

After dark that evening, Alvin pushed open the front door of the *dawdy haus* without a knock. This was, after all, his *daett*'s place, and he was expected tonight for supper. Mildred would have told his *daett* by now, and if the truth be told, his *daett* was probably behind Mildred's invitation. Anything to encourage Alvin's interest in Mildred and distract him from Debbie.

Alvin squinted in the sudden light of the gas lantern hanging from the ceiling. His *daett* looked up from rocker with a pleased expression. "*Gut* evening, son. I see you decided to come."

"I told Mildred I would," Alvin muttered.

Mamm was sitting on the other rocker, and Alvin approached for a quick hug and a peck on the cheek. A faint smile crossed her face. "You've come to visit again."

"*Yah, Mamm.*" Alvin took a seat on the couch. He turned around for a quick smile when Mildred chirped from the kitchen doorway, "It's *gut* you're here, Alvin. I'll have everything ready in a minute."

"No rush," Alvin said, even though his stomach growled. The smells drifting from the kitchen didn't help either.

"I see the deacon was here again," *Daett* said when Mildred had disappeared.

"Are you happy now?" Alvin made no attempt to hide his bitterness. "They're wanting me to stay back from communion."

His *daett* didn't look surprised. "Sufferings and humiliations are always *gut* for a man. And you could use some. You've risen way too fast in life, coming back from your time in the world to take over my farm. If I'd had my say-so, you'd have been left in the *bann* for another year or so."

"That's why it wasn't left in your hands," Alvin shot back. "And what would we do now if I weren't here? *Mamm* needs funds for her doctoring and care. And you sure couldn't supply it for her."

His *daett* didn't appear fazed by the sharp words. He shrugged. "I admit you speak the truth, but it's still not *gut* for you. I'm glad to hear the ministry is taking steps to rein you in. Maybe this will wake you up to what a mistake you're making by dating that girl Debbie. Those *Englisha* girls always had an awful pull on you, Alvin. I see that now, and I pray you will wake up in time."

"Bishop Beiler thinks the world of Debbie," Alvin said.

That seemed to silence his *daett* — at least for the moment. He settled back in his rocker.

Mildred appeared in the kitchen doorway again. "It's ready, everyone! Can't be allowing the food to grow cold!"

His *daett* rose with a smile on his face. "She can cook, that girl can. Think about that, Alvin."

So his *daett* did have a hand in his invitation tonight, Alvin thought as he helped his *mamm* to the table. Well, it made no difference. He was here to eat, and that was all.

Mildred stood by the stove as they found their seats. Then she took the one next to him. Alvin knew it was her usual place, but tonight her presence so close rushed over him. It felt so homey, so comfy, and so pleasantly right. Alvin told himself this was his wounded emotions speaking, but he kept his gaze away from Mildred, all the same.

His *daett* cleared his throat and led out in prayer. When he finished, Mildred handed Alvin the bowl of mashed potatoes so he had to look her way. She was glowing as she smiled . . . and he smiled back. Was she now blushing? *Nee,* that must be from the kitchen heat. Not since their school days had he seen Mildred blush. For a moment time stood still. He was back in the schoolroom at his desk and catching her gaze on him.

Alvin dipped out the mashed potatoes. *Yah,* but those days were over, and he must not imagine things. Mildred was being nice to him, but that was because she worked for his *daett.* And Mildred understood about Debbie. Hadn't Mildred told him so often enough herself?

"Do you like the potatoes?" Mildred's voice sounded cautious.

Alvin's laugh sounded strained. "I haven't tasted them yet. But they look delicious. And the truth is, I'm starving."

"Oh, you poor thing," Mildred cooed. "Doing those chores by yourself every evening. Your *daett* was just telling me tonight I should try to work time into my schedule so I can also help you in the evenings too."

"You don't have to," Alvin managed. He couldn't accept her help twice a day. Debbie would have enough objections if she knew Mildred was in the barn for the morning chores.

"You'd like that, wouldn't you?" Mildred

sounded quite hopeful.

"I'm sure you have plenty of work in the house," Alvin protested. But the truth was, had he not thought of this very thing himself while he worked on the chores tonight after the deacon left? He'd wished Mildred was in the barn to take some of the load off his shoulders. And off his soul, Alvin admitted. Was he to blame if Mildred had that kind of effect on him?

His *daett*'s voice cut through his thoughts. "Mildred's helping you both mornings and evenings from now on. She's willing, and we can make do at the house. I'll do a little more myself. And it's money better spent on the farm than on housekeeping for us."

His *daett* wasn't known for his concern for the farm, Alvin thought. But he also couldn't bring himself to turn down the offer of help. Debbie would just have to understand.

"I'd be glad for the help," he admitted.

Mildred glowed and grinned from ear-to-ear as she gazed at him. Hopefully she wouldn't give him that look at the Sunday services. She would surely have enough sense not to. But neither could he bring up the matter with her. That would be tacky, to say the least, and downright indecent if he even suggested that Mildred might be in

247

love with him.

"Then it's decided!" Mildred beamed. "I'm so glad you're giving me the chance to help out, Alvin. You're such a *wunderbah* family."

"We do have our problems," Alvin said wryly.

Mildred's face fell. "Deacon Mast was back again, wasn't he?"

"*Yah,* he was," *Daett* spoke up. "And it's a *gut* thing. Alvin needs to learn a few hard lessons in life."

Mildred sent a sympathetic look Alvin's way.

No doubt she wanted to say something, but she didn't dare in *Daett*'s presence. But her concern and obvious understanding ran over his bruised emotions like healing oil. And there was nothing wrong with that, he told himself. Hadn't Mildred stated her true role in their home right now — that of a trusted friend here to help out?

Alvin continued to eat, filling his plate twice while Mildred kept an eagle eye on him. "You sure you don't want more?"

Alvin gave her a smile. "I'm sure you have dessert yet. Where am I going to put that?"

Mildred's smile was almost as bright as the lantern light. "Of course there's dessert, Alvin Knepp! I'd be an awful person if I failed to make at least a decent pie for tonight."

Mildred stood up with a flourish and went to the kitchen counter, returning with a whipped-cream-topped cherry pie. Alvin's mouth watered at the sight. The crust looked like it would melt in his mouth.

"Do you think you'll like that?" Mildred teased. "My best, if I must say so myself."

"I'll take a piece," *Daett* said.

Mildred didn't miss a beat. She smiled pleasantly as she cut a large piece. "Is that big enough, Edwin?"

No doubt even *Daett*'s mouth was watering, Alvin thought. And *Daett* has seen many a cherry pie in his lifetime. It wasn't like his *mamm* hadn't cooked before her stroke. It had just been so long since either of them had tasted decent cooking.

"How much for you, Alvin?" Mildred smiled at him now.

Alvin gulped hard. "About what *Daett* had."

"Oh, you can handle more than that!" Mildred said. She cut an even larger piece. "I saw you working in the fields most of the day. Then doing all those chores by yourself. That makes for a healthy appetite, I'm sure."

"It does." Alvin nodded. "I'll eat for the hunger tomorrow," he laughed.

Mildred joined in as if he'd said the funniest thing in the world. "You do that, Alvin. Now let me get both of you glasses of milk."

His *mamm* didn't have a piece of pie yet, Alvin noticed when Mildred was getting the milk. He leaned toward her. "Do you want a piece, *Mamm*?"

His *mamm* smiled weakly. "I don't have an appetite like I used to, Alvin. But thank you anyway."

Mildred was a lot like his *mamm* used to be — before she had the stroke — motherly and kind. *Mamm* had written him letters while he was in Philadelphia, always hopeful that he'd return. She'd helped draw him back. That was a lot like what Mildred was trying to do now. Mildred was encouraging him through this hard time in his life, even without knowing all the details.

Mildred returned with the glasses of milk, and Alvin drank a deep swallow. Out of the corner of his eye he saw his *daett* do the same. He was more like his *daett* than he wished to admit. He had the same temper and stubborn ways; they were just expressed differently. *Yah,* at heart he was his *daett*'s son.

Alvin shifted on his chair as he thought about this. Maybe he should pay more attention to his *daett*'s opinions about the girl he dated. But that would be a leap of logic. Just because they were both comfortable right now after they'd been served supper by Mildred, that didn't mean he should say the wedding vows with her. Mildred had never fascinated him like Debbie had — and still did. That was likely something his *daett* knew little about. His *daett*'s love of his *mamm* had always seemed more of a steady brook compared to the wild dash of emotions Alvin felt for Debbie. *Nee,* he and his *daett* might have a lot of things in common, but not everything.

They finished their pie, and *Daett* led out in a prayer of thanks before he got to his feet. Alvin jumped up and helped take *Mamm* back to her rocker. Mildred followed them and whispered in his ear, "Do be a gentleman, Alvin, and help me with the dishes."

"I don't know," Alvin said. But he glanced at his *daett,* who motioned with his head toward the kitchen in agreement.

"Please?" Mildred cooed. "I help you with the chores, and I'll be out there twice a day now. And I don't bite; you should know that."

Alvin grimaced but gave in. He already was comfortable working with her. This wouldn't be any different from when Mildred helped him in the barn.

"Do you know how to dry dishes?" she teased, holding out a dry towel.

He jerked it away from her. "I've done this before, you know."

"Ah . . ." She smiled sweetly. "Then we're all set."

Mildred filled the sink with hot water while Alvin carried over the dirty dishes. She scraped them clean and slid the plates into the water.

As she began to wash, she gave him a sideways glance. "Do you want to tell me about Deacon Mast's visit?"

Alvin hesitated.

"You don't have to." She gave him another warm smile. "I just thought it might help, you know, being over there in that big house all by yourself with no one to talk to."

He grunted and began, his words coming in short bursts. "It was about Crystal Meyers and my time among the *Englisha* in Philadelphia. Deacon Mast and the others of the ministry, they have suspicions. Suspicions that are untrue. *Daett* told them of the letters *Mamm* used to write me once the committee took over the farm. *Mamm* asked me to return to run the farm. And to make things worse, I had to tell the deacon how Debbie used to drive past our place long before she joined the community. She'd watch me work in the fields. That was the last straw, I think. They want me to voluntarily stay back from communion this fall as a time of mourning and repentance."

"I'm so sorry," she said. "Surely Deacon Mast gives you some hope that the ministry might change their feelings."

Alvin toyed with the dish towel. "If I humble myself, *yah.*"

Mildred reached over to touch his arm. "I think they want the best for you, Alvin. I know that I do. And I think you'll make the correct choices. Your heart's in the right place. You've come back from your time in the world. You've repented. I believe you belong here, on this farm, working in your *daett*'s place. He can't see that right now because his heart is still troubled. You'll make it, Alvin. I know you will."

"Thank you," he whispered. "That's nice of you to say."

"I'm not just saying it. I believe it."

He dried another plate. *Yah,* Mildred was a *gut* friend. Alvin thanked *Da Hah* for sending such a *wunderbah* friend his way. This was much more than he deserved.

TWENTY-THREE

The next morning Ida was washing the dishes at the kitchen sink as the early morning sunlight streamed across the lawn outside. It had only been three days since the awful tragedy concerning Paul Wagler. The area by the silo stood empty now, the tractor and huge corn chopper moved on to the next site. If what she'd heard was right, the machinery was at Paul's *daett*'s place. Emery had told her yesterday the silo crew would begin the week's work at Jay Wagler's after they'd finished the fields at Deacon Mast's farm on Friday.

Paul was still in the hospital, and his *daett* had taken his place on the silo-filling crew. The family could ill afford to have their *daett* away from the farm for the rest of the season, but they would manage. Jay wouldn't allow his son's spot to remain unfilled on the threshing crew. Perhaps a younger man could be found next week to help out, but Ida doubted it. The wedding season was next month, and fall was always a busy time on the farms. She ought to offer her help with the chores at the Wagler farm, but that was out of the question. Not with her own wedding ahead and the help *Daett* and Emery needed at home.

She also didn't want anyone to think she was trying to weasel her way into the Wagler family's affection. Not that anyone would think such a thing, since few people knew of her former crush on Paul. She'd traveled with Paul to the hospital on Thursday, and that had pushed things far enough. She felt no guilt and had only the deepest compassion for Paul and his agony during the ambulance ride. At the hospital she'd stayed with Paul for the few minutes until he was taken into surgery. The family had arrived soon after that, and Jay had brought her home in his buggy while the family waited for Paul to come out of surgery.

Paul's arm was gone now, *Daett* had told them last night. It was taken somewhere above the elbow. The damage had been too extensive. She didn't understand all the medical terms, and neither did *Daett,* but they could understand a man's empty sleeve. Paul would never be the same again.

On the ride to the hospital while the

ambulance's siren blared over her head, a strange thing had happened to her heart. Perhaps it was the sight of Paul bloodied and on that gurney. Whatever the cause, it was *Da Hah*'s mercy because the last of her fascination with Paul's bold ways had vanished. Like snow that melted before the warm spring sun, Ida told herself. That's how it felt. Paul had become an ordinary man to her as he rested sedated on the stretcher. She was ashamed that any of her old feelings had still been there, but they were gone now, and for that she was thankful.

Before her face rose the memory of Ben and how he'd looked on his visit last night. Joy had glowed on his face as he touched her hand in greeting. "Ida," he'd said, "it's so *gut* to see you again. I'm so sorry to hear about the accident on Thursday. I hear you rode with Paul to the hospital."

She had nodded and smiled. The man couldn't be jealous, she figured, not with that look on his face.

"*Ach,* you have a golden heart, Ida," he'd said. "I do declare. *Da Hah* has greatly blessed my aching life with such a deep and *wunderbah frau*-to-be."

She'd turned bright red right then and there. This morning the heat still rose up her neck when she remembered it. How plainly Ben had spoken, and yet it was as if he had the perfect right to. Was she not his promised one? And he would come this Sunday morning again, since there were no services in their district. They would speak more about their wedding plans with *Mamm* and *Daett,* and also have some time alone on the front porch swing, unless the weather was too cool.

Ida's thoughts were interrupted when Debbie came into the kitchen to help.

Debbie picked up the towel. "You're awfully quiet this morning."

"Just thinking about things." Ida lowered her head.

Debbie glanced at her. "Pardon me for asking, but I just have to know. Riding with Paul to the hospital . . . seeing him in such agony — did that change anything for you?"

Ida hadn't planned to go there with any of the family, but maybe Debbie would listen if she spoke plainly. Ida took a deep breath. "In fact, the last of my fascination with Paul left me, Debbie. I fear Paul will never be the same, losing his arm. Men never are the same after something like that."

Debbie nodded. "That's what your *daett* told me."

Ida tried to tease but the words came out tense. "Maybe he'd be about right for you now."

Debbie laughed and concentrated on the dishes.

Ida could say more about that, but it was best to keep silent. But it wasn't lost on her what Mildred was up to over at the Knepp farm. Mildred was capable of a lot, now that she was older and had been passed up by the other eligible Amish suitors. Ida had seen those looks Mildred still gave Alvin at the hymn singing. *Yah,* it was obvious Mildred tried to hide her feelings in public now that Alvin was dating Debbie. But at home and on the Knepp farm, unless she missed her guess, Mildred felt no such restrictions. All while Mildred was taking care of Alvin's *mamm,* which would play well on Alvin's affections. But it was not Ida's place to interfere. Not to that extent anyway.

Debbie gave Ida a quick glance. "I'm quitting my job next week."

Ida's head jerked in her direction. "You're what?" Now that was a change of subject!

"You heard right." Debbie's voice was firm. "I need to help with the wedding next month, and after that I'm the only girl still at home."

Ida didn't hesitate. "But, Debbie, you can't put yourself out like that."

Debbie snorted. "Like you have anything to say about self-sacrifice. Look how you live."

"But that's only me being me," Ida managed. "It's nothing special."

"Don't worry." Debbie forced a smile. "I'll never be you, but I've already spoken to your *daett* about it. He agrees. He likes it that I'm quitting my job and staying home on the farm." Debbie paused to wipe her eye. "He said he'd treat me like his own daughter. He'd take care of me like he's taken care of you and Verna."

"Oh . . ." Ida wrapped one arm over Debbie's shoulder and pulled her close. "You sweet thing. You are something."

Debbie had tears in her eyes when she glanced up. "Your *daett* looks at me as his daughter, Ida. Do you object?"

"Debbie!" Ida wrapped Debbie in a hug with both arms now. "Of course I don't. You don't know how much this eases my mind. I guess I've pushed my concerns to the back of my mind regarding how *Mamm* and *Daett* will handle things on the farm after I'm gone. But you've stepped right up and filled in what's needed. You really are one of us."

Debbie wiped her eyes. "I don't know about that, but I'm trying. And your *daett* and *mamm* do seem to accept me."

"And so do Verna and I," Ida whispered. "Lois would too if she'd come to her senses."

"I miss her," Debbie said. "I know I'm not Lois's real sister, but I feel what your family is going through without her."

"Of course you do." Ida continued to wash the dishes. Perhaps now was the time to tell Debbie. She'd been waiting for just the right moment, and it couldn't get better than this. "Ben is coming this morning. We're making plans for the wedding. And I want you and Alvin to be the witnesses on my side of the family."

Debbie paused with the towel held in one hand. "*Me?* You want me? And Alvin? But what about Emery?"

Ida shrugged. "It's Alvin you're dating, not Emery. We could put you with Emery, I guess." She gave Debbie a crooked smile.

Debbie drew in a sharp breath. "I do think that Emery should be your first choice."

Ida reached over to give Debbie a quick hug. "Maybe, but I want you there beside me on my wedding day. Emery will understand."

Debbie hesitated for only a moment. "Ida,

I know you don't like Alvin, so this is awfully kind of you. And I accept. It's a great honor."

"Then it's settled." Ida was all smiles.

Debbie sobered. "But I'm not staying home today to help plan the wedding. Isn't that what witnesses do? Emery is visiting another district for the services, and I told him I'd hitch a ride and go along."

They heard rapid footsteps on the stairs behind them. "It's okay. I wasn't expecting you to help today. And here comes Emery right now, if I don't miss my guess."

Debbie turned as Emery burst in the kitchen. "Who's going with me?" he sang out. "I'm leaving in a Dutch minute."

Ida felt a warm glow as Debbie snapped back, "No, you're not! It's still early."

"I don't plan to arrive with the old men," Emery said with a laugh as he rushed out the washroom door. He hollered over his shoulder. "You'd better get changed."

Ida smiled as Debbie dropped her towel and beat a fast retreat up the stairs. Emery was teasing, but one never quite knew. He surely wouldn't drive off without Debbie in the buggy. If he did, Ida would rush out of the house herself and flag him down.

Emery needed a girlfriend — badly! No one said much about the subject at home

261

— if they could help it. But neither did *Daett* have his head buried in the sand. They all knew that Emery was growing older every day and that he needed a *frau* to help him run the farm he'd soon inherit. Debbie might think she had solved the problem with her offer to stay home and help on the farm, but that was only a short-term solution. *Daett* and *Mamm* would soon build their *dawdy haus,* and Debbie couldn't continue to live with them. Not and work at close quarters with Emery every day. Debbie was part of the family, and yet she wasn't. Ida scrubbed a pan for a few minutes. She should stop her concerns about this situation. She would soon be married to Ben, and likely Debbie would marry Alvin before long. Emery could trouble himself about his own *frau* problems.

Ida looked up with a bright smile as Debbie reappeared in her best Sunday dress. "Have a *gut* day at the service."

Debbie stepped closer for a quick peck on Ida's cheek. "And may the wedding plans go off without a hitch."

Ida felt the heat rise on her neck as Debbie dashed out the door. So much had happened so fast. Ida had a hard time keeping up. Today Ben would agree with the first Thursday in November as their date for the wedding, she was sure. He had, after all, given *Mamm* and her the privilege of picking the day.

"The sooner the better," *Mamm* had told her. "You'd best not draw this out."

And she had agreed, although she wasn't quite sure what *Mamm* meant. Surely *Mamm* didn't think she had doubts. *Nee, Mamm* probably figured it would be the best for the children — Melvin's and Ben's. Ben had told them the news that they would come to live with Ida and him after the wedding. Ida could tell the mixed emotions from the looks the two oldest, Willard and Rosa, had given her last Sunday at the service. *Mamm* probably noticed it too. With what had happened last time, a long, drawn-out affair wouldn't be in anyone's best interest. Melvin's children would wonder if she'd be snatched away from them again. She could tell it especially in Rosa's eyes. Willard had little more than a frozen look in his — bitter almost, like he hated the disturbance from where his heart had taken refuge.

Ida wiped away a tear as she thought about Willard. He would be her first project when it came to Melvin's children.

Ida finished the last of the dishes and peeked into the living room. *Mamm* and *Daett* were sitting in their rockers. *Daett* had his Bible open, and *Mamm* was reading *The Budget. Mamm* looked up with a smile. "We're going to miss you, Ida. You're leaving us after all these years."

Ida choked up for a moment as she rushed over to give *Mamm* a quick hug. "I'll miss you too."

Daett glanced up from his Bible. "You've always been a *gut* daughter, Ida. I want you to know that. Ben is getting a much better *frau* than he deserves." *Daett* smiled. "But then don't all of us get more from *Da Hah*'s hands than we should?"

"Thank you, *Daett,*" Ida whispered. "I'll have my hands full, I'm sure."

"That you will," *Daett* agreed. "But you're the woman for the task, Ida. You're a credit to the community with your willingness to love Ben and Ben's and Melvin's children. Your life is an example we all should seek to follow."

"Oh, *Daett,* that's too much." Ida felt her face grow hot from all this praise. She hadn't expected this from *Daett.* Ben might say such things, but then he would soon be her husband. *Daett* was usually more restrained. Maybe his old age had cracked open his emotions.

"And *Da Hah* has left us Debbie," *Daett* added, "to comfort us in our old age."

Ida felt she needed to caution *Daett.* "*Yah,* but you know she might wed next year to Alvin, and then you'll be alone."

Mamm reached up and touched her arm. "Don't you worry about that, Ida. That's a while yet. And maybe Emery will have settled down by then."

"*Yah,* maybe," Ida managed. She didn't look at *Mamm.* They must all live in faith, she told herself, and hope for the best. Regardless of how things turned out, there would always be a way to serve *Da Hah* with a whole heart. That was the most important thing, was it not?

"Sounds like Ben's here!" *Daett*'s announcement interrupted her thoughts.

"Oh, *yah!*" Ida gasped. "And I'm still in my chore dress."

Mamm smiled up at her. "He'll like you just fine, Ida. There's no sense in going all fancy this morning. There's just us and the two of you."

Mamm was right, Ida thought, as she hurried to the front door. She would meet Ben out by his buggy in her chore clothes, and they would go from there.

TWENTY-FOUR

Ida waited in the shadow of the barn door while Ben tied his horse to the stall post. Moments before she'd helped him unhitch and followed him into the barn. For some reason they seemed a little nervous around each other this morning. Surely something hadn't happened since last night? Certainly not on Ida's part. So it must be the newness of their relationship that would still take some getting used to.

Ida stepped closer as Ben finished.

A nervous smile crept across his face, and his hands fidgeted.

"It's okay, Ben," Ida whispered, taking both of his hands in hers. "With Barbara so recently gone, it must seem mighty strange to be alone here with me in the barn. And yet I'm your promised one. Isn't that how *Da Hah* wills things?"

He nodded. A smile spread over his face as she continued.

"We must go on, Ben. Even I must forget about Melvin and the plans we had together. Melvin is with his beloved Mary now. They're happier than any of us can even imagine. And Barbara, wouldn't she wish you to seek help raising your children and even comfort for yourself? She has all the joys of heaven now, and a man wasn't meant to live on this earth alone."

Ben's face lit up.

A warm rush of emotion flowed through Ida. She'd said the right thing, even to a stern man like Ben. And he wasn't stern really, not underneath all that strictness.

His hand touched her face. "You never cease to amaze me, Ida. You speak to my heart without knowing much about me. Truly *Da Hah* has sent you to bless my life. I can never thank Him enough."

Ida smiled. She was sure her face burned red from his praise. "You say too nice things, Ben. I'm glad you're comforted this morning. We don't have to be nervous around each other. It's not that long before we'll be living together in the same house."

"I know." He let go of her hand, but his smile never left his face. "So have you and your *mamm* picked a wedding date?"

Ida nodded. "The first Thursday of November. Is that okay?"

Ben's smile grew wider. "*Yah,* that's fine. And maybe there will be less of the others marrying on that Thursday."

Ida tilted her head. "I hadn't thought of that. But ours will be small. I hope you don't have a problem with that."

He gave her a quick peck on the cheek. "As long as you're there, Ida. And the bishop is there to hear our vows. That will be enough for me." He paused as a shadow crossed his face. "But are you sure about a small wedding? That's not fair to you, is it? You've never been married before, and first brides like . . ."

Ida rubbed her burning cheek with one hand. "You have nothing to worry about, Ben. I also asked for a small wedding with Melvin, but *Mamm* wouldn't listen. This time I'm getting my way."

Ben grinned. "Putting your foot down, are you?"

"It's what I want." Ida stepped closer.

Ben shrugged. "It fits you. Selfless, giving, always thinking of others."

Ida looked down. "You believe that because you haven't lived with me yet."

Ben glanced away for a second. "It will make no difference, Ida. I've already seen all I need to see to know you're a woman after *Da Hah*'s own heart. He must have been saving you for my hour of trouble."

Ida decided it was high time they changed the subject. "Come." She motioned with her hand. "Let's find a place to sit, and I'll tell you the plans."

Ben pointed toward a hay bale. "Then why not here? It's warmer with the horses than on the front porch."

Ida smiled. "Why not?"

Ben grinned as he heaved the bale against the wall and spread a clean feed bag across it. "Our couch. Quite nice, don't you think?"

"I like it." Ida sat down comfortably. "Wasn't the Savior born in a barn? Why should we not speak of our wedding plans here?"

Ben grinned. "You don't have to convince me. Not with you here."

"Enough of that." Ida laid her finger on his lips.

He gripped her hand for a moment before he let go. "So tell me. What are these plans of yours?"

"Well, let's start with our witnesses." Ida leaned back against the wood wall. "You mentioned your brother for your side of the family. Is that still okay?"

He nodded. "Phillip and a friend of the family named Carrie. I've already written him to ask. Sort of trying to make peace in the family."

"Okay," Ida said. "And what about Debbie and Alvin for me? That's a given, isn't it?"

She was met with silence. Ida waited a moment before she stole a glance at his face. What had she said wrong? He looked very serious.

Ben hesitated a moment longer. "I suppose you don't know about Alvin?"

"About Alvin?" Ida leaned forward. "What about Alvin?"

"Alvin has church problems." Ben paused. "I guess it's okay if I tell you. You'll soon be my *frau* . . ."

"Go on, I'm listening," Ida said, fear rising up inside her.

"What is your opinion of Alvin?" He regarded her steadily.

She paused a moment. "Does it matter what I think? Debbie's opinion of him is what matters." When Ben didn't speak, she continued, "Okay, I don't care for Alvin, but neither will he be my husband. He's Debbie's choice."

Ben took a deep breath. "Ida, the ministry, myself included, have a lot of questions about Alvin's character. What with his bringing that *Englisha* girl, Crystal, back in from the world. *Yah,* she seems like a decent woman. Of course, if Crystal should want to join the church — that is formally, we'd have to dig deeper. But there are other questions about why Alvin returned when he did. We think the man has a fascination with *Englisha* girls, and this troubles us greatly. Such a man in the midst of the community could cause no end of trouble down the road. If his heart is with us for the wrong reasons, it will surely show up in his children, let alone in what decisions he might make in the future for his family. We're asking Alvin to voluntarily hold back from communion this fall . . . until the matter is cleared up."

Ida forced herself to breathe. "And is he willing?"

Ben shrugged. "I don't know. Deacon Mast went to speak with him last night. I suppose if Alvin agrees that will help restore some trust."

Ida took a deep breath. "But I asked Debbie this morning, and she agreed to be my witness. How do I change that now?"

"I'm sorry, Ida." He looked sorrowful. "Let's just not say anything else until we know more. If Alvin will cooperate, it might be all right to have him sit as a witness for our wedding."

"Oh, Ben!" Ida clutched one of his hands with both of hers. "Already I see that I have

271

much to learn about being a *gut frau.* Please forgive me. I should have waited to ask Debbie until I had spoken with you."

"Ach." He stroked her hand. "There can't be that much harm done. But I see your *daett* is correct. Debbie has grown close to all of your hearts."

"Yah, she has," Ida mused. "But who shall I get if Alvin doesn't work out?"

"Let's hope he will," Ben said. "If he doesn't, we'll have to deal with that then."

"Okay." Ida got to her feet and pulled him up with one hand. "Let's go inside and see if *Mamm* has any questions for you about the wedding plans."

He wiped his forehead and pretended to wobble to his feet. Ida laughed. She had never thought Minister Kanagy could be this much fun, but then he wasn't Minister Kanagy to her anymore. He was *Ben.* Maybe that was what made all the difference.

Ida led the way across the lawn and glanced up at his face. "How's Willard taking the news?"

Ben shuddered. "He's not saying anything. I'm worried about him."

Ida looked away. "That's what I feared. He has gone silent since his *daett* died. With both parents gone, it's no wonder. It will take a miracle from *Da Hah* to break through to his heart."

Ben looked down at her. "If anyone can be that tool in *Da Hah*'s hand, it's you."

Ida didn't meet his gaze. "Should I visit before the wedding? To speak with him?"

Ben didn't hesitate. "*Nee.* He lost the hope of you as his *mamm* once when Melvin died. Let's wait until we've said the vows. I think he'll come around."

When Ida opened the front door and the two of them walked in, *Mamm* and *Daett* looked up with smiles.

"I see our popcorn maker has arrived!" *Daett* teased.

"You're getting none until this afternoon," Ida said. "We have plans to go over."

Out of the corner of her eye Ida saw Ben give *Daett* a wink. "Maybe I'll help with that popcorn making, and then we can talk."

"Spoken like a true man," *Mamm* groused. "And since when do you know anything about popcorn making, Ben?"

"I don't!" Ben laughed. "I did when I was single and at home, but I think I've forgotten."

"Okay!" Ida held up her hand. "The men win."

Daett grinned up at Ben. "You sure you want to marry this woman?"

Ben didn't miss a beat. "I'd say the vows today if we could."

"Oh, that's so sweet of you to say." Ida snuggled into Ben until *Mamm* gave her a sharp glance. Ida stood up straight. Some things weren't meant for public display — even before your parents apparently.

Daett smiled. "I still haven't seen any popcorn . . ."

Ida hurried toward the kitchen, and Ben followed her. She motioned for him to sit on a chair while she worked. It was nice to have his presence to herself. Once they said the vows and began their married life together, these moments would be difficult to find with eight children in the house. She would treasure every second she could catch alone with this man in their brief courtship.

"Surely I can do something," he objected from the chair.

She pretended to glare at him. "You sit right there and talk to me about all the little details of life at the Kanagy farm. I want to learn all I can before the wedding day."

"You're a *wunderbah* woman!" he said.

She shushed him with a finger to her lips, pointing toward the living room.

He laughed and started talking about daily life at the Kanagy place.

TWENTY-FIVE

The following Sunday night Debbie climbed into Alvin's buggy. Alvin asked Star to speed away so quickly that Debbie had to grasp the buggy door to steady herself. Was Alvin hurrying to leave behind his troubled thoughts — whatever they were? That was something people often did in the *Englisha* world. And Alvin was clearly troubled. He hadn't said anything since she climbed in other than "*Gut* evening." And from the brief glimpses she'd had of him at the service today, he wasn't very happy.

Instead of sorrowing tonight, they should both be rejoicing because Ida and Minister Kanagy had announced their upcoming marriage this morning. Ida had whispered the news of the date to her on the way to church this morning. Apparently Minister Kanagy and Ida had spoken with Bishop Beiler last Sunday, and they'd requested the formal announcement of their wedding day

— as was the custom in the community. And all on the same day when pre-communion church had been held.

Debbie hugged herself for a moment. She would get to go along for her first communion in two weeks! Why wasn't Alvin excited with her? Didn't he care? And she hadn't had a chance to tell him of Ida's request that they be witnesses for the Beiler family. Maybe that would cheer his spirits. Surely Alvin wouldn't object to such an honor.

Debbie stole a quick glance at her date. Maybe what he needed was some cheerful chatter from a female. Alvin did, after all, live alone in that big house of his. Unless . . . Mildred was spending time with him. Was she maybe even fixing meals for him? Debbie sat up straight on the seat. She shoved thoughts of Mildred from her mind. She wouldn't let anything interfere with her relationship with Alvin. She'd waited too long for him to ask her home to question him and show her doubt of him. She didn't want him to peg her as a meddlesome, high-maintenance woman. That would not do.

Debbie took a deep breath. "Wasn't that a wonderful time today? I was allowed to sit in on an Amish members' meeting! Maybe I shouldn't be making a big deal out of it, but to me it was a big deal to be at a pre-communion service. And I got to listen to Bishop Beiler go over the *Ordnung* rules — none of which I'm transgressing, if I must say so myself. I can't tell you how blessed I feel, Alvin. And now to ride home with you as my escort. How much more blessed could I be?" She glanced up at his face. He still hadn't said anything. Maybe he'd been caught in some small transgression and was unhappy about that. But how could that be? The Knepps were known for how strictly they kept the *Ordnung.* Verna and Ida had told her this several times.

"You wouldn't have gotten caught in an *Ordnung* breaking?" she teased. "Is that why the sour face all day?"

He still didn't respond.

"I'm sorry, Alvin. I was trying to tease you into a good mood." She reached for his arm and tried again. "Then it must be because you're taking responsibility of your *daett*'s farm, and it's weighing heavy on your heart. Let me assure you that you're not to blame."

"You're right there!" Alvin said with an edge to his voice. "I couldn't have said that part better myself. But that's not all the story."

"I'm afraid I don't understand," Debbie said. "What story? What more is there?"

Alvin slowed down for the Beilers' driveway. He turned and then pulled to a stop by the hitching post. "Maybe we'd better go inside to discuss this."

Debbie climbed down. At least she felt like she could breathe again. Alvin had said "discuss." From the way he'd acted, she'd half expected him to just drop her off and drive off into the night.

Something was seriously bothering him, Debbie acknowledged as she waited for Alvin to secure Star. Whatever the *kafuffle* was, surely it could be fixed. Whatever it was, she would love him through it. She took his arm again and led the way into the living room. Once there, Debbie sat beside him on the couch.

Alvin glanced at her. "You're not making this any easier, Debbie."

Debbie sighed. "Alvin, you're talking in riddles. Why don't you start at the beginning and explain what you mean?" Debbie smiled. After a bit she raised her eyebrows and waited even more.

He refused to look at her. "So you really don't know?"

"Alvin!" She was exasperated. "How *could* I know unless you tell me?" Her heart nearly failed her at a sudden thought. "Is it something about Mildred? Are you in love with her?"

His voice trembled. "I don't know. But that's not what the trouble is." He turned to look at her. "Has Bishop Beiler told you about the church trouble I'm in?"

"No." Debbie could hardly believe her ears. The man wasn't sure if he was in love with Mildred, and yet he wanted to speak of his church troubles? "What have you done?"

"Nothing really! The ministry just thinks I might have."

"I don't understand."

Alvin reached for her hand, and she didn't pull away. "I'm not trying to talk in riddles, Debbie. It's the way we talk . . ." He was struggling. "Did you hear that I won't be allowed to participate in communion?"

Debbie shook her head. "How would I hear that? Wouldn't that be a private matter between the ministry and you?"

Alvin snorted. "Far from it, Debbie. I'm a very public matter now. Not going along with communion is a serious matter — even though I'm supposedly going to do it voluntarily. I'm to 'humble myself,' they said." Alvin's voice turned bitter. "Humble myself over why I have this apparent history of fascination with *Englisha* girls." Alvin jumped to his feet and paced the floor.

Debbie clasped her hands but remained

seated on the couch. She could hardly believe what she'd heard. "You think I'm just a fascination, Alvin?"

He whirled around. "Weren't you? Aren't you? You drove past my place before you even joined the community. Tempting me. And *yah,* I was tempted. By your pretty face, and your fancy ways, and your *wunderbah* charm. And look where it led me. Out into Philadelphia. I was excommunicated, Debbie. Why? That's what I keep asking myself. Over you and the farm, but a lot of it was you. My family isn't like that. We love the community. The old life. My *daett* and brothers would never have done something like that. And yet I did. And now the ministry wonders about me — after Crystal, an *Englisha* girl, follows me home. First you and then Crystal. They think I'm lured to *Englisha* girls. They don't trust me!"

Debbie clutched her chest as stabs of pain ran through her. "You blame me for your leaving the community and that you dated Crystal?"

Alvin resumed his pacing. "*Nee,* I blame myself. But the point is I can't go on like this. I don't want to live life with questions about my character being asked of me all the time. I'm doing my repentance this communion to show everyone that I do doubt myself, and that maybe everything was my fault. But then . . . but then I want to move on. I've too much to lose. So what am I saying? I guess I don't know. But you and me, we can't go on, Debbie."

She said nothing as the tears came.

"I'm sorry." He sat down beside her and took her hand. "I know we've talked of big things, of making this work, and of the days when everything would be right. But it's not all right, Debbie. I'm tired of trying, of dreaming big things. I just want to be a simple farmer, Debbie. I want to live in peace, and raise my family in the community like I was raised. And I don't want any cloud hanging over my children's heads, either."

"So that's what I've been to you, Alvin?" Debbie whispered. "A cloud hanging over your head? A torment in your heart?"

"Nee! Nee!" He squeezed her hand so hard it hurt. "You are not that at all, Debbie. You're way up there. You've always been above me, out of my reach. I knew from the beginning I shouldn't even have tried to think I could ever say my wedding vows with such a woman. But I did think that, and I'm sorry. I want to make it right before it's too late. I want to live where I belong, Debbie. You deserve someone better than

me. You really do."

She tried to stand but didn't make it. "And I have no say in this matter? You would throw away all that's happened between us? You would say that it was nothing? That what I feel for you, and what you felt for me, Alvin, was *wrong*?"

He stood and paced a few minutes before he stopped to look out the living room window. He stared into the darkness outside.

When he didn't speak, Debbie said, "It's Mildred Schrock, isn't it? With her you can have the life you want. The uncomplicated life of a simple Amish farmer who has no 'fascination' with *Englisha* girls."

He froze. His words were clipped. "I won't have you saying bad things about Mildred. She has been nothing but supportive of our relationship."

Debbie flinched. "I'm sorry. I didn't mean it the way it sounded."

Alvin nodded. "This is between you and me. I'm also sorry, Debbie. This is what I hate about this. I don't want things said we'll both regret. But I think we'd better part ways for now — until things are clearer for me and for you."

Debbie struggled to steady her voice. "If that's how you would have it, then that's how it will be."

Pain flashed across his face. "It's not what I want, Debbie. It's just the way things are. You're too good for me." He rushed to the door and fled outside.

She didn't follow him. She watched through the window until his buggy lights disappeared. He wouldn't come back, Debbie told herself. Her dream was gone. With a sob, she sank into the couch and buried her head in her arms.

TWENTY-SIX

In the predawn darkness, Alvin hung the gas lantern on the barn ceiling. He stared at its bright light until his eyes hurt before he turned to kick a hay bale near him. Why had he behaved the way he did last night? Why had he cut off his relationship with Debbie so brutally? Debbie had been the best thing to ever happen to him. She was a dream that had drifted in from the forbidden world out there — from that fancy *Englisha* life. But that was the problem. *Yah,* he would always see her like that — an impossibility that didn't belong in his world. Even though Debbie was Amish now, she would always be *Englisha* to him. She would always bring back memories of what he wished to forget — those months in Philadelphia when he tasted of the world's forbidden fruit.

How could it ever be otherwise? Not one word he had spoken last night hadn't been

284

true, though they had cut him to his heart to say them. From the look on her face, Debbie must have sobbed half the night after he left. How had his world come to such a tortured end? With another kick at the bale, Alvin headed toward the back of the barn.

Mildred's voice stopped him. "Did we have a tough night?"

He whirled around to see her standing there, a questioning look on her face.

"How long have you been here?" he asked.

She gave him a steady look. "Long enough to see you throwing a fit about something by attacking an innocent hay bale." A slight smile played on her face as she picked up a three-legged milking stool.

He managed a slight grin. "I guess I did look foolish." Her wry smile made him feel better at once — and he didn't like it. He wanted Mildred to scream at him, to tell him he was an idiot. That's what he deserved.

Instead she was all sympathy. "Sorry you're not . . . feeling well."

"I'm feeling just fine."

She appeared unperturbed. "Did Debbie feed you sour milk with the cookies last night?"

Alvin cringed. Why had she said such a

thing? Now he found himself saying what he hated to say . . . but must. "Mildred, I want you to leave. I want you to quit working for my *daett* and *mamm*. I'll talk with *Daett* later today about it. Perhaps your sister Bertha can take your place. I'm sorry, but it has to be this way."

The stool clattered to the floor. Tears sprang to Mildred's eyes. "What have I done, Alvin? Did I offend you? Or Debbie? Please tell me what it was, and I'll stop."

He stared at the ceiling. "The truth is that I have to think some things through, and I can't do them with you around. It's not about you, Mildred; it's about me."

"Is Debbie making you do this?" Mildred wiped at her eyes.

"Nee!" he snapped. "I broke up with her last night."

"You *did*?" Her exclamation came in a gasp. She stepped closer. "But why, Alvin? I thought you liked her."

"I did," he muttered. "And I do. I can't explain it right now. Even to myself."

Shock was in her voice. "Did Debbie drop you, Alvin?"

Alvin laughed. *"Nee!* Though I wish she had."

"Then why?" Her voice was insistent.

He paused. "Debbie . . . Debbie is not

286

from my world. She never was. I longed for something that wasn't mine to have. And look what it cost me! Because of that insane fling in Philadelphia, I'm now in trouble with the church. I have to stay back from communion. I can't go on living like that, Mildred. Debbie deserves someone better than me."

She grabbed his arm. "Then there is hope for me, Alvin? We can begin again? I had never dared think this before. I certainly wasn't trying to interfere with your relationship with Debbie. But, please, listen to what you're saying, Alvin."

That wasn't quite true, he thought. Mildred had made her desire plain enough. But she had conducted herself without blame these past few weeks. He met her troubled gaze. "*Nee,* Mildred. It wouldn't work out between us."

Her face fell. "Then you're going to try to get back with her? Make up?"

"I don't know!" He almost screamed it. "*Nee,* I can't get back with her now. Or ever! I'm confused, okay? And you being here isn't helping."

She regarded him for a moment. "We'd better do the chores. Sometimes thinking about things only makes it worse."

"That's the most sense I've heard all

morning," he said, relief flooding through him. As always, Mildred knew what needed to be said and done. He'd already spent hours in thought about this since he came home last night to no avail.

Alvin went about his chores, and when he returned with the first round of cows, Mildred had the feed spread out. He met her pleading gaze for a moment. Her words from earlier buzzed through his sleep-deprived mind. Mildred had clearly offered a renewal of their relationship. She had shown every indication of this the past weeks, but to hear the words spoken made the option all the clearer. This was not a dream. Mildred wouldn't disappear on him sometime in the future. She had no place to vanish to like Debbie did. She was Amish through and through. She had no past beyond what they both knew, and she had no future that was any different from his future. Debbie's *Englisha* past would always be a part of her. She couldn't change that, no matter how Amish she became.

Alvin brought his thoughts about Debbie to a stop. This was not Debbie's fault. She was making every effort to fit in with the community. This was about him. Could he see himself with a right to belong in Debbie's life? And even if he could, would he handle himself as someone fitting for her? Not judging from his recent actions.

Alvin groaned. Mildred was right. All this thinking was getting him nowhere. He'd better forget about it and sink into a day of normal choring with people like . . . Alvin stopped himself again, but the thought wouldn't leave.

Mildred glanced at him from across the back of the cows and smiled. "Stop thinking now!" she teased.

He looked at her and knew what he wanted. *Stability.* And there in front of his eyes was stability. *Yah,* there was no buzz or thrill or dream associated with Mildred, just plain old stability. Stability based on the farming life he'd grown up in. Here was a *frau* who fit into all he'd known in the community, who would be happy to live here with him, who knew how to work this life as her second nature.

Mildred offered all that to him. And she was serious. If he turned her love away now, there might never be another chance. What other girl in the community fit so well with what he was used to? Here was a *frau* who could cook, who overlooked his faults, who didn't fight with him, who didn't ask painful questions, and who hadn't even brought up the fact this morning that he wouldn't

— couldn't — go along with communion this fall.

Alvin swallowed hard and kept busy at his work. If he opened his heart to Mildred, he would have to give up Debbie. But hadn't he already done that? Last night wouldn't be an easy matter to repair. Debbie had overlooked so many of his failures already. He couldn't ask her for more.

Mildred's voice chirped beside him. "I know the real reason you want me to leave, Alvin."

He didn't answer for a moment, and then he gave in. "Okay, tell me."

Her smile was bright. "So you can ask me home sometime in the future, when it's decent of course. Now, with me here, it might not look right. You know what I mean."

He didn't answer so she continued. "It's better if I go now, especially since word will soon get around about your breakup with Debbie. Then it won't look like I had anything to do with it, which, of course, I didn't. But you know how people go by how things look." She paused for breath. "And, Alvin, I think that was a brave and self-sacrificing thing you did yesterday, staying back from communion, taking the blame for something that wasn't your fault in the least."

"I wouldn't say that," he muttered. "I had my share of the blame."

She ignored his comment. "But am I right about why you want me to leave?"

He hadn't quite thought it through yet, but that theory did make sense. It would give him the time to think things out, and Mildred would wait for him until he was ready. "Well, just so you know, I'm not doing anything soon." He gave her a sharp glance.

She giggled. "Oh, Alvin! That's all I need to know!" She clasped her hands for a moment. "I'll be out of here tomorrow. And I will wait, Alvin, until you think a decent time has passed. I'm just so happy I'll have a chance to correct that awful mistake from my youth. What a fool I was to drop you like that, thinking I was better than you were. I'm so sorry, Alvin. Can you really forgive me?"

He allowed a grin to creep over his face. "I forgave you a long time ago, Mildred. But please understand, I'm not making any promises."

"You don't have to," she said, radiant with joy. "This is all I need to know for now. I'm going home and praying like I've never prayed before that the time will be short until you ask me home, Alvin."

The next thought hit Alvin like a ton of bricks. It would be so very easy to end his torture right now. Wasn't it true that Mildred represented all he expected — and all he deserved from life? Wasn't it obvious now that *Da Hah* had brought Mildred here for the very purpose that now lay before him? *Yah,* it was surely so. Why spend more months in agony over this? *Nee,* the thought of continued uncertainty was like a knife in his heart. He would do this and do it now. He stepped out from behind the cow and approached Mildred.

"Well . . ." he reached for her with both hands. "Do you . . . want to . . . I mean . . ."

She hesitated. "Do what?"

"Do you . . . want to . . . wed me this fall?" he squeaked out the words.

"You are asking me to be your *frau*?" Her voice squeaked.

"Yah!" Why hadn't he taken this step a long time ago? "Will you say the wedding vows with me, Mildred? Come live on this farm? Take care of *Mamm* for us? Work with me?"

She leaped forward and wrapped her arms around his neck. "Of course I will, Alvin! You know I will!"

"This fall yet?"

"*Yah,* this fall. We'll make it happen, Alvin. Whatever it takes. My parents will help, and I'm sure your *daett* won't object. If we work fast, we can get it in for the last week of November. The Schrocks can do it, Alvin."

He pulled her close. "Then let's do it."

She looked up into his face. "Kiss me, Alvin. Kiss me like you wanted to kiss me behind the schoolhouse that long ago day and I wouldn't let you. Show me you've accepted my apology."

He didn't move for a moment as he remembered that day. That was a time he'd blocked from his memory. The shame of it had been too great. He'd finally gathered up enough nerve to linger after school on a day Mildred had to stay late to finish an assignment. It had happened near the end of their eighth school year. In his mind she'd grown more beautiful each day while he seemed headed in the other direction — clumsy and full of stammers. But he'd finally worked up the nerve and reached for her hand when she came around the corner of the schoolhouse. Then her scorn and her rapid rush to leave had burned deeper than even he had ever acknowledged.

He dropped his gaze to her eyes now — her deep-brown eyes that contained all the memories of those long ago days.

Her mouth moved. "I love you, Alvin, with all my heart. I'll always be yours."

He closed his eyes and pulled her close. He allowed the years to wash away as he tasted her lips. He was young again. He dared again. He was accepted again. And above all he belonged here — in her arms.

Long moments later, he pulled back. "Well, was that showing you enough?"

She nodded and her cheeks flamed. "We'll make this wedding happen, Alvin. If we have to wed with only the bishop there."

He laughed. "In the meantime, these cows want out of here."

She joined his laughter. "Then let them go, and we'll finish the chores. After that, you're coming over for breakfast. We have much to tell your *daett* and *mamm.*"

He nodded but didn't trust his speech right now. This had happened so fast, but it felt so right. It would put to an end his misery. Mildred as his *frau* would keep him close to the earth, and she would bear him children, like his *mamm* had borne for his *daett.* And they would be the people they were meant to be.

Debbie would find someone who fit her so much better than he ever would have. *Yah,* she deserved someone better. And *Da*

Hah willing, she would now be free to find that someone better. Alvin sent a smile toward Mildred, who glowed almost as bright as the sun peeking above the horizon.

TWENTY-SEVEN

Debbie tiptoed down the stairs in the predawn darkness. Emery's footsteps had gone past her bedroom door moments ago, and she could hear Ida stir in her room behind her. The Beiler household had awakened on this Wednesday morning — a day Verna was due to visit and maybe even Lois would drop by.

Saloma had mentioned this last night with a wistful tone. She missed Lois more than she admitted. With only a little more than two weeks before Ida's wedding, the Beiler family had allowed Lois to help with the food. It seemed strange that she should help given that her family hadn't attended her own wedding, but then that was the Amish for you. Debbie rubbed her head. She too might someday struggle to accept her parents' absence at her wedding, should they refuse to attend.

Debbie squeezed her forehead as a stab of

pain ran through her. Why was she thinking of her own wedding? Maybe from some ingrained instinct in all women to dream and long for that special day. Well, her hopes on that score had been dashed on Sunday evening. After that initial crying spell on the couch after Alvin left, a faint hope had stirred in Debbie. But when morning arrived, there had been nothing but a dull ache. She knew. *Yah,* this was the end of the road for them. Should she tell Saloma and Ida? Not if it would spoil their joy over Ida's wedding. But perhaps she'd spill to Verna today while they cleaned upstairs. She'd weep on Verna's sympathetic shoulder. But no, that was unlikely. She would rather climb in a hole and never come out again. Any further indulgence of her emotions was a waste of time.

Debbie groaned and pushed open the stair door to step into the living room. It was dark with only a dim light from the kitchen doorway splashing across the floor. When she walked in, Saloma greeted her with a cheery, "*Gut* morning!"

"*Gut* morning," Debbie managed to return. Saloma had made sure everyone was in bed by ten o'clock last night so everyone would have plenty of sleep. Still Saloma must have noticed the circles around Debbie's eyes.

"Didn't sleep well?" Saloma asked.

"No." Debbie put her hand to her aching head. "But don't worry about me. I'm good to go."

"You can help chore this morning," Saloma offered. "Sometimes the fresh air is just what one needs to clear a headache."

Debbie glanced up. "You can handle the kitchen by yourself?"

Saloma's bright smile faded a bit. "We might as well get used to it. The wedding will be soon enough, and then there's only you and me."

"That's true," Debbie said as she headed to the washroom to pull on her boots and overcoat. Truth be told, she still preferred the barn chores to food preparation.

Debbie pushed open the outer door to take in deep breaths of the cool morning air. It did help, she thought. At least a little. Hopefully it would also clear out thoughts of Alvin, but that was perhaps too optimistic. Alvin wasn't something she could sweep out the door like the dirt Emery tracked in from the barn. Alvin was a decent human being and would have made a *gut* husband. Why he thought their love was only a fascination, she had no idea. Wasn't that how love began at times? She knew that her attraction for him had been pure on those days she used to drive past his place and catch glimpses of him at work in the fields.

Debbie paused for a moment to take in the great sweep of the stars overhead. The early dawn had begun to lighten the eastern sky and sent streaks of red and orange heavenward. She had so much she could be thankful for, she told herself, even in her sorrow. Here she was, a real Amish girl, at home in the bishop's household. She got to help with the chores and join the family around the breakfast table afterward.

Alvin hadn't taken any of that away. And he couldn't. She had accomplished those cherished goals on her own — aims that had been hers since childhood. And Alvin hadn't been among those goals, not back then. Sure, she had driven past his place all those times and had been drawn to him. But she'd always insisted that Alvin was separate from her desire to join the Amish. And nothing had ever happened to persuade her otherwise. She'd continued that journey while Alvin had spent time in the *Englisha* world in Philadelphia. And she would continue now. It wasn't some harsh determination of her mind, but a simple walk onward in the life she knew God had for her. If Alvin chose not to accompany her, that was his choice.

Life would go on. Was that not the Amish way?

It was, Debbie told herself with one more quick glance up at the twinkling stars. She must not hold this against Alvin. But there she went again. She couldn't make logical sense out of this. Maybe what she needed was a good meltdown, complete with stomping feet and screams that echoed toward the retreating stars. A smile stole across Debbie's face. At least she could still laugh at herself. Maybe there was hope that she could heal . . . in the future. Right now it sure didn't feel like it. Debbie pushed open the barn door and squinted in the light of the gas lantern.

"I see sleepy-eyes is up," Emery teased.

Debbie stuck out her tongue at him.

Emery roared with laughter as he rushed off with milk buckets in his hands.

At least she supplied humor for someone, Debbie thought. Emery was a sweet man, that much was for sure. Which was no doubt why Crystal Meyers wanted to sink her claws into him. The woman continued to attend the Sunday services, and she was eyeing Emery in particular — discreetly, of course. No one else seemed to notice. Not that she should think such awful thoughts about another human being, but it was true.

She knew her own world. To Crystal, Emery was a dream. He was solid. He worked hard. He was faithful and steady. Emery looked like a vision, especially after Crystal's breakup with her husband.

Debbie shook her head. She shouldn't be worrying about Emery. He hadn't responded to Crystal's attentions that she knew of, and hopefully things would stay that way. And perhaps there was something she could do. At least, she could watch for chances to influence Emery away from any fascination with Crystal. Maybe Alvin had been right about the way some Amish men felt toward *Englisha* women.

Debbie jumped when Ida came through the barn door and greeted her with a happy "*Gut* morning! What's up?"

Debbie painted on a bright smile. "*Gut* morning. Your brother's teasing me."

Ida laughed. "I do declare that's one thing I'm going to miss about being home. Emery's teasing — or rather his teasing you. You seem to bring that side out of him."

Debbie smiled. "Emery is a *gut* man. Now if we could only persuade him to marry a decent Amish woman. But I'm afraid I've been of little help in that area . . ." *I can't even keep my love life on the tracks,* almost slipped out.

Ida stared at the milk-house door for a moment. "It's not your fault. None of us can do much either."

"I'm afraid not." Debbie sighed.

"We must pray," Ida said with resolve. "Sometimes that's all one can do."

With Ida here in front of her and both of them alone, Debbie's thoughts turned to whether or not she should tell Ida about Alvin. She thought for a moment and then said, "Ida, I need to tell you something . . ."

Ida glanced at Debbie and, catching the tone, turned pale. "What is it? Not bad news?"

"*Yah,* I suppose it is bad news . . . in a way. Though someday maybe I'll think differently about it. On Sunday night, Alvin cut off our relationship. I don't think he's coming back, which means . . ."

Ida stopped her by wrapping her in both arms and whispering in her ear, "Oh, Debbie! You know I didn't care for Alvin, but I'm still sorry."

"I know." Debbie couldn't pull off a smile.

"Now I know why you've been so quiet these past few days. And to think I didn't ask. I've been so wrapped up in the wedding — but that's no excuse."

"It's okay." Debbie wiped her eyes. "You couldn't have done anything."

"Was he nasty to you?" Ida's look became intense.

Debbie laughed. "No, Ida. He was a perfect gentleman. And that may have been part of the problem. He didn't want to hurt my feelings, so I think he's been keeping things hidden inside. The problem now is that I can't be your witness on your special day. I'm so sorry for letting you down."

A look of brief anger flashed across Ida's face. "Don't be saying that, Debbie. It's not your fault. Alvin is to blame for this! But still, I'm sorry for you that it didn't work out. I know your heart was set on the man."

"I suppose so." Debbie glanced away. She really didn't want a long discussion with Ida on the matter. How Ida felt about Alvin was no secret. But as usual her friend was being supportive.

Ida studied her now. "You know, I still want you to be my witness, Debbie."

Debbie choked. "Not with Paul. Don't even think about it."

Before Ida could answer, the milk-house door swung open and Emery burst in. He took in both of them with a quick glance. "Oh *nee*! Is this trouble I see! What's afoot now?"

"It's none of your business," Ida told him.

But Debbie wanted Emery to know, although she wasn't sure why. The words blurted out. "Alvin terminated our relationship on Sunday night."

Emery jerked his head around. "Now that was mighty dumb of him. A *gut*-looking woman like you."

"Thank you!" Debbie gave him a hint of a smile.

Emery grinned. "Did the man find greener pastures?"

"Emery!" Ida shrieked. "Be sensitive to Debbie's feelings."

Debbie kept her smile pasted on. "I think that's probably a good way of saying it, although I've wanted to avoid such thoughts. I imagine Mildred Schrock has been working her charms."

Emery made a face. "Well, take it from me. It's Alvin's loss — and a big one at that."

Now she was going to really cry, Debbie thought as her eyes stung.

Emery seemed to notice her discomfort. He turned, headed toward the back of the barn to bring in the cows. They were being too nice to her, Debbie thought. She didn't deserve any of this, but God had led her here. He would supply her with what she needed to continue the journey — alone, if necessary.

And she was sure Mildred had much more to do with this than Alvin had wanted to admit. But she mustn't think ill of Alvin or of Mildred. A sob caught in her throat. If Alvin chose Mildred over her, she would bear the shame as any decent woman would. She was not the first woman who'd been rejected in favor of another.

Ida touched her arm as the cows pushed in. "We'll talk later about someone to sit with you on my wedding day."

TWENTY-EIGHT

Debbie stood at the kitchen sink later that morning washing the last of the breakfast dishes. Lois had arrived some ten minutes earlier and was busy at work at the dining room table with Saloma. The two had their heads together with recipe books spread out around them. They were deep in conversation about the menu for Ida's wedding.

As Debbie glanced out of the window, she caught sight of Verna's buggy pulling into the driveway. "Verna's here!" Debbie said as she turned to go out the washroom door.

Lois shouted after her, "Tell Verna *gut* morning for me. I'll give her a kiss when she comes in."

Debbie hurried across the lawn. She couldn't help but find good cheer in Lois's antics this morning. At least the girl had arrived in a decent dress instead of jeans or a cut-off shirt. Lois had even agreed to Saloma's requirement that she wear an Amish

306

dress at the wedding.

Thankfully, Ida had said nothing more about who was to sit with her as a witness at the wedding. No doubt Ida meant to give her feelings a rest before the mention of some distant Beiler relative she'd never seen before. With all that was wrong in her life right now, she could take the consideration with a grateful heart. Hadn't even the brief glimpse of Verna as she came in the driveway choked her up? If she didn't watch herself in the next few minutes, she'd go on her long-overdue blubbering breakdown right by Verna's buggy where the whole Beiler family could see her.

Verna left her horse by the hitching post and turned to greet Debbie with a hug. "It's so *gut* to see you again!"

Debbie smiled. "And you. I'm thinking little Sarah Mae is all bundled up in that buggy somewhere."

Verna glowed with joy. "That she is."

Debbie marched over to peek at the *boppli* wrapped in the quilt Verna had fastened to the buggy seat. Sarah Mae's face scrunched up in a bright smile. "She knows me!" Debbie cooed. "May I carry her into the house?"

"We'd better unhitch Isaiah first." Verna wrinkled up her face. "He shouldn't stand out here all day, especially if it turns cold."

"Of course!" Debbie rushed to help. "How quickly I forget the routines of Amish life. But I'm learning."

"You're doing very well since your baptism," Verna said. "And long before that, really. You almost grew with us."

Debbie lowered her head as she unfastened the tugs. "It's still not quite the same."

"You'll make Alvin an excellent Amish *frau,*" Verna said, her voice lilting.

Debbie bit her lip.

Verna laughed. "Now don't go blushing on me. I know how much Alvin means to you. I'm sure he's thinking the same thing of you. Now that the man has finally gotten around to asking you home on dates. Remember how hard we used to work, Debbie? Scheming to match Alvin up with you at my wedding as a table waiter. I thought the poor man would die of fright. But Alvin has come a long way from such a timid start, if I must say so myself. And I'm not ashamed to claim credit either. You two make a very nice couple."

Debbie said nothing as she held the buggy shaft as Verna led Isaiah forward. Her silence finally drew Verna's attention.

Verna pulled Isaiah up with a jerk and turned. "Debbie, you're sure quiet this

308

morning. Did I say something wrong?"

Debbie dropped the shaft and covered her face with her hands. "Alvin broke off our relationship Sunday night."

"Oh, Debbie!" Verna let the tie rope fall and rushed over. "Surely not! I can't believe it! Why, that man is a hopeless case after all. Oh, Debbie, I'm so sorry this happened." A strain of hope crept into Verna's voice. "Do you think it's final?"

Debbie choked for a moment before she answered. "I'm afraid so. My heart feels like a piece of lead sunk down to the bottom of the ocean."

"Oh!" Verna wrapped her in another hug, and the two clung to each other for a long time — until baby Sarah Mae's cry cracked the air. Verna let go to hurry to the buggy and gather the baby in her arms. "Were you scared that Mommy had left? I'm right here, just taking the horsey into the barn."

"I'll take Isaiah," Debbie said, grabbing Isaiah's tie rope. "You take the baby in out of the cold."

Verna didn't protest as she pulled the quilt off the buggy seat to wrap around Sarah Mae. "Will you bring my satchel in?"

Debbie nodded as Verna sent a mournful glance her way. "We'll talk more about this later, Debbie."

Debbie pulled on Isaiah's tie rope. The horse stared at her and blinked his eyes. "You're coming with me," she said. Isaiah followed as if he understood. He entered the barn and whinnied to the other horses. Debbie tied him in an empty stall and gave him a small bucket of oats. She made sure there was hay in the rack and water. With one last pat on his neck, she left the barn. Verna's buggy door was still open, so she stopped to pick up the satchel and then closed the door. When she walked into the house, all three Beiler women were cooing over baby Sarah. Verna stood beside them with all the glory of motherhood.

Debbie quenched a sob. This was no time for a pity party. But the sight of the women gathered around the baby brought the stabbing thought that she might never get to experience giving birth to her own child.

Debbie pasted on a smile and joined the group. She reached over to squeeze Lois's arm. "How's married life?"

Lois glowed. "It's unbelievable! I'm so in love with the man I can't see straight sometimes. It's what I've always wanted, Debbie."

Saloma sent Lois a sharp glance, and Debbie knew she needed to change the subject to something other than Lois's life in the *Englisha* world. "I'm glad to hear that. And I'm glad you're here to help with Ida's wedding."

"*Yah,* and I will dress Amish. That will seem almost like old times." Lois lost her smile for a moment. "But it's only for the day. Doug won't come. He's sore about, well, you know, about you not coming to our wedding."

Debbie winced but bit her tongue. Lois chattered away. "He'll get over it. He's so understanding. He knows things are different. If I bring him a few pies home from the wedding, and some Amish date pudding, which he's never had, that'll put a smile back on his face."

"Sounds like you have things figured out," Debbie said. She would ask no more questions of Lois. All of them seemed doomed to veer into uncomfortable territory for Saloma.

Lois regarded her for a moment. "I meant to ask you, Debbie. What didn't you like about Doug? I mean, you did date him. I asked Doug, and he mumbled something about you two not being meant for each other."

Debbie's head spun. Now they really were in rough territory.

"Lois!" Saloma gasped. "That's indecent to ask."

"Sorry," Lois said. "I was just curious."

Debbie found her voice. "Doug's right, Lois. You fit him much better than I ever could have."

Lois glowed. "Thanks, Debbie. That makes me feel *gut*. But why are you dating that Alvin Knepp? He's not even close to being like Doug . . ."

"Lois!" Saloma's voice cut her daughter's comment short.

Lois shrugged. "Sorry. I meant no harm, Debbie."

Debbie sighed. She might as well tell the truth. It would come out soon enough anyway. "Alvin ended our relationship Sunday night."

Lois raised her eyebrows. "Can't say I'm sorry to hear that. Do you want me to keep my eye out for a decent date — you know, out *there*?"

"Lois!" Saloma's voice was even sharper. "That's enough!"

Lois wasn't through though. "You don't have to get all snappy, *Mamm*. I like my life out there. I thought Debbie might want to rejoin the crowd."

A deep pall settled over the room. Little

baby Sarah kicked on the quilt, but no one looked.

"We have said enough on this." *Mamm*'s voice hadn't lost its edge. "Only *Da Hah* can know where this all will end. You've left the faith. And I fear for *Daett*'s health at times. This will surely drive him to an early grave. But Debbie is not joining you in your foolishness. Of that I'm certain."

Lois looked like she was ready to say something, but she changed her mind. Saloma gathered little Sarah Mae in her arms and kissed her on the cheek several times. "*Yah,* little dear one. You came along to comfort our hearts, didn't you? *Da Hah* is that way, giving so much more than we deserve. He sends peace again into our hearts."

Ida and Verna glanced at each other and, without a word, headed upstairs. Lois shook her head and left for the kitchen. Debbie turned and followed Ida and Verna upstairs. They had plans to clean the whole house, so she assumed that's where the two were headed. She wondered why they hadn't taken brooms and wash buckets with them. Maybe they planned to assess the situation first.

Debbie reached the top of the stairs to find the two near Ida's bedroom door in

313

animated conversation.

"Sorry," she whispered as she began to back down the stairs.

Ida motioned Debbie over. "I was just trying to get Verna on my side before I told you, but I'm not having much success."

"Tell me what?" Debbie stepped back up. Could this morning get any worse? What did Ida have in mind now?

Verna ignored Debbie and addressed Ida instead. "It's only been two weeks. The man's barely out of the hospital. And he's depressed — extremely. We were over to see him last night and well . . ." Verna let the sentence hang.

Ida's face was set. "All the more reason to ask him." Ida ticked off imaginary numbers on her fingers. "It'll be four weeks by the wedding day. He could use the morale boost. It will get him back into the life of the community. He'll see that nothing has really changed at all."

Verna didn't appear convinced.

Debbie burst in with, "What are you two talking about?"

Verna ignored her again and got in what sounded like a parting shot. "See, Ida, I told you. Now stop interfering." Verna turned toward her. "Ida wants Paul Wagler to fill in for Alvin."

Debbie blanched. "Ida just doesn't give up."

Ida grabbed her arm. "*Nee,* don't think the wrong thing, Debbie. This would be for both of you. It would do you *gut* to keep going with another man in a situation that doesn't mean anything. And Paul needs help after what he's been through. I know him well enough to know that. I did drive to the hospital with him, you know."

"I don't like this, Ida," Verna said. "Let it be."

"Joe can ask him," Ida said. "He's Paul's *gut* friend, and you've already been to visit him."

"What about my opinion?" Debbie got in edgewise. "Don't I count?"

"Oh! *Yah!*" Ida turned toward her. "But surely, Debbie, you can see the sense in this. Besides, it's my wedding. You would do it for me, wouldn't you?"

Ida hit a nerve with that line of thought. Debbie would do just about anything for Ida, and her friend knew it. But still her heart sank at the idea. All she could muster was, "I don't know about this."

Ida seemed content to leave things there for now. "That's okay. Just promise to think about it. Verna, we'll let you know once Debbie decides."

Verna shrugged. "Whatever. Now, we'd better get to work or this house is never going to get cleaned."

Debbie followed the two downstairs, not knowing what to think. Life hurt enough already without any fresh wars that might erupt with Paul. And the last thing she wanted was for Paul to get encouragement for his romantic ideas about her. But neither Ida or Verna had seemed to think this would be a possibility.

Debbie stifled a groan and grimaced as she resigned herself to the cleaning work ahead of them.

TWENTY-NINE

The next Sunday night after the hymn singing, Debbie stood in the line of girls on the sidewalk as they waited for their rides. She'd almost stayed home, but she knew that was no way to act. She had to reject her instinct to crawl into a hole and hide. After all, it would only hurt worse later. One was better off to face things now — even if they hurt.

Debbie peered toward the barn where some of the men were still hitching their horses to the buggies. She was sure one of them was Emery. He'd left for the barn moments ago. Alvin too had scooted out the door some time ago and would be appearing soon. Debbie could feel the other girls glancing at her. Apparently some of them still hadn't heard that she was no longer dating Alvin. But that didn't surprise her. As a couple, they weren't a high priority for the community. Not with other things on people's minds. Paul Wagler was still mend-ing at home, and the wedding season would soon be in full swing.

Ida would be among the first to say her vows. Minister Kanagy had made his appearance again this afternoon. He'd insisted that for once he wanted to take Ida to the hymn singing. Apparently the man wished to give Ida at least the appearance of a formal courtship. Ida had objected to any extra attention expended on her at the expense of Minister Kanagy's children. But the man hadn't budged. He said his sister Lily and her boyfriend, Mahlon, had their own wedding to plan next month. They could do so while they babysat the children. Thus Minister Kanagy had come to pick Ida up that afternoon.

Ida had spurted a few more protests but given in. The two were long gone now. They had been one of the first couples to leave after the parting song had ended. Debbie still couldn't get used to the sight of Minister Kanagy and Ida together. But Ida seemed happy, and what did Debbie know? Look what a mess she'd made out of her dating relationship. Hopefully Alvin had already driven past with his buggy. There would be no reminder that had things gone right, she would be climbing into Alvin's buggy so he could drive her home.

Debbie glanced toward the barn and caught sight of Emery's buggy. She moved toward it but stopped short. Alvin's buggy had pulled out of the line and was waiting by itself. Who was Alvin waiting for? He didn't have any sisters. And Alvin didn't like to wait. Debbie had never made him wait on any of their dates — few though they were.

Then Debbie froze in place at the sound of the washroom door slamming and the sight of Mildred running down the line of girls. A deathly kind of cold crept through Debbie as she wrapped her shawl tighter over her shoulders. Mildred was clearly creating a scene on purpose. She was flaunting her conquest. And it was working. Most of the girls in the line alternated quick glances between Alvin's buggy, Mildred, and Debbie.

Debbie fled into the darkness toward Emery's buggy. She caught a brief glimpse out of the corner of her eye of Mildred climbing into Alvin's buggy. Debbie didn't slow down when she arrived. She pulled herself into Emery's buggy and scrunched down on the seat. "Get me out of here!" she whispered.

Emery stared at her. "Have you seen a ghost?"

"Worse," Debbie managed. "Mildred Schrock just climbed into Alvin Knepp's buggy for everyone to see."

Emery grunted. "Sorry about that." He kept his horse in line for the driveway as they crept past the girls at the end of the sidewalk.

Debbie pulled her bonnet forward and ducked her head out of sight. "Don't stop, please."

Emery clucked his tongue in sympathy. They whirled out of the lane and onto the main road. Emery must think her the biggest failure in Snyder County. The girl who thought she'd become Amish, only to fall over her two big feet and land flat on her face. Emery was so solid, so sure of himself. He'd never understand. Debbie slid even further down on the buggy seat.

Emery gave her a sideways glance. "Don't let Alvin get you down."

"That's easy for you to say," she shot back. "You didn't just see your rival climb into your ex-boyfriend's buggy the Sunday right after he dumped you."

"That *would* be difficult," Emery agreed. "I just think there's plenty of life still open in front of you. Your life isn't dependent on what Alvin does."

Debbie couldn't keep the edge out of her

voice. "Emery, I'm an Amish girl now, and I will be twenty-four next spring. Even if I wanted the attention of another man, which I don't right at this moment, what are the chances for me?"

Emery laughed. "Don't worry, that's all I'm saying. Cry a little maybe. But the morning always comes again."

"That's what they all say," Debbie muttered. "And I'm *not* crying."

Emery gave her a quick look. "He's surely worth a few tears?"

Now she would weep and bawl, Debbie thought. And right in front of Emery. He didn't seem to mind as she pulled out her handkerchief and blew her nose.

"Like I said before, I think Alvin's making a big mistake." Emery smiled at her.

Debbie sat up straighter. "Thanks, but that doesn't solve my problem."

"You're available for Paul Wagler now." Emery's voice was even.

Debbie flinched. "Did you have to bring him up?"

"Sorry." Emery clucked to his horse. "Just trying to help."

Maybe she should ask him about Ida's wild idea. She still hadn't settled on a firm no, not after Ida had rocked her firm resolution to leave the man alone.

Debbie cleared her throat. "Ida wants me to be a witness with Paul for her wedding. Do you think I should?"

Emery's head jerked around. "I thought you didn't care for the man."

"I don't. But Ida thinks the gesture would be nice for Paul. Help him back on his feet and into the community and all that. She claims the event doesn't mean anything. That Paul wouldn't read anything into it."

Emery gave her a sweet smile. "It would be nice of you. I don't see where any harm would be done. But don't encourage the poor man if you don't plan to follow through."

"I wouldn't do that, Emery. I'll think about Ida's suggestion a bit more," she said.

They pulled into their driveway. Emery smiled again when she climbed down to help him unhitch and held the shafts for him.

"Want me to help you put the horse away?" Debbie asked.

He laughed but didn't answer. Emery no doubt knew anything was better than imagining thoughts about Alvin and Mildred together on the couch in the Knepp's *dawdy haus.* Maybe in a way she should be thankful that Alvin had brought things to such a clear end. Perhaps it was better if her dream died a sudden and merciful death. Other-wise in the months ahead she would have been left to wonder whether there could be a chance their relationship might resume. In her head she'd felt like it wasn't possible, but the heart doesn't always listen to reason.

Tears sprang again to her eyes, and Debbie made no attempt to wipe them away. She gazed up into the cloudy sky. So much was over, but no doubt more was to come. Maybe her feelings for Alvin would dribble away in the months ahead. But how did one just walk away from love — or perceived love? She had thought her feelings were real, but apparently she'd been wrong. That was almost an easier thought to bear. Yet it didn't lessen the pain. Was this what Ida had gone through with Melvin's loss? No, a death was much worse than what she was experiencing right now, and yet in some ways this *was* a death. Her hopes must now change, her vision of the future must change, and her expectations of what life would hold must change.

Debbie glanced toward the barn to see Emery reappear. He pulled the barn door shut behind him. He'd already caught sight of her still beside his buggy, so there was no use in rushing to the house to avoid being seen. Emery would know she'd dawdled and was mourning her loss. She decided she didn't care if he knew. His presence soothed her, and he'd already seen the worst of her breakdown when she climbed into his buggy. No doubt she'd made more of a display of her emotions than even she knew.

"Still thinking of Alvin?" Emery teased, coming to a stop near her.

"Maybe, but mostly about how to go on. Seems like everyone else can do it. Ida, for example. With all her losses, how was she able to turn her heart so completely around and love again so soon?"

Emery winced. "Don't ask me about Minister Kanagy or Ida's affections. Not all of us are such self-sacrificing individuals."

"So you think that's all it is? Ida's being self-sacrificing?"

His answer came at once. "*Nee,* Ida's genuine to the heart. It just goes with that type of person, I suppose. You shouldn't try to be like her though."

Debbie laughed but it sounded hollow to her ears.

Emery took a step toward the house, and Debbie fell in beside him.

Changing the subject, Debbie said, "So you really think I should be a witness at Ida's wedding with Paul, even though I will never accept his attention? You said that being a witness with him on Ida's wedding day didn't have to mean anything."

He gave her a quick smile. "I'm glad you're not interested in Paul. That leaves things open for me."

Shocked, Debbie almost stopped walking. She couldn't think of a thing to say.

Emery continued nonchalantly. "And be assured that being matched up as a witness isn't a big deal. Couples do it all the time. Wasn't Ida a witness with Paul at Verna's wedding?"

"She was." Debbie kept a step behind him. "I always thought they should end up together."

Emery gave a short laugh. "You should know by now that Cupid doesn't shoot very straight arrows around here."

Debbie drew in her breath. "How do you know about Cupid? That's not something an Amish man would say."

He grunted. "I heard the story of Cupid in my *rumspringa* time. What there was of it."

"Most men would forget," she said.

Emery held the front door for her.

Debbie pasted on a smile as she stepped inside. She greeted Minister Kanagy and Ida with a "*Gut* evening."

"*Gut* evening," Emery echoed at her

shoulder.

Ida and Minister Kanagy nodded and smiled. They obviously wanted to be alone, so Debbie gave Ida a quick smile and followed Emery up the stairs.

Inside her room, Debbie lit the kerosene lamp and stared at it for a long time before she got ready for bed. Life would go on, she told herself. And she would go on with it. Her heart would mourn when it had to, but it would also heal. She might love again, but she wouldn't concentrate on that right now. She would remember what she already loved — this place, these people, their way of life, their faith. And Emery. He'd driven her home tonight and laughed and teased her like he always did. He'd even joked that he might wish to fill the hole in her heart. That was so kind of him.

THIRTY

Debbie held perfectly still on the hard wooden church bench. This was the most comfortable position at this late hour she could find. The constant adjustment of her position did little to ease the ache that had begun to seep through her whole body. The clock on the living room wall said three, and Bishop Beiler had been preaching for two hours straight now. She'd grown accustomed to the three-hour Sunday morning services, but a service of an equal length held in the afternoon upset any equilibrium she thought she'd developed. But she didn't complain. She'd looked forward to and longed for this day. She would enjoy the day fully. Her first Communion Sunday was finally here.

Even an occasional glimpse of Alvin seated in the unmarried men's section failed to upset her. He didn't look happy in the least. Debbie pushed the pleasure back that had leaped up inside of her earlier. The sight of Alvin in distress wasn't something she should rejoice over. And whatever the cause, it certainly couldn't be due to any trouble he might be having with Mildred. The girl appeared way too pleased for any trouble to have developed in that department. And Debbie wouldn't play that game anyway. If Mildred had won Alvin's heart, Debbie would consider it done fair and square. She'd move on with life regardless how much the loss of Alvin still smarted.

At least she didn't feel much heartache today. And a breakdown of tears right in the middle of the church service would be a disaster. Thankfully, Mildred had the decency to stay out of her way. Even during the noon meal, when each family had spread out in a section of the house to eat, Mildred had managed to stay completely out of sight.

It had been two weeks now since Alvin had cut off his relationship with Debbie. The days seemed longer than that, and yet they didn't. In a way it felt like only yesterday that Alvin had left with his parting salvo: "I think we'd better part ways."

Obviously, Alvin had decided on his own that they couldn't be together. Perhaps that hurt as much as anything — her failure to win his heart. She'd never experienced anything like this before. Always out in the *Englisha* world she'd been the one who held back on relationships. Now she was the recipient of similar treatment. And it stung. Debbie would likely be left high and dry when it came to finding a husband among the Amish — unless she wanted to consider Paul, which she didn't. There were no other unmarried men in the surrounding districts she had the least interest in. True, one could pop up at a wedding or walk in as a visitor. Such an occurrence wasn't uncommon. There could be an unexpected flash of love between their hearts. But she doubted if love at first sight would be her lot. She'd certainly never experienced anything like that before. It didn't fit her. She wasn't one who was easily swept off her feet. Even her attraction to Alvin had grown out of another love — that for the Amish community, she realized.

Debbie shifted on the bench. She really should pay attention to Bishop Beiler's sermon. He was near the part of the story where Jesus suffered in the garden of Gethsemane. The bishop appeared tired; as well he should after, so far, a two-hour sermon. She'd be ready to drop in her shoes. But then she wasn't a minister or used to public speaking.

"And now our Savior entered one of the greatest hours of His trial." The bishop spoke in a steady voice. "The disciples gathered around Him as they entered that garden. But our Savior only took three of them — the ones He'd grown the closest to — further in, that they might be with Him. And so began His sorrows that night, as even those whom our Lord loved the most couldn't stay awake to pray with Him."

The bishop paused to look over the congregation. "How many of us intend to walk with *Da Hah* regardless of how great the trial may be? And yet like those three men, we find our flesh failing us. We must take courage in this story, both in the compassion of our Lord toward the weak and in His strength to complete the journey. In that lies our hope and salvation." The bishop's voice rose in triumph. "Our Lord was able to travel all the way to the cross to bear our sins and to wash them with His own blood. For only through His precious blood can we have hope of obtaining forgiveness of our sins and inheriting eternal life. Thank *Da Hah* that His Son became our Redeemer, that through His name we can be called the sons and daughters of the Most High."

Debbie listened as the bishop worked his way through the rest of the story: the tears Jesus wept in the garden, the arrest, the trial before Pilate, the whipping at the hands of the soldiers, the crown of thorns squashed on His head, the condemnation, the long walk to the cross, those hours of suffering, and His last cry where the Savior commended His Spirit to God.

Bishop Beiler paced for long moments with clasped hands before he continued with the story of the resurrection on Sunday morning. Debbie thought his face almost glowed as he spoke of how the women found the tomb empty and of their wild rush back to tell the disciples of the discovery. And no one believed them!

A smile played on the bishop's face. "This can be a lesson to us. Sometimes our wives see things that we men haven't seen, and we must be open-minded enough to listen. *Da Hah* may have revealed to them what lies hidden to us."

A few of the older men across the room nodded, probably remembering instances when such things had happened in their marriages. Debbie supposed Amish men, just like other Christian men, did need the reminder from time to time of the importance of their wives' counsel. She'd never

331

seen Bishop Beiler run roughshod over Saloma's opinions, but she knew it wasn't unheard of in other marriages. She had only to think of Minister Kanagy seated on the front bench to believe him capable of such a thing. But from what Ida claimed — if she could be believed — even Minister Kanagy had a kinder heart than he let on at times.

Bishop Beiler wrapped up his sermon and called for the bread and wine. Deacon Mast appeared in the kitchen doorway as if he'd waited long for this moment. They all stood for prayer, and the congregation members remained on their feet afterward. From the corner of her eye, Debbie saw Alvin sit down. Then she remembered Alvin had said he had to "voluntarily" stay back from communion. None of it had made a lot of sense at the time. She supposed she didn't understand everything about Amish church maneuvers yet. But Alvin must be surviving his voluntary humiliation if he could date Mildred Schrock so openly and so quickly.

Bitterness ran through her, and Debbie whispered a quick prayer. "I'm sorry, Lord. I don't want to harbor unforgiveness in my heart for Alvin . . . or anyone." The bitterness seemed to fade, and Debbie took a deep breath. If Alvin wanted Mildred

Schrock as his *frau* instead of her, she must not hold that against him. She just wished he'd been man enough to come out and say so instead of going through all that mumbo jumbo about church problems. But then Alvin probably knew more about such things than she did. She must allow for that possibility, and she must forgive.

Debbie gathered her thoughts as Deacon Mast came down the aisle of the unmarried women's section. The deacon broke off pieces of bread from the loaf in his hand for each member. No one had gone over this part of the service with her. Ida or Saloma would have if Debbie had thought to ask, but there had been too much activity recently. Debbie watched out of the corner of her eye as each girl ate the piece of bread given to her and sat down at once. That was different from what she was used to. In her parents' church everyone waited until the entire congregation could eat together.

Debbie took her piece of bread, put it in her mouth, and sat down. She chewed the bitter taste of the unleavened loaf. This was most appropriate, she thought, and so unlike the delicious flavor of the usual Amish homemade bread. They were to remember what the Lord had suffered. Bitter bread made a whole lot of sense.

Debbie caught sight of Alvin's mournful face. As she watched, his face brightened considerably. His gaze had focused on the unmarried girls' section, and he was exchanging looks with Mildred. Her smile had obviously reached his heart.

What did Mildred have that she didn't have? The thought raced through Debbie's mind with a sharp sting. Was that what Alvin had referred to when he'd rambled on at their last date about being "tired of trying, of dreaming big things, of . . ." What had he said? "I just want to be a simple farmer . . . to live in peace and raise my family in the community like I was raised."

Alvin had meant he could do that with Mildred. Debbie didn't want to admit it, but it was true. She'd been rejected for not being good enough. She hadn't supplied the stability Alvin wanted. She would never be a true Amish woman even if she sat and ate unleavened bread for the rest of her life.

The tears stung as they flowed, but Debbie left them alone. If people noticed, they would think she was crying over the joy of participating in her first communion service. *What a disgrace this is! Shedding tears over a man at this most sacred moment.* Maybe she was nothing but a fake. Hadn't she wondered this same thing in those first days when she'd moved into the Beiler home? Maybe she ought to just get up right now and run out. She could let everyone see that Alvin had been right. There would at least be the satisfaction that she'd make one man really happy. Alvin could then congratulate himself for the rest of his life over his wise choice of Mildred over her.

Debbie took several deep breaths. This was only her exhaustion speaking. These feelings of utter failure would soon pass. She knew they couldn't be true. If she needed any proof, she had only to think of Bishop Beiler's confidence in her. He might not know all her secret thoughts about Alvin, but she didn't think that would make much difference to the bishop.

Bishop Beiler's call for prayer brought Debbie out of her thoughts. She stood and remained on her feet with the others when the prayer was completed. The cup of wine was soon handed to her, and Debbie took a sip. When she sat down, the first thought that crossed her mind almost made her burst out in laughter. That had been real wine — and quality stuff at that. Wherever the deacon had shopped, it hadn't been cheap. Now that was unexpected. Her parents' church always used grape juice. Her mom, for all her worldly ways, would pass out in horror if she was asked to drink anything else in church.

Debbie wiped the threat of a smile off her face and put on a sober look. These people had no end of surprises up their sleeves. And none of them were in any danger of drunkenness either. How great of the Lord to send her this little boost of humor right in the middle of the dark vortex she'd almost spiraled into.

Moments later the bishop's voice interrupted her thoughts again as he called for testimonies on the sermon preached. Several more minutes passed as those were given by two older men. A song number was shouted out. After singing, the congregation would wash feet next. Debbie had gleaned this information from past conversations with the Beiler girls. They'd always been glad when the time had arrived because feet washing signaled the end of a long day.

There was more to the practice than simple relief, of course. When they washed each other's feet, the members of the community demonstrated their forgiveness and acceptance of each other and their willingness to serve even the lowliest among them.

Suddenly an unexpected thought entered Debbie's mind. She pinched herself when it first came. She wouldn't do that. It was out of the question. Yet the thought wouldn't go away. If she wanted to live in peace among these people, what better way to continue that journey than to clear the air between Mildred and her? She would wash Mildred's feet.

The thought made chills of rage and fear run up and down her back. She would be admitting defeat by her action, there was no question about that. And what self-respecting girl ever admitted defeat — even in the face of obvious rejection? But that was exactly the kind of worldly thought she wished to leave behind. Debbie decided she *must* do this. For her own sake and for Alvin's. She would release Alvin, and she would forgive Mildred.

Debbie steeled herself with determination. When her row of unmarried women moved toward the wash basins set up in the kitchen, she pushed forward and tapped Mildred on the shoulder. "I'd like to wash your feet," she said with more confidence than she felt.

A look of horror appeared on Mildred's face, but it was slowly replaced with relief as Debbie kept her smile evident. Mildred seemed to know what Debbie was up to as she sat down in front of one of the bowls and held her foot over the water. Debbie sank to her knees and took Mildred's foot in her hands. It was the foot of a farm girl, rough and obviously used to being bare in the garden. Debbie dipped the foot into the basin and splashed water gently over it. Then she lifted Mildred's foot gently and dried it. Then she took Mildred's other foot and did the same.

When she finished, Debbie looked up to meet Mildred's gaze. Her expression was hard to read. The two young women exchanged places. Her own feet in Mildred's hands looked nothing like Mildred's had. Hers were the feet of a city girl, soft and white. She worked outside barefoot occasionally at the Beilers', but she was clearly in another league compared to Mildred. Maybe Alvin had been right in his choice. She wouldn't have wanted to live with a man who always compared her to what he was used to and found her lacking.

Mildred finished Debbie's feet, and the two stood and gave each other the customary kiss on the cheek.

Mildred held her close for a moment and whispered in Debbie's ear, "Thank you for that. I hope you find the love of your life someday."

Debbie nodded, but she didn't trust her voice even to whisper. The two parted, and Debbie found her way back to her seat. This had indeed been a memorable day — way beyond anything she'd expected. Her mother would think she was mad for having washed her rival's feet, but didn't that answer the biggest question of all? She really was Amish, wasn't she? Yes, she was! Debbie answered her own question. And for right now that was all that mattered.

THIRTY-ONE

Ida pushed back the curtains of her upstairs bedroom to look out at the still, dark sky. She'd lit the kerosene lamp moments earlier unable to sleep any longer on this, her wedding day. She glanced at the clock on her dresser. Four-thirty. Ida took a deep breath. She'd been tense all night with a nameless dread that had now disappeared. *Da Hah* had seen her through the days and months since Melvin had passed, and today she would finally be a bride.

Ida rubbed the sleep from her eyes. The faces of Melvin's children had rushed past her all day yesterday. But this wasn't a stuck-together situation with Ben, Melvin's brother, just for the children's sake. Even if it had been, Ida reminded herself that this marriage would have been worth the price to have Melvin's children in her life again. She'd wanted this, and *Da Hah* had mercy on her in granting her desire. He had sent the first feelings of love for Ben into her heart some weeks ago. Who would have thought that Ben had such a tender side to him? Life with him would be pleasant as *Da Hah,* hopefully, would give them many years together. She might actually come to love Ben as deeply as she had Melvin. She was older now, and what she had with Ben would be enough.

"*Yah,* it is," Ida whispered. "It's much more than I ever expected."

Ben had agreed that it would be wise to meet with all the children last night at his place. They had put it off so that Melvin's children wouldn't struggle with the fear of losing Ida again at the last minute. But last night had been a good time to meet. The children were going to be scattered again among Ben's family for a few days. And then they would all be together in one house. Ben and Ida would be back on Sunday night. Ben hadn't requested the time alone with Ida, but wisely she had insisted. They did, after all, barely know each other. Normally a newly married couple had many months together before another person was added to the family. The least she could do was give Ben and her a few days of time alone to begin to establish a solid foundation as a married couple.

341

Ida smiled as she thought about what she'd told Ben. "You might need time to get used to my quirks."

Ben had laughed. "You seem pretty normal to me."

"I might be putting on quite a show," she'd teased. Really, she had been honest with Ben from the start, and so had he been with her. That was a *gut* foundation on which to build a marriage. They could both be thankful for whatever love *Da Hah* had allowed to grow in their hearts for each other.

And by Monday morning, when all the children returned, they would be so buried with work there would be little time for anything else. That was really what had awakened her this morning, Ida mused. Willard, the eldest of Melvin's children. Her largest and most urgent work lay with Willard. He'd never gotten over the shock of finding his *daett*'s mangled body under the cultivator. That was not something a nine-year-old should experience. Willard had been a cheerful, open boy before that day. But he had turned into a ten-year-old who spoke little and walked through life with a closed-off attitude. The happy Willard was inside there somewhere, Ida told herself. If *Da Hah* allowed her to reach Willard, then Ida felt her days on this earth would not have been wasted.

Rosa was eight now, and she had smiled willingly enough last night, clearly happy about this turn of events. At the first chance she had, Ida had drawn Rosa close to her on the couch in Ben's living room and spent an hour alone with her. If nothing else, she wanted to let Rosa see that she would live permanently in her life.

The four youngest had chattered freely last night. Baby Lisa, who wasn't quite a baby anymore at three years of age, kept clinging to Ida's neck. She couldn't imagine that Lisa remembered her from earlier in the spring, but the girl acted like she did. Maybe it was *Da Hah*'s grace showing itself again. Ida wiped away a tear and turned away from the window.

She would love all of the children. There was no doubt about that. Ben's two children had accepted her last night with timid smiles. At least there had been no tense moments, even though their *mamm* had passed away not that long ago. Wilma and John were a testament to Ben's child-raising abilities. He was stern but also kind with his children. Ida liked that combination.

Ida changed into her chore dress as her thoughts turned to Debbie and Paul. If she could only get the two of them together permanently, what an accomplishment that would be. Ida sighed. She really must stop her scheming. That wasn't right. All she could do was pray and help where possible. And at her wedding hadn't Verna tried to help Alvin and Debbie along by having them be table waiters? *Yah,* and so Ida was doing nothing wrong when she'd asked Debbie to be her witness alongside Paul. *Da Hah* knew the man needed to get out of the house and around people again. That had been reason enough to ask him. Ida had thought Debbie wouldn't agree to the arrangement at first. She could be awfully stubborn when it came to Paul Wagler. And Debbie probably had hopes Alvin would return to her someday. Those hopes had, of course, been dashed when Alvin began to date Mildred.

Thankfully Debbie had finally agreed to sit with Paul today. She had given her consent after breakfast on Monday morning. Ida drove to Verna's to inform Joe, so he'd pass the final word on to Paul. The truth was, Ida had Joe approach Paul early last week already to ask him if he'd consider a witness position alongside Debbie. Joe had been told to tell Paul that Debbie hadn't agreed to it yet, that this was all Ida's idea.

344

Ida headed down the stairs with her kerosene lamp. Debbie and Paul were now in *Da Hah*'s hands. The bride-to-be had done what she could. She made her way through the church benches already set up in the living room and entered the kitchen. There were no visitors in the house, which was a strange feeling for an Amish wedding. *Mamm* had actually agreed to keep the wedding small, and all of the immediate families lived in Snyder County. Wayne and Reuben, Ida's two oldest married brothers would come with their wives and family, as would Verna and Joe with little Sarah Mae. Beyond that, Ben's immediate family and the church district had been invited. Ben's youngest brother, Phillip, who was still single, would be up from Lancaster. He'd agreed to serve as Ben's witness from their side of the family, and Ida was glad. Ben's gesture to heal wounds from a past quarrel with the family had been accepted. Quarrels were sad, but their wedding might play a part in the settlement of one.

And Lois would be here — but not Doug. Maybe *Mamm* could have them all back in the house for Thanksgiving, and then Doug and the Beiler family could warm up to each other. Ida doubted it would happen though. The pain Lois had left in *Mamm* and *Daett*'s

345

hearts wouldn't heal quickly.

Ida turned her thoughts back to today. She was happy with her wedding plans. There would be enough people in attendance. And all she really needed was Ben beside her and *Daett* to marry them. That would be a sight, Ida thought, laughing to herself. A couple and a bishop who stood in the living room all by themselves and said their vows.

Nee, she would need more than that, Ida decided. On her wedding day she wanted to be surrounded by her family and the community, and that's just what would happen today. Ben and Ida were not islands in the sea that floated along on their own. They were connected with each other, with family, with the community, each dependent on the aid and love others supplied. This was her world, and she would now go through the rest of her days as a married woman among her people. Even if *Da Hah* should someday choose to take Ben before she passed, she would be known as his widow. Her days as a single woman would never return.

She heard the downstairs bedroom door open. Ida waited until *Mamm* appeared in the kitchen doorway.

"You're up already? Are you okay?"

Ida smiled. "Don't worry, *Mamm*. I'm not having doubts. I woke up thinking about the children."

Mamm sat down on a kitchen chair. "It's hard to let you go, Ida. I guess you know that. But of all my daughters, you're leaving for the most worthy cause."

"Ah, *Mamm*." Ida took a chair beside her. "I love the man too. You know that."

Mamm smiled for a moment. "And I'm glad to see that, but you know what I mean. Don't overwork yourself, Ida. Remember that. And there will be children of your own, I suppose. They take a toll on a woman. You have to pace yourself. You can't carry the whole world on your shoulders."

Ida moved closer. "*Mamm*, please relax. I know all that already. Why are you telling me this now?"

Mamm regarded her for a moment. "I don't know, Ida. Just be careful. No woman knows when it happens until suddenly exhaustion has crept up on her because her life has become nothing but children, and work, and dirty diapers. Don't let that happen to you, Ida. Take time to help with the chores — with Ben. In fact, *make* time. You're not really a house-type woman. Your heart has always been outside. You need that

347

at times. Ben will understand — if you *tell* him."

Ida laughed, the sound soft against the kitchen walls. "You surprise me, *Mamm*. You've never said these things before."

"And you've never wed before, Ida." *Mamm* gave her a direct look. "You don't know how to take care of yourself. You've suffered greatly already, but that doesn't mean you should expect life to only contain pain for you. Make time for you and Ben alone. Even if it means sitting up later to talk *after* the children are in bed. Life can take that away from you, Ida. And it happens easiest for women like you. You need Ben's love, so don't ever be afraid to ask for it, especially when the times get rough."

"Mamm!" Ida felt heat rise on her neck.

Mamm smiled. "I'm afraid the time for blushing is past, Ida. You'll be a wedded woman by tonight. You're getting a *gut* husband, but you're not his first *frau*. He'll have to learn many things over again. You must tell him what's on your mind. Tell him what love means to *you.*"

Ida's face turned even redder. She hid her face in her hands.

Mamm's voice was insistent. "You must listen, Ida. I know what I speak of."

"Ben's been fine about all this, *Mamm*,"

348

Ida protested.

Mamm gave her another look. "It's not Ben I'm worried about. It's you, Ida."

"I'll try, *Mamm,*" Ida said. She really had no idea what *Mamm* was talking about, but she would remember the words for some future time — when and if they were needed. Perhaps there would come a day when the hours were dark and the work of the house too much for her. It would be a relief then to sit down with Ben after everything was quiet and soak in his presence.

Ida got to her feet. "Well, I must get busy."

"Get busy?" *Mamm* glared at her. "Where are you going?"

"Out to the barn. There's choring to do."

Mamm got to her feet. "*Nee,* Ida. It's your wedding day. You'll do no such thing."

Ida allowed a smile to creep across her face. "I want to, *Mamm.* I want to say good-bye to my life as a single girl. I'll be in before long. A few minutes alone in the barn is what I need right now."

Mamm hesitated but soon nodded. "You don't forget what I said now."

"I won't," Ida promised. She slipped into her winter coat and boots in the washroom, lit the gas lantern, and found her way outside. Ida hurried across the lawn and pushed open the barn door. The stillness enveloped her as she hung the lantern on a beam in the barn ceiling. Emery and *Daett* would be out soon, but for now she was alone. Ida walked around and stroked the noses of the draft horses as they stomped in their stalls. She peeked out the back door to where the cows had begun to stir. Several of them noticed her and mooed.

This was a part of her world, and she must not forget it. Whatever *Da Hah*'s plans were for her married life — work, joy, trouble, heartache, loss, and perhaps even *kinner* of their own — she must return at times to this part of her childhood that would always have a special place in her heart.

A lantern bobbed outside. Recognizing the footsteps, Ida turned to greet Emery with a cheery "*Gut* morning."

"What are you doing out here?" he asked with a smile.

"Saying goodbye." She wiped her eyes quickly.

He made a pretend frown. "Don't go crying on me now, Ida." He smiled. "I do wish you the best."

Ida reached out and squeezed his arm. "Thanks, Emery. You've been a kind brother to live with. I hope you find a *gut frau* for your own wedding day."

Emery didn't comment, but he kept smiling as he went to open the barn door for the cows.

Ida lowered her head and hurried out of the barn and across the lawn to the house.

Thirty-Two

Debbie stepped back from the front window to hide behind the curtains as Paul Wagler's buggy turned in the driveway. Minister Kanagy had arrived moments earlier and was in whispered conversation with Ida in the kitchen. The rest of the wedding party was due anytime now. Minister Kanagy's brother Phillip and a friend of the Kanagy family named Carrie would be the witnesses for his side of the family.

Obviously the Amish didn't worry if the couple saw each other before the ceremony like *Englisha* do, Debbie thought. They were much too practical for that. Long before the first guests arrived, the couple would be hidden out in the upper levels of the barn, where the meal would be served. From there they'd make the trek back to the house when it was time for the service to begin. Debbie would be seated on one side of Ida with Carrie on the other. Right up on the front row where everyone could see them. Debbie steadied herself. This wouldn't be too bad. She'd been through much the same thing at the baptismal service. And if she got nervous, she'd remind herself that Ida was the one everyone would be looking at.

Debbie peeked out the window to see Paul's buggy come to a stop. His eldest sister, Esther, jumped down. She proceeded to unhitch the horse. So far there was no sign of Paul. He must be waiting in the buggy, the poor man. He probably hasn't recovered completely from his injury, Debbie thought. Why then had Paul consented to this? Would he take the chance to tease and flatter her again? She didn't imagine that a man in his state would be up to that kind of behavior. Yet one never knew with Paul Wagler.

And that raised the question of why Debbie had consented to sit as Ida's witness today with Paul. The answer was complicated, inspired by her roiling emotions since Sunday and Emery's earlier encouragement. Like Emery said, this didn't really matter in the larger scheme of things. And if it made Ida happy and helped a fellow community member, even if it was Paul, why not? Emery seemed to approve of the gesture. That meant a lot — more than she wished, in fact.

Debbie's thoughts returned to the communion service on Sunday. Her initial euphoria over washing Mildred's feet had soon given way to doubt. What if Alvin thought it was a desperate attempt to win him back? Sort of a show for the whole world that she was able to forgive and leave behind the past. That hadn't been her intention. She'd wanted to create peace between Mildred and her. She hadn't seen Mildred since Communion Sunday, but Alvin's girlfriend had given every sign in the moments after the service that Debbie's gesture had been fully understood, accepted, and appreciated.

Perhaps her desire to move on with her life and truly leave Alvin behind was what motivated Debbie to accept Ida's request. She didn't want a future with Paul, of course, but she did desire a future among the community she loved. Hopefully Paul would understand that her acceptance of being with him for the day wasn't a promise — or even an indication — of interest.

Debbie drew in her breath as Paul finally climbed out of the buggy. His left sleeve hung empty. Debbie knew there hadn't been time yet for fitting a prosthetic limb, so she should have been better prepared for the sight of him in his injured condition. But it was quite a shock. And it wasn't just the missing arm. It was the entire way Paul bore himself. He moved slowly, and his face still bore the marks of pain and suffering. Debbie took a deep breath and steadied herself. It wasn't decent to hide behind the curtain like this. The least she could do was go out and greet him. She was, after all, going to spend the entire day with him. A frank, no-nonsense start was the best approach. They weren't exactly strangers anyway. She and Paul had traded more than one barb, and they'd gone out on a date at a restaurant once upon a time.

Debbie braced herself again, opened the front door, and took the front steps one at a time.

Paul stood beside the buggy as she approached.

His smile was a bit crooked. "*Gut* morning, Debbie." Something of his old attitude flashed in his eyes, but it was quickly gone.

"*Gut* morning," she replied. She fumbled for something more to say . . . but what? Esther had the horse out of the shafts and was leading him toward the barnyard so they were alone. Should she express her regret about Paul's accident? "It's warmer inside. Shall we go in?" she offered instead.

He genuinely smiled this time. "I suppose so." His smile once again disappeared, which was so uncharacteristic of Paul.

Concern surged through Debbie. Maybe she had more of Ida's compassion in her than she knew. She spoke gently. "I'm so sorry about your accident, Paul. It must have been hard. I wish it wouldn't have happened."

He shrugged with his good shoulder. "*Da Hah* makes those plans, I suppose. He strikes down the haughty."

Debbie gave him a quick glance. Did Paul realize she'd seen him clowning around on top of the stack of corn bundles before his fall? He didn't look like he did, but then she'd never seen him quite like this before. Crestfallen. Humiliated. As if the air had gone out of him.

"Thanks for agreeing to this," he said. "I know I'm not much to look at."

"Oh . . ." Debbie tried to keep lightness in her voice. "You shouldn't say that. Besides, this is for Ida and Ben's sake. I'm sure it's good for you to get out of the house too. And you're a *gut* friend of the Beiler family."

He winced. "Nothing like Ida for taking care of people."

"Here." Debbie stepped closer and offered

her hand on his arm. "Shall I help you into the house?"

"Thank you!" He grimaced in pain. "I'd better make my own way. It's not as bad as it looks, although there is still some pain."

But it was, Debbie thought. She watched him out of the corner of her eye as they made their way to the house. The man should really be home still recuperating. His tough constitution from years of outdoor work was probably keeping him on his feet. That and his desire to be out of the house again. That must weigh the heaviest on his heart — besides the loss of his arm, of course.

Paul interrupted her thoughts. "Were you here that day when I fell?"

"*Yah,* I was."

"You told Ida what to do, didn't you?" He stopped to look at her.

Debbie's lips curved up a little. "I said some things. But it was obvious what needed to be done."

He resumed walking. "I thought I heard your voice, but I wasn't sure. Maybe to some people it was obvious, but thanks, Debbie. I could have died, I suppose. Maybe that's what *Da Hah* had planned. You must have changed His mind."

"That's not true!" Debbie gasped. "You

must not think that." This was not good. The last thing she wanted was for Paul to feel he owed her a debt. That would cause a big change in their relationship — and not for the better.

"Thanks, anyway," he said with some of his old determination.

She knew it was useless to protest. Paul would think what he wished. She reached over to take his elbow as they went up the steps. Ida and Ben met them at the front door where they greeted and fussed over Paul for a few minutes. Paul was obviously embarrassed, Debbie thought, but the others didn't seem to notice.

Ben's brother Phillip and Carrie arrived moments later, and the wedding party moved to the upper level of the barn. A temporary woodstove was puffing smoke out of the window. Verna's wedding day hadn't been this cold, Debbie remembered, and no heat had been needed. But they would want all the warmth they could get today.

Paul opened the fire door with his one hand and tossed in a piece of wood. He lowered himself on the bench nearby.

Debbie made a point to sit with him. He needed to be mothered, even if he didn't know it. And this was Ida's wedding day, so some of Ida's ways must be rubbing off on her. They'd be gone by tomorrow, but right now Debbie couldn't imagine the battles she'd often engaged in with Paul or that he'd once openly sought her attention. He looked broken today, as if attracting a girl's affection was the least of his concerns.

She felt drawn to him in a way. Maybe she felt sorry for him. She wasn't sure. Perhaps it was because she knew who Paul used to be that she almost wished he'd be that person again. She glanced around. Ida and Ben were talking in whispers on the other side of the stove. Phillip and Carrie were seated several benches away deep in conversation. Phillip was very handsome. That much Debbie could tell, but she wasn't in the mood to think of that right now.

"Does it hurt much — your arm, I mean?" Debbie ventured.

Paul made a face. "Besides the physical trauma, I'm experiencing 'phantom pains' — that's what the doctors call it. It's when my body says the arm I no longer have is in pain. The doctors don't know when those pains will stop."

Was she also a phantom pain? Debbie wondered. Had Paul forgotten his constant attempts to attract her attention? She'd never thought she'd miss his teasing, but this morning it would have been a pleasure compared to the tortured look on Paul's face. "When will you get a prosthetic arm?" Debbie asked.

"They don't know." He regarded his empty sleeve with contempt. "I have to heal completely first." Moments later he amended his statement. "I have to be ready too, I suppose. That would help."

"You'll be surprised how well they work." She tried to sound hopeful.

He didn't respond and glanced away.

Had she hurt his feelings? She'd only meant to help.

He seemed to read her thoughts. "I'm just touchy about it, I guess. Sorry."

She reached over to touch his good arm. "A man's measure isn't taken by his lost body parts, Paul. It's what's going on in his character that matters."

He snorted. "That's easy for you to say. You're not thinking of living with a man who has a steel arm."

Debbie didn't back down. "If he had a *gut* heart, the arm wouldn't matter."

He laughed but it sounded bitter.

"It's true," she insisted. "Most women don't care about such things."

"Would *you*?" The words came out low.

Debbie didn't hesitate. "Not if I loved him."

He looked away. "Sorry for asking. I'm feeling sorry for myself."

She touched his arm again. "Paul, the right woman will be along for you someday."

A brief look of the old desire flashed over his face, but again it was gone at once. "You're more than kind, Debbie. And thanks again for helping after the accident."

She nodded but said nothing more. This was much more of an intimate conversation than she'd expected to get into. Paul obviously needed encouragement, and he obviously didn't plan to pursue her like he had before. Much had changed between them, and it would take some time for her to adjust.

Minutes later, Paul glanced at her again. "I'm pretty sure you saw me clowning around on top of that wagon, Debbie." He didn't wait for her nod to continue. "Not many people saw that besides you. I'm sorry you had to see me like I used to act." He paused, as if in deep thought.

If Paul was about to say he would change his ways for her attentions, Debbie thought she would scream. She couldn't stand such promises from men, especially after Alvin's repeated and failed promises. Right now she didn't want any assurance from men who needed to mend their ways. She wanted peace. And if God ever sent a man her way, she wanted him to arrive ready to go. Was that too much to ask?

But Paul didn't say anything more.

Ida announced it was time to file into the house for the service to begin.

THIRTY-THREE

Debbie held her breath for a moment as Bishop Beiler concluded his sermon. His face appeared burdened, as if he suffered. Perhaps he was thinking of Lois. He seemed to heave a big sigh before he turned to Ida and Ben seated in front of him. Across the room, in the women's section, Saloma and Verna were trying to smile. They must be feeling the same emotion. Seated between them, though, Lois looked quite happy.

As Ida and Ben stood and stepped forward, Debbie smiled. Bishop Beiler asked the traditional questions, and Debbie watched as the two interacted with the bishop. The bishop would ask a question, Ben would answer, followed by Ida. Their *yah*s hung in the air for only seconds before Bishop Beiler asked the next question.

The words of the vows expressed purpose and determination, just as Debbie thought they should. This befit the occasion of two people promising their lives to each other.

"Do you believe *Da Hah* has led you together?" Bishop Beiler asked.

That question and affirmative answers took faith all on their own, Debbie thought. One could be mistaken, she supposed, as she had been with Alvin. But one must still believe the hand of God worked in one's life. A person couldn't lie about such a thing. And it would be a long time — if ever — before she would venture such an opinion again. Not after the fiasco she'd made of her relationship with Alvin.

Bishop Beiler now joined the couple's hands. A tear was trickling down Ida's cheek, but she didn't wipe it away. Her gaze was fixed on the floor, so typical of her not to want to display her emotions.

Debbie caught Paul's gaze out of the corner of her eye. He had none of his usual teasing look in his eyes. He appeared more mournful than anything. Maybe the exchanging of vows was reminding him of lost dreams and shattered hopes.

Debbie turned her attention back to Ida and Ben, who were retaking their seats. As man and wife! Debbie told herself. A pang ran through her. Ida would never come back to the Beiler household as she'd left it this morning. So much had changed. The upstairs would contain only Emery and Debbie now. It had seemed empty when Verna married last year . . . and even emptier when Lois left. The house will almost seem to ache. Debbie reached up to wipe away her tears.

Seated beside her, Ida seemed to understand. She reached over to squeeze Debbie's hand as the last song was sung. By the time the last note finished, Debbie had herself under control. How strange that she had to fight to not make a bigger public display on Ida's wedding day than Ida herself. As usual, Ida was the mature one.

The service was dismissed by Bishop Beiler, and Debbie waited until Ida stood before she did so. Ben led the way out the door with Ida by his side. Debbie stayed close to Paul as they followed, and Carrie did the same with Phillip.

"Nice service," Paul commented as they made their way across the lawn.

Debbie smiled. "Ida deserved the best."

"She's a self-sacrificing individual, that's for sure," Paul said.

"And kind too," Debbie said, thinking in the back of her mind that Paul could have had Ida's love if he'd pursued her as he had pursued Debbie. Well, it was too late now.

"She'll sure have her hands full with eight

children," Paul said.

"She can handle it," Debbie told him. "I'm wondering if I can handle the loss of Ida. That's what just hit me."

Paul gave her a quick glance. "You've always been close to all three sisters."

"*Yah,* and Ida and I have grown closer since Lois left and Verna married." The observation was perceptive of him, Debbie thought. She wasn't used to this kind of depth in Paul. Perhaps the accident really had changed him like Ida thought it had.

"Do you know him?" Paul nodded off to the side toward Phillip.

Debbie glanced that way. "Not before to-day."

"He's been looking at you all day," Paul remarked, his gaze directed off in the distance.

Debbie laughed. "You're teasing, right?"

Paul shook his head. "You didn't notice during the service?"

Debbie paused a step, but she quickly resumed her pace. "You're not jealous, are you?"

"I'm dying of jealousy." Paul wrinkled up his face in pretend agony.

Debbie laughed. "That sounds more like the Paul I remember."

Paul winced. "It takes more than the loss

of an arm to change a man, I suppose. Although . . ." He shrugged. "Maybe I've been adjusted around my sharp edges. I hope so. I do know I haven't always been . . . appropriate or kind with you, Debbie. Throwing my interest at you like I deserved to be noticed. I'm sorry for all that."

She gave him a steady glance. "You don't have to apologize to me, Paul. And you still are a man, you know."

"A man with feelings," he admitted slowly.

Debbie drew in a deep breath. Was he trying for her attention again? "Paul, don't go there. Not today. Not with me."

Paul glanced at his empty sleeve, but he kept his walk steady as they entered the upper level of the Beiler barn. Paul took his seat without comment. A shaky smile was pasted on his face.

The last thing Debbie wanted to do was fight with Paul on Ida's wedding day.

People came by to express their congratulations to Minister Kanagy and Ida. Debbie snuck a glance at Paul and tried to say something appropriate. "I'm glad you had the courage to come out and attend the service today. It meant a lot to Ida, and I think it's good for you."

He nodded.

She was used to Paul in all his glorified

honesty, even if it made her angry. This new attitude would take some getting used to.

He leaned closer. "I was glad to help out." He looked hopeful. "I know I was clumsy, but perhaps we could have a fresh start now that Alvin . . ."

When she didn't respond a shadow crossed his face. "I was sorry to hear about Alvin. I really was."

"You don't see me dancing in the streets," Debbie retorted.

Paul was silent for a moment. Finally he said, "I guess I was just hoping, that's all."

What was she to say to that? "I'm not the girl for you, Paul," she asserted as gently as she could. "Someday you'll find the woman for you."

"I suppose you're right," Paul sighed.

She reached over to squeeze his hand. That Paul still cared about her was a little bit flattering. She decided to admit it. She gave him a sideways glance. "You're a sweet man on the inside, Paul. Thanks for still thinking about me that way. I'm flattered."

"You're welcome." He added, "So, we're still on speaking terms?"

She returned his smile. "At least for Ida's wedding day."

He laughed, the sound infectious. His laugh sounded almost like it had before his injury. Maybe she had done Paul some good today, which would be a great thing to happen on Ida's wedding day. Ida would appreciate that.

THIRTY-FOUR

The late-afternoon sun hung low in the sky. Ida's wedding was over. Debbie stood beside Paul's buggy as he pulled himself up with one arm. His face was etched with pain as he took a seat beside his sister Esther. With a quick wave Esther took off down the lane. Paul barely attempted a goodbye. He was obviously tired and in pain. He shouldn't have stayed this long, Debbie thought. He was barely fit to leave the house this morning, and yet he had come. If she hadn't insisted over an hour ago that Paul consider a return home, he'd still be here. Paul had exhausted himself well beyond his current endurance level. That wouldn't be good for Paul's long-term health and recovery.

From the other side of the lane where a small group of people had watched Paul leave, Minister Kanagy spoke up. "That was the smart thing to do. He was obviously tired."

Debbie nodded as she walked over and joined the group.

Ida clung to his arm and agreed with her new husband. "He was really suffering." Ida glanced over at her friend. "Now Debbie has no one to sit with her tonight."

Ben's face brightened at once. "Phillip has offered a suggestion, and I kind of like it. He's offered to take Paul's place, and one of our cousins can sit with Carrie. I'm sure Debbie wouldn't mind."

"Oh!" Ida hesitated. "Well, *yah,* if you think so."

Debbie exchanged looks with Ida. She didn't want to reveal that she didn't want to sit with the handsome newcomer because of the many stares he'd cast her way all day.

Ben grinned. "I think this will work out well. Let me go confirm it with Phillip." He sent a meaningful glance toward Debbie before heading to the barn. Debbie let out a sigh. First she had had to deal with Paul's semi-unexpected attention. Now this Phillip cousin. What if he asked her home for a date on Sunday night? That is, if, as expected, he stayed over the weekend to visit family. Well, she would just tell him *no.* That's all there was to it. She wasn't ready for a romantic adventure. Not until she was sure *Da Hah* was behind it.

Ida walked over to Debbie. "I saw the way you were so kind with Paul. That was nice of you."

Debbie shrugged. "He was at the end of his rope and too stubborn to admit it."

"I noticed you spoke with him a lot." Ida continued to probe.

"We had a good time . . ."

Ida brightened a bit. "Maybe the sparks will fly for you yet."

Debbie laughed. "You have some impractical theories, you know that, my friend?"

"I know," Ida admitted. "I guess I should stop worrying about other people and find Lois while I have a free minute. I really need to thank her for making the extra effort today. My wedding wouldn't have been the same without the awesome food she and *Mamm* prepared for the noon meal. And there's more coming tonight, I'm sure." Ida turned and rushed off toward the house.

Debbie waited. Ida would never stop showing her concern for people. It was her lot in life. She always seemed to know what needed doing. Like thanking Lois for her help with the wedding. Lois had appeared cheerful enough all day, but she was here without her husband. That must wear on her. Whether Doug was Amish or not, he was still her husband.

Debbie walked toward Minister Kanagy as he came out of the barn with a big grin on his face. She already knew the answer from Phillip long before she reached him.

"Phillip is more than glad to help us out," Minister Kanagy said. "He said he almost feels like he knows you." The man's eyes twinkled. "I want to take this chance to tell you, Debbie, how much I appreciate how you've been handling yourself since Alvin is no longer seeing you. Ida told me it was all Alvin's doing. And I've noticed he's already dating Mildred. Not that there's anything wrong with that — other than his hurting your heart. Some young women might have gotten bitter through the experience. I'm glad to see you're not holding anything against him. Ida told me about you asking to wash Mildred's feet at the communion service. No one was expecting that of you, Debbie, but you did it anyway. This is something we can all be thankful for — having someone like you living amongst the community. I sometimes don't even think about you coming from the outside anymore. It's as if that never was."

Debbie felt herself turn red. "Thank you, I appreciate that."

Ben smiled. "You're welcome. And I'd best be off to find Ida, my *frau*."

Debbie directed him toward the house with a wave of her hand. When he was gone, she stood silent and amazed. After all his months of scrutiny, she had finally managed to impress him. She had received praise from Bishop Beiler *and* Minister Kanagy.

A shadow crossed Debbie's face at the memory of Paul's assertion that he still cared about her. Paul had probably accepted Ida's invitation to serve as a witness out of his friendship with the Beiler family, yes, but his purpose had gone deeper. He had clearly hoped he'd have a chance to advance his continued affection for her because Alvin was out of the way. Apparently he hoped to win her over before another man got in his way again.

Debbie told herself she ought to be honored with the continued attention from unmarried Amish men. But the one man she'd wanted to marry hadn't seen things that way.

Debbie's brow furrowed as she thought of Paul. The poor man.

But right now she'd better get ready to meet Phillip Kanagy or he would catch her flat-footed. The man was good looking, Debbie admitted.

She walked back into the barn and up the stairs. She stood by the upper barn door looking out. Below her the washroom door opened, and a long line of teenaged girls walked out for the evening hymn singing and supper. The older boys had already gathered outside the barn where they'd pair up with the girls before they took their seats.

Debbie watched Ida come out the front door of the house and run across the lawn to join Ben. They hurried into the barn, and soon Debbie heard them thump up the stairs. She turned and watched them go to the head of the line and take their places at their table. An unfamiliar man was already seated with Carrie, who appeared happy enough with the change in plans. Now what was Debbie to do? Ida hadn't said anything as she zipped past. And she was taken up with Ben at the moment.

Well, Phillip could find his own way, Debbie decided. She would take her seat. She hadn't taken more than a few steps when a man's deep voice stopped her.

"I'm right behind you."

A quick retort sprang to Debbie's lips, but it died when she turned around. Phillip was much more handsome than he'd appeared at a distance. Much more!

"Debbie?" he asked, though it was obvious he knew good and well who she was.

She relaxed. "And you're Phillip."

"That's my name." He smiled. "I hope you don't mind the change in plans. That fellow you were with today seemed like a very decent man. Sorry about him having to leave."

"Poor Paul," she murmured. "He put himself out for the Beiler family today."

"That was very thoughtful of him. Ben told me all about him." Phillip motioned toward the table where Ida and Ben were sitting. "Shall we be seated?"

Debbie liked how he took charge yet wasn't bossy. And he sounded like he cared about Paul's condition, and yet he wasn't full of angst that she'd been with him all day.

"Are you a local?" Phillip asked as he glanced her way.

Debbie smiled. "*Yah,* you could say so." Apparently no one had filled Phillip in on her past history or he was a very good actor. She decided to see how long she could convince him she was raised Amish.

"I know you're Debbie, but that's about all. I don't even know your last name."

"Yoder," she said lightly, watching his face. He didn't register any surprise at the Amish name, but Ida clearly heard. She gave Debbie a sharp glance. Debbie smiled at Phillip. "Actually, I'm a Watson — Debbie

Watson. I was *Englisha* until I graduated from college. I've boarded with the Beilers for a long time, and it seems like I've always been drawn to the life of the Amish community. Now I'm Amish. I joined the church only recently."

The drop of his mouth was unmistakably genuine. And he seemed, well, interested. Intrigued almost.

"Is that really true?" The surprise still lingered in his eyes. "I believed you when you said your name was Yoder. You look quite Plain."

She smiled. "I was raised living next door to the Beilers. I hung around with the Beiler sisters — Verna, Ida, and Lois. When I finished college, I made the jump . . . once Mom pushed me out of the nest, so to speak. And here I am."

"You're baptized in the Amish faith?" His expression revealed his fascination.

She nodded. "This fall, *yah.* I just had my first communion."

He seemed pleased. "And where was this college you went to?"

Debbie hesitated. "Does that make a difference?"

"Just wondering," he said.

"Do you know anything about *Englisha* colleges?"

He laughed. "*Nee,* but you seem to have made it through okay without getting corrupted."

He was hitting all the right buttons, Debbie thought. And he hadn't picked a fight yet. Phillip maneuvered around her feelings like a man sure of his grasp on the tiller.

"Franklin and Marshall was the college." She added, "In Lancaster."

He didn't miss a beat. "Nice college. I've driven past there often. It's a nice choice of location."

Debbie smiled. Maybe this evening wouldn't turn out so badly after all. Then she caught sight of Emery talking with Crystal at the young folks' table. Why on earth was Emery with Crystal? Did he feel sorry for her? Or was there a deeper motive?

"What's wrong?" Phillip asked, noticing her distress.

"Nothing . . . I hope." Debbie forced her attention back to Phillip and resumed their casual chatter.

THIRTY-FIVE

Ida got up from the couch to take another glance out the living room window of the home she now shared with Ben. It was Sunday, and the children ought to be arriving any moment now. She could hardly wait! Ben was reading his copy of the weekly *Budget* and was digging deep into the bowl of popcorn she'd prepared. The past few days since the wedding had gone by so quickly. Ida wondered if they'd allowed enough alone time before the children arrived, but Ben didn't appear unhappy, so he must be okay with the plans.

He noticed her glance and smiled. "They'll be here soon enough."

"You don't mind then?" She hesitated. "All of them coming at once. I will be busy, you know."

He grinned and reached for her hand. "You'll always have time for a kiss, won't you? Like right now? A kiss for an old man?"

"You're not that old!" She playfully slapped his cheek, but then she planted a kiss firmly on it. He set *The Budget* aside and gathered her in his arms. Ida remembered this was how they'd first kissed. Heat still rose in her face being this intimate, even though they were alone in the house. It would take her a while to get used to the fact that she was Ben's *frau* and that kisses could come at unexpected moments like this.

"We can't be doing this when the children are around," she said.

His smile didn't fade. "Then I'll be remembering them in my mind."

"You say such nice things." She stroked his beard.

His eyes twinkled. "That's because you're nice."

"Maybe it's because you're a *gut* man," she corrected.

He grunted. "Now you'll have me blushing."

So he'd noticed her constant blushes. Well, she was a young bride. Young brides were supposed to blush. A shadow crossed her face.

"Did I say something wrong?" he sounded concerned.

"Nee." She gave him a warm smile. "I was

just thinking of Paul and Debbie."

He touched her hand. "I wouldn't worry about that. Would you object to another Kanagy dating a Beiler?"

Ida looked up in surprise. "Phillip? Phillip and Debbie? Why didn't you tell me?"

He shrugged. "I was thinking of other things." He smiled. "And it's not a sure thing. Phillip is interested, but I don't know what arrangements they made, if any. Phillip doesn't exactly talk with me about everything . . . yet."

She gave him a baleful glance. "Then you don't know anything. You're guessing . . . and hoping. Well, I still wish Paul and Debbie would come together someday. Even if Phillip is your brother."

"You never were one to shy away from the truth, Ida." He sounded amused. "I guess love lies in the hands of *Da Hah* . . . and Debbie and Phillip . . . and Paul."

"Yah," Ida agreed. "I must stop trying to help *Da Hah.* I have other things that need doing."

"Yah, I would think so," he said, motioning toward the front door.

Ida jumped up when she heard the sound of buggy wheels in the driveway. Her hands flew to her face. "Oh, Ben, they're here!"

"Yah." He got up and took her hand.

381

"Let's go welcome *our children* home."

She clung to his hand and felt great waves of joy rush through her. She'd never doubted Ben's resolve to take Melvin's children in, but now that the moment had arrived to hear him say *our children . . .* Oh, it was almost too much to take in! She needed to receive this great privilege and blessing one *slow* breath at a time. *Breathe, Ida. Breathe.*

Ben's sister Lily was waiting beside the buggy with a big smile on her face. All of the children except for three-year-old Lisa were gathered around her, uncertain where to go or what to do. Lisa was still sitting on the buggy seat. Ida let go of Ben's hand and headed straight for the little girl. She reached in, gathered her into her arms, and smothered her with kisses. Then Ida set Lisa on the ground and glanced around. Maybe this was a bad start, showing such emotion right away. But Ben had tears in his eyes, as did both of his children, eighteen-year-old Wilma and sixteen-year-old John. They had their *daett*'s gut heart inside of them, Ida decided.

She gave Wilma and John quick hugs. Wilma clung to her for a moment, but John was a little stiff. Ida decided he wouldn't like hugs in the future. And he was almost a

382

man, so that was understandable. And she wasn't his mother, so she'd try to remember to give him plenty of room. The last thing she wanted was for Ben's children to feel uncomfortable around her.

Ida took four-year-old Lonnie into her arms next. He smiled up at her, his face glowing. "It's really you!" he said. "Are we going to live here all the time now?"

Ida choked back the sobs, unable to answer. Five-year-old Ephraim and six-year-old Amos joined their embrace. They created a little circle of heads around her body. Ida was crying with joy. All three of these boys would be hers forever! Their tender hearts were still flexible enough to make room for her with only minor adjustments. And they'd been young enough to have been spared the brunt of sorrow associated with their *daett* and *mamm*'s passing.

Ida untangled herself from the arms of the three young boys. She approached eight-year-old Rosa. She wiped her eyes, and reached for the girl. Rosa's return hug was a little weak. Ten-year-old Willard was totally stiff and unresponsive, but she already knew he would be. Willard was the one she'd prayed for the most, and she could again see why. His heart had been deeply wounded, and only *Da Hah* would be able to break through. Still, she gave Willard a long hug and whispered in his ear, "It's so *gut* to have you home."

He didn't say anything.

Ida stepped back, let out a long breath, and smiled at all of them. "Well, you have come!" She stepped next to Ben. "We welcome you to your new home. Why don't we all go into the house, and we can start getting to know each other better."

That seemed to break their trance. The three boys raced for the house, with Rosa tagging along behind them. Willard headed toward the barn without a backward glance.

"Where's he going?" Ida asked Ben

"Willard has chores to do," Ben said. He glanced toward his two children. John gave his *daett* a quick nod as if he understood and walked toward the barn.

They knew it was best if Willard wasn't alone, even if he wished to be, Ida thought. Deep gratefulness rose up inside her. She whispered, "Thanks for everything you're doing, Ben."

He stepped closer to slip his arm around her. "You were right from the start, Ida. I should have seen it myself about my brother's children. I've always loved them, but they grew even dearer to my heart in the week they were here before the wedding."

"Well, I guess I'd better get out of here," Lily said loudly.

Ben laughed. "You have your own wedding coming up next week. You'll be getting plenty of hugs yourself, so don't look so innocent."

"I can't wait." Lily grinned as she climbed into the buggy. "See you soon!" And with a wave she drove out of the lane.

Wilma was almost at the house, Ida noticed. She left Ben's side to hurry after her. She caught up with her at the front steps and stopped to catch her breath. "Will you fill me in on how you've been running the household? I do declare I'm getting to be an old woman."

Wilma smiled. "You look quite young to me."

"Thank you!" Ida returned. "How did it go with all the children?"

Wilma looked pleased that Ida was consulting her. "We were just doing the best we could. The relatives helped me before the wedding to clean the house." Wilma made a wry face. "That's why things were decent when you got here on your wedding night. It wasn't because of me." She frowned. "I'm glad to hand running the house over to you."

"I'm sure you did great." Ida laid her hand

on Wilma's shoulder. "Between the two of us, we should manage just fine. Now, what kind of meal schedule did you have?"

Wilma didn't answer for a moment. "I kept *Mamm*'s ways, but you don't have to."

Ida drew Wilma close. "I know I'm new here and have my own ways, but that doesn't mean we will change everything. For one thing, that's what your *daett,* John, and you are used to. And we want everyone happy, don't we?"

Wilma glowed. "You're everything *Daett* said you were."

Ida blushed and hid her face for a moment. "I'm sure your *daett* doesn't know everything about me."

Wilma didn't appear convinced. "He's had a few days with you, and he looks quite happy."

Ida took Wilma's arm. "Please know I'm not trying to take your *mamm*'s place, Wilma. And you've been running the household for quite some time now. I don't want to just step in and take over. I hope you know that."

Wilma sighed. "No one can take *Mamm*'s place. Thank you for not trying. *Daett* said you'd be like that too."

Ida looked away. "What else has your *daett* told you?"

Wilma laughed. "Only nice things, believe me."

"Well, that's a relief." Ida let out a long breath.

"We usually have supper at six," Wilma offered. "And I did laundry on Mondays — when I got to it. The situation was getting pretty serious, believe me, with those three boys living here. *Da Hah* knows I love my cousins, but they are a rambunctious bunch. They needed a clean set of clothes every day!"

Ida smiled. "I believe you. We'll have to see what we can do about sharing the load and corralling the boys."

Wilma's eyes widened. "You plan on taming them?"

Ida didn't hesitate. "The truth is, I don't know. I'll consult your *daett,* and we'll do what we can. Boys and girls can learn how to play without rolling in the dirt like farm animals."

Wilma beamed. "You are a *wunderbah* woman!"

"Let's wait and see how things work out," Ida corrected. "I'm sure there will be bumps along the way." Ida led the way into the house. "Shall we begin fixing supper then? I believe you and I handle things similarly, so let's stick with that schedule for the time being. We'll be flexible, of course. One must always be flexible because change happens."

Wilma's smile widened. "I think I'm going to like having you here very much."

"You're a *wunderbah* young lady," Ida said. "Any handsome men knocking?"

Wilma turned all shades of red.

Ida gave her a quick hug. "I'm sorry if that was too direct. You don't have to tell me. But I'm here if you ever want to talk or you have any questions or concerns you want to work out."

Wilma shook her head. "I'm okay. Well, everything seems to be going okay . . . umm . . . I don't have any questions right now."

"That's okay." Ida gave Wilma what she hoped was a helpful smile.

Wilma looked at her pensively. "How did you marry *Daett*? I mean, how did it start? Was it a sudden thing?"

Ida breathed deeply as they walked into the kitchen. She hadn't planned on having this conversation so soon, but why not? Wilma had a right to ask. Ida was, after all, the new woman coming in to take charge of the household. And she did want a close relationship with Wilma. So what better time than now to begin?

"Maybe we'd better sit down." Ida motioned toward a chair and took one herself. "When your *daett* first showed an interest in me, I immediately thought about how the two of us, if we got together, could raise your uncle Melvin's children. But marriage is holy, and it requires much more than wanting to help someone else. I suffered a lot with the death of your uncle Melvin. I thought *Da Hah* had led me to him, and that we would be spending our days getting old together and raising the children."

Ida gave Wilma a quick glance to gauge her interest level. Had she said too much? No, the girl appeared interested.

Wilma reached over and touched Ida's arm. "I can only imagine the sorrow you felt."

Ida continued. "After that I wasn't so concerned about feelings or what I thought life should be like. When your *daett* noticed me after the funeral and I could see his interest, I couldn't think of any reason why I shouldn't say *yah.* I knew he needed more help. And after we talked and he said he was willing to bring all of Melvin's children to live with us, I knew it would be a *gut* situation. Isn't that how *Da Hah* works? And soon *Da Hah* gave me love for your *daett* and all of you on top of everything else." Ida stopped as she blushed. She decided that was enough to say. Wilma would have to be satisfied.

Wilma, though, wasn't finished. "Have you ever loved someone who didn't love you back?"

Ida met the girl's gaze. "Oh, Wilma, is that what you're going through? The boy you're interested in doesn't return the feeling? *Yah,* I once did love someone who didn't return my love."

A tear glittered in Wilma's eye, but she quickly wiped it away. "I don't know. But he . . ."

"I know it's hard. It will be okay, sweetheart." The words spilled out of Ida. "You have nothing to worry about. *Da Hah* will see that the right man loves you someday. If it's not to be this one, you can trust *Da Hah.* He knows what's right."

Wilma studied her face. "You know of this then?"

Ida winced. "*Yah,* I know of it well."

A soft smile spread over Wilma's face. "Thank you, Ida. I'm glad you've come to help us. Our lives will be better for having you here."

Now I will cry, Ida thought. She stood up and wrapped Wilma in a tight hug. Ben interrupted them a minute later when he cleared his throat from the kitchen doorway.

"Is supper coming up anytime soon?"

"Men!" Ida huffed as she wiped her eyes. "They never give women a moment's peace."

Ben laughed and disappeared.

"Thanks for loving my *daett*," Wilma whispered. The two embraced again.

Thirty-Six

Debbie slipped out of the house toward the barn. It was Wednesday, and she shouldn't have waited this long, but she'd wanted to be sure lest she act in haste. Even now she really didn't have the time for this with all the work that needed doing. And yet this had to be done. Emery had shown an interest again in Crystal at Ida's wedding, and Debbie couldn't live with herself another moment if she didn't at least speak with Crystal. Emery obviously had a soft spot for the woman. Bishop Beiler evidently believed Crystal had the same interest she had about joining the church. But it wasn't the same at all! Debbie was sure disaster was lying in wait if some things weren't corrected.

Maybe it had been Ida's wedding day and the sight of Lois there without her husband that had finally made it clear to Debbie. Whatever the reason, urgency had risen up inside her. She must speak with Crystal before an unmarried Amish man fell for her, especially if it was Emery!

She entered the barn and approached Emery as he fed the cows. "Emery, I need the address where Crystal is staying."

"And why's that?" Emery asked in surprise.

"I want to speak with her. I saw you with her at Ida's wedding."

"Yah." Emery chuckled. "What do you plan to do?"

She frowned. "Emery, I just don't like this situation. Someone has to talk sense into that woman, seeing as you don't seem to comprehend the danger."

"You think I'm going to fall in love with her?" He smiled. "You're worried I might love her?" he asked with a sly grin.

Debbie held out a piece of paper and a pen. "I know she has relatives in the area and is staying with them. Please write down the address."

He scribbled on the paper.

Her heart sank. Despite her bravado, she was hoping he didn't know it.

He handed back the paper. "You've got this all thought out, it seems."

She ignored the comment. "Yes, I do. Someone has to speak to her."

Emery shrugged. "She's not staying with a family in the community. She hasn't behaved in a questionable way as far as I know — in the community or outside. You can't just order a person away. Especially one who is seeking faith and peace. Be careful."

She hesitated. "How do you know where she lives?"

Emery met her gaze. "It's common knowledge, Debbie. My knowing means nothing."

Yes, it does. She almost said it aloud, but managed to hold it in. She went instead to catch and harness Buttercup.

Emery helped her, but they said nothing more. They hitched the horse to the buggy, and Debbie climbed in. When she turned down the driveway, she saw him standing in front of the barn watching her drive out.

This morning Debbie had almost spilled her plans to Saloma, but she doubted if Saloma would think Crystal's presence was a matter of concern. Why was everyone so blind when it came to Crystal? Did they think because they'd been wrong about her, that they might also be wrong about Crystal? Debbie pulled up for a stop sign. As usual, blame for all *Englisha* things eventually landed back on her.

She shouldn't blame Saloma for her lack

of interest when it came to Crystal. Saloma was still mourning the loss of Ida not being at home. They hadn't spoken of it, but Debbie knew. Adam and Saloma were both struggling to establish a new routine now that all three of their girls were married and gone . . . now that Debbie was the only girl to help on the farm. Saloma bore the brunt of the loss of Ida since she'd assumed Ida's chores.

Debbie pushed her thoughts away and turned on the lane toward the small town of Penns Creek. Buttercup settled into a comfortable gait that would eat up the distance. Debbie's thoughts drifted back to Ida's wedding and her time with Phillip. She sighed. She really didn't want to think about the man. She wouldn't allow herself to fall for an unobtainable dream again. Alvin had taught her that much. Her heart still needed healing before she could ever consider another man. Phillip would return to Lancaster next Thursday for Lily's wedding. Debbie had agreed to sit with him at the hymn singing in the evening when all the Amish youth were paired up with someone. With that ahead of her, she might as well think about him. The evening wasn't a date, which is why she'd agreed to it. She would have to sit with someone, so why not

Phillip Kanagy? He probably felt the same way, so that was that. Phillip would have come straight out and asked her for a date if he was interested in her that way. It wasn't like he was shy. The man could handle himself quite well.

Paul would be disappointed that she wasn't available to sit with him. But he shouldn't be. She'd told him she wasn't interested in romance with him. She hadn't given him any encouragement even though he continued to express affection for her. Yet Paul was more humble since his accident. He'd come down some from his high horse. And he was a known quantity. But that wasn't enough. She would never marry him.

So why shouldn't she consider Phillip? Was she frightened of being in another relationship? She didn't really know Phillip, but that was why one dated someone. Debbie thought of Emery in the barn this morning and sighed. She was realizing she was drawn to this man who was almost a brother to her. That was the real problem. She had no right to think of Emery as a possible husband, and so soon after Alvin. What was wrong with her? Why was she so tempted with something that couldn't happen? Yet, Emery was a real man, a solid man, and that's why she was on her way to see Crystal. Emery couldn't ever be her husband, but if she could help it neither would Crystal. Crystal was not what was best for Emery.

Debbie sighed. Why she was dwelling on men and romance, she had no idea. She still needed time to heal from the treatment Alvin had given her. But here she was, with the attentions of a possible new beau in front of her — and the wrong one at that. If anyone knew that she harbored even the slightest interest in Emery as a husband she'd be the outcast of the community for sure. "Gold digger" wouldn't come close to what she'd be called.

Debbie pulled to a stop at the lone stop sign in Penns Creek. Enough of Phillip Kanagy. She would deal with him later. She turned left after the road cleared and found the address. An open parking spot was next door, so she tied Buttercup to a telephone pole there.

Going up to the house, Debbie knocked.

The door was opened by a woman who appeared friendly. "May I help you?" she asked.

Debbie smiled. "I was wondering if I might speak with Crystal?"

"You're in luck. Crystal just came home

from Mifflinburg." She held out her hand. "I'm Margaret. Crystal's been such a nice boarder. Are you a friend?"

"No, I'm just . . . an acquaintance. My name is Debbie." Had Crystal lied about having family in the area?

Margaret ushered Debbie into the living room. "Crystal! Someone is here to see you."

Footsteps came down the hall immediately. Crystal exclaimed, "Debbie! What a nice surprise!"

Debbie's resolve wavered. "Good morning. I thought I'd stop by to see you . . . and talk." Crystal was a beautiful woman, even more beautiful in her *Englisha* clothing. She'd been beautiful in Philadelphia, Debbie remembered. No wonder both Alvin and Emery had fallen for her.

"You want to talk?" Crystal was puzzled, but she motioned upstairs. "My room is up there."

Debbie followed her after a brief nod to Margaret. Crystal held the bedroom door open, and Debbie took the only chair in the room.

Crystal made herself comfortable on the bed. "So what brings you here?"

They could be two sisters meeting for an evening talk before retiring, Debbie thought.

Only they weren't. This was much more dangerous business than that, and the stakes were much higher.

Debbie gathered her thoughts. "I know we see each other at church, but let me explain who I am and why I'm here. I first saw you in Philadelphia with Alvin. I'd driven there to talk to him, but he wasn't home. Alvin and I had been interested in each other before he left for Philadelphia. I was waiting outside in my car when Alvin, you, and a large dog walked toward the apartment building. I was so shocked I didn't even get out of my car. Oh, in case you're wondering, I was driving a car because I originally came from the outside world — the *Englisha* world, as the Amish would say."

Crystal nodded. "I knew you were Alvin's ex-girlfriend, and that you came from . . . our world. But I didn't know about Philadelphia. That is interesting."

Debbie continued. "I'm here, Crystal, because I want to straighten some things out. Things can't go on like they have been. No one else has told you this, I'm sure, but I'll be direct. You will never be allowed to marry an Amish man. Within the Amish faith a man cannot wed a divorced woman."

Crystal raised her eyebrows. "I realize

that. I've read some of the *Ordnung* rules and studied the Amish people. I know every community is different though."

"If you join the community, are you prepared to live as a single woman?"

Crystal gazed out of the bedroom window. "I haven't decided about joining. There is another option, you know."

Debbie looked puzzled a moment, and then she gasped. "You wouldn't do that. You couldn't!"

Crystal smiled. "Maybe, maybe not. I have a right to happiness. Even with an ex-Amish man. It's happened before, you know. An Amish man leaving the community isn't the end of the world. You and I both know that."

Debbie clutched the edge of the bed. "That can't happen, Crystal. That would be wrong. Terribly wrong! Leaving the community means giving up everything the Amish person has known and experienced. What if you get an Amish man and one day he realizes what he's lost? You'll lose his heart. The Amish people have deep roots in family and the land. His heart is wrapped up in the community. That doesn't change by saying marriage vows."

Crystal met Debbie's gaze. "Are we in competition by any chance?"

Debbie kept her voice steady. "I don't

know what you mean."

Crystal laughed. "A woman knows, Debbie. I can see it in your eyes. You're in love with Emery and want him for yourself. Well, so am I, and so do I."

Debbie controlled her voice. "No, Crystal. Emery's the bishop's son. He'll lose the farm and anything else he has if he leaves the faith. And if he leaves, Emery may never be allowed back, and he can never just take up where he left off. Especially if he marries you. And what if he finds out he's made a terrible mistake? I guess that's happened to you before."

Crystal frowned. "My past is none of your business."

"When the marriage doesn't work out, you can always find someone else and marry again. Emery would never have that option. He wouldn't be allowed to marry among the Amish. Are you willing to put him through that depth of sorrow? And all for a few years of happiness on your part — if it lasts that long. Your world is not his world. I know. I come from yours, and now I'm in his."

Crystal regarded her for a moment. "So what's in this for me? If I abandon my hopes, what benefit do I get? Am I to do that because I love him so much?"

"I don't believe you love him that much," Debbie said. "I'm hoping I can appeal to your sense of what is right. You surely understand that concept. Leave and let Emery get over his attraction to you. He'll be the better and the wiser for it. If you stay nothing good can come out of it."

Crystal stood. "I'll think about this."

Debbie rose and offered Crystal her hand. "We have all been shown great mercy by the Lord." The two shook, and Crystal led the way downstairs. After saying goodbye, Debbie walked to the parking lot and untied Buttercup. Hopping into the buggy, Debbie drove south with only a brief backward glance. Everything would be okay, she thought. The community would never see Crystal again, and Emery was safe. Crystal would do more than think about this. She would leave now that light had been shed on her plans. "Thank You, dear God, for Your help," Debbie prayed, her face lifted toward the sky outside the buggy door.

THIRTY-SEVEN

Debbie sat quietly beside Emery as the two made their way back to Lily and Mahlon's wedding site for the evening hymn singing. Emery had been cheerful all day. In fact, he'd been extra happy since the weekend when Crystal hadn't shown up. Did Emery approve of what she had done? The thought took her breath away.

But she had other things to think about since Friday night. Alvin and Mildred had shown up at the Beiler place. Seeing them pull into the driveway had sent Debbie in a beeline for her room upstairs even as she wondered what in the world those two wanted with the bishop.

It had taken a while to figure that out, but once she listened to the murmuring of voices downstairs, the reason dawned on her. Alvin and Mildred wanted to be married this fall. There could be no other explanation. Distress should have ripped through her heart, but peace came instead. She'd healed faster from Alvin's betrayal than she'd imagined possible. In fact, she'd considered going down to make the two feel welcomed, but that would have been a little much. Her expression of forgiveness and acceptance to Mildred at the communion service was sufficient.

After Alvin and Mildred left, Saloma told Debbie that she'd been correct. Bishop Beiler would publish Alvin and Mildred's wedding for the last Thursday in November.

And that's what had happened on Sunday.

How Alvin had managed to put their love in the past so quickly did sting a little, Debbie admitted to herself. Obviously she'd been a mere fascination for him and nothing more. How could she have been so wrong? She told herself it was time to move on . . . to look forward to whatever God had in mind for her.

There was so much for her to be thankful for. Crystal hadn't attended the service or the hymn singing on Sunday. Debbie thanked God for His mercy and grace. He had blessed her trip to Penns Creek. Perhaps she should have asked Emery about Crystal on Sunday, but instead she'd waited to see what would happen. She figured Emery would speak about Crystal when he was ready.

On the buggy seat beside her Emery must have read her mind. He turned and asked, "What did you tell Crystal last week anyway?"

"I said only what needed saying, Emery."

He grinned and lapsed into silence.

She ventured a look in his direction. "I wish you hadn't been tempted by her."

"Who says I was?" Emery asked, sober-faced now.

Debbie took a deep breath. "Please don't be tempted to see her or ask her to stay, Emery. She knows what's best."

Emery nodded. "I agree. But honestly, I'm not tempted. Crystal said she was considering joining the community. She liked the peace and harmony we have and I believed her."

Debbie grimaced. "Would she have done it, Emery? I think we both know better. She only wanted to steal you away."

He grinned again. "No one's stealing me."

"That's *gut* to hear." Debbie tried to breathe evenly. She'd said way too much. Thankfully Emery didn't appear offended. "I care about you, Emery. I care about you a lot. I couldn't sit by and watch Crystal destroy your life."

"Nothing was happening," he protested as they arrived at the Kanagy home place. "But thanks for caring."

"I'm glad you think so," Debbie said as she climbed out of the buggy. She reached in and gave his hand a squeeze and smiled warmly. He smiled in return and drove on toward the barn.

Debbie paused to catch her breath before she went inside the washroom. She'd ventured where angels feared to tread for the sake of Emery and had survived by the mercy of God. Beyond that, she'd better not go.

Debbie stepped inside the kitchen to find a roomful of girls spilling into the living room. All of the couple matchups for the evening had been done, she guessed. Two boys with notepads still hung around the front door looking for stragglers like Emery and herself. One of them headed out the door toward Emery while the other glanced her direction. He looked down at his pad and smiled. She had no reason to feel embarrassed. Phillip Kanagy was going to take her to the table tonight. It was an honor to be chosen ahead of time. With her inappropriate thoughts about Emery, she ought to let go tonight and get lost in Phillip's awesome smile, in his understanding of her feelings, in his instinctual touch he seemed to have. Wasn't that what she wanted? A man who understood her for once? Who didn't have to be led along and encouraged constantly like Alvin Knepp and wasn't impossible like Emery?

Debbie's thoughts were interrupted by the sight of Phillip among the crowd of men outside the barn. She caught only a momentary glimpse through the kitchen window. He was as handsome as ever. He seemed so perfect! Can anyone be perfect? She'd heard there was a problem within the Kanagy family. Perhaps Phillip was the black sheep? Had he done something to cause a rift? Minister Kanagy's piercing looks during her months of instruction classes flashed in front of Debbie's eyes. It wouldn't take much to earn Minister Kanagy's disapproval. Ida claimed Ben had a kind heart underneath all that strictness, but that didn't mean he would slack off when it came to church matters and discipline.

Debbie sighed. All this was just to avoid thinking about Emery, which wouldn't work anyway.

Debbie pressed through the crowd in the kitchen and moved into the living room looking for Ida. After searching downstairs, she went upstairs. The first bedroom door was ajar, and Debbie peeked in. Ida was on the bed beside the youngest of Melvin's children, little Lisa, who was fast asleep. Ida noticed Debbie and smiled. She put her finger to her lips before tiptoeing out into the hallway.

"The poor thing is just exhausted," Ida whispered. "I'll wake her in a minute since supper's about ready to start."

Debbie nodded. Ida was clearly in her element now, surrounded as she was by eight children. If there had been any doubt that Ida was up to the task, they'd been vanquished in the two weeks since the wedding.

Ida spoke softly. "How's things going with Phillip?"

"Okay, I guess." Debbie forced a smile.

Ida glanced away. "I'm not getting involved this time, Debbie, I've worked so hard for so long encouraging you to accept Paul's attentions. And you never would consider it. I figured it was time I stopped."

Debbie considered this for a moment. "Well, I know you care about me. But I still want to hear what you think. Don't ever be afraid of advising me. You're like a sister to me, you know."

Ida smiled. "I won't. I care deeply about you. I do have my hands full now with a husband and eight children. In matters of the heart, I'm afraid you'll have to make up your own mind. My advice? Just follow your heart. It led you to us, didn't it? And *Da Hah* will keep you on the right path if you ask Him to help you."

"Thank you, Ida," Debbie said. From downstairs came the rustling of clothing and the decrescendo of voices, so she surmised the girls were heading out. "It sounds as if the girls are leaving. I guess I'd better go join them."

Ida squeezed her arm and disappeared back into the bedroom. Debbie made her way down the stairs and moved to the front of the group of girls. She'd be expected, as one of the oldest unmarried girls, to lead the way just behind the girls who had established relationships.

Soon she would be the oldest unmarried girl. The current wedding season would marry off most of the older dating couples. Maybe the single life was an option for her. It had its pleasant side. She could live on the Beiler farm until Emery married . . . but that might not be so very long. Emery would soon find the right girl and settle down.

Debbie sighed. She should prepare her heart for the single life, but the vision she had of being an Amish farmer's wife was still strong. She envisioned a life of morning and evening chores, of cows that needed care, and, perhaps, children of her own to care for someday. Children who would have what she'd always dreamed of while she grew up — the soil of a farm to call their own. She wanted them to experience open fields in winter right outside bedroom windows, the longing for spring to arrive, and fascinating moments watching a summer thunderstorm move toward the farmhouse, knowing it would bring life-giving water for the livestock and the family for the months ahead. How could she leave that vision behind? That was the question. But it took a man to realize such a dream. And that seemed quite impossible at the moment.

THIRTY-EIGHT

Through the open, pole barn door where Lily and Mahlon's wedding meal had been served this afternoon and the hymn singing would be held tonight, Debbie caught a glimpse of the old woodstove the Kanagy family used to heat the building. Minister Kanagy, his back turned toward her, threw in fresh wood. Her feelings were still mixed toward the man.

Debbie turned her thoughts to what was going on ahead of her. The steady couples matched up first. The boys coming out of the group gathered near the pole barn to join their girlfriends. Debbie drew in her breath as Alvin approached Mildred and took her hand. Mildred glowed, just as she should be. She had, after all, pulled off quite a coup by snatching Alvin from the affections of another girl — her — and now they planned to wed not many weeks later.

A man's voice coming from her side made

Debbie jump. "Lost in your own beautiful world?"

"Not so beautiful," Debbie replied without much thought.

Phillip didn't miss a beat. "That your old flame ahead of us?"

He already knew, so she didn't answer.

His voice was sympathetic. "Maybe we can steer over in this direction instead." His hand touched her arm lightly and guided her to an empty table. He seated her looking away from Alvin and Mildred.

Other couples soon filled in the empty places at their table. They were of a younger age group. Across the room Emery took his seat alongside an Amish girl. At least Crystal was out of the picture! Debbie thought. More power to Emery for seeking an Amish *frau*. Now if her heart didn't stir at the sight of him, she could be more responsive to Phillip's attentions. The least she could do was try, even though she wouldn't get too far.

"Thank you," Debbie whispered to Phillip. "You knew just what to do."

Phillip nodded. "Weddings can make the heart throb again."

"Just for the record, I'm supposed to be over him." Debbie spoke out of the corner of her mouth to avoid detection. "Their

412

wedding date was published last Sunday."

"Don't give up hope. Maybe there's someone else for you."

"Do you plan to take advantage of the brokenhearted?"

He laughed. "A beautiful girl like you? Who wouldn't be tempted?"

Debbie's heart melted a little. He really knew what to say and how to say it.

Minister Kanagy stood and led out in the prayer. As soon as the amen was said, Phillip asked, "What did you think of the wedding today?"

"It was nice, I guess. I wasn't really paying attention. My mind was elsewhere."

"Is Ida settled in with my brother?" His smile was bright.

Debbie was about to answer just as the first dish of food came around the table. She took a portion, passed the dish on, and said, "Ida's taken to the children quite well . . . and to your brother." Debbie took a deep breath. Should she say what she really felt? Now was her chance. "Your brother has always seemed to me to be, well, a bit harsh. But Ida says he's really very kind . . . tenderhearted."

He didn't flinch. "She's his *frau* now. I'd expect Ben to say nice things to Ida."

Debbie ventured further. "From what I

413

gather . . . and I could be wrong . . . his feelings for family don't carry over to you quite as much." She kept her gaze on his face. His smile was gone now. Had she struck a nerve?

"Let's say we have our differences." He took a bite of food and didn't look at her. "Did you figure that out yourself or has Ben been telling tales?"

Debbie hesitated before she plunged forward. "He's told me no tales. In fact, he's the one who persuaded me to accept you as a replacement the evening of his wedding."

"Ben approves of . . ." his eyes were wide, ". . . of you and me?"

Debbie finished her bite of food. "I suppose so. Did you think otherwise?"

For the first time he stumbled for words. "I, well, I thought Ida was behind it. She's on the kinder side, you know."

"Yes, I know. But not this time. It was your brother."

"Ben shouldn't have done that."

They ate in silence, uncomfortable with each other for the first time.

"Confound that Ben!" Phillip finally said. "He messes in everything I do."

"What is there between the two of you?"

"I'd better not say. One doesn't go spilling family secrets."

"Fair enough." She decided to change the subject. "What do you do in Lancaster?"

He grinned. "I run a siding crew for a large company. Nothing illegal."

"No interest in farming then?" The words slipped out.

He snorted and passed her another plate of food. "That's one irritation between Ben and me. He can't imagine a Kanagy who isn't a farmer. I was the youngest boy — the one who wouldn't follow the family tradition."

"That doesn't sound serious enough to split a family." Debbie motioned toward the center table where Lily was laughing with her new husband. "Why didn't your sister ask you to be her witness today?"

His face darkened. "Tread softly, my dear."

Debbie glanced away from his gaze.

He touched her hand under the table. "I'm perfectly safe, Debbie. Even with your charming face, your beauty, your . . . well, everything about you."

She tried to breathe. If Ben's words to Ida were anything like this, no wonder Ida's heart had melted like butter. The Kanagy men sure had a way with words.

Debbie sighed. "Maybe we'd better just enjoy our food."

Phillip smiled. "Enhanced, of course, by the presence of a gracious lady."

Debbie cringed as her gaze settled on Emery seated beside the Amish girl she didn't know.

Phillip's hand found hers under the table once more. "I must have said something wrong, so let's try this again." He paused for a moment with his fingers wrapped around hers. "I'm Phillip Kanagy. I left the family farm some years ago to work in Lancaster, Pennsylvania. It was after a tiff with my family, I admit, but now I'm happy as a bug in my own little rental outside the small town of Whitehorse. I'm living amongst the rolling hills of Lancaster County Amish country."

"That's good, but it still doesn't work for me." Debbie couldn't help herself. The sight of Emery with his head bent toward the Amish girl pushed her over the edge.

His fingers tightened on hers. "Now why would a beautiful girl say such a thing?"

She pulled her hand out of his. "Because you and I don't work."

"Fair enough," he sighed. "You're an honest, wholesome soul. That's important to me."

Debbie waited as the dessert bowl came around. She kept her gaze away from Emery.

Phillip took his time dipping out a small portion before he held the bowl for her.

"No hard feelings then?" He regarded her with interest.

She shrugged. "No, no hard feelings."

He took a bite of date pudding.

Debbie went on. "I've had some practice in the art of trying to draw wandering Amish prodigals back to the faith. I lost someone I consider a sister — Lois Beiler — and I was worried about losing someone I consider a brother. An old boyfriend wandered into the world for a time too. And now there's you. Perhaps that's all I'm good for in the community."

As the meal concluded and the singing began, Debbie was relieved at the opportunity to focus on something else. She wasn't surprised that Phillip didn't reach for her hand again, although he was nice enough and she enjoyed his presence. Clearly the wind had gone out of the sails of any possible romance. She knew he wouldn't ask her for a date on Sunday night. When the last song was sung, he'd walk out the door to return to Lancaster. She would not hear from him again, but her heart simply couldn't open up under the circumstances.

As they parted when the singing ended,

he leaned over and whispered, "The best to you, beautiful one. I wish it could have been different."

She didn't have a response, so she didn't say anything.

Across the room Emery and the Amish girl shared a hearty laugh.

THIRTY-NINE

Ida rose before dawn on Thanksgiving morning. Ben was still asleep and the alarm wasn't set to go off for another ten minutes. She lit the kerosene lamp on the dresser and changed into a work dress. She was ready to slip out of the bedroom when Ben stirred.

"*Gut* morning," he called sleepily. "What time is it?"

"Time to get up." Ida shut off the alarm. She stepped over to the bed to kiss Ben on the forehead.

He groaned. "Can't we sleep in on Thanksgiving morning?"

"It's up to you," she said on the way out. "I'll have breakfast ready soon."

She knew he'd be up and dressed soon now that he'd awakened. Ben didn't need an alarm clock, and neither did she. They were creatures of habit, and already their household routine was well-written in their minds and hearts. Ida smiled to herself. She'd never imagined that life could hold so much happiness. The work was intense, of course, but she'd never minded work. And the children made the love in her heart bloom. Ben was all a husband should be — tender with her heart and firm with the children. All these *gut* things were so much more than anything she'd expected even in her wildest dreams.

Ida wiped away a tear as she entered the kitchen. Perhaps this was one of the blessings that came because she hadn't had dreams about Ben. She'd had dreams about Paul Wagler, and look how that had worked out. This was much better than anything she'd imagined with Paul. Leave it to *Da Hah* to know what's best.

Ida heard footsteps approach and a smile softened her face. Ben was up, and his voice soon hollered up the stairs, "Time to get up, children!" Moments later he was in the kitchen where he paused to give her a playful kiss.

"I'm busy," she protested, but she allowed herself to be gathered in his arms for a quick hug. Ben's beard brushed her face. Ida hoped her face wouldn't still be red when Wilma came down. She was a young bride, and her love for Ben was nothing she needed to feel ashamed of. Still . . .

Ida bustled about the kitchen, and moments later Willard was the first child down the stairs.

"*Gut* morning," Ida greeted with a warm smile.

"What's for breakfast?" he asked.

Ida gave him a quick hug. He didn't usually stop to chat, so she wanted to grab this moment. She smiled down at him. "Not much. Just cereal. We'll have a big noon meal over at *Mamm* and *Daett*'s place later."

"At your *mamm* and *daett*'s place?"

She ruffled his hair. "*Yah,* mine."

Out of the blue, he blurted, "Why did my *mamm* and *daett* have to die?"

The question took Ida's breath away. She'd expected it, but not now. Not on Thanksgiving morning right when breakfast needed her attention. And the other children would soon be down. In fact, footsteps were already sounding on the stairs. A moment later Wilma and John appeared in the doorway. She greeted them, and John went out into the washroom where he banged around as he pulled on his winter clothing. Wilma appeared perplexed as to why Willard was still standing in the middle of the kitchen.

Ida took Willard's hand. "We'll be a moment, Wilma. Will you please put the water on to boil for the oatmeal? We're just having cereal this morning. And then I'm going out to help chore."

Wilma headed toward the cupboards while Ida took Willard by the hand and led him into the living room. Once they were seated on the couch, she answered him. "I don't know why your *mamm* and *daett* were taken. Sometimes we have to just trust in *Da Hah*'s wisdom when our own wisdom and knowledge fail us. I'm glad you trusted me enough to ask."

She stroked his forehead while Willard seemed to be processing the information. At least the boy was talking to her. She'd waited so long for this moment.

"Why is *Da Hah* so mean?"

Ida pulled Willard tightly against her. "He isn't mean. What He does is always for our best because it's for His best. And He never leaves us or forsakes us — if we don't forsake Him."

"Did Barbara have to die so you could be our *mamm*?"

Ida was surprised. *What a horrible thought,* she wanted to say. But that wouldn't help. Clearly, Willard had been thinking long and hard in his silence.

"*Da Hah* is good," she responded. "He

doesn't do wrong things and then try to make them right. Barbara was diagnosed with cancer around the same time as your *daett* passed on. God must have wanted and needed both over there. It just took Barbara longer to leave."

"Did Barbara look like *Daett* did when I found him?"

Ida pressed back the tears. Of all *Da Hah*'s ways, this one she'd struggled with the most. Why had Willard been the one to find his father? She choked back the sobs. "I wish you hadn't found your *daett* that way, Willard. That must have been extremely hard to see."

"*Daett* would still have been like that even if someone else had found him."

"*Yah,*" Ida said. What else was there to say?

"Did *Daett* do something very wrong? Like when I need a whipping?"

"No!" Ida clung to Willard and buried her face in his hair. "You must not think that. It's this awful world that we live in. The sin, the evil that people do, the wickedness. Life can be like a bucket of slop, and we get splashed sometimes. You mustn't blame *Da Hah*. He uses the wrongs of the world to make us right."

"Will I die under a cultivator too? With my bones sticking out?"

Ida struggled to control her voice. "We all die differently, Willard. And on the other side is joy beyond what any of us can imagine. Hasn't *Da Hah* given you back to me? Isn't there joy growing in our hearts? Maybe *Da Hah* allowed our great sorrow because He knew there was a way we could still be together."

Willard nestled tightly against her side. Ida reached into her dress pocket for her handkerchief. Willard straightened and got to his feet. "I'd better be going to help chore."

Ida nodded. "I'll be out soon."

"Don't cry too much." He stroked her arm, and she dissolved into fresh tears.

"I'm crying because I love you, and I'm sorry you had to experience that."

The boy stared at her for a second and then quietly slipped away as Ida dried her eyes.

She got up and went into the washroom. Pulling on her winter coat and boots, she stepped out under the star-studded sky. When she entered the barn, Willard glanced up from where he was milking the cows. He gave her a slight smile.

"Thank you, dear *Hah,* for reaching that boy's heart," Ida whispered.

"Coming out to help?" Ben asked in greeting. He sent a quick glance toward Willard. "Why was he late?"

"We were talking," Ida said. Ben seemed to notice her tear-stained face for the first time. A look of comprehension dawned. He nodded.

Ida got busy. As she helped with the cows, her thoughts turned to last night. She'd finally asked Ben more questions about Phillip, mostly because he seemed so interested in Debbie.

"I said some things to Phillip I shouldn't have said," Ben admitted. "All of us boys at home were farmers, but Phillip hated the life. He didn't just leave, Ida; he shook the dust off his feet. He said things he shouldn't have said. I, in turn, said things about his heart not being right with *Da Hah* and that Phillip thought he was too high and mighty for Snyder County. We all thought he was going *Englisha,* and he still might."

"Have you told him you're sorry?" Ida asked.

Ben nodded. "Many times. But Phillip doesn't want to open himself to his family again. He's thrown us all into one basket, even though I was mostly to blame. It's a miracle he agreed to be my witness at the wedding. I don't think Lily dared ask him."

"That seems a little harsh on his part,

turning away from his family," Ida commented. She didn't want Debbie married to a man who had this kind of reaction to his family.

"Debbie can do him a lot of *gut,*" Ben said, as if reading her thoughts. "It may be *Da Hah*'s way of bringing our family back together. The right *frau* can help a man greatly. Look at how much *gut* you've done me already."

She colored then and changed the subject. Ben was prone to exaggerate. His explanation of his brother didn't quite fit. There must have been harsher things said than Ben let on. That was how such things went in the heat of the moment, and later they could be difficult to heal. Perhaps Debbie was the one to heal the Kanagy family? Ida would have to pray and hope things would turn out for the best. She wouldn't interfere this time, that was for sure.

After finishing her part of the chores, Ida returned to the kitchen to find the table set and the oatmeal steaming. She gave Wilma a warm smile and went to get the smaller children up.

By the time the men returned from their chores, all the children were gathered around the table. Ida had little Lisa in the high chair, and she almost didn't fit anymore.

Willard looked happy this morning as they bowed their heads in prayer. While Ben spoke, Ida breathed her silent thanks. "O, dear *Hah,* the Maker of all that's *gut.* Thank You for what You've done in my heart and for the love I have for Ben and for these children. You've allowed so much into my life. You've even given me Wilma and John's acceptance. They could have made a fuss about me trying to take their *mamm*'s place, but they have shown me nothing but love." She wiped the tears from her eyes as Ben said "Amen."

No one seemed to notice her tear-stained cheeks as they passed the food and chattered softly around the table.

"When are we leaving for the turkey dinner?" John asked.

"Around ten or so, I believe," Ida answered, giving Ben a quick glance to make sure.

"That sounds fine with me," he said between spoonfuls of oatmeal. "We can be very thankful the Beilers are opening their home to us this year. For Christmas, we'll be over at my family's home farm."

"Sounds good to me," Wilma said.

Ida detected a touch of sadness in her

voice. "Are you missing your *mamm*'s side of the family today?" Ida ventured.

Wilma nodded and looked away.

Ben cleared his throat. "I'm thinking you and John might want to drive over to the Yoder farm this afternoon to say hello. That's where the family's gathered this year. Everyone should be there, and I'm sure they'd love to see you."

Gratefulness flashed across Wilma's face.

How kind of Ben, Ida thought as she gave his hand a quick squeeze under the table.

"You don't mind, Ida? Do you?" Wilma's timid question broke into Ida's thoughts. "I mean . . . I do enjoy your family, but . . ."

"Sweetheart," Ida responded gently, "I have no problem with that. You mustn't ever lose contact with your *mamm*'s side of the family."

"Then it's settled!" Ben declared.

He didn't like weepiness, so Ida gave him a warm smile of appreciation.

Moments later they gathered in the living room for their morning devotions. Ben read a portion of Scripture from the book of Psalms, chapter 80, where David wrote, "Give ear, O Shepherd of Israel, thou that leadest Joseph like a flock . . . Turn us again, O God, and cause thy face to shine; and we shall be saved."

Ida thought how that could be her prayer for the days ahead. She pulled little Lisa against her. She hoped *Da Hah* would continue to keep His face turned toward all of them — and Debbie too. Debbie needed comfort and direction. And something wasn't right between her and Emery. Ida sensed an unsettling tension between them.

FORTY

The Thanksgiving meal lay spread out on the Beilers' table. Debbie paused for a moment to catch her breath. Verna and Ida were both working in the kitchen, and Lois stood at the table putting the last touches on the tossed salad by sprinkling cheese over the bowl.

When Debbie let out a sigh, Lois sent a smile her way. "Tired are we?"

"A little," Debbie admitted. She sent a quick glance toward the men in the living room. "I think we ought to sit around like they do." Lois didn't say anything as she continued to work. Debbie glanced at the group of menfolk again. They were all sitting around lazily on the couch and chairs, deep in conversation about their farms. Emery was in the middle of a story about an incident that happened this week. She wondered if he had that Amish girl from the wedding dinner in the back of his mind as he talked. But that wasn't her place to imagine. Emery's thoughts were none of her business — as long as they didn't involve Crystal. Emery had every right to take any Amish girl to the table he wished to.

Debbie hadn't asked the Amish girl's name, but from the look on his face the next morning, Emery had enjoyed his evening with her. Debbie considered teasing him about the mystery girl while they did the chores, but she knew he'd shoot right back about Phillip. Still, Debbie wanted to know more. She felt like she wouldn't be able to completely put the evening behind her until she did. Maybe tonight after a happy Thanksgiving meal . . . with pumpkin and pecan pie for dessert . . . Emery would be in a talkative mood.

Debbie rallied her spirit as Saloma approached Lois, who was still bent over the salad bowl. "Is there anything I can do?" Saloma asked, her voice rising above the men's conversation.

Lois shook her head. "We're ready."

Saloma seemed happy today. Maybe she could forget for a few hours that her youngest daughter had gone *Englisha.* Lois hadn't dressed Amish, but she had on a deep-blue, solid-colored dress. It could pass for an Amish imitation if one didn't look twice. At least Lois had finally learned how to deal with her parents. Maybe the day would come when Doug would consent to visit.

She should visit her parents this afternoon, Debbie reminded herself. Things had been very tense these past months because of not helping with and attending Lois's wedding. Debbie admitted that she'd been too wrapped up in her own world to think of a visit home, which wasn't good. She'd have to remedy that soon. Maybe Verna and Ida would walk down the road to her parents' place with her. It would be like old times.

Debbie allowed a smile to creep over her face. So much had changed since those days. And most of it for the better, even though there had also been plenty of sorrow and heartbreak. Lois moving to the *Englisha* world. Alvin deciding to marry his childhood sweetheart. On the last, so much for her pride, she thought.

Saloma walked into the living room and whispered in her husband's ear. Debbie jerked herself out of her thoughts to hurry into the kitchen. The family would soon be seated, and here she was lost in her own thoughts.

"It's ready!" Verna said, greeting her with a smile.

"You did such a *gut* job helping *Mamm,* Debbie," Ida added. "I don't know what she'd do without you."

"I didn't do that much," Debbie protested. "Would the two of you consider walking down with me to my parents' place this afternoon?"

Before they could answer, Saloma called from the kitchen doorway, "Time for prayer, girls!"

"Of course," Verna and Ida said together in answer to Debbie's request. Then Ida led the way to the table. The rest of the family filed into the dining room. The two oldest sons, Wayne and Reuben, seated themselves first, and their wives and children clustered around them. Lois fussed over everyone. Debbie wondered if Lois realized that she'd always be Amish at heart, even if she denied her heritage.

Verna sat down at the other end of the table where Joe had positioned a high chair for Sarah Mae. Ida blushed as she took her seat beside Ben and their eight children. The table had been stretched out yesterday to the fullest, with four leaves added from the upstairs storage room. Still they barely fit.

Debbie waited to take her seat, in case they'd missed someone and needed another chair. Saloma gave Debbie a grateful smile. Today Debbie was taking her place in the family like she'd never done before. In more ways than one, she was the Beilers' daughter. This was how the three Beiler girls would be behaving if they still lived at home.

Debbie finally seated herself across from Wilma and John. They both smiled. Wilma whispered, "Everything looks very *gut,* Debbie!"

"Thank you," Debbie whispered back just as Bishop Beiler led out in prayer.

With the "Amen" said, the food was passed and the turkey was carved by the bishop himself.

"Now watch that hand!" Wayne hollered out. "We don't want you in the hospital on Thanksgiving Day."

"I'm not that old," Bishop Beiler grumbled as everyone laughed.

He was though, Debbie thought. His age showed. They could all laugh, but they also knew the truth. Adam and Saloma were getting up in years. And Debbie was here to help them in their old age. This was an honor she never imagined would be hers. She decided she'd even follow them to their *dawdy haus* if they'd let her. That way she could still help, and Emery would be able to settle on the farm with his *frau.* Perhaps he was already contemplating vows with the mystery girl who had finally won his attention. At least this girl wasn't *Englisha.* Debbie wiped away a tear before she passed the mashed potatoes. John caught her eye and she whispered in his direction, "Just thankful, that's all."

He nodded as if he understood. "We too have much we can give thanks for. Ida's blessing our home with her presence. We all think *Daett* chose well in picking a new *frau.*"

"That's nice of you to say," Debbie told him. "Be sure to tell Ida that."

He nodded again before saying, "I will."

Conversation continued around the table as the turkey, dressing, potatoes, and cranberries were eaten. When everyone was finished, Debbie stood up to clear some dishes from the table and make sure Saloma kept her seat. Lois jumped up at the same moment to add her support.

Saloma gave in with a sigh. "I guess I am getting old."

"Nee," Lois said, patting her *mamm* on the shoulder, "it's just your turn to be served."

Debbie and Lois took the dishes to the sink and returned with some of the pies Lois had baked yesterday.

Reuben, the second of the Beiler boys,

took his piece with wide eyes. "I need a pie maker like this at my house!" He glanced at Lois.

"Yep! No one can match Lois for pie making," Wayne seconded.

"Now, now," Lois chided. "You're hurting your *fraus'* feelings. And who said I made these?"

"We know you did," Reuben said. "And our women are quite secure. They know that all men are attached to their family's cooking."

"They can outdo you in other things," Wayne added, and Reuben nodded his agreement.

When the first pies were devoured, Debbie went to the cupboard and pulled out two more. After she took more empty plates to the sink, she picked up several pie crumbs from an empty pie pan with her finger. They melted in her mouth. No one could match Lois's piecrusts. She deserved all the praise she'd received from her brothers and then some.

By the time the last pie had been passed around and eaten, everyone was talked out. The men took their seats again in the living room and leaned back for quick naps. Debbie helped the women and girls clear and wash the dishes. With so many willing hands, the task didn't take that long.

Verna went upstairs to put baby Sarah Mae down for her nap. Debbie waited until Verna returned to bring up the subject of visiting her folks again. Lois was still in the kitchen, but the other women had pulled up chairs beside their husbands.

Debbie took a quick glance around before she asked Verna, who was standing at the bottom of the stairs, "Would it be okay to leave now? Or do you need to stay here for a while?"

Verna smiled. "*Mamm* can keep her ears open for Sarah Mae's cry, and Joe can live without me for an hour or so."

"You want to ask Ida then?" Debbie asked. "She's already in the living room next to Ben."

Soon the three put on their winter coats and were on their way out the driveway. Wilma and John were in the yard, their horse hitched to a buggy. Ida hurried over to speak with them. Verna and Debbie waited at the end of the lane until Ida caught up.

"Wilma and John are leaving to visit their *mamm*'s folks," Ida explained. "They want to keep contact with that side of the family. I think that's a very *gut* idea."

"As always you're thinking of others,"

Verna said with a smile. "I agree that is the right decision."

"How do you know your parents will be home today, Debbie?"

"Unless they've changed their habits, they will be."

"Old people rarely do," Verna volunteered.

"We're all getting older," Debbie said.

Verna gave her a sharp glance. "You don't sound so happy about it. I heard you sat with a very handsome man the other day. Tell me about him."

Debbie laughed abruptly. "Phillip Kanagy. He was very good looking, but I'm sure he's not going to call on me."

"Are you sure?" Verna asked.

"Nothing's happening with him," Debbie asserted, looking the other way.

"She sounds bitter." Verna glanced at Ida.

Ida nodded. "I know. I'm worried about her."

Debbie frowned. "Stop it, you two! I'm resigned to being an old maid if I must."

"That won't happen!" Verna declared. "Look at the two of us! We're married and some people thought we never would be."

"Maybe we'd better stay out of Debbie's love life this time." Ida's voice was sober. "I know I've meddled enough. I'm sorry, Debbie. I'll pray instead that *Da Hah* will make His will known."

Debbie nodded.

They walked in silence, and then Verna admitted, "I suppose my meddling hasn't done any *gut* either. Look at the Alvin situation."

When they approached Debbie's old home, the front door opened before Debbie could knock. Her mother's smiling face appeared.

"Herbert!" her mother called back into the house. "Our long-lost daughter has returned!"

Debbie wrapped her arms around her mother for a hug. Callie returned her hug and then greeted the other two girls, inviting everyone to come inside. Debbie's dad rose from the couch to give Debbie a hug. He shook hands with Verna and Ida. He grinned from ear to ear. "If it isn't the Beiler sisters! But where is Lois?"

"Back at the house," Debbie said. "I asked Verna and Ida to come with me."

"Why, Debbie? You're not shunning Lois, are you?" Callie sounded indignant.

"Of course not, Mom. Lois was never a formal member of the Amish church, so shunning was never considered."

"Oh, I didn't know that. I just know Lois is sensitive about such things." Callie motioned for them to take a seat.

"How have you been doing?" Debbie asked as she took her dad's hand in hers.

A broad smile spread over his face. "Much better now that I'm seeing my daughter again."

"I'm sorry." Debbie tightened her hand on his. "I should visit more often. I've been so busy and life has been ruffled."

Her dad just smiled at her.

Her mother responded though. "Amish life ruffled? Now I've heard everything!"

Debbie stroked her dad's hand. "We're human, Mom. Even if we live in a culture that doesn't prefer technology, we still have plenty of issues to straighten out and work to do. That's what makes it so busy. It's not like what they show on TV."

Verna must have thought it was high time the conversation moved to safer ground because she jumped in. "Did you have a nice Thanksgiving?"

"The turkey was moist," Debbie's dad, Herbert, said. "Some members of my side of the family were here earlier. My brother Thomas and his wife, Emerald. They left about an hour ago."

"Of course the turkey was moist! He just likes to make it sound like I can't cook," Callie said.

As they all laughed, Debbie decided she was glad she'd come. Now that things had quieted down, she needed to visit her parents more often. And she would. Certainly at Christmastime — and hopefully several times before that.

FORTY-ONE

Two Sundays after Thanksgiving, Debbie was sitting on the front row bench of the unmarried women's section at the hymn singing. The last song had been given out, and through the living room window she could see the *Englisha* neighbor's Christmas lights twinkling in the distance. They looked dreamy, Debbie thought, as she turned to the correct page.

Tonight she was the oldest single girl sitting on the front row. The wedding season had thinned out the line. It seemed like a dozen girls were gone, if you counted all the neighboring young people who attended the hymn singing in Bishop Beiler's district on their "off" Sundays. But perhaps she was exaggerating. Right now she felt weary to the bone and glad the hymn singing was almost over. Hopefully Emery would leave right after the dating couples did so they'd be on their way home quickly.

For a few more minutes the sound of the young people's voices hung in the air. Conversations started almost immediately after the last note died down. Debbie tried to join in, but she soon lapsed into silence. She just wanted to get out of there. The place was too empty with Ida and Verna gone. It even felt strange not to have Alvin and Mildred on the front row, even with Mildred aglow over her anticipated wedding, which had happened last Thursday. They would be at home together tonight. She didn't begrudge them their togetherness. She was long past that point.

There was one *gut* memory that lingered from Alvin and Mildred's wedding. Emery had asked her to the table for the evening supper and hymn singing intead of his mystery girl, of whom he was still tight-lipped about. No one had looked crossways at them even though she lived with the Beilers. Maybe everyone thought they preferred each other's company over some random matchup. Which was the truth — at least on her part. She'd been able to relax. There were no arguments or poundings of the heart — just delicious peace as she and Emery made small talk. To top things off, Paul had been matched with a visiting girl so his attention was elsewhere.

One thing Debbie knew for sure: Emery was a dear. At Alvin's wedding he must have been trying hard to keep her spirits up. And he didn't bring up the mystery girl either. Debbie had found out the girl's name was Laura, and she was from Lancaster — according to Ida. Had Emery been interested in her?

Ida had said that what happened among the young people at Amish weddings didn't usually mean a thing, but Debbie was realizing more and more that she hoped Ida was wrong. Tonight she was becoming more aware of her feelings for Emery Beiler. Could Emery ever care for her in a romantic way? The thought brought a quick lump to her throat. That was simply not possible. Would it even cross his mind?

Debbie pulled in a sharp breath when she saw Emery get to his feet. She hadn't said a word in the past five minutes, and she didn't want to. But if she sat here like a mute, she would soon draw attention to herself. Debbie got up to make her way to the washroom. Emery wouldn't be ready with his horse when she got outside, but she'd help him hitch up. That wasn't the usual Amish practice, but things were a little upside down right now. Besides, she and Emery were like brother and sister, were they not? Right now she wished that wasn't the case . . . but then she wouldn't be free to follow him out to his buggy either. Well, she'd enjoy his company while she could. Emery was such a comforting presence. He'd eventually marry, and she'd deal with it like she had with all the other changes that had happened this year.

A few of the dating girls gave her warm smiles as she walked into the washroom, probably expecting she had a date with someone. Why else would she be out here this early? Well, she wished she had one — and they would never guess with whom! Not Phillip Kanagy, or Paul Wagler, or Alvin Knepp. No, someone more solid, more mature, more manly, and certainly more godly than all three of them put together. Debbie banished the thought as she absent-mindedly returned the girls' smiles. No one said anything as they searched through the clothing pile to pull out their shawls and weather bonnets. Debbie hung back until the first wave of girls went out the door. She found her own wrap and went outside. She left the line and crossed the lawn in the moonlight, only slowing down when she approached the long line of buggies parked along the back fence. The men with steady dates were busy hitching their horses to their buggies. They were too busy and focused to notice her. By the lights of the men's lanterns, Debbie found Emery's buggy. She stepped into the shadows to wait for him to come out of the barn. When he reached the buggy, she stepped out to meet him.

Startled he stopped for a moment. Then he grinned. "I don't remember asking anyone if I could drive her home."

Debbie reached down and lifted the buggy shafts. "Sorry. It's just little old me. I can walk home if you want to take someone else. I'll even ask her for you."

His laughter was full and bright, just like the Christmas lights that flashed across the road. His words were gentle. "Why, I'd be honored to have you along for the ride."

She went along. "Well, we *are* going the same way, and if there's no one else . . ."

"There's no one else," he said after he finished connecting the tugs. "Hop on in!" He helped her into the buggy and then handed the lines to her.

Debbie settled on the seat and handed the lines back when Emery joined her. They were both quiet as he maneuvered his horse past the buggies in line to pick up passengers.

Now that they were alone, the last thing

Debbie wanted to do was make Emery angry, but curiosity got the best of her.

Hesitantly she asked, "Emery, why did you take me to the table at Alvin's wedding?"

When he didn't respond she continued. "If it's because Laura wasn't there so I was your backup choice, I can't say that I blame you. She's much better looking than I am."

He grunted. After a minute or two he said, "Debbie, Laura never meant anything to me. You know how wedding match-ups are."

He didn't sound harsh, but the words still cut. She regarded him out of the corner of her eye as he drove through the night. Was he going to say something more? When he didn't, she couldn't believe her boldness when she asked, "Does that also cover Alvin's wedding?"

"You don't have to look so nervous," Emery finally said, as if that was an answer. "I asked you because I knew I would enjoy your company."

"You did?" Her voice caught.

"I've always appreciated you, Debbie. There'll be someone for you, if that's what you're worried about. The unmarried men won't let a sweet girl like you sit around alone for long."

Quick tears burned her eyes, but Debbie left them alone. Emery wouldn't see them in the dark, and after all, how could she expect him to even consider her in a romantic way?

"Thank you for your concern," she said in a steady voice. "I'm sure the same holds true for you. I don't understand why you don't have a decent girl in the buggy with you right now."

He chuckled. "Who says I don't?"

"Emery!" Her voice squeaked. "Emery, don't tease me tonight. My heart can't take it right now."

"I'm sorry." He glanced at her. "Did the handsome Phillip Kanagy love you and leave you in one night?"

"Emery," she begged, "that's not how it was."

He didn't look convinced. "You two seemed to have a great time — at least from what I could see."

"I could say the same thing about you and Laura." The words slipped out, and she was sure they sounded bitter.

He turned and regarded her for a long moment. "There's nothing between Laura and myself, Debbie. She's from Lancaster."

"I know." Debbie took a deep, calming breath. "Who you sit with at the table at an Amish wedding doesn't mean anything."

"You keep saying that." He held onto the

reins as they turned into their driveway. "Did I offend you?"

Debbie suppressed a sigh. "No, Emery. I'm glad for an evening with you, even if it doesn't mean anything,"

Emery stopped his horse at the hitching post, but he didn't climb down from the buggy. "What is it about the heart?" he mused. "Why is love so hard, so complicated, so unexpected?"

Debbie didn't dare move lest she break the spell of this moment. Never had Emery opened up like this to her.

"I don't know much about women, Debbie. I'm a common, ordinary man. I don't have the flash of a Phillip Kanagy or the boldness of a Paul Wagler. I plod along with my responsibilities. I know I need to wed, but why? I ask myself. Just because it needs done? And to whom? And when I consider what I would like in a *frau,* it doesn't seem quite possible to find a girl like that." He gazed across the dark fields.

Debbie held her breath. What kind of life did Emery want? What was he looking for in a *frau*? Was it also what she wanted? Could she come close to being what he desired?

Emery's voice broke the silence again. "Maybe we'd better go inside. *Mamm* and

Daett will think someone has brought you home . . . and you're sitting out here kissing him."

Debbie laughed. "They know me better than that."

Emery was halfway down the buggy step, but he paused to look up at her. "I want to thank you, Debbie, for who you are. It took a lot of courage to come from your world into ours. I've never told you this before, but I've thought it often. You'll make your mark in life with your steady and unbroken spirit, with your fear of *Da Hah,* and with so much of the specialness that makes up you. You've been a blessing to our family, and you've helped out more than you can know."

He finished climbing down and she followed on her side. She undid the tugs on her side, while he undid them on his. She held the shafts while he led his horse forward. As she set the shafts down, he took the horse into the barn. She waited until he returned and fell into step with him as they walked toward the house.

Did she dare do what she wanted desperately to do? Slowly Debbie slipped her hand into his. She looked up at his face in the moonlight. "I haven't made you angry, have I?"

He grinned. "You'd have a hard time making me angry, Debbie."

The words came easily. "That's because you're such a sweet-tempered person."

He laughed. "You do my heart *gut,* Debbie."

"And you mine," she whispered.

He paused at the front steps to give her a quick, sideways hug. His chin pressed into her *kapp* for a moment. "I'm sorry life dealt you such a difficult hand with Alvin, Debbie. I really am."

She glanced up at his clean-shaven face. "I guess I was wrong about Alvin . . . and about my heart."

He nodded.

She touched his face with her finger. "You'll soon be growing a beard, I'm thinking. You'll look right handsome."

He grinned. "Does that mean I'm ugly now?"

"Laura didn't think so," Debbie pressed back a tear. "And neither do I. We can't both be wrong."

He cleared his throat. "I'm thinking we'd better get our sleep or neither of us will be worth much tomorrow."

"Spoken like a true farmer," she teased and followed him through the front door.

He cast a final smile her way and then went up the stairs. Debbie slipped into the kitchen. Saloma had cleared the supper dishes away, and the kitchen sparkled in the soft moonlight coming through the window.

Returned love might not come her way, Debbie thought as she pressed back another tear. But for right now she had this — the Beiler family's love, a wonderful place to live, her Amish community, and enjoyable evenings like the one she'd had tonight. Perhaps that could be enough. At least until Emery found himself a *frau*.

FORTY-TWO

It was Christmas Day, and Debbie was sitting in her bedroom upstairs. Bishop Beiler and Saloma were napping downstairs after the hearty breakfast Debbie had fixed of pancakes, bacon, eggs, and potatoes. The day would be a quiet one. On Thanksgiving, Saloma had declared to her children that Christmas should be spent with their in-laws and other family. "It's only fair that everyone's elsewhere on Christmas," Saloma had remarked. "The children need to spend time with both sides of their families."

Debbie didn't mind the quiet day at home. The Beilers could have visited among their widespread family connections, but the bishop and Saloma seemed content to stay home. Debbie had awakened early to spend the first part of the day with her parents. She'd told them last week that she would. And on the visit this morning, she'd taken Christmas presents along — a knitted sweater for her dad, which she had slaved over under Saloma's tutorage. Her dad had seemed pleased and thanked her for the gift. She'd given her mom an embroidered doily. That hadn't been as big a hit, but her mom was hard to please.

Still, the effort had been worth it. And the four yards of dark-blue dress cloth her mom had given her warmed her heart. At least Mom had taken the time to figure out what she could use as an Amish woman. She'd given her mom a big hug. Her dad received an equally tight hug for the little box of chocolates he'd given her. The box was sitting on the dresser right now. Debbie glanced at it with a smile. She'd only eaten two. Perhaps she would share several with Emery later. He liked chocolates even more than she did.

She'd come back in time to fix a late breakfast for the Beilers. There had only been the four of them sitting around the table and making small talk. After they had prayer and the bishop read the Christmas story, Emery had vanished. She'd heard his buggy back in their lane some ten minutes ago.

Debbie smiled as she thought of Emery. They'd had such a nice talk that night on the ride home from the Sunday-night hymn singing. None of the rides since had been as momentous, but Debbie felt they'd grown closer each week. They chatted often during chore time, and she managed to keep foolish thoughts of Emery as a husband out of her mind. She was honored to share even these few precious moments of friendship with Emery. She would cherish them forever in her heart even after Emery found himself a woman he could love and marry.

Debbie stood and walked over to the window to look out. Perhaps that had been where Emery had gone — to visit a girl he'd had his eye on. It didn't seem reasonable though. Amish people didn't usually take such liberties on Christmas Day.

A soft knock sounded on the bedroom door.

"Come in!" Debbie called. No doubt it was Saloma on her way up for a motherly chat and probably concerned that she might be lonely. To her surprise, it was Emery who opened the door.

"Okay if I come in?" he asked.

"*Yah,*" Debbie answered, her voice a bit squeaky.

When he entered, she said, "My dad gave me chocolates." She pointed to the box on the dresser. "Help yourself. I know you love good chocolate."

Emery ignored the remark as he seated himself on the bed.

He seemed tense, Debbie thought as she faced him and leaned against the window frame.

Emery studied the floor for a moment before he looked up and met her gaze. "I've been thinking about you, Debbie."

Debbie's brow furrowed. "Have I done something wrong?"

He shook his head. "On the contrary, Debbie. You do a lot of things right. I was thinking of you . . . of you and me."

She waited and hardly dared breathe. Her face flamed red.

"Surely you know what I mean. I . . ." Emery searched for the right words. "These feelings . . . these feelings for you, well, they've been in my heart for a long time. Longer than I've wanted to admit."

"You mean . . . you and me together, Emery?" she dared ask. "Are you saying . . ."

He met her gaze. "You do care for me then? In that way? I had hoped so because of the way you were worried about Crystal . . . and then Laura. But I wasn't sure. There were always other men around you. And you seemed interested in Phillip."

She glanced away. "I do care about you, Emery. But would it be right? I mean, it wouldn't look right to people. We live in the same house. People think you're like a brother to me."

He stepped closer. "But I'm not your brother, Debbie. No one thinks like that. When I took you to the table on the night of Alvin's wedding, no one thought us a strange couple." He gently gripped her upper arms. "Look at me, Debbie. *We are not family.* Not in that way. And you know that."

Heat burned like fire in her face. "But . . . but Emery . . . How can we . . . we . . ."

He continued. "How can we not, Debbie?" He seemed to know what she was thinking and what to say, as if he'd thought through the situation. "First, we need to tell *Mamm* and *Daett* that we're thinking of each other in this way. That is, if you want to see me that way. I don't expect you to make your mind up for sure right away. But I do think they should be told that we're interested in each other. I'll start sleeping in the basement or in the barn so it will look right. We don't need to date officially until you decide *yah* or *nee.* But the truth is that I'd wed you tomorrow — if you'd agree and if it were possible."

She tried to breathe.

He paused and then said, "Debbie . . . Debbie, if . . . if you tell me *nee,* no one will ever have to know. We can go on like before. I'll straighten up my feelings the best I can. But I feel that you and I together would be so right. You love this place like I do. You're committed to my people as I am. You belong here with me."

When she still said nothing, Emery let go of her and stepped back. "You will at least consider it?"

She finally answered slowly. "This is not how I thought life would turn out. I always thought I'd marry Alvin. But obviously God had other plans. You are . . ." She took both of his hands. "You are too good for me, Emery. But, yes, love for you sneaked into my heart when I wasn't looking."

He gently pulled one of his hands out of hers and touched her face. "Who knows how the heart works, Debbie? We don't have to figure it out. What we can have here would be ours alone. A new love would grow strong in our hearts. Our *kinner* would be on this place. And we would love each other, Debbie. I know we would!"

Her voice trembled. "And your sisters and parents? What will they say?"

He didn't seem fazed. "I don't know, but we're not doing anything wrong."

She touched his smooth face. "I guess I'll get to watch your face grow a beard — from close range."

He smiled and she giggled. They sat on the bed.

"So the answer will be *yah*?" he asked. "You know already . . . for sure?"

She smiled at him. "The answer is *yah*! More than *yah*!"

He drew her close. "We'd best tell *Mamm* and *Daett*."

"I can't tell your parents," she managed. "I just can't. They'll be shocked. And what if they disapprove?"

"I'll tell them for us." He hesitated. "They do have to be told."

She nodded. There was nothing wrong with what she felt for Emery, and yet she felt like a thief or a schemer. Maybe they would think she'd moved in to snatch the prize — their son.

"I can move back in with my parents," she whispered. "That might be for the best. I can still come and help with the chores and the housekeeping."

"No, you won't." Emery regarded her for a long moment. Then he rose and made his way out of the room.

Debbie heard his footsteps on the stairs. She sat still and listened. She could hear the murmur of voices from the living room. Suddenly she found herself in tears. She'd just been offered a fresh start. A husband better than insecure Alvin, or Paul and his bombastic ways, and even the handsome Phillip. Emery was solid. He would stand the test of time. And he loved her. And she loved him! So why was she crying as if the world were coming to an end? Hadn't Ida shown her the way?

It seemed like hours before she heard footsteps and the stairs creaking. A soft knock sounded on the door frame. "Come in," she whispered.

Saloma entered and sat on the bed. She slipped her arm around Debbie's shoulder and hugged her. "You poor thing," Saloma cooed, comforting Debbie as if she were comforting a baby.

"I didn't mean for this to happen," Debbie said through sobs. "I really am sorry."

Saloma continued as if she hadn't heard. "*Da Hah* has brought you a long way, Debbie. You've become like a daughter to us, so maybe we're partly to blame for the mess Emery and you are in."

"It is a mess, isn't it?" Debbie asked through her tears.

Saloma looked at her with compassion. "*Yah,* Debbie, but it's nothing that can't be fixed. *Daett* and I feel quite badly for what has happened. It was our selfishness in taking you in like we did and not looking forward to see what might come to pass. So dry your eyes, and we'll see what can be done about this."

"You're blaming yourselves?" Debbie didn't hide the shock in her voice. "But I'm the one to blame."

Saloma gave Debbie a soft smile. "*Nee,* this is not your fault, dear. That's the last thing that crossed our mind. *Daett*'s down there giving Emery a talking-to. This situation should never have happened like this."

Debbie gulped and stopped crying. Saloma was right, the murmur of voices downstairs was still going on. "So you and the bishop disapprove?"

"Oh, *nee,* Debbie. We approve! We just believe Emery should have handled things better. If he's had feelings for you, we should have been told long before now."

Debbie lowered her head, still not sure. "Don't blame him for everything. There were warnings for both of us. I think we just didn't want to believe them."

"*Daett* and I should have been on the lookout ourselves," Saloma said. "Now come downstairs. *Daett* wants to talk with you."

Saloma stood and offered her hand to Debbie. Debbie took it and stood. After squeezing her hand, Saloma turned and headed downstairs with Debbie following close behind. In the living room, Debbie hardly dared to look up and meet Emery's gaze. She sat down on the couch beside him. He looked chastened but still happy, which was a good sign.

Bishop Beiler regarded her for a moment. "Debbie, first I want to apologize for Emery's behavior. We should have been told about his growing interest in you a long time ago. And it was most indecent of Emery to speak with you so suddenly about this matter. I can imagine how you feel. But now that it's out in the open, *Mamm* and I wish to help where we can. And the first thing that must be done is getting Emery out of the house. He will move into the barn with his blankets tonight. The stove is still out there from Ida's wedding and working just fine. We'll get him set up in there."

"But I'm the one who should leave," Debbie interrupted. "I could go home to my parents."

The bishop glared at Emery and then smiled at Debbie. "*Nee*, he needs a little suffering before he gets handed a decent *frau* like you, Debbie. Emery won't freeze, and it'll do him a lot of *gut.* And we'll get our *dawdy haus* built by late spring. You can then move into it with us, and Emery will move back into this house. Until that time, you're not to date officially. Is that understood?"

"*Yah,* I understand," Emery said as he looked at the floor.

"And you?" Bishop Beiler asked, turning his gaze in Debbie's direction.

"Of course." Debbie stole a glance at Emery, and found he was stealing a glance at her. The corners of his lips turned up.

Saloma rose. "Well, let's get Emery moved then." She turned to face Debbie. "And you're not to help. This is between Emery and us."

"Are you sure? I can help . . ." Debbie paused as Saloma shook her head. "Is it okay if I go up to my room for a while?"

"That sounds like a good plan, Debbie," Saloma said.

Debbie stood and slipped up the stairs. She heard Emery say, "I'm going to get some of my stuff." Then his footsteps were behind her. She turned to wait for him at her bedroom door.

He paused close to her. She looked up and his eyes were shining.

"I love you, Debbie!" he whispered. "And

watch out because I'll be stealing kisses whenever I can!"

She smiled, turned, entered her room, and closed the bedroom door, all the while thinking she should have stuck out her tongue at him at such a remark. But then she'd probably end up in a kiss with him, and that would have been good — too good.

FORTY-THREE

New Year's Eve found Debbie upstairs in her bedroom changing into a Sunday dress. She'd helped Saloma all day with the food preparation. They'd added all the extra leaves to the dining room table. Everyone was coming today. They'd been told there would be a family related announcement, and it was important to be there. Reuben and Wayne had arrived with their families a short time ago. Verna and Ida, with their families, were expected soon. To Debbie's surprise her parents had accepted their invitation and were coming too. Lois and her *Englisha* husband, Doug, would round out the guest list. Bishop Beiler had decreed the family gathering the day after Christmas. Saloma and the bishop had insisted the news of Debbie's engagement to Emery remain a secret until New Year's Eve so the entire family could hear about it first.

"This is not our normal practice for

engagements," he'd told Debbie. "But under the special circumstances, we believe it would be best to clear the air with everyone in the family first — and with your parents especially."

"Thank you, *Daett.*" Debbie gasped, horrified by the slip of tongue. But when she looked up, a smile had crept across the bishop's face. Saloma had heard from the kitchen. She came to the doorway. "And, Debbie, you are to call me *Mamm* now."

Debbie pressed back the tears as she hurried to Saloma and answered with a tight hug.

Saloma glowed with happiness.

Debbie smiled as she remembered the scene. She paused to look out the window. The only darkness on the horizons in the lives of the bishop and Saloma was Lois. But *Da Hah* was working in their hearts because the bishop had invited Lois and Doug to the gathering. Debbie hoped she'd played a small part in healing the rift. Debbie hugged herself at the thought. She would be Emery's bride the next wedding season, and in so doing would truly become a sister in the Beiler family. What Lois had left, she'd replaced. Who would have thought things would turn out this way?

Debbie's thoughts whirled until the sound

of buggy wheels in the driveway interrupted them. She turned and hurried to pin on her *kapp*. She'd hoped her parents would arrive first so she could speak a few words with them. The news of her engagement should come to them through her first, she thought. Debbie was sure her mom suspected something like this anyway. Hadn't she made the wry remark soon after Debbie had decided to board at the Beilers about a dozen children? Debbie felt the heat rise up her neck at the memory. Her mother might have been on target all along. She could easily imagine the farm filled with *wunderbah* children — Emery and hers!

A knock on the door made Debbie jump. Would Saloma have come up for a final word? No . . . this wouldn't be Saloma. There could only be one other person outside her bedroom door at this moment. Debbie rubbed her face with vigor, but that wouldn't deceive Emery. He already knew her too well. With a quick pull she opened the door. *"Yah?"*

Emery was leaning against the doorframe grinning. His look took in her flushed face. "Nervous are we?"

"Maybe a little." A smile spread over her face, and she felt blood rushing into her cheeks. Emery was much too manly for his own good! Thankfully he didn't seem aware of all his charms, which added to his attractiveness.

"I'll be sitting beside you at suppertime." His grin was still broad. "I just wanted to make sure you were comfortable with that."

"You know I'd love it!" The words slipped out so easily. She'd not dared imagine this engagement would ever happen, but now that it had her moments with Emery were the most natural in the world. It was like they'd always been meant to be together. And perhaps they had.

His grin turned wicked. "It will be a pleasure on my part."

She wanted to kiss him right then and there, but this wasn't the time. "You'd better go on downstairs. I'll be there soon."

He didn't budge. "You look ready to me." His gaze took in her dress and shoes. "Pins and needles all in place?"

"Okay, I'll come now." She took his arm and marched down the stairs with him. At the stairway door, she released him as he led the way. Debbie entered the living room close behind him. Verna and Ida had both arrived and were standing there with puzzled looks, obviously unaware of the news about to be announced.

"What's this all about?" Verna asked

Debbie, as if she suspected it had to do with her friend. That Emery was with her caused a light to go on in her eyes.

Ida too was now staring at them. She clapped both hands against her face. "Oh! Don't tell me that . . ."

"Both of you be silent now," Saloma commanded from the kitchen doorway. "You're not to breathe a word more."

Verna ignored her *mamm* and drew in a long breath. "My own brother and Debbie?" She wrapped Debbie in a tight hug. "I can't believe it!"

"Believe it!" Emery said with a sly grin.

"Now we are sisters! *Really* sisters!" Ida had tears on her cheeks. Her hug was even tighter than Verna's had been. "You and my little brother! How did this happen?"

"You showed me the way," Debbie whispered.

"Enough of this now," *Mamm* interrupted. "Debbie's parents just arrived, and she needs to welcome them."

As soon as Debbie and Emery were on the porch, he said, "I'll give you some time with your parents." He turned to head toward the barn where Joe, Ben, Wayne, Reuben, and *Daett* were talking.

"You're not scared are you?" Debbie teased.

Emery rubbed his forehead with his forearm. "Maybe a little."

She laughed and shooed him toward the barn.

He grinned and walked away.

Debbie approached the car as soon as it pulled to a stop in the driveway.

"Debbie!" Her mom gave her a long hug when she got out of the car. "What's this all about?" Her mother looked around, and her gaze took in the gathered knot of men by the barn.

"Bishop Beiler wants to make an official announcement at suppertime, but I wanted to let you know ahead of time. I'm engaged to Emery Beiler!"

"Engaged!" both parents said at the same time.

"Yes! Can you keep the secret until suppertime so Bishop Beiler can make the formal announcement to the rest of the family?"

"Secrets, secrets!" Herbert laughed as he embraced his daughter. "You look very happy. And that makes me happy too."

"Do you love this young man?" her mom asked.

"Yes, Mom, I do. I really do."

"Okay, we'll keep your secret."

Just then Doug and Lois drove into the lane.

"Well, if the wayward daughter and her worldly husband have also been invited, all must be forgiven and forgotten."

Debbie had no reply to that. The Beilers would always feel the pain of their daughter's departure into the *Englisha* world. But they would also always love Lois.

Callie walked over to greet Doug and Lois. Debbie and her father followed. After the hellos, they turned and headed toward the house, the men following behind the women. Lois rushed ahead and was already at the front door, smiling and feeling perfectly at home.

There are indeed *wunderbah* things afloat tonight, Debbie decided.

As they entered the house, Lois was already talking to her *mamm*. She turned around to look at Debbie. "I can't wait to hear what this is all about. Will you tell me now?"

"I'd better not," Debbie said. "You'll find out soon enough."

Lois didn't pursue the subject as she chattered on. "I was telling *Mamm* she should have asked, and I'd have come over earlier to help with supper."

"Well . . ." Saloma hesitated, obviously

471

not sure if they would have felt comfortable with Lois and Doug coming that early just yet. Healing was going to take some time. "I'm just thankful you're here, Lois. And Doug too."

Lois's face softened a little. "I do understand how things are, *Mamm*. But just know I'm available if you need my help. Remember that, okay?"

Saloma nodded and took Lois by the arm. Together they walked toward the kitchen.

Debbie watched with contentment. Each time they got together was another opportunity to help heal the hurt. She would help all she could in that direction. As Emery's *frau,* the opportunities would abound.

Minutes later, Saloma ushered her girls out of the kitchen and into the dining room, their arms filled with food bowls. Debbie hurried to help, and moments later the table steamed with a delicious supper set out.

Saloma went to the living room doorway and announced, "Supper's ready!"

Debbie waited in the background as everyone traipsed in and was seated at Saloma's direction. She then slipped in beside Emery. Ida dabbed her eyes and Verna glowed as if she'd birthed another *boppli.* From the look on Lois's face, she too had finally figured things out.

Bishop Beiler cleared his throat. "Before we eat, I have something to say. First I want to welcome everyone, especially Debbie's parents, Herbert and Callie. You are always welcome in our home."

All eyes turned to Debbie's mom and dad as the bishop paused, cleared his throat, and continued. "Lois and Doug, we welcome you too. We thank *Da Hah* for His blessings this past year and ask that His grace continue in the next. May His hand be with us as we gather to celebrate a most happy occasion." A smile crept across the bishop's face. "An occasion that has surprised even me."

Minister Kanagy grunted from his place at the table, and Bishop Beiler gave him a brief look before he continued. "I'm sure all of us here will want to join in the joy that my youngest son, Emery, and our dear friend Debbie feel tonight. I'm pleased to announce that Emery has asked Debbie to be his *frau,* and she has consented."

There were small gasps of surprise and joy, even from Verna, Ida, and Lois, who had guessed the news. The bishop continued. "Because of the . . . unusual circumstances involved, Saloma and I thought it best to gather you all together for this announcement before it was published in the church service."

"Thanks, everyone, for coming," Emery said. "I'm sorry we didn't give you more notice. I guess I never thought this *wunderbah* woman would consent to be my *frau*. But she has said *yah,* and my heart sings!" Emery stopped as if overcome by his own flowery thoughts and words.

Debbie clung to his arm and kept her eyes on the table, mostly so no one would see her tears. She couldn't say anything even if she knew what to say.

Herbert spoke up. "When Callie and I raised Debbie, we always prayed for her to be happy as an adult. We were puzzled when she made her decision to . . . umm . . . join the Amish faith, but indeed our prayers have been answered. We're overjoyed that she's found happiness in her faith and now in love." He looked at his wife.

Callie just nodded. For once she seemed without words.

After congratulations were said and the talk flowed, the bishop finally boomed, "Okay, I'm hungry. Let's pray and then eat!" The room got quiet as everyone bowed their heads and prayed silently. The bishop said "Amen," and everyone looked up.

Saloma wiped her eyes before she passed

the first of the dishes around the table. Verna and Ida also had tears to wipe away. Emery turned to Debbie, squeezed her hand, and mouthed, "I love you."

Debbie wondered that she wasn't a blubbering mess. She leaned against Emery's shoulder with the realization that she was now home — truly home. There was no question about that. She would find Emery after everyone had left and kiss him for a few precious moments. They had waited long enough.

DISCUSSION QUESTIONS

1. In what ways could you have shared Debbie's joy on her baptismal day?
2. Would you have any advice for Ida as the recently widowed Minister Kanagy begins to pay her attention?
3. Why do you think Emery, the youngest son of Bishop Beiler, shows no interest in the community's unmarried women?
4. Do you think Emery is interested romantically in Crystal Meyers once she shows up in the community?
5. Why is Alvin blamed by the community for Crystal's arrival?
6. What do you think of Alvin's character when he tells Debbie why he has waited so long for the date he has promised her?
7. Was Paul Wagler's accident at the silo filling deserved? To what extent

did his character improve? Should Debbie have opened her heart romantically to him?

8. When Deacon Mast arrives to speak with Alvin about his past, how does he handle the pressure? Could Alvin have done better?

9. Do you blame Mildred for seizing the opportunity to rekindle her past romance with Alvin? Do you approve of her methods?

10. How did Alvin handle his breakup with Debbie?

11. Should Debbie have been open to Phillip Kanagy's attentions?

12. Did Debbie make the right choice when she took Ida's example and followed her heart into unexpected territory?

ABOUT THE AUTHOR

Jerry Eicher's bestselling Amish fiction (more than 600,000 in combined sales) includes The Adams County Trilogy, Hannah's Heart series, The Fields of Home series, Little Valley series, and some stand-alone novels. He's also written nonfiction, including *My Amish Childhood* and *The Amish Family Cookbook* (with his wife, Tina). After a traditional Amish childhood, Jerry taught for two terms in Amish and Mennonite schools in Ohio and Illinois. Since then he's been involved in church renewal, preaching, and teaching Bible studies.